PENC

A Christmas Mira

A Christmas Miracle on Sanctuary Lane

KIRSTY DOUGAL

PENGUIN BOOKS

PENGUIN BOOKS

UK | USA | Canada | Ireland | Australia
India | New Zealand | South Africa

Penguin Books, Penguin Random House UK,
One Embassy Gardens, 8 Viaduct Gardens, London SW11 7BW

penguin.co.uk
global.penguinrandomhouse.com

First published 2024
001

Set in 12.5/14.75pt Garamond MT Std
Typeset by Jouve (UK), Milton Keynes
Printed and bound in Great Britain by Clays Ltd, Elcograf S.p.A.

The authorized representative in the EEA is Penguin Random House Ireland,
Morrison Chambers, 32 Nassau Street, Dublin D02 YH68

A CIP catalogue record for this book is available from the British Library

ISBN: 978–1–405–95868–4

www.greenpenguin.co.uk

Penguin Random House is committed to a sustainable future for our business, our readers and our planet. This book is made from Forest Stewardship Council® certified paper.

To John, Tom, Charlotte, O and O.
With love, as always.

Dear Readers

I've been delighted to receive so many lovely messages telling me how much you enjoyed getting to know Ruby and her family and friends in Wartime on Sanctuary Lane, *and how excited you are to find out what happens next. Well, wait no longer, because the next instalment is finally here!* A Christmas Miracle on Sanctuary Lane *was a joy to write; it covers some difficult themes, but I love the festive season and it has been great fun 'seeing' the animal hospital up and running in all its glory and following Ruby as she struggles to understand who she is in an ever-changing world.*

As ever, I've tried my best to stay true to the spirit, if not to every detail, of the age. The Battle of the Somme was, of course, an absolute tragedy, with nearly 20,000 Allied troops killed on the first day alone. Rabies had been eradicated in the UK in the nineteenth century, but really did threaten to make a resurgence towards the end of the First World War as soldiers attempted to bring home abandoned animals they had 'adopted' in France and Belgium. And, despite the East End of London being a real melting pot of different nationalities and cultures, it really was not a good time to have German heritage – or even a German surname.

I really hope you enjoy the story and thank you again for all your support.

Love, Kirsty xxx

Prologue

Tuesday, 19 December 1916

Boom!

The sound came from nothing . . . turning the world upside down.

A second later, the lights went out. Where once had been a little group of people chatting around the oil heater at the Sanctuary Lane Animal Hospital, there was now just inky blackness.

Ruby was hurled from her chair. There was the shattering of glass, the rumble of collapsing masonry, and then something hard landed – crack! – across one of her legs.

Ruby lay there in shock and disorientation and tried to control her raggedy breathing.

What on earth was happening?

What had happened to the others?

And would they all get out of there alive?

I

Friday, 27 October 1916

'Is this the Sanctuary Lane Animal Hospital, Miss?'

Ruby smiled at the girl with the dirty face and the patchwork dress who had poked her head around the door from the street. 'Yes,' she said. It wasn't the name written on the posters plastered in all their windows, but that hardly mattered. 'Yes, it is.'

'And is it really all free?'

Ruby's smile widened. It didn't matter how big the writing on the posters or how many flyers they handed out informing people about the Silvertown Animal Hospital, people still continually wanted to be reassured that they wouldn't have to pay an extortionate amount to have their sick or injured animals treated there. Ruby must have fielded half a dozen such queries already – and the hospital had only been open an hour or two that damp autumn morning. She supposed she shouldn't really be surprised; the young girl probably couldn't read. Everyone around here had grown up knowing that vets were prohibitively expensive, so the very idea of the hospital probably seemed too good to be true.

Ruby nodded at the dirty-faced girl. 'Quite free,' she said. 'We ask for a donation from those that can afford it but if you can't, we won't charge a penny.'

The girl's face split into a gap-toothed grin. 'Thank you ever so much, Miss,' she said. 'Me friend said it were free but I didn't quite dare believe it. I'll go and get Teddy now and join the queue.'

She turned on her heel and, with a little wave, was off at a run, disappearing around the corner and onto the high street. Ruby shut the door behind her, wondering idly whether Teddy was a dog, cat or a rabbit and what ailed him or her.

No doubt she would find out soon enough.

Before she returned to her duties, Ruby stood with her back to the door, surveying the little scene in front of her. The morning clinic was in full swing and the reception was already packed to the gills with owners and their assorted sick or injured pets. Chairs had been pulled out of their neat rows to accommodate the animals and a dog was straining at its lead in an effort to get at a miserable-looking moggie three chairs away. It was the usual organised chaos! Mr Atkins, who had known Ruby since she was a little girl and who lived in one of the nearby houses on Sanctuary Lane, was also in attendance; he *always* seemed to be at the hospital even though he didn't own an animal. Ruby suspected he had nipped inside to avoid having to light the fire at home. She didn't mind – Mr Atkins was getting more and more confused these days and probably relished the company – although if dozens of other people started having the same idea now that the nights were drawing in and the days were getting chillier, she might have to act.

Nellie was going from one owner to the next with her

clipboard and pen, assessing which animals needed to be properly examined and which could be simply dealt with then and there.

'So, what's wrong with your fella, then?' she was asking a tall, gangly youth with a miserable-looking mongrel almost as spindly as he was. She took hold of the dog's face and peered into its mouth. 'Looks like you both need a good tonic,' she added. 'I've got just the thing for your boy, but can I recommend a pint of stout at the Queen's Head for you?'

To his credit, the youth grinned as a little titter went around the room. Lovely Nellie – straight-talking and blunt she might be, but she always dispensed a potent mix of wit, warmth and wisdom as she did her rounds. Nellie must have been sixty if she was a day, but she was full of energy and good humour; so what if she was a little slower than she had been and her arthritic fingers were beginning to give her gyp? Silvertown born and bred, Nellie ran the dog food barrow up at the market and had taught Ruby much of what she knew about animals. Ruby strongly believed that what Nellie didn't know probably wasn't worth knowing.

'I'm almost certain your boy ain't got distemper,' Nellie was saying. 'But I wouldn't mind bouncing it off someone round the back to make sure.'

'I'll take him,' offered Ruby. 'I think Robert's free; I saw the lady with the ginger cat leave just now.'

Hopefully, it wasn't distemper. Ruby didn't have much experience of the virus, but she knew that once it hit a community, it could run amok. If they did have a case, she wanted to be the first to hear about it. She took the clipboard from Nellie, checked the names, and then smiled reassuringly at the youth. 'Would you bring Dexter and come with me, Mr Andrews?'

Ruby led the way to the back of the reception room and into a narrow corridor. A few months ago, this had been a haberdashery, but the plethora of storage rooms behind the shopfront now served very well as two consulting rooms, a recovery room and a variety of storerooms. Robert Smith, their qualified veterinary practitioner, had taken the larger room with its window looking over the back courtyard. The other was used mainly by Jack Kennedy, who might not have any formal veterinary qualifications but who had worked extensively with dogs and horses at the front – even operating, on occasion, under supervision – and who had such a way with animals that he had already thoroughly impressed Robert Smith.

Jack Kennedy also just happened to be Ruby's sweetheart.

Goodness, that sounded good.

It *felt* good, too.

Jack and Ruby had been stepping out for a few months now; in fact, Jack had first kissed Ruby the day the Silvertown Animal Hospital had opened, and the two had been going strong ever since. To be honest, it had passed in a blur because all of them had been run quite ragged managing the weekly animal hospital clinics in addition to their paid jobs. But it really had been the most wonderful blur and Jack was part of the family now. In fact, the animal hospital was quite the family affair: Ma worked in the bakery next door and popped in with tea and buns on a regular basis and Aunt Maggie volunteered at the clinic too. Even Ruby's brother Charlie popped in after school from time to time and, to Ruby's relief, they all got on like a house on fire. Jack and Aunt Maggie were in the second consultation room at that very moment; Ruby could see Jack bent over the table examining a fractious terrier whilst Aunt Maggie was doing her best to keep the poor animal still.

Ruby knocked on the door of Robert's consultation room and ushered Mr Andrews and Dexter inside. Robert and Leah Richardson were standing perfectly properly on either side of the consultation table – both, as ever, professional to a fault. But Ruby fancied that Leah's cheeks were a little too flushed for the chilly day, and Robert's eyes were far too twinkly for ten o'clock on a busy Friday morning. Neither Leah nor Robert had confirmed that the two of them were stepping out together – but something was definitely afoot . . .

'Hello, M'Leah,' said Ruby.

'Ruby!' cried Leah, in mock frustration, her eyes round and indignant behind her thick-rimmed glasses. 'When are you going to stop *calling* me that?'

'I'm trying,' said Ruby. 'It's *hard*.'

Ruby and Leah both worked at the government munitions factory down by the river. Although the two young women were fast friends out of work, Leah was a manager from a well-to-do family and was by far the senior on duty. Ruby had become so used to calling her 'Miss' that it was proving very difficult to break the habit, although sometimes, at work, she had the opposite problem and Leah's name came out as 'L'Miss'!

'Who have we got here then?' said Robert, turning away

from his paperwork with a professional smile on his thin, clever face.

Getting Robert on board with the hospital had been a real coup. Despite being less than wholly enthusiastic when Ruby had first mooted her idea, he had turned out to be a complete stalwart, turning up to volunteer at most of the weekly clinics with grace and good humour – and there were naturally many times when his five years' training and experience simply couldn't be beaten. In this case, it only took a couple of minutes before Dexter was pronounced clear of distemper and was prescribed aspirin and a tonic instead.

A very relieved Mr Andrews was just preparing to lead Dexter away when a loud commotion in reception made them all jump. Shouts, screams and – thank goodness – the odd cackle of laughter as well. As one, Ruby, Leah and Robert ran down the corridor, with Jack and Aunt Maggie joining them on the way . . .

'What's on earth's going on?' asked Ruby, looking around in confusion.

The young girl with the dirty dress and the patchwork pinafore was back, standing in the middle of the room looking anxious and distressed. Everyone was staring intently at the top of the shelving unit behind the reception desk. When the shop had been a haberdashery, the shelf would, no doubt, have been stuffed full of wool in some of the less popular hues. Now, however, it was totally empty . . . save for a small, light-brown monkey staring back at them all and clutching something furry to his chest.

Teddy was a monkey.

A very cheeky monkey at that!

'What's he holding?' Ruby muttered to Nellie, praying that it wasn't someone's precious pet mouse or hamster.

Nellie gave a discreet little cough. 'I believe it's Mr Arnott's toupee,' she said, gesturing to a bald, red-faced man sitting over by the door.

Ruby found herself fighting an overwhelming desire to giggle.

'I'm ever so sorry, Mr Arnott,' she said, as seriously as she could. She turned to the young girl. 'Can't you call him down?' she added gently.

The little girl shook her head, looking close to tears. 'I've tried,' she said. 'He don't always take much notice of me and me pa's working at the market today.'

Now Ruby recognised the girl. She was Mabel, the organ grinder's daughter.

'Don't worry,' said Robert kindly. 'I'll go up and encourage him down. There doesn't seem to be much wrong with the little blighter's climbing ability, anyway.'

There was a movable ladder attached to the shelves and Robert pulled it around until it was directly under where Teddy had taken refuge. He climbed a few rungs and stretched out his arm for the little monkey.

Too slow!

Quick as a flash, Teddy had reached out for *him*. The toupee was discarded, tumbling forlornly to the floor, as Teddy grabbed the stethoscope around Robert's neck. As Robert cried out, Teddy swung himself casually around the shelves and over towards the front window.

Nellie clutched Ruby's arm, and Ruby could see that

the old woman was nearly doubled up in silent laughter, which made Ruby's desire to giggle even stronger.

'I'll grab him,' said Jack, setting off in hot pursuit.

And then Ma appeared through the front door laden with her mid-morning tray of cakes. Without warning, Teddy dropped the stethoscope and launched himself through the air, landing smack bang on Ma's left shoulder. Ma shrieked but managed to keep the tray of cakes admirably level.

'What do I do now?' she yelled.

'Don't worry, I'm coming,' said Jack.

He was fast closing in on Teddy but . . .

Wham!

A cream bun caught him squarely on the cheek.

Whack!

A Chelsea bun hit Robert right in the middle of his forehead.

Smash!

Poor Mr Arnott had no sooner picked up his discarded toupee and carefully replaced it on his head than a jammy bun landed on top of it and duly exploded.

Ruby looked around at the little scene – at all her wonderful friends and co-conspirators – and collapsed into laughter.

Whatever she might have expected – and no matter that they were all exhausted to the bone – working at the Silvertown Animal Hospital certainly wasn't dull.

2

Of course, life wasn't all fun and games, nowadays.

Not a bit of it.

Zeppelin strikes continued to plague the city every couple of months – striking fear into everyone's hearts – food was getting ever more scarce and ever more expensive and, of course, Ruby's older brother, Harry, was away 'doing his bit' for King and Country.

Conscripted into the army – 47th (London) Division – earlier in the year, Harry had recently been deployed to France. And not just to *anywhere* in France, but to the Somme Valley where fighting had been raging ever since the summer. No one knew exactly where Harry was, but Ruby and her family *did* know that this was the last place on earth anyone would want a loved one to be sent.

At first, the newspapers had been deceptively coy on the casualty count of the 'Big Push' – and some had printed downright lies – but no one had been in any doubt that the campaign had got off to a disastrous start at the beginning of July. It had taken weeks before the government had finally admitted that almost twenty thousand British troops had been killed on the first day alone – the greatest daily loss for any day in any war – but the signs had been everywhere. When a young telegram boy or girl had visited a neighbourhood to deliver the very worst of news, they had often crisscrossed the street visiting multiple homes. People working in the hospitals had known that the wards were crammed to overflowing leaving wounded soldiers sleeping in corridors; people working at the Army Post Office's Home Depot in Regent's Park had known that there were hundreds of sack-loads of letters marked 'Killed in Action' being returned . . . and so it went on.

The high casualty count had been obvious at the munitions factory, as well. Leah was a personnel manager and it was part of her job to fetch a white-faced employee from one of the offices or factory floors to reunite them with a weeping relative who had arrived at the factory carrying the dreaded telegram. Leah, naturally, hated that aspect of her job with a vengeance.

At least the newspapers had stopped trying to hide the obvious. From mid-July, they had started publishing lists of the soldiers who had been killed, wounded or reported missing in action and also gave a running commentary on activity at the front.

But July had given way to August and September and the battle had just gone on and on with virtually no let-up in the fighting.

And then the mud had arrived.

By October, the rain and the shells had turned the battlefield into a quagmire, making it almost impossible to advance, transport supplies and provide medical care. As the papers reported, the mud was not, of course, only a physical obstacle but also a psychological one; making the already challenging conditions of trench warfare even more unbearable.

And it was to this hellscape that Harry had been sent barely two weeks previously. That day had been a long time coming – Harry had been training in Blighty for the best part of six months. His intended destination had always been something of a foregone conclusion, but it had all still come as a terrible shock to Ruby and the family when he had written to say that he was off to France only a few weeks after he had turned up at the hospital opening. To be honest, they didn't yet know if Harry had reached the Somme; his latest letters talking only of arriving at a large army base camp on the French coast at Étaples for more training. Who knew whether, since then, Harry had joined his unit at the front line or if he was still safely by the sea?

Ruby and her family – like millions of families up and down the land – could only hold their collective breath and anxiously live from letter to letter.

As soon as she got home from her shift that afternoon, Ruby's eyes went instinctively to Harry's photograph in his army uniform on the mantlepiece to see if there was a letter propped in front of it.

Ma looked up from her place at the kitchen table and gave Ruby a tiny shake of her head and Aunt Maggie, sitting beside her, pursed her lips and said that hopefully something would arrive first thing in the morning.

Ruby swallowed her anxiety, patted Mac – her little black-and-white dog – on the head and poured herself a cuppa from the ever-present teapot on the kitchen table.

'Oh, you're making the Christmas cake!' she exclaimed with pleasure, noticing the little piles of cherries and candied peel on the table for the first time. The fruit was twinkling in the gaslight and looked so opulent – to say nothing of delicious – that Ruby couldn't help stretching out her hand for a piece of angelica.

'Just soaking the fruit,' said Ma, gently slapping her hand away. 'And we've barely got enough as it is, so mitts off.'

'Here, have a couple of raisins instead, child,' said Aunt Maggie. 'We've got plenty of *those*.'

Ruby popped the raisins in her mouth. 'It seems like summer has barely finished,' she said, sitting down and stroking Tess, the little black cat who had been rescued from the munitions factory. 'I can't believe we're already thinking about Christmas.'

'It's already the twenty-seventh of October,' said Aunt Maggie. 'And we need time for the fruit to plump up in the rum.'

'Besides, with all the talk about shortages this year, we thought we shouldn't hang around,' added Ma. 'Can you imagine your brother arriving home for Christmas and there ain't being a cake?'

'There would be hell to pay,' agreed Ruby, helping herself to another raisin. 'Our Harry likes his cake.'

'He does. He'd scoff the whole thing by himself given half the chance! And don't forget the mince pies. Remember the year he ate six all by himself and was promptly sick?'

As the family laughed easily together, Ruby found that she was pleased the old rituals and routines were still being observed, even more than two years into the war. Take the recent harvest festivals, for example. They might have been a little more subdued than usual, but they had continued in earnest despite the war. This year, in particular, they had been used as an opportunity to collect donations and contributions for the boys at the Somme and the emphasis had been all about patriotism, sacrifice and recognising the contribution of farmers – and the agricultural industry in general – to the war.

And it looked like Christmas was going to be much the same. Oh, she knew that the likes of Mrs Henderson – her old employer from her days in service – would be pushing the boat out as she always did; only the tallest tree, the fanciest icing and the most elegantly wrapped presents would ever have been good enough. But Ruby *had* wondered if the East Enders would be taking a much more low-key approach this year now that the shortages were really beginning to bite. Luckily, if Ma and Aunt Maggie were anything to go by, not a bit of it.

Look at them now.

Were they really toasting each other with tots of rum sloshed into teacups?

'For shame,' said Ruby, mock-primly, pushing Mac's enquiring nose away from the dried fruit. 'You look like a couple of old soaks.'

'We just need to make sure the rum ain't gone bad over the past year,' said Aunt Maggie with a wink.

'Of course it ain't,' said Ruby. 'That's the whole point of alcohol.'

'Come on, get a nip down yourself,' said Ma. 'You're looking altogether too pasty for me liking nowadays. All that working at the factory and the animal hospital on top.'

She poured a tiny measure into a rose-patterned teacup and handed it to Ruby. Ruby, for her part, gave an exaggerated shrug, screwed up her face in anticipation of the fiery bite and took a dainty sip. Actually, it was lovely. Rich and warming and comforting . . .

'I've been meaning to ask you something,' said Aunt Maggie, pouring the rum into the measuring jug and then into the big cream mixing bowl. 'I were wondering if there were cotton wool I could take from the hospital.'

'Whatever for?' asked Ruby, taking another sip of rum.

'I want to hang balls from thread to make snowflakes,' said Aunt Maggie. 'I'll hang them from me front window and it will look ever so festive to people walking down Sanctuary Lane. I can make some for the hospital windows too, if you'd like?'

Ruby swallowed the rest of her rum whilst she considered the request. Her instinctive reaction was a firm 'no'. It would, of course, be a matter of moments before any 'snowflakes' hanging in the hospital reception were either destroyed or consumed by the animals waiting to be treated. Besides, she could hardly just start giving away the hospital supplies to her relatives in order to make Christmas decorations. At the end of the day, it wasn't her money that had purchased the cotton wool and, even if no one noticed on this occasion, it was the principle that mattered. After all, the whole enterprise was built on trust . . .

But then again, her aunt just wanted to do something nice to brighten up the street during these cold, dark days. They *all* needed cheering up nowadays. She would give Aunt Maggie the cotton wool, tell Leah what she had done and pop sixpence from her wages into the hospital donation box to make up for it . . .

But, before she could answer, there was a knock at the door and Mac duly started barking.

Ruby's heart started hammering loudly and her breathing

changed to raggedy little gasps. Ma's hands shook as she added the last of the fruit to the alcohol and Aunt Maggie let out a little yelp as she returned the bottle of rum to the larder.

Was it a telegram boy or girl – the so-called 'Angels of Death'?

That would teach them to relax, even for a second.

'It don't have to mean anything,' said Aunt Maggie resolutely, wiping her hands on her pinny.

'Of course, it don't,' said Ma, stoutly, giving the fruit a stir. 'It could be a thousand and one people. A thousand and one reasons.'

No one moved and there was another knock at the door.

'Oh, this is ridiculous,' said Ruby. 'We're spooking ourselves over nothing.'

And, before she could change her mind or question herself, Ruby marched down the passage – Mac, Ma and Aunt Maggie in tow – and flung the front door wide open.

It was Jack, face creased into his trademark lopsided grin.

Ruby sagged against the front door jamb as Ma and Aunt Maggie melted away, muttering in relief and annoyance.

'Why on earth didn't you use the back alleyway?' said Ruby, clutching her chest theatrically to make her point. 'You've given us all a heart attack.'

'I'm so sorry,' said Jack. 'I didn't think. I had something important to tell you and I just rushed straight down the street . . .'

He looked so crestfallen that Ruby's irritation quite melted away. She put her arms around his neck – feeling his loop around her waist in reply – and gave him a huge hug. He smelled of leather and animals . . . and Jack.

'Wait – can I smell alcohol?' said Jack, pulling away and looking down at her in amusement. 'Have you been *drinking,* Missy?'

'Just a tot of the rum from the Christmas cake,' said Ruby with a giggle. 'Rather nice, actually.'

'Ha! We'll make a soldier of you yet,' said Jack. 'Me ma were steeping the fruit for the Christmas cake yesterday and all,' he added. 'Said we'd better get on with it before rationing starts – although at least that would stop the rich from hoarding . . .'

They were interrupted by a small canine cannonball hurtling down the passageway. It was Mac, who had been originally owned by Jack but who, unbeknownst to Jack, had been sold to Ruby by his mother whilst he was still away at the front. Jack crouched down onto his haunches and took Mac's face in his hands and the little dog, by way of reply, wriggled with delight and started licking Jack's face over and over again.

And here was Ruby's younger brother, Charlie, sauntering up Sanctuary Lane without an apparent care in the world. It was a good few hours after school had finished and Ruby felt a wave of frustration wash over her. It was only a matter of months since Charlie had admitted to throwing bricks through the windows of premises owned or run by Germans . . . and here he was, if not exactly running wild, certainly not rushing home to complete his homework or help around the house.

'Where have you been?' asked Ruby, slightly tartly, as Charlie approached.

She was struck how much he looked like Harry at the same age; half-man, half-boy, with the same slanted hazel eyes and full mouth. But, goodness, he reeked! He badly needed a decent bath, but he wouldn't get one of *those* until Sunday.

'Out,' said Charlie, with fourteen-year-old insolence.

'Oi,' said Jack, mildly enough. 'Don't talk to your sister like that.'

Charlie paused, clearly wondering whether it was in his best interests to cheek a man who was a head taller and a good couple of stone heavier than he was.

'Sorry,' he mumbled. 'I were out with me pals.'

He pushed past Jack and Ruby and, without a backwards glance, headed inside the house.

Ruby gave an exaggerated sigh at his departing back and then turned her attention back to Jack. 'Sorry about that,' she said. 'So, what were the very important thing you wanted to tell me?'

Jack straightened up, one hand still on Mac's head and smiled sheepishly. 'I applied for a job at the munitions factory,' he said.

Oh!

Whatever Ruby had imagined he might say, it wasn't . . . that.

'You never said!' she replied indignantly, punching him lightly on the chest.

'If I didn't get in, there would have been nothing to say,' said Jack. 'And it were hardly the thing to start talking about it at the hospital. Besides, we was rushed off our feet and there were never a chance to talk to you, even if I'd wanted to.'

'That monkey . . .'

'I *know*. I had to go and have a good wash after that, I can tell you. What a waste of a cake!'

'And . . . ?'

'And what?'

'Did you get the job, of course?'

Jack smiled with satisfaction. 'I've been invited to start on the main factory floor tomorrow morning,' he said.

Ruby gave him another hug. 'Well done,' she said. 'Not that it were ever in doubt.'

'You don't mind?' said Jack. 'Please tell me if you do. Because I promise I won't take it if so . . .'

'Mind?' said Ruby, sitting down on the scrubbed door-step. 'No, of course I don't mind. I'm perfectly resigned to me sweetheart turning bright yellow as he does his bit.'

Jack laughed, sitting down next to her. 'I were worried you might think I were stepping on your toes,' he said. 'But I couldn't carry on running dunnage from the docks, and I can't face the thought of starting up me stepdad's old costermonger business, neither. Besides, I felt I had to do *something* to support the war effort after being invalided out and the powers that be were suggesting I work at the Home Depot, sorting post for the soldiers at the front. But that's in Regent's Park; three trains away . . .'

'Of course,' said Ruby, shuffling up as Mac tried to wedge his way between the two of them. And with you hating trains as much as you do . . . But what will happen to Mayfair? You won't need a donkey no more if you're working at the munitions and we really need her at the hospital on a Friday. Who will ferry animals and supplies to and fro otherwise?'

'Don't worry,' said Jack. 'Mayfair is in high demand from costermongers and stallholders and me stepdad has written to tell me to continue to stable her at the depot and to rent her out as and when. He's happy with her helping out at the hospital on a Friday and me pal Tarroc likes doing his bit too – so no change there.'

'Marvellous,' said Ruby. 'And obviously we'd be happy to pay your stepdad to use Mayfair so he ain't out of pocket. Oh, it will be wonderful having you at the factory, Jack. It's like a small town, so it's plenty big enough for the two of us, if that's what you're worried about. We won't be able to eat in the same canteen if you're on the main factory floor, but we'll see each other around the place and we could even walk there together if we're on the same shift.'

'Marvellous,' echoed Jack. 'I'm so pleased you don't mind.'

'I'm only jealous of one thing,' said Ruby.

'What's that?' said Jack, his brow furrowing.

'You won't have had to drop your skirts to prove you ain't a man trying to avoid the call up.'

3

Tuesday, 31 October 1916

A couple of days later, Ruby and Leah were heading to 'their' bank of grass at the munitions factory during their lunchbreak. After a few months on the night shift, Ruby had asked to switch back to daytime working to better fit with her weekly shifts at the animal hospital and Leah, as her personnel manager, had been more than happy to oblige.

This bank was the spot where the two had met and bonded several months ago over a mutual affection for the cats who hung around the factory canteen kitchen. Nowadays, with more and more people working at the factory, spots on all the grassy spaces were at a premium whenever the weather was good enough, but the two still sat there whenever they could. Ruby would have loved it if Jack could have joined them as well, but his shift pattern had turned out to be slightly different than hers. Starting a couple of hours later, his breaks didn't overlap with hers at all.

No sooner had they sat down than Leah suddenly coloured prettily and said, 'I just wanted to let you know that Robert and I are stepping out together.'

Finally!

'Oh, that's marvellous,' said Ruby, clapping her hands

together in delight. 'I'm so happy for you both. Robert's wonderful, he really is. And you ain't bad, neither!'

Leah grinned. 'That's not what you said a couple of months ago,' she said dryly. 'I distinctly seem to recall you saying that Robert's eyes were too close together, his face was too thin and that he reminded you of a ferret. Oh, and that he was an odious little man, to boot.'

Ruby buried her head in her hands.

Had she really said all that?

'It's fair to say Robert didn't start off in me good books,' she admitted. 'But you can't blame me; he complained to his pa about me and his pa had me chucked out of the room at the depot we was going to rent. I'd say I were quite within me rights to call him a ferret!'

'True,' said Leah. 'But he didn't mean for us to be chucked out of the depot and, besides, the building we've ended up in is far better, is it not?'

'It is,' agreed Ruby. 'Anyway, I trust you ain't going to tell Robert what I said?'

'Oh, I'm not sure,' said Leah with a smile that set her dimples dancing. 'Probably not if you make it worth my while.'

'Ha!' said Ruby. 'Don't forget that *you* once said Robert were a dreadful sap your mother were trying to marry you off to.'

Leah threw her hands up in mock surrender. 'I know,' she said, with a laugh. 'I can't believe that I ever said that. Isn't it funny how feelings can turn on a sixpence?'

Ruby nodded. It had been different with Jack, though, of course. Ruby's heart had started beating that little bit faster from the first moment she'd ever set eyes on him and the swooping in the pit of her stomach showed no sign of abating.

'Anyway,' said Leah, 'we will, of course, be consummate professionals at the clinic, so you don't need to worry about that. But we *did* wonder if you two would like to come to the cinema with us and maybe for a bite to eat beforehand? We feel we should really join the rest of the country and finally see *The Battle of the Somme*.'

Us.

We.

Ruby suppressed a smile. It really was the loveliest news.

She wasn't sure about the cinema, though.

Robert and Leah were lovely, but the two couples were from very different classes and, before the war, socialising together would simply not have been entertained. Even now, it was sure to invite comment. Besides, even after a few months, Ruby was still at the stage in her relationship where she wanted to hug Jack to herself; it was nothing against Leah – who she considered to be her very best friend – she didn't want to share Jack with *anyone* just yet. She wanted to carry on going out for walks with him, snatching the odd coffee in a café, watching football matches together. It was hard enough finding the time to be with him anyway, what with all their commitments and now the nights were drawing in, there seemed less and less opportunity to be alone. They could go to Ruby's house after work, of course, but the kitchen was always a crush – and she hadn't yet been invited around to Jack's. She wasn't particularly worried about this; her first meeting with

Mrs Driscoll months earlier had hardly been plain sailing and Jack had already told her that he had never taken any girl back to meet his mother. When – if – she was invited, it would be a red-letter day indeed . . .

All that aside, did she really want to watch a film about the Somme when Harry had so recently arrived out in France? On balance, she supposed that she should, even though she had been avoiding it for months. The papers had reported that the Prime Minister himself was encouraging all patriotic Britons to see it, so it was probably her duty to do so. Anyway, if Harry was going to have to face the fighting, surely the very least *she* could do was watch a film about it. Goodness knew what Jack would make of it, though, having recently fought out there. She would ask him and let his reaction make or break the idea.

Ruby was saved from having to answer Leah one way or another by someone flopping down onto the grass beside them. It was pretty, blonde Elspeth who had started at the Brunner-Mond munitions factory on the same day as Ruby and who was now one of the stars of its football team. Strictly speaking, it was pretty, blonde, *yellow* Elspeth because Elspeth worked directly with the chemicals and her skin was fast turning the very colour that had the Munitionettes dubbed 'The Canary Girls'. Ruby now considered Elspeth a firm friend and, although Elspeth didn't directly volunteer at the animal hospital, a few months ago she and her mother had offered to organise a Christmas bazaar to raise much-needed funds.

'Hello, Elspeth,' said Ruby in surprise. The last Ruby had known, Elspeth had been working night shifts on the main factory floor. 'You switched to the day shifts and all?'

'I have,' said Elspeth with a grin. 'Special request from the captain of the football team herself! We've got a couple of important matches coming up and this fits much better with our schedule.'

'Any news of your pa, Elspeth?' asked Leah.

'Still at Étaples, I think,' said Elspeth. 'How about your brother, Ruby?'

'Same,' said Ruby. 'Hoping we get a letter very soon.'

Elspeth nodded. 'So are we,' she said, with a little grimace. 'By the way, I've seen your Jack on the factory floor.'

'I hope he's getting on alright,' said Ruby. 'He barely talks to me about it at all.'

'Well, he throws those sacks of chemicals around like they weigh nothing at all,' said Elspeth with a little laugh. 'He had three over his shoulders at one point yesterday and I told him he were showing the rest of us up. Doesn't seem quite so keen on the noise, though.'

Ruby grimaced. 'I don't blame him,' she said.

Ruby had been relieved to leave the main factory floor and to start assembling detonators for that very reason. The main factory floor was absolutely deafening. Clangs and bangs and rumbles and people shouting and . . .

Hopefully, Jack would get used to it. The war had left him deaf in one ear, so maybe that would actually help . . .

'I just wanted to have a chat with you about the Christmas bazaar before I head off to training,' said Elspeth, cutting across her thoughts.

'Oh, Lord, Christmas is going to be upon us before we know it,' said Leah, gloomily.

'Too right it is,' said Elspeth. 'It's already All Hallows' Eve. I can hardly believe it.'

'Are you doing anything to mark it?' asked Leah.

Ruby and Elspeth both shook their heads. All over Silvertown, families would be bobbing for apples, telling ghost stories, and carving faces into hollowed-out turnips and – whilst she definitely considered herself too old to get involved – she *had* wondered if Charlie would twist Ma's arm to celebrate the occasion. But even her brother had pooh-poohed the idea this year; what was the point, he'd said, when you were no longer allowed to illuminate the Jack-o'-lanterns with a candle and display them on windowsills or front doorsteps to ward off evil spirits?

'Me neither,' said Leah. 'I plan to totally ignore it. But Christmas is a different matter. Mummy keeps sending me details of all sorts of ghastly soirees and parties that I'm supposed to be showing my face at. I keep telling her that there's a war on, and that excess is frowned upon, but she's already been up to Selfridges and bought the most vulgar Christmas decorations you can possibly imagine. Huge gold baubles and red velvet bows you could make a sash out of and . . .'

'It's all cotton-wool snowflakes on Sanctuary Lane,' interrupted Ruby with a grin. 'Aunt Maggie's already asked if I can raid the hospital supplies for her. Don't worry,' she added, seeing Leah's horrified face, 'I'll make sure the hospital ain't out of pocket.'

'I know you will,' said Leah, 'but if it's cotton wool one week, it will be people helping themselves to tweezers and scalpels the next . . .'

'Actually, cotton wool ain't a bad idea for decorating the hospital with for the bazaar,' interrupted Elspeth.

'Decorations was one of the things I wanted to bounce off you today. I were thinking paperchains, but snowflakes would be ever so festive.'

'Especially as you never seem to get a proper white Christmas in the East End,' added Leah.

'As long as they don't get a freezing Christmas at the Somme, I don't care what we get here,' said Ruby. 'But, yes, snowflakes is a good idea for the bazaar. Maybe we could all get together one evening and rustle some up.'

'Count me in,' said Leah. 'Especially if it's on the same day as one of the parties. That way I can legitimately claim "charity work" and Mummy won't have a leg to stand on.'

The three women laughed easily together and Ruby thought, for about the millionth time, how strange it was that they had become fast friends. She had initially dismissed Leah for being insufferably po-faced and la-di-da and had written Elspeth off for being irritatingly vapid and frivolous ever since they had been pupils at the same school. It just showed that you really couldn't judge a book by its cover.

'Most things for the bazaar are already in place, but December twenty-second will come around quickly,' Elspeth was saying. 'We have the whole of the hospital *and* the courtyard behind it with all the stables and garages – so we'll have plenty of space. I've already got people from church and from the factory allocated to sort out all the main stalls. It's going to be grand. We've got stalls selling animal tonics and the like, loads of bric-a-brac and all the usual games like lucky dip and tombola. And I might just know someone at the market who can find us a couple of coconuts for a shy, which would just be the icing on the cake.'

'I reckon we would make the most money from auctioning them off afterwards,' said Ruby with a wry smile. 'You can't get coconuts for love nor money nowadays. But that all sounds fabulous, Elspeth. Thank you ever so much.'

Elspeth beamed with pleasure. 'Is there anything else you can think of?' she said.

'Pin the tail on the donkey?' offered Leah.

'Everyone comes dressed as their favourite animal?'

They all burst out laughing at this last, not entirely serious, suggestion from Ruby.

'Seriously, though, the bazaar will be a great way to really put the hospital on the map,' said Leah. 'The concert in the West End was all well and good, but most of the audience were rich and don't live in Silvertown. We need to keep building awareness so that everyone round here knows about what we offer.'

Ruby nodded. 'Talking of which, I've been thinking of changing the hospital name. Instead of the Silvertown Animal Hospital, what do you think of the Sanctuary Lane Animal Hospital? We haven't got a proper sign up yet – it still says Mullers Haberdashery, for goodness' sake – so we can still change our minds.'

Elspeth clapped her hands together. 'I think that's perfectly marvellous,' she said. 'Most of your customers are from Silvertown anyway and this tells them exactly where in town it is.'

'And doesn't everyone seem to call it the Sanctuary Lane Animal Hospital anyway?' said Leah. 'Besides, it's such a perfect street name. Even though we aren't a sanctuary as such – well, we aren't a sanctuary at all – the word just conjures up all the right connotations, doesn't it?'

'It does,' said Ruby, smothering a smile. Leah's turns of phrase were just so impossibly la-di-da sometimes! 'So, that's decided. The Sanctuary Lane Animal Hospital it is.'

Elspeth stood up and brushed the grass from her trousers. 'On that note, I'd better get a move on,' she said. 'I don't want to be late for training *again* – Mr Leadbetter would have me guts for garters.'

She gave a little wave that encompassed them both and was off.

'Should you two be sitting so close to the perimeter fence?' said a voice that Ruby vaguely knew.

She spun around, but the short, stout Woman Police Officer staring down at them and bristling with aggression was not one that she recognised.

Leah was looking up at the policewoman in irritation. 'I've been sitting this close to the perimeter fence for the past year,' she said shortly.

That wasn't strictly true.

The bank was much busier than usual and Ruby and Leah had inadvertently moved closer to the fence that bounded the site. In fact, they were close enough to smell the curry-leaf plants that had been planted by the Cat Committee to deter unwanted cats from entering the site.

Ruby was about to apologise and to shift closer to the canteen when she noticed that Leah was rigid with annoyance beside her.

'I'm one of the personnel managers here,' she said stiffly, 'so I'm well aware of the rules, thank you ever so much. And I think I can safely say that if we *are* closer than three yards to the fence, it will be by a matter of inches.'

'And I think *I* can say that the rules apply to everyone, regardless of whether you're a manager or not,' replied the policewoman curtly. 'Perhaps I can trouble you to move, *Miss*,' she added, in a tone that dripped with sarcasm.

'Come on, Leah.' Ruby kept her back firmly towards the police officer in her embarrassment. 'Let's just move closer to the canteen, shall we?'

'For goodness' sake, we're just sitting here chatting,' said Leah tetchily. 'We're hardly passing secrets to the Germans. We're nowhere near the fence and we're certainly no threat to national security.'

'That ain't the point,' said the policewoman. 'Rules is rules. It ain't up to me nor you to interpret them as we see fit. You're wasting me time and I've got a good mind to take things further.'

Oh, really!

That was a bit rich.

Ruby was about to interrupt again – this time in Leah's defence – but something made her hesitate.

She really did recognise that voice – that *tone* – and she was still trying to work out from where. She spun around again and, for the second time, took a good look at the face beneath the hat. A good twenty years older than Ruby, a wisp of sandy hair, a snub nose . . .

'Cook!'

Ruby had been a housemaid before she had left to do her bit – and Cook had worked at the same large apartment in Hampstead in the service of Mr and Mrs Henderson.

To be fair, she knew that Cook had handed her notice in to join the police but, nevertheless, it was a huge coincidence.

Cook had been glaring down at Leah, hands on hips, but now she turned and her gaze settled on Ruby.

'Well, well, well,' she said in a much softer tone. 'If it ain't little Ruby from Hampstead. Fancy seeing you here! You scarpered from the Hendersons without any notice and left them well and truly in the lurch, didn't you, girl?'

Ruby made a face. 'I did,' she admitted. 'I do feel a bit guilty . . .'

'Don't,' said Cook, shortly. 'The Hendersons deserved all they got. Bleeding misers, the pair of them. Barely gave me a pay rise in ten years.'

'They wanted me to start doing their cooking after you said you were leaving,' said Ruby with a grin. 'Me! I could barely boil an egg. And it would have been for the same wages, of course.'

'Says it all,' said Cook with a sniff.

Ruby turned to Leah. 'This is Cook – I mean Mrs Lillie Fletcher – from the Hendersons' house in Hampstead,' she said.

'So, I gathered,' said Leah. 'Pleased to meet you,' she added to Cook in a voice that suggested she was anything but.

'Likewise, I'm sure. *Miss*,' replied Cook.

Leah stood up.

'I'm going to head back on duty, Ruby,' she said stiffly. 'Lots to do. I'll see you on Friday, if not before. And do let me know about joining us at the flicks to watch *The Battle of the Somme*.'

And she was gone in a swish of skirts.

Cook gave a little snort. 'I might still have to work every Saturday here, but it's nice having a bit more power over our so-called betters, ain't it?' she said with satisfaction. 'It felt good taking Miss La-Di-Da there down a peg or two, I can tell you.'

Ruby hesitated.

'I don't really think of it like that,' she said, carefully. 'After all, surely we're all on the same side nowadays? All of us making munitions together. Us against the Hun.'

'Of course, we are,' said Cook. 'But, even so, things are changing in the right direction, ain't they?'

'They are,' Ruby said cautiously. 'But Leah – Miss Richardson – is a decent sort and, believe me, she's as much for change as we are . . .'

'I didn't like the tone she took with me.'

'She won't have meant to cause offence,' said Ruby. 'Honestly, I think you need to work with her. Things is hard enough as they are without making any more problems for ourselves.'

'And I think *you* need to be careful,' Cook retorted. 'Seems like you've found your tongue since you left service, but Miss Richardson and her sort will have us back below stairs as soon as the war is over, you mark my words. I'm going to do everything in my power to make sure that don't happen and, if I were you, Ruby, I would look sharp and start doing the same. Nice to see you again and good day to you.'

'Good day, Cook,' said Ruby, heading slowly back to work in the detonation shed.

That was not at all how she'd imagined her lunchtime would end.

4

Thursday, 2 November 1916

Despite her initial reservations, Ruby agreed to meet Leah and Robert for an evening at the flicks.

Somewhat to Ruby's surprise, Jack seemed keen on the idea and, at the end of the day, why not? Robert and Leah had been so supportive of the animal hospital – indeed, had both been absolutely instrumental to its success – and it seemed churlish not to accept their invitation.

Really, it should be *her* inviting *them* out for an evening on the tiles!

But then Leah suggested meeting at the Tivoli on the Barking Road. Ruby had never been there before and would probably have preferred to go to Sweetingham's on Albert Road, which was a stroll away in the heart of Silvertown and only cost sixpence for the whole programme. The Tivoli was a much grander affair; a bus ride away, Ruby had heard it cost well over a shilling apiece. Ruby didn't particularly mind for herself – the munitions factory paid well and she could afford the odd treat – but she was worried for Jack. He had barely started work at the factory and, on more than one occasion, he had made it clear that the money he'd received when he was invalided out of the army had already been swallowed up by this and that. The last thing Ruby wanted was for him to feel in any way embarrassed. She could offer to pay for him, of course, but that might just succeed in making matters worse. Knowing Jack and his silly, adorable pride, he would probably feel he should be paying for her, quite forgetting that this was 1916 and that many women had their own money nowadays and were quite happy doing things for themselves.

Why was it all so *complicated*?

Ruby broached the subject as they were taking Mac for a walk down by the river in Victoria Park a couple of mornings after Leah had issued her cinema invitation. Sometimes meeting up for a stroll before work felt like the only time the two could be alone and Ruby treasured this time together. Autumn was her favourite season anyway – the leaves in the park turning orange and drifting lazily to the ground to be crunched underfoot, the smell of the woodsmoke, the caw of the gulls as they wheeled overhead – but sharing it with both Jack and Mac made it all even more special. She would tuck her hand into the crook of Jack's arm as they promenaded up and down the gravel pathways – stopping for the occasional chaste kiss and cuddle – and Mac would bound at their feet. Ruby loved it all – loved *them* – and was the happiest she had ever been. If only she could bottle this on-top-of-the-world feeling.

To her relief, Jack didn't bat an eyelid about splashing out to go to the Tivoli.

'I'm not *that* short of cash,' he said, throwing a ball for Mac along the towpath and narrowly avoiding the navy-blue water. 'The Tivoli will be grand and no less than you deserve. And, before you protest, I insist on paying, of course.'

Ruby took a deep breath. 'Only if I can take care of supper before,' she said, as she had already planned to do. 'I'm very happy for you to actually pay for me in the restaurant if you'd like, but you must let me pay you back.'

Jack hesitated; his handsome face screwed up in concentration as he considered her request. 'Oh, you modern girls,' he said, with a grin that creased up his face. 'Still, I don't want to stand in the way of progress – anything that gives you women more freedom is absolutely fine by me – so I will just thank you kindly and accept your offer.'

'Thank you,' said Ruby simply. 'And are you sure you're alright seeing a film about the Somme? We could suggest something else if you'd prefer. I still ain't seen *20,000 Leagues Under the Sea*.'

Jack bent over to retrieve the ball from Mac, straightened up and threw it again. 'It will be fine,' he said shortly. 'I need to do me social duty and see it along with everyone else.'

'But you was there. I'd say you've already done more than your duty . . .'

'Ruby, it will be fine,' interrupted Jack. 'Might even be interesting to see it all in context.'

'You'll be able to tell us which bits they got wrong . . .'

'That I will.'

Ruby stopped still as Mac galloped towards her at full tilt. The little dog stopped in the nick of time in front of her and she duly reached down to take the ball from his mouth. 'Oh, Mac; that is just revoltingly slobbery,' she added, wrinkling up her face in distaste. 'You've got it all over me skirt and I've got to go straight to work after I've dropped you off at home.'

'There's something you can do for me,' said Jack, taking hold of her slobbery hand. 'I warn you though, it might make you want to turn tail.'

The smile had gone from his face and he suddenly looked a little nervous.

Oh, Lordy.

'What's that?' asked Ruby, heart beginning to beat like the clappers.

'Me ma wants to know if you'd like to pop round for a cuppa,' said Jack. 'You know, to meet her properly.'

Oh.

Whatever Ruby had thought Jack had been about to ask, it certainly hadn't been . . . *that.*

Jack was looking at her, head on one side, waiting for an answer and, a dozen thoughts suddenly competing for attention, Ruby gave him a weak smile.

'Oh, Lordy,' she said.

Out loud, this time.

When Jack's mother had sold her Mac, Ruby hadn't known the little dog actually belonged to Jack, who was away fighting in France. In fact, back then, she hadn't known that Jack existed! All she had known was that Mac was disfigured because Mrs Driscoll had poured paraffin into his ear and set fire to it in a bid to get rid of his canker – and that Mac had gone partially deaf as a result. Because Mrs Driscoll needed a guard dog who could actually hear, she had been forced to purchase a second dog, Rex, who had taken an instant dislike to Mac and made his life a misery. Ruby had truly believed she was doing the right thing by buying Mac and had paid Mrs Driscoll way over the odds. What she couldn't possibly have known was that – when Jack finally returned from the war – Mrs Driscoll would tell him that Mac had died. The resultant hoo-hah when Jack had discovered both that Mac was still alive *and* was now owned by the girl he intended to court had resulted in a heartbroken Ruby returning Mac to Jack and vowing never to speak to him again. It had been weeks before the situation had been resolved and before Mac had been returned to Ruby's care and, although things between Ruby and Jack were now fine and dandy, Ruby knew it continued to be a source of ill-feeling between Jack and his mother . . .

That said, it was surely a good sign that Mrs Driscoll now wanted to meet Ruby. And it was an even better sign that, despite the circumstances, Jack was prepared to let her.

So, she just smiled at Jack and said simply, 'That would be lovely.'

Jack's face melted into a smile. 'Why don't we go just before we go out on Saturday?' he said. 'It's the perfect excuse to keep things short and sweet.'

'Splendid,' said Ruby. She gave Jack a wide grin. 'Shall I bring Mac and all?'

'Not if that revolting hound makes your hand as slobbery as it is now.'

Ruby crouched down and wrapped her arms around Mac's neck. 'Don't listen to him,' she crooned. 'You're not a revolting hound. You're the best boy in the whole world.'

'What, even better than me?' said Jack, with mock affront.

'That's for me to know and you to find out,' said Ruby pertly, standing up and giving Jack a kiss on the cheek.

Another wave of happiness swept through her. Jack really was the loveliest man and he had just invited her to meet his mother.

Despite everything, life was good.

Saturday, 4 November 1916

Ruby was exhausted when Saturday finally arrived.

The weekly clinic at the animal hospital the day before had been bedlam. Despite how hard they all worked, the queues stretching down the street never seemed to get any shorter and – although rewarding – there had hardly been a moment to catch her breath.

Ruby could, quite happily, have gone to bed at five o'clock in the afternoon.

Instead, she dressed carefully for the occasion.

For both occasions.

Until very recently, her wardrobe hadn't included clothes suitable for an evening excursion such as this. It simply hadn't needed to! But an incident at the theatre a couple of months previously – when Ruby had been embarrassingly mistaken as one of the theatre staff – had forced her to reassess all that. With no time in her busy days – and very little inclination – to make her own clothes, Ruby had saved her wages for a few weeks and dragged Leah off to Selfridges to buy some new-fangled ready-to-wear dresses. And how glad she was that she had done so, because she was now the proud owner of three new dresses in various colours and designs. Nothing too fancy, of course, but tonight Ruby felt fresh and pretty in a light green serge dress and a matching cloche hat. It was just the sort of thing that Leah might wear and Ruby fancied that the casual onlooker would not immediately know the huge class difference between the two women. The dress was modest enough with its high neckline, long sleeves and semi-fitted silhouette, but Ma and Aunt Maggie had – predictably – spluttered good-naturedly over the midcalf hemline. No matter; Ruby loved it all and fancied that the colour brought out the golden highlights in her dark-blonde hair and the greenish flecks in her otherwise blue eyes. She tied her hair into a loose plait – just the way that Jack liked it – and even contemplated applying a little rouge and lipstick from the dainty – thus far unopened – boxes also purchased from Selfridges and hidden in her bottom drawer. In the end, she decided that Ma and Aunt Maggie would certainly have something to say about *that* – cosmetics, in their mind, were only worn by certain ladies of ill repute – and settled for pinching her cheeks to bring a little colour to her creamy complexion and biting her lips in search of the perfect rosebud pout.

Jack was certainly most appreciative of Ruby's efforts when he picked her up from Sanctuary Lane.

He gave her a cheerful wolf-whistle as she opened the door and then bent over and kissed her hand in a formal little courtly gesture. Ruby decided then and there that she wouldn't swap the admiration and attraction in his eyes for all Leah's fine jewellery, even if Jack *had* promptly let go of her – definitely *non*-slobbery – hand and dropped to his haunches to make a thorough fuss of Mac.

'Ready to face the enemy?' he said, cheerfully, straightening up and offering Ruby his arm.

Ruby's heart started to pound as the two set off down Sanctuary Lane together.

She hadn't been particularly nervous before, but Jack's words had rattled her.

'Stop it,' she said, firmly. 'Your mother ain't the enemy. I've met her before and she's . . . ever so lovely.'

That, of course, wasn't entirely true.

Mrs Driscoll hadn't been particularly lovely in her dealings with Ruby to date. In fact, she had been short-tempered and sarcastic – and sometimes barely the right side of downright rude. Still, everyone had their off days – or off months! – and the circumstances were entirely different now that Ruby was stepping out with Jack. She was completely prepared to give Mrs Driscoll a second chance and she hoped that Mrs Driscoll was ready and willing to do the same.

After all, they both loved Jack – and she was pretty sure that Jack loved them both in return.

Surely that was enough.

Like Ruby's home on Sanctuary Lane, 39 Victory Lane was a small redbrick terrace opening straight onto the street at the front. At the back, as with Ruby's home, there was a small yard opening onto the rear alleyway that ran parallel to Victory Lane and connected all the houses. The internal layout of Jack's home was also exactly the same as Ruby's, the only difference being that there was no one sleeping in the front parlour at Jack's house as Aunt Maggie was at Ruby's. Nevertheless, it would no doubt still be a tight squeeze for them all.

'How do you all sleep?' Ruby wondered out loud and then, when Jack smothered a smile, she could have kicked herself for asking such a potentially forward question.

Nerves getting the better of her, as usual.

'Well, now,' replied Jack, seemingly not minding the question at all – random though it might have been. 'Archie is in with me ma; Maude has the box room and I have the back room. It's easy now the children are little more than babies.'

Ruby nodded. That made sense. Jack's father, she knew, had died when Jack was ten – a short, sharp respiratory illness one particularly cold winter which had also carried away his younger brother Alf. For a few years, it had just been Jack and his ma, but then Jack's mother had met and married Bert Driscoll, had moved from East Ham to his house on Victory Lane and had given birth to Maude and Archie in fairly quick succession. By all accounts, it was a happy family and Jack often spoke fondly of his stepfather who was away fighting in Mesopotamia.

'If we're talking about sleeping arrangements, how about your house?' said Jack, cutting across her thoughts. 'There's more of you than there are of us – well, more adults, at least.'

Ruby grinned at him. It seemed that Jack could be just as forward as she was.

'Well, Aunt Maggie you know about,' said Ruby. 'She sleeps in the parlour so the kitchen is really the only room we have to live in. Ma's in the main bedroom, Charlie's in the back bedroom and I have the little boxroom at the back. It works fine at the moment, although I suppose

Charlie and Harry will have to share again when Harry gets back from the front.'

Jack nodded. 'It seems a little rum that you have the tiny room when you're both older than Charlie and you're working and paying rent as well,' he commented, mildly enough.

Ruby blinked at him. She had never thought of it quite like that and it simply hadn't occurred to her to question the sleeping arrangements at home. It was partly, of course, that her brothers had always shared the bigger bedroom growing up, so Ruby still viewed it as 'the boys'' bedroom. When Ruby had moved away into service, Harry had stayed in the larger bedroom and Charlie had moved into her small one – only reclaiming the larger one again when Harry enlisted. That, of course, had only been a matter of weeks before Ruby returned home. Maybe she *should* have kicked up a fuss. After all, she was the elder child and, as Jack had just pointed out, she was earning a good wage and contributing heavily to the family finances whilst Charlie had just started his last year at school and was contributing absolutely nothing. But she hadn't thought to question the status quo because . . . well, Charlie was a boy and that was just the way things were. But, if you factored Aunt Maggie into the equation, things got a little more complicated. Aunt Maggie certainly hadn't moved into the boxroom in Sanctuary Lane when she had first started renting out her house in Whitechapel all those months ago. And she hadn't even displaced Charlie and moved into the larger back bedroom. No – she had bypassed all that and moved straight into the *parlour*, thank you very much. And there she had stayed. Despite a rocky start, Ruby was fond of her aunt and knew that she contributed some of the rent from her house to Ma. And then there was the small matter of her arthritic knees, which she claimed made navigating the stairs tricky and painful (although Ruby had seen her bounding up them two at a time when she wanted to bawl somebody out.) But Aunt Maggie was Ruby's elder and better and therefore was entitled to the better room, and Ruby hadn't thought to question it.

It just was.

But maybe it shouldn't be like that anymore.

Ruby might be a girl and she might be younger than Aunt Maggie – but she was earning by far the most out of all of them.

'Here we are,' said Jack, cutting across her thoughts.

To Ruby's surprise, he was steering her down the rear alleyway and through the gate into his backyard. It wasn't what Ruby had expected – not using the front door *was* a little unusual – but it was surely a good sign? It meant that Jack saw Ruby as someone he felt comfortable and familiar with. Almost like one of the family . . .

'The back alleyway!' came an indignant voice. 'For *shame*.'

Mrs Driscoll had obviously seen them arrive through the kitchen window and had bustled out indignantly, hands on hips.

'Hello, Ma,' said Jack, bending to kiss his mother's cheek.

'This is no way to treat a guest to our house, now, is it?' barked Mrs Driscoll, fairly wagging a finger in his face.

Ruby was shocked. Her own family was far from

perfect, of course, but Ma would never tear her off a strip like that – especially the first time she was introduced to someone important. Ma might have given Ruby a piece of her mind later, or even made a pointed joke about whatever it was at the time, but Mrs Driscoll didn't sound like she was joking. She sounded harsh and critical and Ruby burned with embarrassment for poor Jack.

Before Jack could say anything, Mrs Driscoll turned her pinched, perennially disapproving face in Ruby's direction. 'I'm so sorry,' she said, pointedly. 'I can assure you me son *has* been brought up to know his manners.'

'That's quite alright, Mrs Driscoll,' replied Ruby with a careful little laugh, disappointed that she obviously *wasn't* viewed as part of the family. 'We can walk round to the front door and do it properly if you would prefer?'

It was a joke.

Clearly a joke.

But Mrs Driscoll just gave her a sharp look. 'There's no point in doing that, is there?' she said, a trifle sharply. 'You're here now. I only hope me son didn't arrive at your house the same way to pick you up and escort you here, although I really wouldn't have put it past him.'

Oh, dear.

Mrs Driscoll obviously didn't appreciate her – admittedly feeble – attempts at humour. And there had been absolutely no suggestion of calling her Annie going forwards.

It seemed that both she *and* Jack were in the doghouse.

Ruby smiled demurely. 'He arrived at the front door like a perfect gentleman,' she said. 'Although, of course, he comes around to ours quite often and he works with

Aunt Maggie at the animal hospital and Ma is only in the bakery next door, so we don't tend to . . .'

'Shall we go inside?' interrupted Mrs Driscoll, shortly.

There was clearly a battle still to be won.

Ruby had assumed that the three of them would have a cuppa in the kitchen but, to her surprise, Mrs Driscoll led her and Jack down the passage and into the parlour at the front of the house. A table covered in a lacy white tablecloth was centre stage, carefully set out with a silver tea service. Ruby, unexpectedly, suddenly had a lump in her throat. Despite the afternoon getting off on the wrong foot, this was exactly what her mother would have done when she wanted to impress in the days before Aunt Maggie had taken up residence in the parlour. It was really rather touching – to say nothing of flattering.

Maybe Mrs Driscoll wasn't so bad after all.

They sat down, fluttering open snowy white napkins, and Ruby glanced around the room. It was jam-packed full of highly polished heavy wooden furniture – rather as the parlour on Sanctuary Lane had been before Aunt Maggie had moved in and they had had to get rid of it all – and there was rather a dashing photograph of Jack in his army uniform on the mantlepiece next to one of – presumably – his stepfather. As was the case at home, there were no other photographs, which was a shame. Ruby would have loved to have seen a picture of Mac as a puppy!

Mrs Driscoll poured the tea and passed around bread and butter spread liberally with raspberry jam. It was all quite delicious and Ruby, ravenous, quickly wolfed down a couple of slices. Who cared that she and Jack were meeting Leah and Robert for supper in less than an hour? There might be no compulsory rationing as of yet, but everyone knew it was coming and, anyway, it was already getting harder and harder to get hold of staples like butter and sugar at a price that wouldn't break the bank.

She simply couldn't pass up a treat like this.

Conversation started with the success of the animal hospital and how busy it always was – and quickly turned to the war. Jack had clearly briefed his mother about Ruby's family situation and the fact that her brother had recently arrived in France.

'Is he on his way to the Somme?' Mrs Driscoll asked, topping up the tea.

'We don't know for sure,' said Ruby, her heart beating a little faster. 'We ain't had a letter in nearly over a fortnight. But we think he must be headed there judging from where he landed and the base camp he were sent to.'

'It's a terrible, terrible thing this war,' said Mrs Driscoll, face towards the window, a deep furrow between her brows. 'Me Bert is out there somewhere in Mesopotamia and goodness knows when I'll see him again.' She turned back towards Ruby. 'Me only comfort is that Jack has come home more or less in one piece although, of course, he ain't quite himself no more.'

'Thanks, Ma,' said Jack bitterly.

Ruby's eyes met his for a second before he looked away. He was clearly furious – there was a muscle going like the clappers in his cheek and he was clenching and unclenching his hands on the table as he gently exhaled.

Ruby debated how to reply. She didn't want to say

anything that sounded too flippant or pert after Mrs Driscoll's earlier reaction to her attempts at humour.

'Well, he seems marvellous to me,' she murmured. 'You must be very proud of him.'

But Mrs Driscoll just pursed her lips. 'He's just done his duty to King and Country as he should,' she said. '*Everyone* should have signed up as soon as they could have done.'

Oh!

There was no doubting the rebuke in Mrs Driscoll's words and in her accompanying tone. And there was absolutely no doubting her inference. Jack had been patriotic enough to enlist voluntarily whilst Harry had ignored the call to arms until he had had no choice and had been swept up by the compulsory conscription introduced earlier in the year.

How *dare* Mrs Driscoll?

Ruby felt herself blush with embarrassment and anger and opened her mouth to reply – but Jack got in first.

'Ma!' he said, angrily. 'This ain't the time or the place.'

But Mrs Driscoll just pursed her lips together piously before taking another sip of tea.

Ruby decided to bite her tongue.

Her usual reply in such circumstances was that Harry had stayed at home because Ma had been fairly recently bereaved, having lost Pa in an accident at the docks in 1912. However, this would no doubt fall on stony ground here because *both* Mrs Driscoll's husband and son had signed up at the same time, leaving her home alone with two small children. Besides, that wasn't the whole truth in any case. Harry had mainly refused to sign up until he had no choice because he simply didn't support the war. Pa had drummed it into them all from an early age that 'King and Country' was all well and good but that the poor needed to stick together. The working classes ultimately had the most to lose in any conflict. Pa had been fond of saying that a docker in England had much more in common with a docker in Germany than either of them did with their bosses of the same nationality. He had also been fond of telling his children that during the dockers' strike – just a few months before he was killed – their German counterparts had sent them considerable monetary support. Pa had always said that it would be better to rise up against the establishment than against working men abroad and – like Ruby – Harry had been inclined to agree with him.

Ruby was just composing a bland retort in her mind about how she hoped that Mr Driscoll was safe and well out in Mesopotamia when there was a little knock at the parlour door. It was Maude, Jack's seven-year-old sister, with Rex the dog at her heels. Maude greeted Ruby politely with a little bob and was then sent to fill up the teapot and to fetch the biscuits. Ruby smothered a smile at this obviously pre-planned little interruption, but she couldn't help being particularly struck by Rex, who had trotted meekly in and out at the little girl's heels. The last time Ruby had seen Rex, he had been a snorting, snarling tyrant, out of control and making poor Mac's life a misery. The contrast was almost unbelievable . . . and thank goodness for the perfect excuse to change the subject.

'Look at Rex,' she smiled, clapping her hands together in glee. 'He's like a different dog.'

'He should never have been here in the first place,' muttered Jack bitterly – and you could have cut the atmosphere between mother and son with a knife.

'I needed a guard dog,' said Mrs Driscoll defensively.

'Because you'd poured petrol down the ears of your old one!'

Goodness – this was excruciating.

'Well, it's nice to see how well-behaved Rex is now,' interjected Ruby brightly.

'He just needed training,' said Jack grimly. 'He needed a firm hand and to be shown who's boss and what is and ain't allowed around here.'

Oh!

Despite his grumpiness, Ruby suddenly found herself having the most irrelevant and impertinent thoughts about Jack. Being trained by him really might be rather fun! And then, shocked by her own sauciness, she could feel herself blushing.

'Well, whatever you've done, it certainly seems to be working,' she said in the same silly, cheerful tone.

'Let's just hope it stays that way,' replied Mrs Driscoll.

'Yes, let's,' said Jack. 'Or I might get back from work one day and find that he's been sold for ten bob.'

There was another awkward silence.

The whole occasion seemed to have continually lurched from one uncomfortable conversation to the next.

And then Ruby found her tongue. With a bit of luck, she could turn things around and help patch up Jack's relationship with his mother to boot.

'I've kept meaning to apologise to you, Mrs Driscoll,' she said, putting her teacup down carefully.

Two faces craned in her direction, one curious, one openly suspicious.

'Whatever for?' asked Mrs Driscoll, ungraciously.

'Well, for the day I bought Mac, of course.'

'I don't know what you mean . . .'

'I more or less forced you into it, didn't I?' said Ruby.

'I'm not sure . . .'

'I am,' said Ruby firmly. 'I could tell you didn't want to sell him, but I kept right on at you. Afterwards, I wondered if I had fairly bribed – if not blackmailed – you.'

Jack was frowning. '*Blackmailed* her?' he echoed in amazement.

'Well, blackmailed might be a bit strong,' Ruby conceded. 'But I were furious about the petrol and I might have come across a bit strong with me threats to report her. I'm so sorry, Mrs Driscoll. I think I were . . . unbearable.'

It was partially true, Ruby admitted to herself – although she was definitely overegging everything in order to make her point. In fact, she couldn't actually remember if she *had* threatened to report Mrs Driscoll and, if so, to whom, but she had definitely gone in with all guns blazing.

'I didn't realise,' murmured Jack. He suddenly looked very serious with a muscle pulsating in his temple.

Oh, Lordy.

Had she gone too far?

'Of course, if I'd known Mac were yours at the time, I would never have presumed to do anything like that,' she added hastily.

'I know you wouldn't,' said Jack. 'But I think I assumed

Ma practically threw Mac at you once he were no more use to her as a guard dog.'

'I wouldn't do that, son,' said Mrs Driscoll, reaching out and patting Jack on the hand. 'I'd never do that.'

'But I thought you *had*,' said Jack. 'And imagine how that made me feel. Getting rid of Mac because he could no longer hear very well – and then your own son comes back from the war with exactly the same disfigurement. You couldn't make it up. But now I know that this little Miss wore you down in a battle of attrition – and I know just how dogged and how determined she can be when she sets her mind to something! – well, I suddenly feel very much happier about the whole thing.'

He sat back with a smile and took a sip of tea.

Ruby and Mrs Driscoll locked eyes.

'Have another custard cream,' said Mrs Driscoll.

After that, conversation started to flow freely – the animal hospital, plans for Christmas, the upcoming bazaar. And it seemed like mere minutes later that Jack started hauling himself to his feet.

'We must be going, Ma,' he said.

Ruby glanced at the handsome clock on the mantlepiece.

'Goodness; it's already half past five,' she said in surprise. 'Thank you very much for having me, Mrs Driscoll. It were lovely to meet you properly.'

'You too, Ruby,' said Mrs Driscoll. 'And please call me Annie.'

5

Ruby found herself in high spirits as she and Jack caught the bus to Barking.

She had handled all that particularly well, she thought. In fact, she would go so far as to say that she had quite turned things around. She and Mrs Driscoll might never be the best of friends, but they had faced the Mac issue straight on and they had all come out smiling. The next time she went round to Victory Lane – and she was quietly confident that there *would* be a next time – things would surely be less awkward. The fact that she had potentially helped to repair the relationship between Jack and his mother was just the icing on the cake.

Oh, wasn't life wonderful?

Less than six months ago, Ruby had been in service, bopping curtseys and minding her p's and q's with barely half a day off from her duties every week. And now look at her. She had a job at the government munitions factory – in fact, she had recently been promoted to table supervisor in the detonation shed – she had lovely friends *and* she had opened a weekly animal hospital. Most importantly, she had Jack. The three months they had been stepping out together had been totally magical. Ruby might be the type of person who had her feet firmly on the ground a lot of the time, but there was no doubt that her head was in the clouds whenever she was with Jack. And the most exciting thing was that he seemed to feel the same way. He hadn't yet said 'I love you' but she could see it in his eyes and hear it in his voice when he spoke to her . . . surely it was just a matter of time.

Oh, Ruby.

For shame!

Why should it always be the man doing the running?

Why shouldn't she tell him that she loved him if that was what she felt?

And she did feel it.

She *did.*

'I know what you did back there, Missy,' said Jack, cutting across her thoughts.

Ruby turned from staring at the grey, greasy streets and a little group of urchins with their carefully assembled 'guy' on a street corner. Tomorrow was Guy Fawkes Night and, although the Defence of the Realm Act had put paid to bonfires and fireworks for the duration, nothing was going to stop children demanding a 'penny for the guy' and singing '*Remember, Remember the fifth of November; gunpowder, treason and plot.*'

'What did I do?' she answered Jack carefully.

'Letting me ma off the hook for selling you Mac,' said Jack. He was smiling, but his jaw was set firm and his eyes were steely. 'I ain't daft, you know.'

Ruby thought about demurring, of feigning ignorance – '*Whatever can you mean*?'

But . . . no.

There were to be no lies between her and Jack – not even white ones.

'It were partly true,' she said. 'I *did* go in all guns blazing and she *did* put up some resistance. But maybe not as much as I implied.'

'I knew it,' said Jack, with a satisfied smile. 'Currying favour, was you? You can't pull the wool over my eyes . . .'

'I weren't currying favour,' burst out Ruby indignantly.

'I were only joking,' said Jack. 'You was trying to help me mend me relationship with me mother and that were a very kind thing to do. In fact, it's one of the things I love most about you, your kindness . . .'

Ruby smiled at him, her heart suddenly aglow. Was loving something about someone the same as loving *them*? Not really, but maybe as near as dammit for a tongue-tied young chap.

Say it, Ruby.

Say it.

But the bus was pulling into their stop, and the moment was lost.

As Ruby and Jack alighted the bus outside the Tivoli cinema – all fancy columns and elaborate mouldings – Ruby could see Leah and Robert already waiting for them on the other side of the road. Despite herself, Ruby couldn't help comparing Robert and Jack. Robert might be the superior in social standing, his suit might be better cut and better fitted, but no one could argue with the fact that Jack was taller, broader and blessed with far more regular and handsome features.

It was safe to say that no one would ever suggest Jack resembled a ferret!

Still, Ruby told herself sternly, looks weren't everything. It was a person's character and moral fibre that really mattered. Then she gave a little giggle to herself as she realised that Jack won hands down here too. Jack had bravely served King and Country on the Western Front and had been discharged with honour on being injured.

Robert had avoided conscription claiming flat feet!

'Where would you like to eat?' asked Leah, once they had all greeted each other with handshakes and kisses.

Robert glanced at his pocket watch. 'We haven't got a great deal of time,' he said. 'Not if we want to catch the whole programme.'

Seeing the whole cinema programme was part of the experience. From the newsreel to the serials, to the comedies, to the occasional cartoon – Ruby loved it all.

'At more than a bob a ticket, I'm determined not to miss a second,' Jack said good-naturedly, echoing Ruby's thoughts. 'I suggest we pop into a mash-house.'

'A mash-house, old chap?' said Robert, looking perplexed.

Ruby smothered a smile. Leah, despite her upper-class origins, was living in digs in Silvertown for the duration and was used to going native in the East End. Ruby had seen her getting down and dirty in the filthiest railway arches and the prickliest bushes trying to help Silvertown's stray cats. She had also sheltered from a Zeppelin attack under the Old Woolwich Road, visited the market and the depots – and she had certainly eaten in a mash-house on more than one occasion with Ruby alone. Robert led a far more rarefied existence. He was based in gentrified Hackney and, as he almost exclusively tended to the horses of the rich, he had had very little to do with the working classes until he had started volunteering at the animal hospital. And clinic days were so busy that none of them had the chance to swan off around the local pubs and restaurants at lunchtime – preferring to bring in something from home or to buy a sandwich or a pastry from the bakery next door.

Perhaps, it wasn't surprising that the delights of the mash-houses had passed him by.

Jack was looking at Robert with amusement. 'You ain't heard of a mash-house?' he said almost in wonderment. 'It's a pie and eel shop, pal – and ruddy good they are too.'

'And you don't have to have eels,' giggled Ruby, as Robert's expression switched from confused to disgusted. 'They do all sorts of pies – including a marvellous beef one. All served with mashed potato and lashings of liquor, of course.'

'Liquor?' echoed Robert, screwing up his face in distaste. 'You pour rum or brandy over your pie like a Christmas pudding? Well, I'll be blowed.'

Ruby burst out laughing. She simply couldn't tell if Robert was joking or not.

'It's a parsley sauce,' she said. 'It's really tasty. You're going to love it.'

Leah linked her arm with Robert's. 'Have you finished showing your ignorance yet, darling?' she said with an affectionate smile. 'Come on; time to educate you in the mysteries of the East End.'

Ten minutes later, the four of them were installed in E. O'Malley's Pie and Mash shop, squashed onto wooden benches around a communal table, and tucking into their chosen meals. Robert, to give him his due, piled into his beef pie with gusto and even tried a tiny mouthful of Ruby's jellied eels, pronouncing them 'really quite passable.' And, if he was maybe trying a little too hard – with just a touch of forced bonhomie and heartiness about his manner – Ruby was determined to let it pass. To his credit, Robert was letting them all rib him with grace and good humour and, of course, Ruby would be every bit as ignorant and out of place if she was ever lucky enough for someone to take her to dinner at The Savoy.

Conversation was flowing easily – the hospital, the war, the monkey (that monkey would have them all dining out for a lifetime!) – and to a casual observer, the four of them no doubt looked like longstanding friends on a regular evening out together.

'That was delicious,' said Leah, when all the plates were practically licked clean. 'It's a good thing we'll be sitting down this evening. I'm so stuffed I can hardly move.'

'If your mother could hear you now,' Robert said with a laugh. '"For shame, Leah",' he mimicked in an even more exaggeratedly upper-crust accent than his own.

'I know,' said Leah, eyes dancing. 'She would have a fit. But it's true.'

She opened her leather handbag and pulled out a blue, lacey handkerchief, using it to delicately dab at her mouth and wipe her fingers. Then she placed it on the table whilst she finished her glass of water. The door to the restaurant opened suddenly, the accompanying breeze catching the hankie and sending it flying over Ruby's shoulder and into the furthest reaches of the restaurant.

'Damn,' said Leah, in frustration. 'That's one of my favourites.'

'I'll get it,' said Ruby.

She stood up, clambered over the bench she was sitting on, and went to track the handkerchief down. It didn't take long. A young woman, no older than Ruby and sitting in the corner with a young man, had already picked it up.

'I think your mistress dropped this,' she said, proffering the handkerchief almost reverentially to Ruby. 'Beautiful, ain't it? The stitching . . .'

'Pardon me?' Ruby was so shocked that the words came out more harshly than she had intended.

'Your mistress – the lady?' The young woman looked confused. 'Her handkerchief fluttered over here. I thought that were why you were . . .'

'Yes,' she said. 'Ta very much but she ain't me mistress. She's me friend.'

Ruby reached out and almost snatched the handkerchief away. Delicate and lacey with Leah's initials, LER, embroidered neatly into one corner, it was in complete contrast to the simple muslin handkerchiefs that Ruby owned.

A little of the excitement and fun from the evening suddenly ebbed away. As if Ruby would ever possess anything like this.

The devil was in the detail. Ruby could try to emulate Leah's smart white shirts and tailored skirts, but she would never be able to imitate Leah's elaborate silver and mother-of-pearl hatpins – one of which was even now lying on the table – or her embossed leather handbag, which was placed neatly on the floor.

It was futile.

As if anyone would ever mistake Leah and Ruby for friends.

The world might be going topsy-turvy but some things, it seemed, really hadn't changed at all.

'Are you alright?' asked Leah, linking arms with Ruby as the two women crossed the street to the Tivoli with Robert and Jack chatting behind. 'You suddenly went very quiet in the restaurant.'

Ruby nodded. 'Quite alright, thank you,' she said, firmly. None of this was Leah's fault and there was no point in burdening her with it. 'I'm just a little worried about the film, if I'm totally honest.'

'It's a bit close to home for you, isn't it?' said Leah, sympathetically, giving Ruby's arm a little squeeze.

'It is,' said Ruby. 'I know I need to see it but . . .'

She trailed off. It was only a half-lie. Harry was never far from her mind and the film *was* going to be a tough watch . . .

'And, of course, it's even closer to home for Jack,' Leah was saying. 'I did wonder if we'd been insensitive in suggesting it. Maybe we should have gone to see *Vagabond* instead and had a good laugh at Charlie Chaplin.'

Ruby pushed away a flicker of foreboding. 'I asked him and he said it were fine,' she replied. 'He said he wanted to see how accurate it were.'

Ruby's mood picked up again as they went into the Tivoli. Even with the propaganda posters outside – '*Wheat is needed for the Allies*' – and the blackout curtains over the windows, the whole place was just so glamorous and exciting that it was impossible to feel down for long. As Ruby swept through the grand lobby on Jack's arm, she told herself that it didn't matter what the woman in the mash-house had thought or assumed. She and Leah *were* friends – even if they happened to own very different handkerchiefs.

This was 1916 and the world was changing.

To hell with old-fashioned notions of mistress and servant!

And then they were entering the auditorium and settling down into the luxuriously comfortable seats. Jack took hold of Ruby's hand as soon as they were seated, resting it on his knee, and Ruby leaned her head against the rough wool of his jacket, breathing in the aroma of tobacco and carbolic and . . . home.

There was really nowhere on earth that she would rather be.

And now the programme was starting. A brief newsreel, showcasing current events, news stories and highlights from around the world. Of course, today's whole main presentation was a news story as such, so there was bound to be a little overlap, but there were still all the social events and other noteworthy occurrences to catch up on. It seemed strange to see the plays and the sporting fixtures that were taking place in the midst of all the carnage overseas and, at this time of the year, there were all the Christmas Music Halls and fetes and fairs being advertised for good measure.

Still, as Ma said, life had to go on.

Next up was the movie serial – an episodic film with a continuing storyline. This one was a crime caper but, as Ruby hadn't been to the cinema in weeks, she had missed the preceding instalments and didn't have much of a clue what was going on. After a bit, she gave up trying to work out the plot and instead cast a look at Leah out of the corner of her eye.

Leah was holding hands with Robert!

Ruby stifled a smile.

Whatever would Leah's mother have to say about *that*? It was one thing for a working-class girl to go to the cinema with her sweetheart, but quite another for an upper-class lady to be cavorting in a public place without a chaperone.

For shame, indeed!

Ruby turned her attention back to the screen in time for the comedy short. Today's was Harold Lloyd in a typical silent romp centred around painting a house which, of course, quickly descended into comedic chaos. Ruby loved Harold Lloyd and his meticulously executed stunts and, well before the ten minutes were up, both she and most of the rest of the audience were engulfed in fits of laughter.

The atmosphere quickly changed when the main presentation began and Ruby felt another flicker of foreboding.

The Battle of the Somme had been released back in August – just a month after the initial stages of the most brutal battle of the war. The film aimed to provide a realistic portrayal of events at the front and had already become a major box office success, drawing in millions of viewers. It was still doing so as Christmas approached; the entire auditorium was packed.

Ruby largely knew what to expect.

There had been much chatter about the film at the munitions factory and the hospital – to say nothing of it being all over the papers – so Ruby was well aware that it would show real battles with footage of trench warfare, artillery bombardments and soldiers going over the top into no-man's land.

But knowing what to expect and actually seeing it magnified many times over on the big screen were two entirely different things. Even though Ruby knew that some of the scenes had been staged and reconstructed, the film certainly didn't pull its punches and, more than once, she found herself squeezing Jack's hand as hard as she could. And, by the time the soldiers were filmed climbing over the top into battle, she shut her eyes almost involuntarily.

This was all too close to home.

Much too close.

But she had to bear it. If Harry was going to be asked to live it – and there was almost no doubt that he was – then the very least that she could do would be to watch what he would have to go through.

It wasn't easy, though.

Ruby had heard that one of the aims of the film was to boost morale and to recruit more soldiers but, patriotic as the portrayal of the conflict might be, Ruby wasn't at all sure that it would end up having the desired effect. In fact, Ruby deemed it far more likely that it would simply result in potential recruits running for the hills in order to avoid conscription.

Poor Harry.

Poor *all* of them.

Goodness knew what Jack was making of it all. They were 'just' watching a film – but a film depicting the very horrors that he had, until fairly recently, been living through.

A loud boom from the film shocked Ruby back into

the here and now. On one side of her, Ruby sensed, rather than saw, Leah jump. On her other side, Jack stiffened and it was his turn to hold her hand in a vicelike grip.

Another boom.

Ruby stole a glance at Jack's face. His eyes were still open but they were fixed – almost glassy – and there was a muscle going like the clappers in his cheek. He looked like he was miles away . . . perhaps reliving another time and another place.

A third boom . . . and a little yelp escaped Jack's lips.

Ruby found that she had been almost waiting for it to happen.

She had hoped it wouldn't, of course, but, somehow, she had known that it would. Exactly the same thing had happened the first time she had met Jack . . . or at least the first time she had properly talked to him. Then, of course, the two of them had been huddled together with thousands of others in a pitch-black foot tunnel – and the booms had been real bombs being dropped not five miles away from a Zeppelin floating grotesquely overhead.

Should she nudge Jack; get his attention and gently bring him back to the present?

Or was it already too late for that?

Another boom . . . and the yelp from Jack was a little louder. A couple in the row in front turned around with curious, judgemental glances and, next to her, Leah gently touched her hand.

'Everything alright?' she whispered. Her eyes were wide in the semi-darkness and, on her far side, Ruby could see Robert glancing over in their direction as well.

Things were far from alright – but what on earth to do?

Ruby's mouth opened by itself and she said the first thing that came into her head.

'I don't like this,' she hissed back. 'Sorry I yelped, but I need to get out right now.'

Oh, goodness.

Why on earth had she done that?

Why had she claimed Jack's discomfiture – his *panic* – as her own? Of course, Ruby was hardly enjoying the film herself but she was a long way from screaming or otherwise drawing attention to herself. But the instinct to protect Jack was obviously deep-seated and the words seemed to have bypassed her brain and to have come out fully formed.

'Oh, I thought it was . . .' Leah started doubtfully.

'It were *me*,' interrupted Ruby, firmly. 'I have to go. It's all . . . too much.'

Another loud boom and another moan from Jack threatened to make Ruby's words a lie.

Leah either didn't hear or she was too diplomatic to say anything. 'Shall we come with you?' she asked.

'No, no,' whispered Ruby. 'Jack will escort me home. I'm so sorry to spoil the evening and I'll see you at work next week.'

She stood up, tapped Jack on the shoulder and gathered her hat and bag. As if in a dream, Jack got to his feet as well, blinking in confusion. There were a couple of disapproving mutters from behind them but nothing compared to what would have happened had they blocked people's view during a normal presentation. After all, this film was different and a handful of people had already left, shocked that the harsh realities of the battlefield had been dragged into the public consciousness. Still, there was no time to linger. Grabbing Jack's hand, Ruby almost propelled him past the two long-suffering people at the end of their row and then up the aisle towards the exit.

She led Jack through the now deserted lobby and out onto the street. Outside, all was calm. A lone horse and cart clip-clopped up the darkened street – lit only by the full moon – and a motor swooshed past in the other direction. Across the road, a couple walked by arm and arm, the woman smiling up at her man and then the door to the public house opposite opened momentarily, spilling light and a couple of drunkards onto the pavement.

No bombs.

No trenches.

No terror.

Just an ordinary evening in the East End of London in the run up to Christmas.

Beside her, Jack was bending over, hands on his knees. He straightened up and looked Ruby straight in the eye.

'Did I shout out?' he asked, directly.

'No,' said Ruby. 'But you yelped a couple of times. It weren't very loud but I thought it might get worse if I didn't get you out.'

'Thank you,' said Jack. 'It took me back. It were like I was actually there. It were awful.'

'I'm so sorry,' said Ruby. 'We should never have come. Even though you said it would be fine, I should have realised . . .'

'It ain't your fault,' interrupted Jack. 'I thought it would be alright – or at least I hoped it would. Either way, I wanted to put a brave face on it so as not spoil the night out. Stupid really . . .'

'Not stupid at all,' said Ruby sympathetically. 'It ain't the same, but I hated it too, seeing exactly what Harry is going through.'

Jack nodded. 'Keep writing to him,' he said. 'It really does make all the difference. But write about nice things too. Normal things. About children still touting guys and your ma making the Christmas cake ready for his homecoming . . .'

'I will,' said Ruby. She gave a little shudder and wrapped her coat more tightly around herself. 'Goodness; that film really made me realise exactly what those shells we spend all day making are doing to real human beings.'

'Those poor, poor saps,' agreed Jack. 'It don't really matter whether you're English or German. At the end of the day, those are just boys dying out there.'

'I know.'

'You don't think I'm yellow, do you?'

The words came from nowhere, shocking Ruby to the core.

'Don't be daft – of course I don't,' she said, gently, giving Jack a little shove.

'Sure? Even though I shouted out during the film?'

'Absolutely sure,' replied Ruby firmly. 'As your mother kindly reminded me earlier on, you chose to sign up early on when many millions – including me own brother – didn't. You fought for your country and you were given an honourable discharge when you got injured. There ain't nothing cowardly about that.'

'Thank you,' said Jack softly. 'I love you for understanding.' And then, even more quietly, 'And I love *you*, Ruby Archer.'

Oh, goodness!

'I love you too, Jack Kennedy,' Ruby replied, burying her head into his chest.

There.

It was said and it couldn't be taken back.

Jack bent his head to hers and the two sealed their unspoken pledge under the winter moon.

6

Friday, 10 November 1916

Jack's declaration of love burned within Ruby, warming her heart, and buoying her spirit, and fortunately the upset at the cinema seemed to have been forgotten.

Ruby had already decided to continue the pretence that it was she who had had to make a hasty exit – it just seemed easier that way – but, in the event, it hadn't been necessary. The next Monday at work, Leah had merely said that she had enjoyed the evening and that they must all get together again soon – and when Ruby saw Robert at the next animal hospital clinic the following Friday, *he* didn't comment on it at all.

Thank goodness for that.

Anyway, they all had another issue on their minds and that was how busy the animal hospital continued to be. The problem was that no matter how quickly and efficiently they all tried to work, there were long lines of people and their animals stretching down Sanctuary Lane before each clinic started and the queue didn't seem to get much shorter as the day progressed. Even though they often worked late, Ruby had been acutely aware that a number of animals *never* got to the head of the queue and even though they would make a point of prioritising these patients the following week, the situation was far from ideal.

As the weeks had gone by, Ruby had experimented with different ways of alleviating the pressure on the hospital. One of the best, she found, was sending someone outside to work their way down the raggedy line, triaging the animals and picking out those that could be quickly sent on their way without ever even setting foot inside the hospital. Sometimes there were pills and potions that could be quickly dispensed – often the owners had correctly diagnosed a problem and knew exactly what their pet needed but simply couldn't afford to buy it – or other times, Nellie or Ruby or Leah could simply give advice and reassurance on how to get on top of whatever an animal's problem seemed to be and then send the owner on his or her way.

That had all gone some way to helping to reduce the perennial queues, but it wasn't enough.

They clearly needed to do more, but it was difficult to know exactly what the 'more' should be. Recruiting more volunteers – especially those who knew at least a little about what they should be doing – would be difficult. Besides, their premises in the old haberdashery shop – although marvellous – was already running at pretty much full capacity.

The answer, clearly, was more shifts.

But even that wasn't straightforward.

All the volunteers already worked full time and it was difficult enough coordinating for everyone to get a Friday off. Robert, as a self-employed veterinary practitioner, was just taking the hit on his income, but Ruby, Jack and Leah still had to work a five-day week at the government munitions factory – Leah had already made it perfectly clear that there was no question of the factory agreeing to them cutting it down to four – and so they were all only getting one day off work a week as it was. Ruby couldn't ask everyone to give up their second day off – she simply couldn't. And even planning the odd ad hoc clinic on a national holiday tended to backfire. Back in the summer, Ruby *had* intended to open the clinic on the late August Bank Holiday but, to her chagrin, the munitions factory decided to cancel the holiday at the last minute because of the increased demand for shells from the Somme. If the ghastly battle dragged on, no doubt the same thing would happen at Christmas too. Ruby understood that the war came first – nobody wanted the boys at the front to run out of ammunition – but it did seem a little as if the factory was sometimes conspiring against her truly making a success of the hospital.

'What about an evening shift?' suggested Robert as they all grabbed a quick lunch at the hospital the week after they had been to the cinema.

Ruby looked at him gratefully. 'Would you really do that?' she asked, taking a huge bite of pasty.

It never failed to amaze her that Robert – a bona fide vet who had trained for five years at the Royal Veterinary College – was so willing to give of his time and his expertise to her little venture.

'Of course I would,' said Robert. 'It's a very important thing that we're doing here. I only wish that we could all turn ourselves into ten people and replicate this hospital throughout the East End.'

'Wouldn't that be marvellous?' said Ruby with a grin.

'Maybe one day that will be possible! It might be more realistic to inspire other people to do the same thing where they live. Or maybe we could start doing rounds? We could load up Mayfair's cart with everything we need and go off into Whitechapel and Bow and Tower Hamlets . . .'

Jack laughed. 'You and your fancy ideas, Missy!' he said. 'I'm sure Mayfair would love it, but shall we concentrate on the here and now? An evening shift really ain't a bad idea. It will allow people who work all day to bring their animals along without taking time out from their jobs.'

'Maybe we could tack an evening session onto our existing Friday clinic?' suggested Leah.

There were groans all round.

'I'm exhausted as it is by the time the shift finishes,' said Robert. 'I'd be seeing double by the evening. No, I suggest we run an additional evening shift during the week or at the weekend – it's up to you exactly when, Ruby.'

Ruby shot him another grateful glance. She wasn't the one with a fancy string of initials after her name and she really appreciated the fact that Robert never tried to pull rank.

'I'd love to go for a regular Tuesday evening,' she said. 'But twice a week is a lot to ask of people.'

'Remember, we don't all have to be here every session,' said Robert, standing up and brushing himself down. 'I'm the only one who can operate on animals – although I'd trust Jack with most things – but together we're a competent team. You and Leah are getting pretty good at diagnostics.'

Everyone smiled around at each other and then Ruby clapped her hands together in excitement. 'Maybe we could have different themes for some of the evenings,' she said. 'Worming dogs – so many people come in about that – or treating wounds or whatever the greatest demand seems to be at a particular time.'

'Marvellous idea,' said Robert.

'Or even some education sessions,' continued Ruby, warming to her theme. 'Dot – who lives next door at the bakery and who also works with us at the factory – is really involved with education at the East London Federation of the Suffragettes. Over there, they make a big deal of prevention being better than cure and I think that's something we could be making more of here too. She's promised to get involved – to run it, even – but the trouble is that she's stuck on nights at the factory. She's badgering to be moved to the day shift but there ain't too much she can do at the moment and the rest of us are so rushed off our feet that we ain't had a chance to do anything about it as of yet.'

'Well, if we do get it off the ground – and it sounds like a marvellous idea – can we please put feeding dogs over Christmas right at the top of the list,' said Robert with a world-weary air. 'I can't count the number of animals I've had to treat after the festive period over the years because their owners have insisted on feeding them onions or turkey bones or something else quite unsuitable to the poor dog's digestive system.'

'Understood,' said Ruby. 'At the very least, we can plaster posters warning against it all over the hospital for those who can read. In the meantime, let's press ahead with the idea of a Tuesday evening clinic. Oh, this is quite marvellous. Thank you all so much.'

By five o'clock that evening, Ruby was bone tired.

The sign on the hospital door had been switched to 'Closed' and the reception was empty, but there was still all the clearing up to do. Aunt Maggie and Nellie had already left for the day and Ma had waved through the window as she passed on her own way home from the bakery next door. Robert was packing up his smart mahogany case in one of the consulting rooms, Leah was sweeping the floor whilst humming 'Roses of Picardy' quietly to herself and Jack was helping Ruby replace products onto shelves and generally restore order from the chaos that resulted from a busy clinic.

'I'm knackered,' said Ruby, stacking a pile of leaflets neatly on the reception desk, putting another pile of paperwork into a drawer and then perching on the desk herself with a weary sigh.

'Me too,' said Jack, leaning over and kissing her on the nose. 'I think this just proves that none of us would be able to do an evening clinic after how hard we work here all day. I'm not saying the munitions factory is exactly *easy* work but at least it's different and, as me ma says, a change is as good as a rest.'

'Hear, hear,' said Leah, sweeping the detritus into a little pile and scooping it up with a dustpan and brush. 'And less of that kissing stuff in here, you two, thank you very much.'

'Sorry,' said Ruby, with a grin. If Ma could see her now! 'Goodness, I'm so exhausted and so footsore I don't even think I can walk home!'

'I've got Mayfair outside,' said Jack with a grin. 'The old girl would be happy to give you a lift home when we've finished here.'

Ruby laughed. 'I wouldn't do that to her,' she said. 'It's less than two hundred yards and Mayfair's probably even more exhausted than I am after carting stuff around all day! But I'll come outside to say hello to her and Tarroc before she goes back to the depot. I could do with some fresh air.'

She swung herself off the desk with a little grunt and followed Jack out through the front door and onto the street outside. There was Mayfair, standing placidly by the kerb, whilst a couple of local children patted her nose and her flanks. Ruby took some deep breaths whilst she waited her turn. It was so lovely to be outside – not that the smoky East End air could ever truly be described as 'fresh' – after having been cooped up in the stuffy hospital all day. It was a still autumn evening, the sun was about to go down and, just for a moment, all seemed well in the world. The world was bathed in gold and everything seemed to be moving in the slow motion that they often used in the flicks. And then, as if by magic, Dot suddenly appeared saying that she had *finally* been moved to the day shift at the factory, so that she *would* be able to help much more with the hospital. It was all so wonderful and so coincidental after their conversation earlier that day that Ruby just started laughing. Suddenly, she felt the happiest that she had done in a long time. Leah was still singing 'Roses of Picardy' through the open hospital door and Jack was smiling cheerfully at the children who were petting Mayfair and telling Tarroc that *he* would take Mayfair back to the depot that evening. Any moment now she would go over to him and he would put his arm around her and . . .

Everything was perfect.

It really was.

Even Sanctuary Lane, never the most beautiful of roads, looked soft and hazy and positively genteel as the evening light spun and danced and fingers of gold stretched along the street. That young girl or boy, just crossing the street in the vicinity of Ruby's house, was a romantic, blurred silhouette gliding along like a silent little ghost.

Suddenly, an icy finger ran down Ruby's spine.

No, Ruby.

The blurred silhouette, that silent little spectre, was a telegram boy or girl. It was impossible to tell from this distance which house he or she was heading for, but Ruby knew it was in the vicinity of her home. In fact, was that her brother Charlie standing stock-still outside?

Time abruptly sped up.

The fingers of gold disappeared as the sun set behind the factory at the end of the street and Sanctuary Lane was as grimy and soot-blackened as ever.

Leah's 'Roses of Picardy' and its lyrics bewailing the roses dying as autumn began, suddenly took on an ominous undertone.

The Somme was in Picardy.

Oh, God.

The lightness in Ruby's heart congealed to a cold lead weight and, with a strangled little cry, she started running.

'Ruby!' shouted Jack from behind her. 'Ruby, where are you going?'

But Ruby didn't stop.

She didn't even turn around.

She kept running, feet pounding the pavement, arms pumping by her sides, until her breath was coming in gasps and the cold air was stinging her lungs . . .

The Angel of Death was heading to their house to tell them Harry had died.

Ruby knew it.

Deep down in her bones, she just *knew* it.

No.

You *don't* know it, Ruby.

The telegram girl – because she could see now that it *was* a girl – could be heading to any one of a dozen houses. The trouble was that Ruby was sure that no one in any of the houses immediately around them had a relative at the front . . .

But surely, all was not lost?

Even if the telegram girl *was* on her way to number 139, she could be bearing any number of messages. Harry might be missing in action . . . he could be injured . . . God willing, he might even be letting them know he was heading home on leave. Or Ma's Uncle Paddy very occasionally sent them a telegram to say that he'd be visiting . . .

Ruby was nearer now – closing in all the time – close enough see the little tableau playing out in front of her.

The front door opening . . .

Ma framed in the doorway . . .

The solemn handing over of the telegram . . .

Time seemed to slow down as Ma opened the envelope.

Ruby was still too far away to see her expression, but there was no mistaking the sudden sagging of her body, nor the high wail that escaped her lips and floated all the way down Sanctuary Lane, piercing Ruby straight in the heart. An answering moan escaped Ruby's lips. She stopped running – despite her best efforts, she hadn't got there in time – and placed her hands on her knees, bent over and gasping for breath.

Harry was dead.

As if in a dream, Ruby walked the rest of the way home. There was no point in running now. Ma, Aunt Maggie and Charlie were standing in a semi-circle, stock-still, as if stunned. A little throng of people – neighbours, tradesmen, passers-by – had stopped too and were standing a respectful distance away, faces transmitting a curious mixture of sympathy and relief.

'Killed in action,' confirmed Ma almost conversationally, as Ruby approached them. 'Your beautiful, brave brother has paid the ultimate price and is with your father now.'

The Angel of Death was still standing there, regarding them all impassively. Ruby noticed that she had a hauntingly beautiful face with a rosebud mouth and huge, violet eyes ringed by long, dark eyelashes. But she wasn't an angel – not a bit of it; she was something sent from the depths of hell itself and, for a fleeting second, Ruby hated her with a deep-seated rage. Then the moment passed and Ruby could see that she was just a child; a little girl, out of her depth, with trembling lips and eyes rapidly filling with tears.

'Thank you,' said Ruby, touching her on the shoulder.

The girl nodded vaguely, turned on her heel and trudged off down Sanctuary Lane.

'Right,' said Ruby briskly. 'Shall we go inside?'

'No point in making a spectacle of ourselves out here,' agreed Aunt Maggie.

'It doesn't really matter what we do now,' said Ma flatly. 'And it never will do again.'

Charlie burst into tears.

And then the little family went back inside 139 Sanctuary Lane, shutting the door firmly behind them.

It wasn't how it happened in the flicks.

That was Ruby's first thought after the front door slammed shut.

In the films, the family would be huddled together in each other's arms, howling in grief. Someone might faint. Someone might scream. It would be noisy and messy and intense and . . . well, whatever it was, it would be *something.*

What it wouldn't be was Ma and Aunt Maggie making a brew together and calmly stating that Harry had done his duty to King and Country and had died a hero. What it wouldn't be was Charlie quietly slipping upstairs alone without a word to anyone. What it wouldn't be was Ruby herself sitting down at the kitchen table, picking up the telegram and reading the familiar words – '*We regret to inform you*' – as casually as if it had been the local newspaper.

There really should be special words and actions that were reserved only for when something as dreadful as this took place. Ordinary behaviour and vocabulary just didn't cut it.

Because her lovely, laughing brother was no more.

Ruby suddenly remembered playing hide and seek down by the river with him as a child. It had been the day they had stumbled across a man drowning kittens in a bag and Harry had waded into the river beside her in a largely successful bid to rescue them. She could remember that day as though it was yesterday – the gunmetal-grey Thames water, the limp, little feline bodies, the sting of the thrashing she had received later for getting her clothes wet and muddy. And, all the while, Harry had been there by her side, receiving his own beating without comment or complaint, even though the whole thing had been at her instigation, indeed at her insistence.

Oh, Harry.

Harry!

Had it been written in the stars that he would die when he was barely twenty-three? Had Ruby always known, at some level, that she would lose him so young? Why had she not written to him more often? Told him she knew how terrible it was going to be out at Somme, because Jack had spelled it all out to her?

It was just unbearable.

And then there was a knock at the door.

Calmly, Ruby went to answer it. There was nothing left to fear now – the worst had already happened. She blinked on finding that it was Jack, suddenly remembering that she had left him shouting behind her and had totally ignored him. Mayfair was standing behind him, munching placidly from her nosebag, and, beyond them, little knots of people were huddled together conspiratorially, still looking at the house with 'that' expression. Ruby had, no doubt, had that expression on her face several times over the past few months, and she supposed she would just have to get used to it being turned in her direction.

Ruby transferred her attention to Jack and remembered that she had been talking to him not ten minutes before outside the hospital.

It felt like a lifetime ago.

She vaguely remembered taking to her heels on sighting the telegram girl and Jack shouting urgently after her. Even through her shock and her grief, it suddenly occurred to her how rude and thoughtless she had been by going inside the house and slamming the door without giving him a second thought.

But the truth was that she simply *hadn't* given him a second thought.

'Was that . . . ?' Jack started, pointing in the direction that the Angel of Death had departed. 'Is it . . . ?'

His voice was muffled and seemed to be coming from a very long way away – like the time she had gone to Southend-on-Sea for the day with her family when she was ten and had got water in her ears. But, despite that – and the fact that Jack's words had really made no sense – Ruby knew exactly what he meant.

She nodded her head – yes, to both questions – suddenly not trusting herself to speak. And then she was in Jack's arms and he started stroking her hair and murmuring comforting words in her ear . . . to hell with what the neighbours thought.

And finally, the tears came and Ruby sobbed inconsolably against Jack's shoulder for her darling older brother who wouldn't be coming home, no matter how brightly they had tried to keep the home fires burning.

7

The aftermath of Harry's death was a hideous blur.

There could be no funeral, of course, for the very simple reason that there was no body. The vast number of dead soldiers at the Somme and all the ongoing battles was making recovery and repatriation to England impossible and so what remained of Harry would remain in France. Soldiers were being buried close to where they had fallen, in makeshift graves near or even on the battlefield. Assurances were constantly being given that these burial sites were marked and recorded but the point was Harry had probably already been laid to rest far away in the corner of a foreign field and was not coming home to Silvertown.

As far as Harry's family was concerned, 'The Somme' might as well have been on the moon and it was a very bitter pill to swallow.

It had been dreadful when Pa had died, of course; the accident had been an awful shock and losing her father had rocked Ruby to the core – even though she had been living far away in Hampstead at the time. But at least Pa had had a funeral and they had all had a chance to say goodbye. Ruby remembered the elaborate ritual as though it was yesterday; the high plumes on the horses pulling the carriage, Ma leading the black-clad procession that wound its way through Silvertown, the vicar solemnly officiating the service and then the coffin slowly being lowered into the black earth. Ruby remembered commenting to Ma at the time that people in the East End tended to be laid to rest much more grandly than they had lived and wouldn't Pa have preferred that they spent some of the money on themselves? And Ma had hushed her and said their weekly premiums to the Burial Club meant that they could afford all this and hadn't it been exactly what her father deserved? Ruby, not terribly convinced, had nonetheless duly hushed – and it was only now that she could see the sense in her mother's words. As well as being able to say their farewells, there was also a grave and a gravestone; somewhere they could visit to pay their respects to Pa every week after church.

Harry deserved all of this too – and much, much more – but the ghastly war that had taken his life had also denied this to him.

To them *all*.

The vicar at St Barnabas was so under siege with requests for private memorial services that they couldn't even schedule in a date for Harry. Instead, they had to make do with his name being read out at church the following Sunday – along with an obscenely long list of other names. Ruby had listened to them all numbly – too numb even to cry, unlike the pretty blonde girl sobbing on the pew in front who wouldn't have known Harry at all. It was all scant comfort; as was Harry's name printed – alongside thousands of others – in the newspaper later that week. Fallen Officers had their photographs printed, but if mere privates were afforded the same privilege, the newspaper would probably be too heavy to carry.

It was all just grim beyond hell.

But the real demons came when Ruby was in bed.

Every night, she tossed and turned, her mind invaded by thoughts and images that she didn't want to see. She dreamed of Harry as she remembered him – his tousled hair and sparkling eyes, his cheerful chatter about the sugar and spices and tobacco he unloaded at the docks and about how, one day, he would visit all the countries they had come from. (He hadn't visited any of them, of course; the sad irony was that France was the first time Harry had been overseas.) And throughout these dreams, Ruby would try and tell her brother that something terrible was going to happen to him and that he must listen to her. Try as she might, however, she couldn't get the message across to him. Her words would be hurled away by the wind, or she would open her mouth and her teeth would crumble into her hand or she would try to follow Harry but it was as though her feet were trapped in quicksand. She would wake, heart pounding, chest slick with sweat and, for a blissful moment, she would wonder if it really had just been a nightmare. And then the awful reality would hit her like a tidal wave.

Sometimes, Ruby would try to stay awake so that she didn't have to go through the whole ghastly thing again – sneaking Mac up to her room and lying next to him with her arms wrapped around his neck. But that was almost worse because then she started torturing herself with questions that she simply couldn't answer. The truth was that they hadn't had a letter from Harry for ages and so they had absolutely no idea of the events leading up to his death. The last missive they had received had been written and sent from the base camp at the coast; cheerful and positive, his words had lulled them all into a sense of false security. And, of course, they knew nothing of how Harry had died. All Ruby knew was that he had been 'killed in action', but that, of course, covered a multitude of sins? Had he gone 'over the top' with his comrades and been taken out by machine gun fire. Or had he been hit by a shell in no-man's land – the same type of shell that she spent her days helping to manufacture? Had he made it all the way across to the enemy trenches, or had he not even had a chance to leave his own? Had he died instantly, or later, of his wounds? Had he been alone or was there someone there to comfort him?

Had he known he was going to die?

Had he been afraid?

Had he called out for Ma or for any of them?

And how could she simply carry on making shells and detonators designed to kill other young men? Because somewhere, over the Channel, there were other mothers, other sisters, other families mourning the loss of their lovely, laughing sons and brothers – dead because of something she had helped to manufacture . . .

There were so many questions that Ruby wanted the answers to.

The trouble was, she simply didn't have anyone to ask.

And what of the living?

Through it all, Jack was a stalwart – always by her side

when she needed it and melting away without complaint when she wanted time on her own – and she loved him for it with all her heart. Those early morning walks along the river became her saviour – the chance to get some fresh air and exercise with her sweetheart – even though she now hated autumn with a vengeance and the brown leaves clinging onto the trees and lying on the ground only served to remind her of death and decay. It was Jack who told her she had to keep plugging on – that the war had to be won and the weapons had to be made . . . no matter the cost.

Her family was a different matter altogether.

Initially, Ruby had wondered if Harry's death might bring them all closer together but in the first few days it seemed to be doing the opposite. In fact, to Ruby's sadness, it seemed to be in danger of deepening existing fault-lines and creating new ones. When they were at home, she, Ma, Charlie and Aunt Maggie circled each other warily, rarely speaking about Harry even though his absence dominated their days and nights. Even the animals seemed quieter and more subdued than usual. More than once, Ruby had gone looking for Tess and found her curled in a perfect circle on Harry's pillow. It was almost as if Harry had become the sun and the rest of them were planets, circling him on separate orbits, never deviating from their own path or crossing the paths of others.

It was awful.

How Harry would have hated it.

In the past, Ruby knew that she had been guilty of becoming so overwhelmed with everything she had going on that she had little time left for the people she lived with. Aunt Maggie had taken her to task for that a few months back and, since then, Ruby had really tried her hardest both to be around a little more and to muck in with the household chores when she was able. This time she wouldn't be found wanting, even though it would be more difficult than ever to manage to get the balance right now they had committed to *more* shifts at the hospital. Nonetheless, she would try her hardest to be the glue that stuck the whole family together.

But it was hard.

Really hard – and especially because no one seemed to *want* to be stuck together.

Ma seemed to turn in on herself the moment Harry's death was announced. Oh, she kept up her usual routine – and said she fully intended to go back to work at the bakery – but she began to be plagued by crippling headaches and her mind and her spirit seemed to be far, far away. She turned the mantelpiece in the kitchen into a shrine for Harry – the photograph of him in his Army uniform had been joined by a couple of candles and mass cards, some sympathy cards from neighbours and friends and an old woollen cap of his – and she spent a good deal of her spare time just sitting on a chair and staring at them.

Aunt Maggie took to spending more and more time out of the house. She *said* she had problems with her house in Whitechapel and was struggling to find the tradesmen to sort them out, but Ruby had a sneaky feeling that she felt like she was in the way and was leaving Harry's mother and siblings to grieve on their own. And that didn't help at all.

And as for Charlie!

Charlie had taken to staying out after school and coming in after dark. After the brick throwing several months ago, this really worried Ruby. He had got away with a police caution that time and Ruby had been convinced that he had put all that behind him. She had made a concerted effort to talk to him and to include him and his friend Joe in the set-up of the animal hospital and she had really felt that he had turned a corner. But, as soon as Harry had died, he seemed to have changed and Ruby knew that his hatred of the Germans would no doubt have escalated. The trouble was that Ruby didn't know what was going on in his head. If they were planets, Charlie was Neptune: the furthest planet in the solar system and a bit of a mystery. Ruby was very worried that – fuelled by rage and grief at what had happened to his brother – he might try to step up his activities.

It was all just dreadful.

Ruby did her best. One evening, about five days after Harry had died, she was heading upstairs to bed when, on a whim, she knocked on Charlie's door. Ma had retired early with a 'head', but Ruby could see a sliver of light still glowing underneath Charlie's door, which suggested that he was still awake.

There was a questioning grunt in reply to her knock and tentatively Ruby cracked the door open.

'Just wondered if I could have a chat,' she said quietly.

Mac was on Charlie's bed and thumped his tail at Ruby's arrival. Ruby ignored the fact that he wasn't supposed to be allowed upstairs.

'What about?' said Charlie ungraciously.

At least it wasn't an outright no.

'About . . . well, things. Harry . . .' She trailed off.

A shrug. 'Suppose,' said Charlie noncommittedly.

Ruby slipped into the room and shut the door behind her before her brother had a chance to change his mind. Charlie was sitting up in bed, propped up by a pile of pillows and was regarding her suspiciously. Ruby sat down on a pile of clothes thrown over his chair. The discarded clothes surprised and worried Ruby; not that she would have expected Charlie to have hung them up or folded them away himself – or even to have registered that they were there – but because Ma tidied Charlie's room on a daily basis, always leaving everything ship-shape and Bristol fashion. The fact that she hadn't even been in was concerning. She looked a little further and realised that Ma *had* been in at some point since Harry had died – because everything belonging to her older brother had been removed. Harry's tatty old Hammers jacket and cap were gone from their habitual place on the back of the door. The wooden boat he had made as a teenager was missing from the shelf on the wall. Even his slippers were gone from his side of the bed.

Suddenly, Ruby had a lump in her throat.

She took a deep breath and bent down to pat Tess who had wandered into the room en route for Harry's bed. She resisted her initial temptation to tell Charlie to put his clothes away by himself; he would never open up to her if she went in on the offensive. That was a battle for another day – should she choose to fight it.

Then she noticed in the dim light that Charlie had a

little pile of what looked very much like bricks on his bed. There were three of them, one whole and two halves, looking totally incongruous on the blue, patterned counterpane. She was surprised that Charlie hadn't tried to hide them away as soon as she came in and, remembering the bricks through Muller's window, she swallowed hard before speaking.

'What are these?' she asked, trying to keep her voice neutral.

'Bricks,' said Charlie.

'Yes, I can see that.' Ruby gave a silly, high-pitched laugh. 'But what are they *for*?'

'They ain't for nothing,' said Charlie dismissively. 'They *was* for building a house but now they're just souvenirs. I like looking at them.'

'Souvenirs?' Ruby was totally confused. She'd got a little vase on her windowsill from the long-ago family trip to Southend but, if she recalled correctly, bricks certainly hadn't been one of the trinkets on offer. 'Souvenirs from where?'

'From the Zep strike last month,' said Charlie. 'I went over to Liverpool Street the next day to take a look.'

'Shouldn't you have been at school?' asked Ruby, automatically.

Listen to her.

She was like a stuck record on a gramophone player.

'I *did* go to school,' said Charlie. 'This were earlier. As soon as it got light.'

'Alright.'

Charlie was still talking. 'The whole house fell down,'

he was saying. 'And look; these bricks are totally black from the blast. It's marvellous.'

His enthusiasm was boyish and almost contagious.

Almost.

Ruby gave a cursory glance at the bricks. She hadn't immediately noticed it in the gaslight but, yes, the bricks did indeed appear to be black. 'It ain't marvellous,' she said tetchily. 'It were someone's home. People probably died there.'

'They didn't,' said Charlie. 'They all got out. Anyway, it weren't just me who took something. Everyone takes mementoes.'

'That still don't make it right,' said Ruby. 'And what exactly do you intend to do with them?'

'Nothing,' said Charlie, sulkily. 'They're just to have.'

Everything about Charlie – from his crossed arms to his eyes, which were suddenly focussed on the corner of the room – told Ruby that that was clearly a lie. She could suddenly see, with the utmost clarity, *exactly* what her younger brother intended to do.

'Charles Edward Archer,' she said sternly. 'I very much hope you're not planning to throw all or any of them bricks through the windows of German businesses. You got away with it before, but you won't be so lucky again and it would break Ma's heart. After all she's been through . . .'

Charlie's lack of response told Ruby that she was thinking along the right lines and she felt her cheeks growing hot with anger and exasperation. 'Charlie,' she hissed. 'It ain't the way. It ain't what Harry would want you to do.'

Charlie's eyes snapped to hers. 'How do *you* know what Harry would or wouldn't want me to do?' he shot back. 'He ain't here to tell us.'

'True,' said Ruby. 'But, believe me, there's better ways of remembering him and honouring his memory.'

'Like what?' said Charlie, picking up one of the half-bricks and throwing it from hand to hand. 'I will never forgive the Hun. *Never.* I wish I could kill whoever did this to Harry.'

Ruby gave her younger brother a sad smile. The same wavy hair as Harry, but Charlie's was lighter in colour – almost the same honey-blond as Ruby's. But his hazel eyes glowing in the light from the oil-lamp – well, they were all Harry's. Half child and half adult, his features and his teeth were still too big for his face, but his Adam's apple was definitely growing and there was a light fuzz of growth on his upper lip and his chin. Who was going to teach him to shave now that Pa and Harry had gone? Who was going to teach him to grow into a man to be proud of?

Ruby sighed. 'I know exactly how you feel,' she admitted. 'But we have to try and remember that it ain't the fault of whoever fired the bullet or launched the shell that killed Harry. They was just carrying out orders. It's very likely that Harry killed people too and we both know that he weren't the sort of person who would have done that lightly. I'm making weapons that will kill people too – and I have to learn to live with that . . .'

'I don't care that they was just following orders,' interrupted Charlie, staunchly. 'They still did it and I still hate all Germans. And when it's my turn to fight, I will make a point of killing as many as I can, you see if I don't.'

Ruby sighed. 'Oh, Charlie,' she said. 'God willing that by the time you are old enough to enlist, it will all be over.'

But, even as she spoke, the words rang hollow to Ruby's ears.

The way it was going, who could say *when* the blasted war would be over?

8

All in all, it was almost a relief to go back to work – although Ruby held off returning to the surgery for a further few days. Jack, Robert, Leah and the others were more than happy to hold the fort and, to Ruby's delight, Elspeth volunteered to step forward as an extra pair of hands.

Like everyone else, Ruby and the rest of the family were just expected to carry on as normal. After all, they were surrounded by women – at the factory, at the clinic, on Sanctuary Lane itself – who were trying to do exactly that. Stiff upper lip, keeping calm and carrying on, for King and Country . . . everyone knew the drill and it applied to the Archers as much as everyone else. So, less than a week after Harry died, Ruby was reporting back on duty at the munitions factory, desperately trying to quash her reticence at continuing to manufacture the very weapon that was likely to have killed her brother.

Mary, the middle-aged woman who had shown Ruby the ropes a few months previously and who had recently lost a son herself, rushed over and wrapped Ruby in a bosomy embrace the moment she was back through the door of the detonation shed.

'My poor lamb,' she said. 'You're one of us, now. It's a club none of us wanted to join, but here we are and we've got to make the most of it. Hold your head up, pet, and be proud of your brother. Our men are heroes – *heroes* – and don't let anyone tell you no different. But if ever you feel your guard slip and you need a good old blub, come and find me. We'll find a quiet spot and you can let it all out.'

'Thank you,' said Ruby fervently.

She'd dreaded that first moment – dreaded the swivelled glances and the pitying expressions – but Mary had succeeded in taking the sting out of it all. How glad she was that Mary had coincidentally also transferred from the night shift and would be there to offer support. Of course, so many people were in the same boat nowadays that the sense of isolation Ruby assumed one would usually feel at being bereaved was missing. It might be a club that no one wanted to join, but at least there was some scant comfort in there being a club at all. There was also an element of relief – that Harry had died on active service, unlike poor Connie on the main factory floor, whose brother had allegedly been executed for cowardice . . .

How much harder would that be to bear?

For the first couple of days, Ruby slotted back into work with little trouble. She was still plagued with misgivings about manufacturing weapons designed to kill, but Mary told her to push those thoughts firmly to one side. Britain hadn't started the war but – by Jove – they needed to win it and, like it or not, they all needed to play their part. Leah, Elspeth and Dot were kind and supportive, as Ruby had known that they would be. There always seemed to be one of them around at lunchtime or during her breaks, happy to listen to her talking if that was what she needed to do, but not demanding anything of her if she wanted to be quiet. Not for the first time, Ruby could only wonder at the tightknit band of women she had managed to surround herself with. It was the first time in her life that she had had such close friends and now she wondered how she could have ever done without them. Their friendship cushioned any disappointment she might otherwise have felt at Jack being on a slightly different shift pattern than herself and thus unable to share lunch and breaktimes with her, although they were still walking together in the park most mornings.

Overall, Ruby soon found herself soothed by the rhythms and routines of work; even the evermore demanding quotas her team had to deliver helped by giving her something else to focus her energies on. She still had a lump in her throat every time she heard the name 'Harry' and she heard it a lot: sometimes it seemed that every other man at the factory shared the name. And she still felt like crying every time the women in the detonation shed sung 'Roses of Picardy' and she didn't think that that feeling would ever leave.

But, apart from that, she was doing fine, thank you very much.

Just fine and dandy.

Tuesday, 21 November 1916

A few days after she went back to work, Ruby was in the canteen with Elspeth and Dot.

Strictly speaking, the three women weren't meant to eat together; Elspeth, working on the main factory floor and thus exposed on a daily basis to TNT, was restricted to a different canteen. It was a ridiculous system, everyone agreed; TNT poisoning was hardly contagious and, besides, everybody mixed freely elsewhere. Elspeth, herself, played football in close proximity with the very people she wasn't allowed to share a canteen with.

During the summer, and when the weather was clement, the friends had got around the problem by eating outside on one of the grassy banks between the various, hastily erected factory buildings. But, as it got progressively colder and wetter, this was proving more difficult, so they had decided to simply ignore the rule. Any attempt to 'smuggle' Elspeth into Ruby and Dot's canteen would be unlikely to succeed because Elspeth's skin already bore the telltale yellow tinge of toxic jaundice – and so Ruby and Dot went to Elspeth's canteen instead. They didn't avail themselves of the free milk provided there in an attempt to protect the workers – that simply wouldn't be right – but, apart from that, they couldn't see that they were doing any harm.

Anyway, on this particular day Ruby was sitting toying with her oxtail soup – she had, she found, totally lost her appetite since Harry's death – and letting the conversation twist and turn around her. And then Elspeth turned to her.

'Is it too soon to talk about the Christmas bazaar again?' she asked gently.

Ruby started as though she had been slapped. To be honest, it seemed too soon to talk about *anything* – Christmas was the last thing on anyone's mind and the bazaar itself just seemed so futile as to not be worthy of mention. The animal hospital itself seemed futile at the moment. She might be able to help clear a dog's mange or heal a cat's broken leg but what did that matter when she had been unable to save her own brother?

What was the point of *any* of it?

'Pardon me,' said Elspeth, correctly interpreting Ruby's hesitation and, no doubt, her expression. 'It's just that it's a few weeks to Christmas now and we've still got to get some of the details ironed out – to say nothing of sorting out the decorations.'

Ruby shook her head in an attempt to clear her rambling thoughts.

Elspeth had a point – of course she did – and it had been very kind of her and her ma to offer to coordinate the fundraiser on behalf of the animal hospital in the first place. And she knew that time was marching on, even in the midst of her grief, and that the bazaar would be on them all before they knew it.

Ruby also knew she was comparing apples with plums.

Her thinking made no sense at all.

Harry might be dead . . . but the animals of the East End were still suffering and in an ever more parlous state. Closing the clinic or stopping the fundraising activities wouldn't bring Harry back and it wouldn't be what he would have wanted. Harry hadn't been directly involved with the animal hospital but he had coincidentally turned up at the opening and quite made everyone's day. He had also told Ruby – both in person and in his letters – how proud he was of her for following her heart and for getting everything up and running against all odds. Furthermore, Harry had loved Christmas and he would have thoroughly approved of an all-bells-and-whistles Christmas bazaar to celebrate the occasion. And he would also have approved of the first animal hospital evening clinic, which – as luck would have it – was being held that very evening and was the very first clinic that was being staffed by Silvertown staff alone – Robert and Leah having a commitment together elsewhere.

It was preposterous to even consider calling a halt to the venture.

So, Ruby turned to Elspeth, plastered a smile on her face and said determinedly, 'It ain't too soon at all. Christmas is rushing up on us all and we need to get our ducks in a row. Tell me what you've got in mind?'

'Pudding first, I think,' said Dot with a grin. 'I always find I concentrate better when I've got something sweet inside me.'

'A baker's daughter through and through,' said Elspeth, giving her a friendly shove. 'Always thinking of your stomach.'

'Always,' echoed Dot, good-naturedly. 'Dead man's arm all round?'

Dead man's arm.

The affectionate name for jam roly-poly.

Ruby had grown up eating the comforting steamed suet pastry rolled around raspberry jam and had called it dead man's arm without a second thought. In fact, Harry had always used to press down hard on the sponge with his spoon until the jam oozed out and stained the custard red. Then he would put his bowl under Ruby's nose with a delighted grin. 'That's the blood,' he used to say. 'It's the blood of a dead man and if you eat it, you will die too.' Ruby would squeal in horrified fascination and the meal would either end with indulgent smiles or a swift dose of the strap all round, depending on which way the wind was blowing and whether or not Pa had been down the boozer.

Dead man's arm.

As an adult, Harry's arm had been tanned and muscled from lugging sacks around at the docks. He had had a distinctly working-class arm – a Silvertown man's arm . . .

Dead man's arm.

Ruby pushed her chair back.

She needed some air.

And then she was heading for the doorway, weaving as quickly as she could between the tightly packed tables and chairs, ignoring the curious faces turning towards her and Dot and Elspeth calling after her, concern in their voices.

Bile rising in her throat, she pushed through the door, blundered past a couple of women waiting to come in and then broke into a run. She ran around the side of the building and onto the grassy bank beside the canteen kitchen door – the place she had first met the cats and first talked to Leah all those months ago. And then she stopped, bent over, hands on knees, gasping for breath.

And here were Dot and Elspeth – Leah now in tow – rushing around the corner in hot pursuit. Ruby, still battling waves of nausea, flapped her hand at them in a bid to communicate that she was alright.

Elspeth reached her first and put a reassuring arm around her shoulders and then suddenly all three were talking at once.

'Such a terrible name for a pudding; I promise, I'll never call it that again.'

'You poor thing, Ruby; no wonder you're upset.'

'I'm ever so sorry – I'm such a clot.'

Ruby gave them all a shaky smile and reached out, patting Dot on the arm.

'Don't be silly,' she said. 'It ain't your fault. It just made me think about Harry and . . . and . . .'

And suddenly Ruby found she was crying – huge tearing sobs, which started from somewhere deep inside her and wrenched themselves free. Elspeth's arm tightened around her shoulders, rubbing the top of her arm.

'There, there,' she murmured comfortingly, just as Ma always said . . . or, at least, she used to say when you could still reach out to her for comfort.

And it really helped.

Ruby lowered herself onto the grass and the others sat down beside her and, if it was a little cold and wet, no one mentioned it. They just sat calmly, encircling Ruby, and talking inconsequentially amongst themselves, whilst Ruby's sobs turned into hiccups and eventually dried up.

'I'm sorry,' she said, wiping her eyes. 'I don't know where that came from.'

'Don't be daft,' said Leah, patting Ruby's knee. 'We know exactly where it's coming from and I'm so glad you're finally letting it all out.'

Ruby took a deep, shuddering breath. 'But we ain't supposed to let it out, are we?' she said, a trace of bitterness in her voice. 'We're supposed to carry on being strong and in control. Bottle it all up, hide it away, carry on for King and Country. That's what we're supposed to do, ain't we?'

Leah shrugged. 'Maybe,' she said. 'Maybe on duty. Maybe at the hospital. Maybe even at home whilst you comfort your Ma and your brother. But here? I'd say there's absolutely no need to keep up appearances with us.'

'Hear, hear,' said Elspeth, stoutly. 'We're your friends

and you can share exactly how you're feeling here. In fact, I think that you *must*. After all, what's the whole friends' thing for if we ain't honest with each other?'

'I agree,' said Dot. 'Let's make a pact between the four of us. A pact to share what's important to us without fear of being judged. No matter how much we have to hide our feelings "out there", between the four of us we can just be open and honest.'

'I think that would be marvellous,' said Leah. And then her smile broadened as Balthazar, one of the munitions factory mousers, stalked over and sat down next to them. 'Oh, Balthazar, you want to join us, do you?' she said, stroking the moggy's ginger head. 'Well, I'm very sorry but I don't think that you can. This little club is for females only.'

Everyone roared with laughter.

Elspeth picked up Balthazar. 'I rather hate to point this out,' she said, inspecting the poor cat's undercarriage. 'But it rather appears Balthazar is actually a girl. Shame on whoever named her!'

'That would be me,' said Ruby, giggling through her tears. 'Sorry, old girl,' she added, shaking Balthazar's paw. 'In that case, you are very welcome to join our merry band of female friends and, on top of that, I formally rename you . . . er . . . Balthazar*a*. Or, shall we say, plain old Zara for short.'

The laughter around her intensified and Ruby felt her spirits lift. Then, out of the corner of her eye, she saw Jack walking towards the canteen with an easy, loping grace.

Her heart leapt. Maybe he had been put on a different shift that at least partially coincided with hers and they could finally spend some time together during their breaks at work.

How wonderful that would be.

Ruby's second thought was that there was almost no sign of Jack's limp in the way he was walking and, for some reason, that niggled her . . .

Then Jack's eyes met hers.

Pleasure at seeing her and confusion that she was there jostled for supremacy on his face – and he changed course towards her little group. Then, as he crossed the grass, a stray football from one of several impromptu kick-arounds taking place around them crossed his path.

Jack didn't hesitate.

Jumping up, he twisted around in midair and kicked the ball from behind – sending it flying through the 'goal', which had been marked out by two coats on the grass. It was an undeniably neat manoeuvre and it didn't go unnoticed. The lads and lasses playing football started cheering and whistling – 'Why aren't you in the first team?' – and, out of the corner of her eye, Ruby saw a couple of girls sitting nearby giving Jack appreciative glances before turning to each other and giggling behind their hands.

Ruby could have expected to feel proud . . .

Or perhaps amused . . .

Maybe even a tinge of jealousy . . .

So why, then, did she just feel irritated?

An irritation underscored by another emotion – one that, again, slithered away before she could put a name to it.

'Hello,' said Jack, arriving by her side and smiling around at the little group in general.

Her friends all smiled back and Elspeth gave him a wave for good measure.

Jack was popular.

Everyone seemed to like him.

'I didn't expect to see you chaps out here,' Jack continued. 'Have you changed shifts or something?'

'Not at all,' said Leah, jumping to her feet and brushing down her skirts. 'In fact, seeing you out here has made me realise that I'm late reporting back on duty. I really should get a move on.'

'Glad to be of assistance,' said Jack dryly.

Leah laughed and then her eyes narrowed as Cook patrolled close to them. 'I think you'll find we're *well* within the three-yard rule here, WPC Fletcher,' she said, before Cook had had a chance to say anything. Then, with a flick and a swish of her skirts, she was gone, leaving Cook staring open-mouthed after her.

Jack's eyes found Ruby's again. 'I say,' he added quietly, peering more closely at her face. 'Are you quite alright?'

Ruby's irritation intensified.

'Perfectly,' she replied ungraciously. 'Do carry on playing football, if you'd like. Don't let us stop you.'

Jack raised an eyebrow. 'I ain't playing football,' he said. 'I were just walking to the canteen and I saw you all sitting here and then the ball flew towards me and . . .'

'We saw what happened,' Ruby interrupted tersely. 'Very athletic, I must say. And now if you'll excuse me, I'd better get back to work and all. I'll see you at the clinic this evening.'

*

She was being unreasonable.

Jack hadn't done anything wrong. In fact, he was totally blameless. He had come over to see her, he had expressed concern at her obviously still tear-stained face and what had he got for his troubles? A sweetheart who had been bad-tempered and rude to his face – and in front of her friends to boot. She was completely out of line. She needed to apologise and she would do so as soon as she saw Jack at the clinic that evening.

But something was still troubling Ruby. As she doggedly screwed fuse caps into place and kept half an eye on her quotas, her mind was far away. And, as the shift began to draw to a close, she finally realised what it was.

Jack had been invalided out of the army on relatively minor issues. In fact, he was so good at covering for his hearing loss – standing in the right place so that his 'good ear' was always to the fore – that it was sometimes hard to remember he was deaf in one ear at all. And as for his damaged leg! Jack might have been in hospital on the Isle of Wight for several months on his way back from the front whilst the doctors battled to save it . . . but look at him now. The way he had twisted and leapt for that ball would have put many able-bodied men to shame!

None of this was Jack's fault, of course, but the simple reality was that war had cost Harry his life whilst Jack, by contrast, had got away relatively scot-free.

Ruby tried hard to push those thoughts to one side but nothing could get away from the fact that the difference in sacrifice was very stark.

*

Jack was waiting for her outside the detonation shed as she finished work.

Ruby had feared that he might be there, even though his shift didn't finish for another hour. In fact, she had even considered leaving the denotation shed by the side door that led to the far side of the compound and then walking the long way home in an effort to avoid him. It would have been a futile gesture as they were all meeting at the clinic that evening, so she would hardly be putting off the evil hour for too long.

And why was she even trying to avoid him?

She *loved* Jack.

She had told him as much a matter of weeks ago – and she hadn't said those words lightly. She had meant them with all her heart and soul.

'Hello,' said Jack, transferring his weight from foot to foot.

Rationally, Ruby knew that he was nervous and determined not to upset her further by doing or saying the wrong thing. But the movement only served to annoy her further. He looked exactly like a small boy desperate to go to the lavvies.

'What is it?' she said shortly.

So much for saying sorry.

'I wondered if you'd heard the news?' said Jack.

Ruby looked at him blankly. 'What news?'

'The Battle of the Somme is over,' said Jack simply. 'It finished a couple of days ago. It's all over the afternoon papers.'

Ruby shut her eyes.

It had been a long, brutal and bloody battle and the fact

that it had now concluded was objectively a good thing. But, of course, it wasn't as simple as that.

If only Harry could have hung on a few extra days.

Ruby opened her eyes slowly. 'What happened?' she asked. And then, hopefully, 'Did we win?'

Jack shook his head. 'No clear victory, I'm afraid,' he said. 'The mud saw to that – and the weather, and the German defences.'

Ruby swallowed hard.

Thousands and thousands of lives lost – including that of her own brother – and all to end in a stalemate.

It was almost unbearable.

She gave Jack a little smile. 'Well, thank you for letting me know,' she said sadly.

'I thought I might walk you home,' said Jack.

Ruby felt another, inexplicable, rush of irritation.

'Don't be silly,' she said, making a conscious effort – despite her words – to sound conciliatory. 'You don't finish for another hour. No point in getting into trouble.'

'I can make an exception,' said Jack. 'You was upset at lunchtime and it ain't great news for you about the Somme. I want to help.'

'You can't help, Jack,' said Ruby, wearily. 'Not now. Not ever. Not with this, anyway. And if you don't get back on duty, old Mr Briggs will have your guts for garters and then where will you be?'

'But . . .'

'No buts,' said Ruby. 'I'll be alright and hopefully by the time we meet at the clinic this evening, I'll be right as rain. Go. *Go*.'

She reached out to give him a little push, but Jack caught hold of her hand. He pulled it towards him almost fiercely and, bending over, kissed the back of it. He released it and then, without a backwards glance, he was gone, leaving Ruby staring at his retreating back.

9

The queue for that first Tuesday evening clinic was barely shorter than those for the regular Friday daytime sessions.

At least, thought Ruby, it would give her something else to think about. Since returning to it, the clinic in general had been such a comfort to her. After all, the focus was on healing, not on manufacturing weapons of war . . .

Ruby had put big signs in the hospital windows making it clear that there would be no qualified vets on duty and that it was not a regular clinic. They had decided in advance that the focus for the evening would be dogs; there would be no operations and the skeleton staff were there primarily to diagnose and to give advice. Jack and Nellie would be on hand to examine animals in the consulting rooms and Ruby and Elspeth – now fully on board in the clinic – would be manning the reception area, booking everyone in and treating directly where they felt comfortable to do so.

In addition – and to Ruby's delight – Dot would be running what they all hoped would be the first of many educational classes in one of the old stables – since converted to a room – off the courtyard at the back of the building. This first one would concentrate on digestive issues in dogs; most working-class people in Silvertown simply fed their pets on leftovers from their own table and, as Robert had already pointed out, often what was on offer was supremely unsuited to the poor animals' digestive systems. As an incentive to attend this inaugural class, Ruby had ordered in extra bottles of Day & Son's tonic to give away. Hopefully, in time, all this would filter through to the number of owners presenting with animals with tummy troubles.

By six thirty, the queue, as usual, stretched all the way down Sanctuary Lane with every type of – mainly mongrel – dog under the sun barking, or straining on their leads or simply having a sniff around. It was a wonder that they hadn't yet had any complaints from the residents of this end of Sanctuary Lane, who were regularly having their front doors thus blocked. So far, the hospital had had nothing but goodwill and support.

Ruby felt a twinge of nerves as she swung the sign on the front door to 'open' and the front of the crowd duly started to shuffle inside. Supposing people couldn't read the signs and had assumed it was a regular clinic? Supposing the skeleton team on duty weren't able to get to all the animals and some ended up queuing to no avail? Supposing – and this was a recurrent worry underpinning everything they did, but particularly applied that evening – they were found out for being as supremely unqualified as they mostly were?

Then Jack arrived – later than the others because his shift at the munitions factory had only just finished and he had barely had time to change and eat a sandwich before presenting on duty. He gave Ruby a tight smile as he entered and, despite her current antipathy towards him, she started to feel much happier. She was surrounded by her friends who all knew their stuff despite their lack of formal qualifications and, besides, there were simply no other options available to most animal owners in Silvertown.

The clinic started without incident, everyone busy and focussed on their individual tasks. It turned out that much of the queue had come to hear Dot's talk and headed straight into the courtyard through the side entrance – so making the number of those waiting to have their animals checked over in the clinic proper much more manageable.

Ruby breathed a sigh of relief.

Then a soldier arrived; a blond man in an army greatcoat with a scar on one chiselled cheek. Ruby went over, idly wondering whether he was home on leave or whether, like Jack, he had been invalided out and had a month to return his greatcoat to one of the London railway termini and a shilling for his troubles. Either way, he had clearly survived the Battle of the Somme, the lucky bugger. His dog, a border collie and spaniel mix called Chien, was apparently weak and lacking in energy. Ruby could feel herself flushing slightly as she booked him in because his owner – one Private W Reid – really was *very* handsome.

Ruby turned, almost in relief, to the next owner and dog. Only there was no dog. It was forgetful Mr Atkins who lived more or less next door and who liked to come inside the hospital for the warmth and company. Ruby was just bidding him welcome and realising with a jolt of sadness that he no longer remembered who she was, when a commotion made her start with shock. Chien – the dog allegedly so weak and lacking in energy that he could barely stand up – was up on his hind legs, straining at his lead and barking at a small female dog minding her own business next to him. The handsome soldier barked out an order and yanked on the rope halter for good measure, but Chien took no notice. He carried on straining towards the cowering bitch, snapping and snarling. A couple of dogs sitting a little further away starting growling and barking by way of reply and anxious owners started pulling their animals closer towards themselves, out of harm's way. Then, the solider got to his feet and pulled harder on his leash, fairly dragging Chien back to his side. He kept on repeating the same words in a low, calm voice – they sounded like nonsense to Ruby but, of course, there was a good deal of cockney or coster-slang that she *didn't* know – his outstretched hand, palm down, a clear sign he was instructing Chien to sit down. Finally, *finally*, the dog complied; sitting down he then – incongruously – started to lick Private Reid's face over and over again with a wet, slobbery tongue.

Ruby – along, no doubt, with everyone else – breathed a sigh of relief. Dogs barked and snarled and strained in the hospital all the time, of course. They were mostly poorly and no one expected them to sit neatly and primly awaiting their turn, but there was something particularly feral and ferocious about the way that Chien had behaved.

Weak and lacking in energy indeed!

As she turned her attention to the next customer, Ruby wondered what the soldier had said. It had sounded like '*assay twa*'. The soldier had a typical Silvertown accent but it certainly hadn't been anything that Ruby had ever heard before. Not that it mattered, per se, but it didn't harm to keep on top of how the residents of the East End spoke to and referred to both animals and ailments.

After all, it was all part of the job.

The door opened as Elspeth ushered out one owner and let in another. But no sooner had the thin, sandy-haired man and his thin, sandy-haired dog taken a seat than Chien was at it again, straining at his lead, barking and snarling.

Ruby swallowed a knot of anxiety.

There was something about Chien that she didn't trust. Fortunately, his owner seemed to be a strong man, but, even so, Ruby feared they were only one step away from disaster. Chien wasn't huge, but, with that level of aggression, he was certainly capable of maiming, or even killing, one of the smaller dogs.

'You need to get that dog out of here,' one of the other owners said to the soldier. 'He's going to do someone a mischief otherwise. Miss,' he added to Ruby. 'Turf him out, will you?'

Ruby hesitated and flicked a glance at Elspeth, busy handing over a vial of liquid to the owner of a rheumy-looking pug. Elspeth gave a tiny I-don't-know-what-to-do-either shrug and Ruby sighed inwardly. There was no doubt that she *would* have to intervene, but she was loathe to simply throw the soldier and his dog out onto the street. She wanted the hospital to have a reputation for being inclusive – for *everyone* – no matter how an animal – or its owner, for that matter – might behave. East Enders were so used to being judged, marginalised and excluded and she wanted this clinic to be different.

Then again . . .

'Private Reid, if you'd like to bring Chien and come with me,' she said firmly to the soldier. 'There's a quiet room out the back where you and Chien can wait and where, er, you won't be disturbed.'

Private Reid nodded and started fairly manhandling Chien through reception. Chien resisted him every step of the way – growling and baring his teeth at all and sundry – until they reached the tiny room out the back, which was used as part-storeroom and part-coat cupboard. Ruby flicked on the electric light and pushed a jumble of sweaters and bags off a low bench seat.

'If you wouldn't mind waiting here,' she said. 'I'll try and get you seen to as soon as possible. Although,' she couldn't help adding, 'I rather think being weak and feeble is the least of Chien's problems!'

Private Reid gave her a rueful smile. 'Ta,' he said. 'And I'm ever so sorry; I really don't know what's got into him. He ain't always like this.'

'Hopefully we'll be able to get to the bottom of what's going on, Private Reid,' said Ruby.

'Thank you. And, please, it's Billy.'

Ruby, flushing slightly again, gave him a non-committal and, she hoped, professional smile but didn't otherwise reply.

Billy.

Back out in the corridor, Ruby debated what to do next.

Maybe she should ask Nellie or Jack to cast a quick eye over Chien right away. Even though it wasn't his turn – and even though Ruby hated to reward bad behaviour – Chien had already started barking up a storm behind the closed door and who knew what damage he might do in there. Surely it would be best to process him quickly and thus restore harmony to the hospital.

Nellie was busy. Ruby could hear her through the door of her consulting room, berating some poor owner for feeding scraps to his dog and suggesting that he join Dot's lecture forthwith. But, at that moment, the door to Jack's room opened and he ushered out a limping greyhound and his bluff, cheerful owner.

'Could I have a quick word?' said Ruby awkwardly as the man and the greyhound disappeared.

She had hardly said two words to him since their conversation outside the detonation shed earlier that afternoon and she knew that she still owed him an apology.

'Certainly,' said Jack, without smiling. He jerked a thumb towards the cupboard door – and the thunderous barking emanating from behind it – and raised an eyebrow at Ruby. 'What on earth's going on in there?'

'That's what I want to talk to you about,' said Ruby. She would apologise later. 'That dog was going berserk out the front, trying to attack all and sundry. I were quite scared, I can tell you. His owner keeps yelling gobbledegook at him but the dog don't take a blind bit of notice.'

Jack raised a quizzical eyebrow. 'Gobbledegook?' he echoed, with the ghost of a grin. 'Surely you ain't dismissing back-slang that you don't understand as *gobbledegook*? Where's your respect to the ancient dialects of the East End, I ask you? Shame on you, Missy.'

Ruby grinned and something inside her began to thaw. Jack and his throwaway comments; he never failed to make her laugh.

'"Assay-twa" ain't back-slang,' she said. 'I'm pretty sure of that.'

Jack pursed his lips. 'Is the chap French?'

'No?' Ruby wrinkled her nose in confusion. 'He's no more French than we are. In fact, I think he might have been a few years above me at school.'

The thought had only just come to her, but hadn't Harry played football with a blond chap called Billy Reid back in the day?

Jack grinned. 'Not very French then,' he said. 'A soldier?'

'Yes.'

'Only *assieds-toi* is French for "sit down". What's his dog's name, out of interest?'

'Chien,' said Ruby, impatiently.

What on earth did that have to do with anything.

'Aha!' said Jack, triumphantly, as though he had solved some particularly tricky conundrum. '*Chien* is French for "dog"! There's definitely a theme here . . .'

'That's all very well,' interrupted Ruby, shaking her head with frustration as the barking from behind the door grew in volume. 'But, regardless of whether the blasted thing is called Rex or Max or Chien, can you please take a look at him before he destroys the place?'

'Remind me of his symptoms?' said Jack in an altogether more serious tone.

'Aggressive . . .'

'Yes, I can hear that. What else?'

'Tired and listless a lot of the time, or so the soldier says. He also licks his owner a lot.'

Jack pursed his lips. 'Frothing or foaming at the mouth?' he asked.

'Not that I've noticed,' said Ruby. 'Take a look at him, please, Jack. Surely that's the best way to make an assessment?'

Jack put a finger to his lips, beckoned Ruby into his consulting room and shut the door behind them both. Ruby looked at him in confusion.

'I'm sorry for how I behaved earlier on,' she blurted out.

There.

Said it.

That was, no doubt, why Jack had dragged her in here, after all. He probably wanted to clear the air after Ruby's grumpiness that afternoon.

'Thank you,' he said. 'I accept your apology. But that isn't what this is about.'

'What then?'

'I think your soldier in there has been at the front and has smuggled a dog back from France.'

'Oh,' said Ruby, completely nonplussed. She had never heard of such a thing. 'Do you think Chien were one of those dogs who were brought out there to carry telegram wires or to relay messages. And, if so, ain't that stealing?'

Lordy; were they going to have to get the police involved?

Or wouldn't they be interested in a crime technically committed in France?

But Jack was shaking his head. 'Unlikely,' he said. 'Not if Chien responds to French commands, that is. No, the countryside out in France were full of stray dogs. Families who lived in the farms near the battlefields usually moved away as the fighting came closer and often left their dogs behind to fend for themselves. The poor things was often in a dreadful state and it weren't uncommon for them to be informally adopted by Tommies for a bit of comfort and companionship. Officers turned a blind eye to that although it were, of course, completely forbidden to try and bring them back to Blighty.'

'I see,' said Ruby. 'But that don't mean that we shouldn't treat him now he's here, do it?'

Jack puffed out his cheeks. 'From what you've told me of his symptoms – and I know we ain't examined him yet – it sounds very much as though he might be infected with rabies.'

'Rabies!' repeated Ruby, stupidly.

Oh, goodness.

Ruby knew that rabies was a nasty disease that could easily spread between animals and humans; indeed, she knew that it was nearly always fatal. But she also knew that there had been no rabies in England since she was a little girl. It had been completely irradicated and Ruby had simply never given it a second thought.

Had she been naïve?'

Jack pulled a face. 'The vet I worked with out at the front thought it only a matter of time before a dog that were smuggled home brought the disease back to Blighty,' he said. 'Looks like he might have been right, but I never thought one might turn up on our watch, so to speak.'

'What did you do to dogs you thought had rabies in France?' asked Ruby, knowing – dreading – the answer.

'I'm not sure I ever saw one,' said Jack. 'But if we had, it would have been a bullet to the back of the neck, for certain. That were how we dispatched all sick, injured or unwanted animals out there. By far the quickest and the kindest way.'

There was a bark and the sound of a small scuffle from the coat cupboard and Ruby's hand flew to her heart.

'So . . . you're thinking the lethal chamber,' she said miserably.

'I am,' said Jack. 'Anything else just ain't worth the risk.'

'But you ain't even examined him yet,' said Ruby.

'And get bitten and infected for me troubles?' said Jack. 'No, thank you. I'm just glad he didn't attack you and also that you had the sense to remove him away from everyone else. Please tell me he didn't bite anyone in reception before you got him out?'

'He didn't,' said Ruby. She paused and then added, 'We've got a muzzle out the front. If we get his owner to put it on Chien, would you at least take a look at him . . . ?'

'No,' said Jack. 'Rabies is life-threatening, and I've had enough of life-threatening situations for a lifetime, ta very much.'

'So, you're sure it's rabies, then . . .'

'No. Not at all . . .' He shook his head. 'But I don't want to underestimate the danger we'd all be in if he does have it. Then again, if we muzzle him, I suppose it's only fair to give the poor creature a chance.'

Ruby didn't need telling twice. She ran back to reception and took the muzzle down from one of the shelves behind the desk. Everything was as it always was – a crush of animals and owners, an air of busy enterprise, Elspeth bustling around . . .

Jack was waiting for her outside the small storeroom door when she got back. There was no mistaking the worry on his face and Ruby's apprehension grew as a result. Meanwhile, the barking and growling from within showed no sign of abating.

'Careful,' Jack cautioned as Ruby rapped loudly on the door.

It opened immediately and the soldier poked his head out. Chien, thankfully, had been tied to one of the coat hooks and was safely out of harm's way. 'Could you please put this on Chien and bring him through to the consultation room?' she asked.

The soldier nodded and closed the door. Seconds later it opened, to reveal a duly muzzled Chien. Billy untied him and followed Ruby into Jack's consulting room.

Jack turned to Billy. 'From what I've been told, I'm assuming you've stolen Chien and smuggled him back from France?' he said without preamble.

Stolen.

Smuggled.

Jack certainly wasn't mincing his words.

Billy looked shocked and shamefaced. 'You don't miss a thing, do you?' he said almost admiringly to Ruby. 'And you're right, of course. At least, I didn't steal him – he'd been abandoned – but I did bring him back from France. The old boy saved me life and it were the least I could do.'

'But how did you get him into Blighty?' asked Jack, gesticulating for Billy to lift Chien onto the examination table. 'He's not a particularly large dog, but he would have been difficult to hide away.'

Billy shrugged as he lifted a surprisingly compliant Chien onto the table. 'When a trainload of us soldiers arrives back on leave at Waterloo – hundreds and hundreds of us all pushing and shoving – believe me, there ain't much they can do. There *certainly* ain't no opportunity to check each of us and our possessions individually. If you'd served at the front, you'd be amazed what's brought back in.'

There was an edge to Billy's voice that didn't go unnoticed by Ruby and, beside her, she felt Jack stiffen.

'Oh, I were at the front, alright,' said Jack matter-of-factly. 'But I were transported back to hospital on the Isle of Wight on me Todd and I didn't have the chance to bring back anything without the orderlies and nurses knowing about it.'

'You was invalided out?' asked Billy, a new note of respect in his voice. He held a wriggling Chien firmly whilst Jack began his examination.

'Yes,' said Jack, shortly. He pressed Chien's flanks gently and then very cautiously turned his attention to the dog's mouth.

'Lucky bugger,' said Billy. 'I might not be as lucky as you – I may not come back at all – but I thought the least I could do was get this chap out whilst I still had the chance.'

The long look exchanged by the two men spoke volumes but then Jack exhaled loudly and ran his hand through his hair.

'All very admirable, pal,' he said. 'But you didn't stop to consider you might be responsible for reintroducing rabies back into the country after the best part of twenty years?'

'Rabies!' Billy recoiled, looking genuinely horrified. 'Bloody hell; do you think that's what the poor bugger's got?'

'I can't be sure,' said Jack, straightening up. 'Probably

not. He's got some of the symptoms – certainly not all – but either way, it's too big a risk to allow you to take him home.'

Billy looked stricken. 'You can't destroy him,' he said. 'Not if you ain't absolutely sure what's wrong with him. I won't let you.'

He made as if to grab Chien and Jack went to stand in the doorway.

'Careful,' warned Ruby. 'Don't let him bite you.'

It was still a possibility, despite the muzzle.

'I won't,' said Jack, calmly. 'I suggest you don't try and make a run for it,' he added to Billy.

Ruby could almost see the soldier weighing up the pros and cons of doing just that and she went to stand beside Jack.

'Even if you do manage to get past us and out of here, remember that you gave me your details when you signed in,' she said, trying to keep her voice equally calm. 'If you don't cooperate, we'll have no choice but to contact the police and let them know you've admitted to smuggling an animal that might have rabies into the country. I've no idea what the penalty is for that, but if they decide to throw the book at you under the new Defence of the Realm Act, I'd say you'd be looking at a long stretch in prison at His Majesty's Pleasure. Perhaps even worse. Times is brutal at the moment if you're branded a traitor.'

Goodness.

That had all sounded rather impressive – even to her own ears. Jack gave her a nod of approval and, across the room, Billy's shoulders slumped in apparent defeat.

'But you can't just kill a dog who might not have rabies,' he said desperately. 'What about if I promise to confine Chien until we know one way or another what's wrong with him?'

Jack shook his head. 'From someone who didn't think to muzzle a clearly violent dog when he brought it into a public place, I'd say doing the right thing isn't exactly your strong suit,' he said.

'I thought bringing me sick animal to your animal hospital *were* doing the right thing,' the soldier shot back.

'Could we quarantine him?' interrupted Ruby, a plan slowly taking shape in her mind.

'Ruby . . . don't,' said Jack. 'Rabies ain't something you mess with. Far better we call Father Murphy and his lethal chamber.'

Billy put a reassuring hand on Chien's shoulder as if the dog could understand talk of his potential demise. The dog lay down with a little sigh and regarded his owner with a baleful eye.

'Hear me out,' implored Ruby. 'If we put Chien in one of those large cages that I spent a fortune on and still really haven't had a chance to use, I can't see what the problem would be. Then we wait – what? – a week, and if Chien doesn't develop rabies, we let Private Reid take him home. What would be the problem with that?'

'The cage lock breaks . . . Chien bites the hand of whoever's feeding him . . . a Zeppelin drops a bomb nearby and smashes the cage to smithereens . . . someone breaks in and lets him out with an ulterior motive . . . shall I go on?' replied Jack dryly.

'Things might go wrong, but they probably won't,' countered Ruby. 'I'd say we give it a try.'

What if it was Mac?

She would be desperate for someone to give him a chance – to at least *try* to save him.

'It's not our role to make that decision, Ruby,' said Jack. 'We have to follow the establishment policy on rabies prevention.'

'Is there one?'

'I don't know.'

'Look,' said Ruby. 'This is wartime. Lots of people and institutions – including the Royal Veterinary College, which is pretty much as establishment as it is possible to be – said it weren't our role to set up an animal hospital. But we didn't let that stop us, did we? We thought they were wrong and we carried on anyway. It's the same thing here. At the end of the day, I don't want to destroy a much-loved dog if all he's got is a cold.'

Jack held up his hand in mock-surrender. 'All right, all right – you win,' he said. 'But can we agree on ten days – just to be on the safe side.'

'It's a deal,' said Ruby. She turned to Billy who – naturally – had been avidly following the twists and turns of the conversation. 'I trust this is acceptable to you, Private Reid?' she added. 'You'll leave Chien here with us for the next ten days and, if he's no longer showing symptoms that might be linked to rabies, you can take him home. If, however, it becomes clear that he *does* have rabies, we agree to dispatch him humanely in Father Murphy's lethal chamber.'

The truth of the matter was, of course, that if Chien

had contracted rabies, he was unlikely to survive the next ten days anyway.

But Billy just nodded. 'In ten days' time, I shall be back at the front,' he said. 'Which front, I have no idea after the recent news, but I certainly won't be here. But me sister has agreed to care for Chien whilst I'm away, so she can hopefully fetch him home then. But might I visit him in the meantime?'

Ruby and Jack exchanged a glance.

'As you'll appreciate, this is a new policy,' said Jack. 'You'll need to allow us a little time to iron out all the details.'

'Exactly,' said Ruby. 'We'll take Chien now and we'll let you know what we decide about visiting him in due course. We'll also let you know where we'll be holding him. It won't be here, of course – our landlords would never allow it.'

Jack shot her a surprised glance but didn't otherwise comment and soon afterwards, Billy was on his way. Ruby escorted him through the building and out the front door and, if anyone wondered why Chien was no longer with him, no one said a thing.

'Do you really think the Fishers won't let us keep Chien here?' asked Jack when Ruby returned.

'I'm pretty sure they will,' said Ruby with a smile. 'Particularly if we're sketchy on the details and just tell them we suspect a contagious disease – which could be anything from distemper to flu.'

'We'll have to tell Dot the whole truth, though,' said Jack. 'She's one of us.'

'You're right,' said Ruby. 'We'll tell her what's happened

and she can decide what, if anything, to tell her parents. Either way, I just didn't want Private Reid coming back and springing a break.'

'You're a suspicious little Miss,' said Jack, with a smile. 'I'm sure he wouldn't do that.'

'He might,' said Ruby, shortly.

She might have been tempted to spring a break if it was Mac, regardless of the consequences.

Shortly afterwards, Dot reappeared – her serious, freckled face flushed with pleasure at the success of her first lecture.

The clinic was still ongoing – Elspeth and Nellie manfully holding the fort alone – but Ruby and Jack immediately took Dot to one side and explained the situation – rabies and all.

As Ruby had anticipated, Dot was sanguine – even excited – about it all. More and more soldiers would no doubt want to bring animals home as the war progressed and providing quarantine for suspected rabies cases was an important social service – as important as anything she was involved with at the East London Federation of the Suffragettes. Provided the cage was secure, the stable door firmly locked, and no one else was allowed to be near the animal, she was happy to be involved and she saw no reason to burden her parents with the fact that rabies was suspected.

So, Mrs Fisher was duly summoned and she, too, was relaxed about Chien being quarantined in one of the rooms off the courtyard. She told them she had assumed there would be some overnight guests connected with the hospital – as well as a certain degree of noise – and that it was all no problem at all. There was an empty stable-cum-garage at the end of the courtyard that they were welcome to use; it had a sturdy door and a secure lock and it should be safe as houses.

Then it was just a case of letting Nellie and Elspeth into the secret, getting a large cage secured in the stable and moving Chien. Ruby marvelled at how Chien calmed down when Nellie spoke gently to him and how he trotted off obediently at her side to his new quarters, allowing his muzzle to be removed – a scary moment – with barely a flicker.

And that was that.

Just another day and another challenge at the Sanctuary Lane Animal Hospital.

Once the clinic had finished, Ruby, Jack, Dot and Elspeth sat together, planning how they would care for Chien over the next few days. Nellie offered to have food brought over for him from her dog food barrow at the market each morning and they agreed that Ruby would feed and check on Chien in the morning and that Dot would do the same in the evening.

'What do you think Robert will make of it all?' asked Dot, as they all began to tidy the reception room after the evening clinic.

Ruby hesitated.

She had already started to fret that Robert might disapprove of them taking matters into their own hands without so much as a by-your-leave. After all, whilst the clinic had been her brainchild, and she was – sometimes it felt nominally – in charge, Robert was a qualified vet with a string of initials after his name and he potentially had the most to lose from not following the letter of the law. Ruby didn't want to anger him – and she certainly didn't want him to report her or to lose his support at the hospital.

'I was thinking that I might write to him and explain what we've done,' said Ruby. 'Although we all know what the postal service is like nowadays. He probably wouldn't get it until Friday.'

'No need for that,' said Jack, as the doorbell jangled. 'Speak of the devil . . .'

And in walked Leah and Robert, all dolled up in their finery and bringing in a gust of cold, winter's air with them.

'Should our ears be burning?' said Leah, cheerfully, the jewels in her ears and around her throat catching the electric lights. 'We're on our way home from *the* most tedious veterinary function, but we just had to find out how the clinic went.'

'Yes, how did it go, chaps?' said Robert, rubbing his hands together briskly and looking very dapper in a newfangled dinner jacket.

'Not exactly as planned,' said Jack slowly.

Robert frowned. 'Lecture not go well?' he asked Dot.

'No, that went very well,' said Dot with a broad smile.

Heart thumping, Ruby stepped forward and told Robert and Leah what they had done. There was a short pause and then, to Ruby's relief – and somewhat to her surprise – Robert gave a bark of laughter and clapped his hands together.

'One thing the function this evening confirmed is that

the veterinary profession has its head buried in the sand,' he said. 'They refuse to take the treatment of small companion animals seriously and they simply can't see – or don't want to acknowledge – the speed with which we're moving away from a horse-based economy. If they carry on as they are, pretty soon they'll have nothing left to treat!' He paused to take breath. 'I honestly think, for the medium term at least, animal welfare will be in the hands of small charities like this. So, I heartily approve of what you're doing; I'd go as far as to say that you're at the vanguard of veterinary practice. If soldiers carry on bringing animals back into the country, the government will be forced to copy you and start offering formal quarantine facilities.'

Thank goodness for *that*,' said Ruby, with a sigh of relief.

'Come on, let's have a look at this dog, then,' said Robert.

They all trooped out to look at Chien in his cage. The dog was asleep and, to Jack's evident relief, Robert came to the same conclusion as he had. Judging from his symptoms, there was a chance he may have rabies . . . but there could be many other reasons for his behaviour. Only time would tell.

Then Dot trooped upstairs to her flat and made hot chocolate for them all and it was a very happy little group that sat around and chatted until late in the evening.

Despite her worries about someone in authority finding out what they had done, Ruby wouldn't have had it any other way.

*

'We're a good team,' Ruby said to Jack when everyone else had gone and the two were preparing to lock up.

'That ain't what it felt like this afternoon,' said Jack with a grin. 'You wanted to have me guts for garters then.'

'I know,' said Ruby. 'I'm sorry. I don't know what came over me . . .' She trailed off, unable to find anymore words.

'It's alright,' said Jack, putting his arm around her shoulder. 'You've just lost your brother and you won't be yourself for a goodly while.'

He reached up to get his cap from the coat stand and stumbled, his expression dissolving into a grimace.

'What's wrong?' asked Ruby. 'Have you hurt yourself?'

'It's me leg,' said Jack. 'Me Blighty wound has been playing up like buggery all evening.'

'I'm so sorry,' said Ruby, sympathetically. 'You should have said.'

'It's me own fault,' said Jack, ruefully. 'It were jumping up and twisting around to kick that bleeding football at lunchtime that did it. I think I were trying to impress you, to be honest, but I need to remember that there are some things I could do before the war that I simply can't do anymore. There's Before-Jack and there's Now-Jack and I'm sorry to say that you're lumbered with Now-Jack.'

Any vestiges of annoyance and irritation that Ruby might have been holding onto melted away. She reached up and kissed him on the cheek.

'Lucky, then, that Now-Jack is the one that I want,' she said lightly.

He wasn't a shirker or a malingerer.

He had been trying to impress her!

Suddenly, she knew for certain that she loved him with all her heart and she simply couldn't imagine ever feeling any differently.

What a difference an afternoon could make.

10

Monday, 27 November 1916

As agreed, Ruby had started popping into the hospital early each morning to check on Chien.

It was another thing to squeeze into her already busy day, but Ruby soon found that she didn't mind her new routine a bit. There was just something about the morning solitude there that soothed her soul. It was almost funny, because Ruby absolutely *hated* the quiet at night when she was alone in bed, battling with fitful sleep and unwelcome thoughts about Harry and the unwanted images that took up residence in her head. But at the start of the day, when everything was fresh and new, being in the hospital all by herself could be very calming and comforting – despite the fact that the guest in the stable might be harbouring a deadly disease. Jack had offered to come in with her but, if truth be told, she preferred being by herself. It was welcome respite between Ma's misery and Charlie's moodiness and her busy, stressful day at the factory.

And, to Ruby's relief, Chien seemed to be getting better.

She was no expert, of course, but his temperament seemed to have quite turned around. He greeted Ruby with a little whine of pleasure each morning and looked up at her with such beseeching brown eyes that Ruby was sorely tempted to reach between the bars of the cage and give him a little pat. In fact, one day she threw caution to the wind and did just that – and was then horrified when Chien licked her bare fingers. Scrubbing her hand over and over again with carbolic soap in the little scullery, she counted her lucky stars that she didn't have any scratches or open wounds on her skin and vowed never to be so foolhardy again.

Several mornings after Chien had been admitted, Ruby arrived at the hospital to find a little pile of letters waiting for her.

Leah was great at dealing with the administration side of things, but Ruby liked to keep on top of everything that was happening and so she made a point of making all the correspondence her business. Today, most of the letters were addressed to the hospital and were clearly boring bills or circulars, but one looked much more interesting. Addressed to Ruby by name and written in a distinctive purple ink with a flamboyant looping script, there was no doubt who it was from. Ruby flicked the envelope over.

Mrs A Henderson, Carson Mansions, Hampstead.

Yes, it was her old employer; the lady of the house from her time in service.

Curiously, Ruby ripped the envelope open, not bothering to use Leah's smart silver letter-opener, which lived in the top drawer of the reception desk. The letter wasn't entirely a bolt from the blue, of course; Mrs Henderson had attended the fundraising concert Leah had organised at the Adelphi Theatre a few months previously – what a dramatic night that had turned out to be! – and had made a large donation to the hospital to boot.

Ruby was curious to discover what she had to say this time.

Inside the envelope were two sheets of wafer-thin blue paper . . . and what was this fluttering onto the floor? Another cheque addressed to the hospital and made out for a really very generous amount. Now Ruby thought about it, Mrs Henderson *had* mentioned that she was going to make a further donation, but Ruby hadn't given it too much thought. So many people told her that they planned to donate this or that and then failed to follow through, that she had learned not to get her hopes up. After all, this was wartime and people didn't have much spare cash.

Ruby gave a little whoop of exhilaration. This donation would keep the wolf from the door *and* enable them to run the evening clinics all the way to Christmas, to say nothing of buying some new examination lights that she had seen in one of the glossy sales brochures she was sent and had had her eyes on ever since.

Wasn't it strange how one could still feel happiness and excitement in the midst of great grief?

Ruby placed the cheque carefully on the table and turned her attention to the accompanying letter. Mrs Henderson started by expressing her sincere condolences for Harry's death and asked that Ruby extend those condolences to Ma and the rest of the family. A little taken aback – and easy tears pricking at her eyelids – Ruby sat down heavily on the corner of the desk.

How on earth did Mrs Henderson know about *that*?

Ruby had written to several people to inform them of the sad news, but the Hendersons certainly hadn't been amongst them.

Surely Mrs Henderson didn't scour the unbearably long columns of the fallen soldiers printed in the newspapers every day; surely, she would just look at the photographs of the dead officers who were deemed worthy of a more detailed inclusion.

Maybe Cook had told her. Ruby had no idea if Cook even knew if Harry had died – let alone whether she was still in touch with Mrs Henderson – but it was certainly a possibility.

Or possibly the news had worked its way to Mrs Henderson via Robert's father Sir Emrys, a business associate of Mr Henderson.

Either way, it was very kind of Mrs Henderson to take the trouble to express her condolences and Ruby felt a surge of gratitude amongst the tears.

She wiped her eyes and read on.

'*As I explained when we met at the concert, I intend to come along and offer my help to the hospital in a more practical way as well,*' Mrs Henderson wrote. '*I do a good deal of charity work and am very happy to share my expertise. Please let me know at your earliest convenience when the clinic is next open and I will make it a priority to attend.*'

Oh, goodness.

That seemed rather more a command than a suggestion.

But still, Mrs Henderson had been terribly generous on the monetary front and it would be churlish to refuse her a visit. Perhaps they could just give her a nice cup of tea and make a good old fuss of her and she would go away happy. In either case, Ruby couldn't help feeling that she didn't have much choice in the matter, so she quickly penned a letter to Mrs Henderson confirming that the hospital was open every Friday and that she was, of course, very welcome to come along and take a look. Perhaps Ruby might suggest the first Friday in December – ten days' time – when the whole team would be in attendance and could thank Mrs Henderson for her generosity in person. This, of course, was slightly disingenuous; the whole team was pretty much in attendance *every* Friday, but at least this would give them a little time to prepare for the visit.

That dealt with, Ruby turned her attention to the rest of the post.

The first couple of letters were – as she had expected – bills for the various medicines and other supplies she had ordered. There were a couple of circulars advertising new surgical products and a lovely – if barely legible – card of thanks from an old gentleman whose lame donkey Robert had treated. Ruby put the card on one of the shelves behind the reception desk with a couple of others they had already received and which served to remind Ruby – if she was ever tempted to forget – that what she was doing here was both very necessary and much appreciated. Then she picked up the last letter; a thick, creamy envelope – more expensive than the others – neatly typewritten and addressed to the hospital. In the top lefthand corner were the initials RCVS and Ruby's heart gave a thump of excitement. It was the Royal Veterinary College. Ruby had visited them in person several months ago outlining her plans for the hospital and had been given short shrift by a particularly unpleasant and condescending man called Mr Cotter. Maybe now the hospital was up and running he had had cause to reconsider his patronising putdown and was writing to offer support.

Ruby started reading.

Dear Miss Archer,

Subject: Notice of Non-Compliance and Request for Closure

Ruby put the letter down.

Oh, Lordy.

That wasn't what she had expected at all.

She took a deep breath and, with some trepidation, ploughed on:

The administration of the Royal College of Veterinary Surgeons (RCVS) is writing to address a matter of significant concern regarding the operation of the Sanctuary Lane Animal Hospital.

As an institution committed to the advancement of veterinary medicine and the welfare of animals, we hold ourselves accountable for upholding the highest standards of professional practice. It has come to our attention that the Sanctuary Lane Animal Hospital, an unregulated establishment, has been operating without adhering to the required industry standards and regulatory guidelines.

Our primary concern is the health and wellbeing of the animals entrusted to your care. Reports and observations from concerned individuals have raised several alarming issues related to substandard medical practices, chief amongst which is the fact that the animals are not always treated by qualified veterinary professionals, as well as an apparent lack of proper sanitation protocols and insufficient record-keeping. These violations not only compromise the health of the animals but also reflect negatively on the entire veterinary profession.

We acknowledge the challenges faced by independent animal hospitals, but we cannot overlook the potential harm caused by unregulated establishments. Therefore, we instruct you to immediately cease operations until such time that the Sanctuary Lane Animal Hospital can meet the necessary standards and obtain the appropriate licenses, certifications and affiliations.

It is imperative that you acknowledge the seriousness of the situation and take immediate steps to rectify the noted violations. Failure to do so may result in the involvement of the relevant authorities who will take necessary legal actions, including closure orders.

We request your prompt response outlining your plans to address the concerns raised and a timeline for achieving compliance.

We appreciate your attention to this matter and your commitment to the welfare of animals in London.

Your sincerely,
B. Loddon, Esq.

Ruby let the letter flutter from her fingers onto the desk and, from there, onto the floor.

What on earth was that about?

It was absolutely ridiculous.

The implication was that she had not only set up an animal hospital behind the back of the Royal Veterinary College but had then done her utmost to keep it a secret thereafter.

There couldn't have been anything further from the truth.

There had been *nothing* underhand about what she had done.

Nothing!

In fact, she couldn't have been more upfront about it all if she had tried. She had gone – in person – to the college in Camden Town, outlined her plans in some detail and then asked for support from the College. That request had been denied – somewhat aggressively and patronisingly so – but at no time had anyone suggested that she shouldn't go ahead with her plans.

It was all exceedingly frustrating.

And as for claiming that their concern was for the well-being of the animals in her care, well, that was just plain insulting.

The Royal-bleeding-Veterinary-College couldn't give a stuff about the animals of the East End. That undeniable fact was at the root of everything Ruby had set out to do. The complete and utter lack of affordable options for animal owners was the simple reason there were currently so many sick and injured animals in Silvertown. The only thing she had slight qualms about – and she really didn't want the College to discover – was harbouring Chien, and even that had been done with absolutely the best intentions.

More to the point, who had put the Royal Veterinary College up to this?

Who, exactly, had told them about the Sanctuary Lane Animal Hospital?

Maybe they had clandestinely had their sights on her

ever since her disastrous visit to Camden Town. Or maybe Mrs Coleman or her son James had said something: Mrs Coleman was the receptionist at the College and her son James was a veterinary student there and both were occasional volunteers at the hospital. Ruby knew there would have been no malicious intent had they said anything, but it might have got the ball rolling.

Then again, it could have been Sir Emrys, Robert's father, who had never exactly seen eye to eye with Ruby and who would definitely have reported the hospital with malicious intent . . .

Oh, at the end of the day, it really didn't matter who it was.

What mattered was that she had received this damn letter and she had no idea what to do about it. She had, of course, absolutely no intention of shutting the hospital down and, really, she didn't have the energy or the inclination to even think about replying.

Wearily, Ruby rested her head in her hands on the desk and shut her eyes.

The expression 'it never rains but it pours' had never seemed more apposite. Surely there should be some rule of the universe that if someone was grief-stricken and struggling, they should be spared further problems – at least for a while. But life didn't seem to work like that and it just all seemed so unfair. Out of nowhere, a couple of tears appeared in Ruby's eyes and she dashed them angrily away.

There was no point in feeling sorry for herself.

She could almost hear Harry telling her to pull herself together . . .

Oh, Harry.

Ruby tried to recall her brother's face, but to her shock – her horror! – she couldn't conjure up a complete image. She hadn't seen him for a month or so before his death and she just had a faint impression of a blurry figure with a broad face and a messy shock of hair and, try as she might, it refused to come into sharp focus. Maybe it was just the stressful morning but, if it went on, it would be a disaster.

It would start to feel as though Harry had never existed and, for some reason, that upset Ruby more than anything.

A rap on the front door shocked Ruby out of her wildly spiralling thoughts.

It was Dot, peering with concern through the glass. Goodness knew how long she had been standing there. Wearily, Ruby stuffed the letter under a pile of correspondence in the bottom drawer of the reception desk and went to open the door.

'I'm so sorry to frighten you,' said Dot, face screwed up in concern. 'Only, I were on my way back from running an errand and I just wanted to check that you're quite all right.'

'I'm fine, thank you,' said Ruby, tucking a couple of loose strands from her plait behind her ears. 'Just checking in on Chien and seeing to one or two things here and then I'll be off to work.'

'All fine with Chien?'

'Yes. He seems to be getting better.'

'Well, maybe a quick cuppa before work?' suggested Dot, gesticulating upstairs. 'Just to give yourself a chance to calm down.'

'I *am* calm,' said Ruby.

Dot smiled. 'Apart from being in floods of tears,' she said gently.

Ruby put her hands to her cheeks and was surprised to find that they were wet. Oh, goodness; she *was* crying . . . and somehow that made her cry even more. If only Jack was here – he somehow always knew how to make her feel better. She would make a point of seeking him out at the factory later on and make sure that they scheduled their walks in for the rest of the week. She missed him.

'I'm sorry,' she said, furiously wiping her eyes. 'It's Harry. I miss him so much – even though I didn't see him very often. He was just my brother. And sometimes I think I've forgotten what he looks like.'

Dot didn't hesitate. She stepped forward and wrapped Ruby into a tight hug. 'I know,' she murmured. 'Come along upstairs and have a cup of tea.'

'We'll be late for work.'

'No, we won't. We've got a while before we have to leave. And, tell me if I'm being insensitive, but I stumbled across an old class photograph with Harry in it in one of our albums the other day. Perhaps you'd like to take a look at it? To remind yourself of what he looked like.'

Ruby nodded, perking up.

What a wonderful coincidence.

Photographs of Harry were few and far between. The only photograph of Harry at home was the one on the mantelpiece and it would be simply wonderful to see another image of him.

She locked the front door to the hospital and followed Dot down the passage, past the storerooms and the consulting rooms, through another door and up the stairs. Chien's barking could be heard loud and clear from here and Ruby wondered how many other people might hear him. Oh, goodness, what if the Veterinary College came unannounced to inspect the premises? Chien would certainly be the nail in the coffin of the whole venture. She pushed the thought away as she followed Dot up the stairs and into the flat above – stretching over both the hospital and the bakery next door – where Dot and her family lived. Dot led Ruby into the parlour overlooking Sanctuary Lane and vaguely gesticulated at one of the worn brown sofas.

'Make yourself at home,' she said.

Ruby duly sat down, trying both to contain her ragged breathing and her wildly conflicting emotions. This really wasn't how she had thought her morning would begin.

At least she couldn't hear Chien from here.

Dot went over to the bookcase that lined the wall between the two windows and ran her finger along a series of thick, red-bound volumes. She slid one out and brought it over to Ruby, placing it carefully on the low table in front of the sofa. Flicking through the pages, she stopped at a photograph of a couple of dozen ten-year-old schoolchildren.

'There's Harry,' said Dot, without preamble, stabbing a finger at one end of the top row.

Ruby followed Dot's finger and – oh, goodness! – there he was. Curly hair, dancing eyes, merry lopsided grin. Despite the – presumedly – best efforts of Ma and his teachers that day, his hair was characteristically tousled and his striped tie was defiantly skew-whiff.

Now she remembered what he looked like.

Lovely Harry.

She was crying again, she realised, bubbling over with tears and Dot patted her kindly on the shoulder.

'Have a good blub,' she said, gently removing the album. 'But preferably not all over the photographs! Ma and Pa are both downstairs in the bakery, so you won't be disturbed. I'll pop the kettle on and make you a cuppa.'

She squeezed Ruby's shoulder gently and was gone. Ruby gave into her sobbing for a moment and then determinedly dried her eyes. She wouldn't have access to the photograph for long and she didn't want to waste another second. She picked up the album again and traced Harry's lovely face with her finger and then looked at the photograph as a whole. She recognised most of the children, of course, but because they had been a couple of years above her at school and because the photograph had been taken almost fifteen years ago, she found she couldn't put a name to many. But – yes! – on the bottom row, there was Dot, with her cloud of dark frizzy hair and her freckles, and her brow creased in characteristic concentration. There was Harry's best friend, Alfie, his sharp, pointed chin and challenging expression instantly recognisable over the years, even if his bright red hair and freckles couldn't be captured by the black-and-white photograph. And there was Tommy, Harry's other close friend, standing head and shoulders above the children on either side of him, his angular face stretched into his trademark toothy grin. What had happened to both of them, she wondered? Were they also at the front, caught up in the tentacles of this wretched war? Did they know that Harry had died? Or maybe – and it was, of course, a distinct possibility – one, or both, of them had already pre-deceased Harry.

It was a sobering thought and Ruby suddenly found that she was on the verge of tears again. With a touch of desperation, she turned the page. She didn't want to be greedy, but was there any chance there might be a second school photograph? Another Harry? Almost guiltily, she started flicking through the pictures. There were images of the Fisher family thronged outside an unfamiliar house, groups of solemn-looking older relatives, the staff of the bakery arranged in neat rows on the front steps – all neatly labelled in a meticulous script – sadly, there were no further images of Harry.

Never mind.

One had been more than enough; certainly, more than Ruby had ever thought she would see. Her parents had never been able to afford the annual class photographs and this was a treat, indeed.

She was just returning to the original photo to further feast her eyes when something caught her attention. A large family grouping in a wide-open square outside the sort of turreted castle that Ruby associated with the illustrated Hans Christian Andersen fairytales book they'd had at school. That was interesting enough, but what really piqued Ruby's curiosity was the caption underneath . . .

Fischer family holiday, Neuschwanstein, Bavaria, 1905.

Fischer.

Not Fisher.

Fischer.

Ruby swallowed hard and looked more carefully at the photograph. There was Dot at roughly the same age as in the school photograph and with the same scowling expression and there were her mother and father standing immediately behind her – younger, obviously, but still instantly recognisable. There were a further half a dozen people that Ruby didn't recognise, but the family resemblance in several of them was immediately striking.

Were Dot and her family *German*?

At the very least, they had taken a holiday to visit a family with very nearly the same surname in Germany a decade earlier, so it looked like they had, at the very least, a close connection.

Oh, Lordy.

Ruby knew – because Dot had told her – that Mrs Fisher's sister was married to a German man called Mr Muller. He and his son were currently interred in a camp on the Isle of Man – as were many German men of fighting age living in England. Their business, Muller's Haberdashery Shop, had been spared closure on the grounds that Mrs Muller, who ran it, was British, but that hadn't been enough to stop the shop being attacked by disgruntled locals – including Charlie – every time there was a Zeppelin attack or the war took a particularly nasty turn. Eventually, Mrs Muller had had enough and had retired to the West Country and the Fishers (or should Ruby now say the Fis*c*hers?) had offered the building to Ruby to house her animal hospital. The point was, of course, that if Dot and her family were also German, then, strictly speaking, Mr Fisher should be interred as well and the business should probably be closed . . .

It didn't bear thinking about.

Of course, based on what she knew to date, Ruby had no proof one way or another. Just a grainy photograph and an extra 'c' in a name. She glanced at the caption under the school photograph again and, yes, Dot's name was spelled in the anglicised manner without the 'c' there. The bakery, known throughout Silvertown, was spelled the same way. Everything seemed fine and above board . . .

And yet were the Fishers really all that they seemed?

Ruby could hear Dot pottering around making tea in the kitchen down the hallway and knew that she didn't have long. Without really thinking about what she was doing – and *certainly* without knowing what she was looking for – she was on her feet and padding as quietly as she could around the parlour. Furtively, she looked for anything that might solve the mystery one way or another. There were a dozen or so other photograph albums on the shelves. They would probably be a sensible place to start. If confronted, she could even pretend that she was looking for other photographs of Harry, but she really didn't have the time to start getting them all down and looking through them.

Instead, she turned her attention to the framed photographs on the mantelpiece. There was nothing of interest there – an innocuous and uncaptioned series of family portraits such as might grace any lower middle-class home. But behind them was a small silver trophy. Nothing fancy or elaborate, it was the sort of thing that might be distributed at a school prizegiving or for the best-behaved dog (*there* was an idea for the Christmas bazaar) at the annual Silvertown show. It was somewhat tarnished – the engraving faded and initially hard to decipher – but eventually Ruby deduced that it was a prize awarded for winning a wrestling match back in 1899. She couldn't work out *where* the award had been presented, but the name on the cup was clear.

Friedrich Fischer.

Dot's father's name was Fred . . .

But, was it enough?

Something propelled Ruby back to the bookshelves and, this time, her gaze fell almost immediately on an old, battered Bible on the middle shelf. It was sandwiched between some dull-looking books about wrestling that – together with the trophy – Ruby felt sure must be another clue. With a guilty glance over her shoulder, Ruby slipped the Bible clear of its neighbours and took it down. Then, with trembling fingers, she opened the front cover and . . .

Wow.

Written under the front matter, in a looped and spidery hand, were the words *Fischer Familienbibel,* followed by a long list of names and dates. Ruby's grasp of the German language was non-existent, but it didn't take a genius to deduce that this translated as 'The Fischer Family Bible'. Ruby ran her eye down the page. It was a little harder to work out what was going on here, but Ruby surmised that it was listing the births, deaths, baptisms, confirmations and marriages of each successive generation. The first dates were almost a century ago . . . but the most recent addition was one Dorothy Elizabeth Fischer. As if to confirm matters, a piece of paper fluttered from the Bible and down onto the floor. Hastily picking it up, Ruby found that it was none other than what appeared to be Dot's baptism certificate, issued in German.

'Here we are!' came Dot's cheerful voice.

Hastily, Ruby crammed the certificate back between the pages – any pages – of the Bible and shoved it back into position between the wrestling books. She had only just plonked herself back onto the sofa and picked up the photograph album when Dot re-entered the room carrying a tea tray. And then they were busy with the pouring and the adding of milk and sugar. Ruby tried very hard to chat to Dot and to seem normal and unconcerned, but inside she was reeling.

The Fishers were German.

Dot was German; she had been born there or, at the very least, she had been baptised there.

The whole damn family hadn't breathed a word.

Mrs Fisher had let her own sister – Mrs Muller – be fairly drummed out of Silvertown for having married a German. No wonder she had been so keen for all the fuss to die down because she had done exactly the same thing – and her own husband, far from being interred, was still holding down a business in the heart of the East End. In fact, maybe it was no wonder that Mrs Fisher had been so keen for Ruby's defiantly East End animal hospital to take over her sister's vacated premises and thus to generate goodwill for the Fisher family.

Ruby took a deep draught of scalding tea and looked at Dot through new eyes.

Dot was a lovely friend and a good person. She spent so much time helping those less fortunate than herself and, of course, she was now invaluable to Ruby at the hospital. She was fierce and loyal and funny.

But she was also German.

And the Germans had killed Harry.

Oh, what on earth should Ruby do?

She really didn't want to risk losing both her premises and Ma's job, but, surely, she should say something? At the very least, the hospital could become a target if word got out that the building was owned by Germans and she couldn't bear that. But, more fundamentally, she had to consider the seemingly hitherto preposterous thought that the Fishers might be up to no good. What about the time Dot had worked so slowly at the factory that she had been almost single-handedly responsible for the department missing its quotas that week? Given what Ruby knew now, could that possibly have been deliberate sabotage?

Oh, for heaven's sake, Ruby.

Sabotage, indeed!

'Goodness, you don't half look pale,' said Dot, cutting across Ruby's thoughts. 'I'm sorry if the photograph has made everything worse. I'd hoped it might help.'

Ruby gave her friend a wan smile. Now wasn't the time or place for confrontation; Ruby was too tired and too sad.

Given her newfound knowledge, could the Fishers have written to the RVC?

Could it somehow be in their interests to scupper the hospital?

'I'm alright,' she said. 'And it has helped. It were wonderful to see Harry's face again.'

That much, at least, was true.

'Maybe you should take the day off work,' Dot persisted.

'No need,' said Ruby, draining the last of her tea and standing up. 'Thanks for the brew but we really should get going.'

It was too much.

She would think about it all later.

11

Tuesday, 28 November 1916

At seven-thirty the next morning, Ruby and Jack were walking arm in arm along the river, Mac bounding at their feet. The sun had barely risen above the choppy-grey water – pretty soon it would be too dark to take these strolls before work – and it was *cold*. Jack Frost nipped the tip of Ruby's nose and her fingers, even in her gloves, were becoming slightly numb.

But Ruby barely noticed. She was deep inside her head, mulling over what she had discovered the day before. She knew she had to do something both about the letter from the Royal Veterinary College and, perhaps more pressingly, about what she had discovered about the Fishers. Again, the uncomfortable thought crossed her mind that maybe the two were linked.

'Are you alright, sweetheart?' asked Jack, giving her arm a little squeeze. 'You don't seem yourself today.'

Ruby hesitated. She wanted to tell him what she had found out – she wanted to share *everything* with Jack – but something held her back. She had a horrible feeling that he would take the RVC letter personally – after all, he was actively treating the animals and didn't have an official qualification – and the last thing she wanted to do was to undermine his confidence. And, as for the Fishers; well, once that genie was out of the bottle, it could never be put back in there again. Maybe it would be best to talk to Dot before she approached anyone else.

And so, she just smiled and said. 'I'm sorry. I'm just a bit tired today.'

Jack gave her a lopsided grin. 'I'm not surprised,' he said. 'I'll pop in and see Chien this morning if you'd like?'

'Would you?' said Ruby gratefully. 'Thanks ever so much. It will give me a chance to chivvy Charlie off to school.'

'Least I can do,' said Jack, stopping to pick up a stick that Mac had dropped at his feet and hurling it towards the trees. 'I should have suggested it before. Sooner he's sorted, the better – it has been on me mind. And the other thing I wanted to talk about was Christmas. I know it seems a long way off, but it's nearly December and I wondered if we should start making plans? We could spend it together – at least part of it – and . . .'

Ruby stopped walking and held up a hand. She was thrilled Jack wanted to spend Christmas with her and how wonderful it would be sitting together around the fire, roasting chestnuts and opening presents . . .

'Oh, Jack, I'd love to,' she said. 'But I just don't know if it's the right thing to do this year after Harry. He loved Christmas and . . .'

'Of course,' interrupted Jack quickly. 'You should spend it with your family. Sorry, I should have thought . . .'

'It's just me ma's in a bad way,' said Ruby. 'It feels like the rest of us is slowly getting over the initial shock but she's getting worse and worse. She don't reply when we speak to her and she goes to bed with 'a head' straight after supper most nights. It's nearly three weeks since Harry died and that telegram's still all we've got. I keep thinking that when his personal effects is returned or we get a letter from his commanding officer, she'll start to get better, but at the moment she's all at sixes and sevens. So, I can't possibly think about leaving her for Christmas – or even inviting anyone round.'

Ma was the very heart and soul of their little family – the one who kept the whole show on the road. She oiled the routines of their daily lives and was master of ceremonies at special occasions like Christmas. And she was the only one who had any chance of keeping the ever-elusive Charlie under control: Charlie who had barely been home before five o'clock in the afternoon since their chat about the bricks.

How would they all cope when Ma blatantly wasn't?

'Have you tried talking to her?' asked Jack.

Ruby made a little face at him. 'Of course,' she said. 'I've tried everything – even telling her that this ain't what Harry would have wanted. Nothing's worked. She's just letting things slide and Aunt Maggie ain't no use, either. She's always out and about on some excuse. Now I come to think about it, they ain't even finished the Christmas cake yet. The fruit's still sloshing about in the rum in the pantry.'

'I'm sorry,' said Jack. 'What else can I do to help?'

'What are you like on Christmas cakes?'

'Not really me department,' said Jack with a self-deprecating grin. 'But I will take over looking after Chien for the rest of the week and how about a trip to the flicks at the weekend? We could see *The Floorwalker*. Charlie Chaplin's bound to cheer you up.'

Lovely Jack.

Whatever would Ruby do without him?

Ruby arrived home feeling all the better for her conversation. She packed Charlie off to school and then had a quick peek in the pantry. Maybe she'd been maligning Ma and Aunt Maggie and the cake had been done and dusted whilst she'd been at work or at the clinic. She couldn't believe that they would just forget.

But, no. The cream bowl containing the fruit was still where they had left it all those weeks ago. How long ago it seemed that Ma and Aunt Maggie had been getting tipsy and giggling like a couple of schoolgirls together. It seemed like another world.

Still, maybe she had got it wrong. Maybe the cake *didn't* need to made for another week or so – and all was well in the world. She would make a point of asking Dot at work – and then she could move seamlessly on to . . . the other business.

If necessary – even though she didn't have a clue how to – Ruby would make the bleeding cake herself.

Ruby's day at work didn't start off well.

A girl she didn't recognise started kicking up a fuss in the shifting shed because she had mislaid an item of jewellery she had brought in by accident the day before. Firstly, she thought she'd left it in a coat pocket, next she assumed she'd left it at home and then the infuriating Miss practically barricaded the door and insisted everyone look through their possessions . . .

Ruby could barely conceal her impatience.

You were allowed to bring jewellery into work – just not onto the factory floor – and things were often going missing; there were several handwritten signs on the noticeboard in the shifting shed asking people to look out for this or that – and they usually turned up. Besides, if you were silly enough to leave anything expensive in the shifting shed . . .

All in all, by the time Ruby finally escaped, she was a good ten minutes late reporting on duty.

The morning didn't get any better. Ruby had several new recruits who were taking their time getting up to speed with assembling the detonators and who were putting that week's quotas of finished product in jeopardy. Today they seemed far more interested in discussing last night's Zeppelin raids over the Midlands and Tyneside than inserting springs or tightening screws. Although the Battle of the Somme was over, the demand for munitions didn't seem to have abated and there had been no relaxation of their demanding – and often seemingly impossible – targets.

Finally, *finally*, it was lunchtime.

Ruby emerged into the pungent winter air in relief, and as luck would have it, there was Dot, right in front of her and heading off towards the lavvies.

Ruby hurried to catch her up.

'Dot,' she called and her friend duly turned around, wreathed in smiles.

She didn't look like a German spy . . .

'Hello,' said Dot warmly. 'I were hoping to bump into you. I've got something for you in me bag.'

'Oh,' said Ruby, a little taken aback. 'What's that, then?'

'That school photograph with Harry in it,' said Dot. 'Me ma said she were happy for you to have it, but I didn't want to just drop it through your door after the note I sent you a few months ago went missing.'

And she didn't much sound like a German spy, either . . .

To be fair, Ruby wasn't sure what a German spy looked or sounded like but, either way, that really was an extraordinarily generous gesture.

'Thank you so much,' she said cautiously.

Dot shrugged. 'We're friends,' she said, simply. 'You'd do the same for me if the tables was turned.'

Ruby didn't answer.

She didn't know what to say.

Start with something easy.

'I just wanted to ask you something about Christmas cakes,' she said as the two approached the washrooms. 'Have you made yours yet? Or is the fruit still steeping?'

Dot laughed. 'Why are you asking *me* this?' she said. 'Your ma will know. Quite apart from anything else, she works at the bakery.'

'I know,' said Ruby. 'But she's acting really strange and . . .'

Dot was all solicitous concern. 'I'm sorry,' she said. 'I suppose it's to be expected given everything that's happened. And, to answer your question, ours were all baked a couple of weeks ago. Me ma has had me feeding about fifty of them with rum! It seems people are still going all out to celebrate Christmas, despite the circumstances.'

Ruby nodded. She vaguely remembered Cook regularly poking holes in the Christmas cake with a skewer and drizzling alcohol over it.

‘It ain’t too late to make the cake now though, is it?’ she persisted.

‘I shouldn’t think so,’ said Dot. ‘It might be a little dryer and less flavoursome than usual, but it will still taste good. Otherwise, I’m sure Ma could put one aside for you?’

‘No, no,’ said Ruby. ‘But thank you. The fruit’s steeped and ready to go and we’ve got the ingredients in the pantry . . .’

‘Can I ask *you* something now?’ interrupted Dot. And then, without waiting for a reply. “Have I done something to upset you? I’d got the impression you was trying to avoid me over the last day or so.’

Oh, goodness.

Ruby had planned to confront Dot, but now Dot had got in first and Ruby had rather had the wind taken out of her sails. There was nothing for it but to say her piece.

‘I know you’re German,’ she blurted out.

There!

She’d said it and she couldn’t take it back.

The world stopped whilst Dot registered the words. Dot, for her part, started as if she had been slapped. ‘I beg your pardon?’ she said stiffly.

But Ruby knew that she had heard every syllable.

‘Please don’t deny it,’ said Ruby, as Dot opened her mouth to speak again. ‘The German spelling of your surname were all over your parlour. The photographs, the silver cup, the family Bible.’

‘My,’ said Dot, with an ironic little smile. ‘You certainly had a good snoop around whilst I was making you a cup of tea. And here were I thinking you was grieving your brother and just wanted to see a photograph of him.’

Despite it all, Ruby could feel herself blushing. She squared up to Dot in the middle of the compound and tucked a stray lock of hair behind her ear. 'I weren't snooping,' she replied hotly. 'I just flicked through the album because I wanted to see if there were any more photographs of Harry and I saw the ones with the different spelling of your surname.'

'Well, there ain't no law against that, is there?' said Dot, equally hotly. There were people streaming around them on all sides, some turning to give them curious glances. 'People change how they spell their surnames all the time.'

'No, they don't,' said Ruby. 'And it ain't just that. You was baptised in Germany, for goodness' sake. It were written on your baptism certificate, clear as day.'

'My baptism certificate?' echoed Dot, her face screwed up in anger. 'And you say you wasn't snooping?'

'Alright, that one involved a bit of snooping,' conceded Ruby. 'But the point is that it's true, ain't it? You're all German.'

'My *family* came over from Germany a long time ago,' said Dot, hands on hips. 'I were born here. I do not consider myself to be German at all.'

'You was baptised in Germany!'

Dot sighed.

A long, drawn-out affair.

'I were,' she said. 'But only on a family holiday so me uncles and aunts and grandparents could be there. I'm as English as you are. Me parents moved over here a long time ago and became naturalised British subjects. Why are you being like this? We're friends, ain't we?'

Ruby hesitated. She knew she was coming across as unfeeling and unsympathetic and she was also acutely aware that she was also being hypocritical; after all, hadn't she been at pains to make clear to Charlie just three weeks previously that you couldn't blame all Germans for what had happened to Harry. But this felt different. As Dot had just pointed out, the two had been friends for several months and it suddenly seemed an awfully big secret to have kept all that time. And, of course, it wasn't the Fishers' fault that Harry had died – rationally, Ruby absolutely knew that to be true – but the Fishers had turned out to be German and the Germans had killed Harry and it was all just so confusing . . .

Oh, how it hurt.

But Ruby didn't know how to communicate any of that to Dot – not here, not now – so she just shook her head in frustration. 'I can't believe that you told me all about the Mullers and how dreadful it all was that they were German, but you didn't admit that your family are, to all intents and purposes, German too. I can't believe that you *lied* to me.'

'I didn't lie!' There was real anger punctuating Dot's words and she took a step closer to Ruby. 'And if I weren't totally transparent, it were because I were worried that you would react like this if you found out.'

'How can you blame me for that?' Ruby cried, reaching out and shoving Dot away. 'Me wonderful brother is dead before he had a chance to really live because of the Germans and I miss him so much. And yet you're all going about your day-to-day business as though nothing has happened. Shouldn't your father be interred on the Isle of

Man like your uncle and your cousin? Surely, I've got an obligation to tell someone . . .'

'Tell someone?' said Dot, her voice rising, and apparently oblivious to people standing and staring. '*Tell* someone? I understand about your brother, Ruby, but just listen to yourself. I'm working in a munitions factory, manufacturing shells designed specifically to *kill* the Hun. Ain't that enough? And, if you want more, me ma has given your ma a very good job in our bakery *and* we have rented you the premises for your animal hospital at far less than we could have got elsewhere. Just today, I've offered you a precious old photograph and I've offered to give you a Christmas cake. I've let you keep an animal that might have *rabies* in our stables, maybe putting us all at risk. And yet, apparently that ain't enough for you! You snoop through our belongings and now you talk about "telling someone" that we ain't British enough for you. I can hardly believe it.'

Ruby opened her mouth to reply – to say there were laws they all had to abide by – but, suddenly, the air raid alarm blasted out, making both women jump. All around them, people stopped whatever they were doing and started anxiously scanning the skies.

There hadn't been a Zeppelin raid over London for weeks but, much more to the point, attacks only ever happened at night, under cover of darkness.

'What's happening?' said Ruby, blinking around herself in surprise.

There was no answer.

Dot had gone; stalking off without a backwards glance.

*

Ruby stood stock-still for a moment, unsure what to do next.

Maybe the siren blaring was simply a mistake. She craned her head back and squinted up at the clear, blue sky.

Nothing.

Mistakes happened and they happened much more often during a war when there weren't the parts available to make repairs. One of the gas lamps in Aunt Maggie's room had been out of action for weeks and Robert was always moaning that he couldn't get various bits and bobs for his motor . . .

No need to panic.

A shrill whistle from behind made her jump again.

'Take cover everyone,' a woman shouted. 'Incoming attack . . .'

Ruby glanced up at the skies again.

Still nothing.

All around, people started muttering about heading for the foot tunnel but then the whistle blew again.

'Listen everyone,' the same woman shouted. 'This is an aeroplane – or several of them. They could be upon us very quickly so there's no time to leave the site. Stay calm and take cover in the cellars and bunkers as you've been instructed.'

Ruby's heart started thumping uncomfortably.

An aeroplane?

Dropping bombs?

No one had ever heard of such a thing.

Zeppelins were terrifying enough but at least they moved very slowly. Aeroplanes were fast and nippy and there was every chance they couldn't be shot down before they reached their target. A target that very well might include a government munitions facility . . .

Where was Jack?

Maybe he hadn't heard the siren?

Perhaps she should peel off to the main factory floor in search of him . . .

No, of course he would have heard it! Anyway, the police officers wouldn't let anyone get left behind . . .

Anxiously scanning the skies, Ruby set off at a clip towards the main building. All around her, people were streaming in the same direction. Police officers – Cook among them – were pointing the way to the nearest shelter.

'Hurry up,' said Cook, as Ruby panted by. 'Apparently the aeroplane's over the West End at the moment. It could be here in a jiffy if it puts its mind to it.'

Oh, goodness.

Ruby reached the wide steps leading to the basement and shuffled down them with everyone else. Everything was orderly and calm – no pushing or shoving; no shouts or screams. They had trained for this; they knew what to do and what was expected of them. She was swept deep into the dark, cavernous space. There were chairs and benches around the edge, but not nearly enough to go around and, anyway, those seemed to be reserved for older workers and those with disabilities. So, Ruby sat cross-legged on the floor as everyone around her was doing, trying to get comfortable on the hard, cold stone slabs. From her vantage point, she could watch workers continue to stream into the cellar and she was mightily relieved to spot Jack carefully making his way down the stairs to safety. The first time she had properly talked to him was under very similar circumstances, holding his hand whilst sheltering from Zeppelins in the foot tunnel under the Old Woolwich Road. Suddenly she wanted nothing more than to be sitting with him again; to feel his shoulder brush hers, his eyes caressing her, voice reassuring in her ears. If this was to be the end, she wanted him by her side. Maybe he could pick his way over to where she was sitting and squeeze in beside her. Maybe they might even get away with holding hands . . .

Ruby waved to Jack, trying to make eye contact. But he didn't see her. He had already turned away and was making his way over to the right to where Elspeth was sitting.

Ho hum.

Ruby had no idea how long she had been sitting there in the semi-darkness – letting waves of anxious conversation wash over her from all sides – before there was a resounding crash. There were a couple of ear-piercing screams and, before Ruby could react, a ripple of laughter spread throughout the cellar, growing louder and louder as it did so . . .

Thank goodness for that.

'What on earth was that?' came a woman's hushed tone from behind her.

'I think one of the benches tipped up,' came another female voice. 'What a crash, though – I thought it were the Hun bombing us all to kingdom come.'

'I think we all did,' came a third voice, a male one this time. 'Especially the screamers. Sounds like one of them were a chap, and all. Whatever happened to stiff upper lip in front of the ladies?'

'It were funny though,' came a female voice. 'Especially the way we all laughed when we realised the crash weren't nothing serious.'

'It were like being back in the school hall, weren't it? The way we all laughed if someone let off wind.'

'At least there ain't no one's backside going to be caned today.'

The little group behind Ruby burst into laughter and, just at that moment, one of the managers appeared at the top of the cellar stairs and blew a whistle.

'All clear,' she shouted. 'We're getting reports that the aeroplane has bombed the West End and headed back over the channel. Back on duty everyone.'

Feeling somewhat lightheaded, Ruby hauled herself to her feet and dusted herself down.

How awful.

If the Germans had switched to bombing raids in broad daylight, they would now all be on tenterhooks night *and* day. When would there be any let up from all this relentless misery?

Ruby followed the stream of workers up the cellar steps with something else gnawing at her.

The man who had screamed at the crash when the bench or the chair had toppled over . . . ?

That had been Jack.

Ruby was sure of it.

She had recognised the pitch and timbre of his voice. There was no doubt at all about it. And, even though logically Ruby knew that the laughter that had followed it had been pure relief that the place wasn't being bombed – and nothing directly to do with the screams at all – to Ruby's ears it had sounded very much like everyone was laughing at Jack.

Harry wouldn't have screamed like that.

The trouble was, far from feeling sorry for Jack and his demons, a single word had formed in Ruby's mind and was, even now, demanding to be set free. A word that she didn't want to associate with anyone, let alone with her sweetheart, whom she loved with all her heart.

And that word was 'coward'.

Ruby arrived home that evening tired, grumpy and hungry.

Her mood didn't improve when she discovered her mother sitting on the sofa, staring at the photograph of Harry on the mantelpiece, and with no evidence of supper having even been started. It was chilly too in the kitchen – horribly chilly – and with a shiver of misery as well as of hunger, Ruby realised that the kitchen range was out. Even with the recent coal shortages and hike in fuel costs, that rarely happened. On a cold winter's evening such as this one, the family *needed* the range for heating, for cooking and for hot water, and Ma and Aunt Maggie always made sure it was alright when Charlie got back from school and she returned from work.

It just went to show how bad things had become.

Even Mac and Tess – who were usually cuddled up together on the hearth rug – had obviously wandered off in search of warmth elsewhere in the house.

Not that they were likely to find any.

'What a day!' said Ruby, as she took off her hat. 'What's for supper?'

Maybe she had misread the situation.

Maybe Aunt Maggie or Charlie had already gone for takeaway fish and chips or maybe they were all invited round to Annie-Next-Doors for one of her famous hot-pots or maybe Ma had already planned for them all to go out for pie and mash and had deliberately let the range go off as a result in order to save on coal.

Something.

Anything.

But Ma just shook her head. 'I'm sorry, love,' she said. 'I left work early with one of me heads.'

Oh.

'I don't suppose that blasted plane earlier on helped?' said Ruby, trying to be sympathetic. 'Did you have time to shelter under the table?'

But Ma just looked blank. 'What plane?' she said.

Lordy.

The Germans had made their first daytime aeroplane raid on London. Hoping to hit the Admiralty, they had dropped six 22lb bombs between Victoria Station and the Brompton Road . . . and her mother had had no idea.

'Where's Aunt Maggie?' persisted Ruby.

'Popped round to Whitechapel again,' said Ma. 'More trouble at her place – a burst pipe this time – and the tenants have written threatening to withhold rent.'

Ruby pursed her lips. 'She were even closer to the plane then! But she'll be hard pushed finding a plumber these days,' she said. 'And where's Charlie?'

Ma shrugged. 'Not back from school yet,' she replied.

Ruby's anxiety was physical. She could feel a hard knot

of it underneath her breastbone. Charlie was *never* back from school on time nowadays.

He could be throwing anything.

Doing anything.

A shiver rippled through Ruby; a shiver that was only partly to do with the frigid air. This was no time to think about Charlie or to worry Ma further. She needed to get the range alight and some food on the table before they all either froze or starved to death.

'Don't worry, Ma,' she said, much more confidently than she felt. 'We'll get this room warm in a jiffy and then I'll pop out for fish and chips.'

Ma didn't answer. She just blew on her white, bony fingers and carried on staring at the photograph on the mantelpiece. With a sigh, Ruby crouched down and opened the little door at the bottom of the range. The ashes were stone cold. How long had Ma been sitting there in the cold? More to the point, how long would it be before the range was warm again? If only they had one of those portable oil-filled heaters that they had at the hospital here. Maybe she could nip down the road and borrow one? No, she really didn't want to see Dot – or her family, for that matter. Anyway, it would be far better to get the range alright so that she could make a brew for them both.

So, Ruby busied herself with clearing out the ash, getting coal in from the back yard and getting the fire lit.

'I discovered something strange at work today,' she said, as she worked. 'Or, rather, I already suspected something, but today I had it confirmed. May I tell you about it?'

'Fire away,' said Ma.

But she sounded as if her mind was far, far away.

Ruby started talking, telling Ma all about what she had discovered at the Fishers and how Dot had confirmed that her family were from Germany. She offloaded it partly because she really did want to know what Ma thought, but mainly because she hoped that it would get some reaction – *any* reaction – from her mother. It was this terrible apathy that was so difficult to bear.

Her mother listened, sinewy arms crossed around her body, eyes on the mantelpiece, not saying a thing. Even when Ruby had finished her tale with Dot marching away from her at the munitions factory, her mother didn't react. Despite everything, Ruby had half expected Ma to grab her coat and, without another word, to march down to the police station and report what Ruby had told her.

There were Germans living amongst them and the Germans had killed her son . . .

But there was nothing.

Ruby distracted herself by making a fuss of Mac and Tess, who had both sidled back into the room now that the range had caught and the room had started to warm up. Tess was waddling and looking positively porky and Ruby made a mental note to get her looked over at the hospital on Friday. So many cats presented with huge benign cysts in their sides and Ruby was pretty sure that it was one of those . . . but it really wouldn't hurt to get another opinion.

'What do you think?' asked Ruby, a little miffed when Ma *still* hadn't answered. Surely her news deserved more of a reaction than this. 'What should we do? Ain't it our duty to report the Fishers?'

Finally, Ma held up a hand. 'Quiet, child,' she said.

'Quiet?' Ruby was confused. 'I've just told you that the Fishers are *German*.'

Ma gave her a small smile. 'Everyone in the East End is from somewhere else if you go back far enough,' she said. 'Me ma – God bless her soul – used to say we was like the ingredients in a cake. All quite different from each other but mixed and baked to perfection.'

Ruby sat back on her heels. She had never heard that before.

'But . . .' she started.

'Have you ever stopped to think where your own grandparents were from?' interrupted Ma, looking more animated than Ruby had seen her in ages.

Ruby sighed.

She hadn't – not really – but what did that have to do with anything?

'Weren't they East End through and through?' she asked, wrinkling up her nose.

She knew about Pa's parents, who both had died when she was a little girl. Grandpa Joe had worked down the docks and Grandma Ruby – who Ruby was named after – had known everything about everyone in Silvertown, so she must have been local too. But Ma's parents had both died of diphtheria before Ruby was born and she didn't really know the first thing about them.

How strange that seemed.

If she ever had children, it was funny to think that *their* children might not know anything about her. She would just be forgotten, lost in the mists of time.

'Irish,' said Ma, bringing her back to the here and now. 'The lot of them were Irish.'

'Really?' said Ruby.

She had had no idea.

'Really,' said Ma. 'Me parents and your pa's parents were born here, but your great-grandparents came from Tipperary and Kerry way back in the middle of the last century.'

'I never knew,' said Ruby almost accusingly.

'No reason that you should,' countered Ma. 'It's all ancient history. But me point is that the Irish are waging a campaign for independence from Britain as we speak – we've both seen it all over the papers – and we ain't making that our business, are we?'

Ruby stopped and considered.

It was interesting, but it wasn't really the same.

'But this is *Germany*,' she burst out. 'And we're at war with Germany.'

Ma shrugged. 'It looks very much like we might soon be at war with Ireland as well,' she said. 'Do you think that means that we should be rounded up and interred?'

'No,' said Ruby. 'But this ain't Dot's grandparents or some long-lost ancestors we're talking about. It's her *parents*. She herself were christened in Germany.'

Ma held up a hand again. 'Don't you think we should judge people on what they do, rather than where they come from?' she said. 'The Fishers – with or without a "c" – have been very good to us. They've given us me job – which I don't want to lose, ta very much – your premises and more free bread than we can shake a stick at. She's letting you keep a sickly dog in her stables and you really don't want her talking about *that*. Probably best not to make a fuss.'

Ruby straightened up from the range with a little grunt. She didn't physically need to grunt, of course – she was a young, healthy woman, no problems with her joints or muscles – but she was so used to Ma and Aunt Maggie emitting a groan as they stood up that it almost seemed to be required.

'I've already made a fuss,' she admitted. 'I laid it on quite thick this lunchtime. It hit me hard coming so soon after the news about Harry.'

Ma smiled. 'Maybe a quiet word that you've had time to reconsider?' she suggested.

Ruby nodded, mutely.

Her mother was full of surprises.

That wasn't at all how Ruby had expected her to react but, on the other hand, it was good to hear her engaging and putting forward a point of view again, even if Ruby wasn't a hundred per cent sure that she agreed with her.

Either way, Ruby decided to press home her advantage.

'Aunt Maggie and Charlie are bound to be home soon and, when they are, I'll nip down the road to the chippie,' she said. 'But, in the meantime, how about finally making the Christmas cake?'

Ma gave a deep sigh. 'Not tonight,' she said as, right on cue, Charlie came in through the scullery door. 'My head is pounding something awful,' she added. 'Besides, what's the point? Your brother ain't here to eat it.'

'I'm Ruby's brother too and I'm here to eat it,' said Charlie, putting his arms around his mother from behind and kissing her sandy hair.

But Ma just sighed and didn't answer.

The moment was gone.

And Ruby didn't feel that she could ask her mother about the other matter that was pressing firmly on her mind.

Jack.

12

Thursday, 30 November 1916

Jack hadn't done anything wrong.

In fact, he had pretty much done everything *right*.

By all accounts he had served bravely on the Western Front and had even been mentioned in dispatches. It really wasn't his fault that he had been badly injured and had then been invalided back to Blighty and discharged, with honour, from the army.

Ruby *knew* all that.

She knew it.

And so why, then, was she comparing Jack with Harry and finding her sweetheart wanting? Why was she constantly testing her feelings towards Jack as one might prod an aching tooth. And why had the word 'coward' suddenly popped into her brain and seemingly taken up residence there?

Ruby didn't have the answer to any to those questions but, what she did know, was that she heartily disliked the version of herself that turned up for her early morning walk with Jack the next day. She hated the way that she answered all Jack's questions in clipped monosyllables, then found a way to steer the conversation round to them sheltering in the munitions factory basement the day before and finally made it perfectly clear that she knew it was he who had shouted out at the furniture falling over.

Why had she done that?

It wasn't clever and it certainly wasn't kind.

Jack, for his part, had gracefully admitted both that she was right and that he had been embarrassed and ashamed by his totally involuntary response . . . and *still* Ruby found that she couldn't be supportive.

Harry wouldn't have shouted out.

Ruby didn't say that, of course, but she had muttered something about it being 'only a chair' and then had started moaning on and on about the light but persistent rain, which was in danger of ruining her hat.

Eventually, even the usually placid Jack had had enough. If this really was such a hardship, he suggested that they abandon their walk and meet up the next day at the clinic, when hopefully she would be in a better frame of mind. In the meantime, he would nip home and grab a bit of extra kip before his later shift started, thank you very much.

And, thus, the two had parted on somewhat frosty terms and Ruby had walked to the factory to start her own earlier shift feeling angry with the world and totally at odds with herself.

She loved Jack – she knew she did – so why was she being such an old trout towards him? If she didn't buck her ideas up, it was surely only a matter of time before he told her to sling her hook.

Besides, what on earth was the point of constantly comparing Jack with Harry? Apart from anything else, Ruby still had no idea what had happened to Harry at the front, nor how he would have performed under pressure.

She was being totally ridiculous.

In a bid to feel a bit better about herself, Ruby made a point of tracking Dot down as soon as she arrived at the factory.

She found her friend in the shifting shed, pulling heavy-duty blue overalls over her everyday skirt and shirt. Ruby duly stammered out a heartfelt apology – explaining that she had spoken out of turn and that it had taken Ma to remind her that just about everyone in the East End came from somewhere else. Dot, looking a little surprised and discomfited that Ruby had confided in her mother, had simply said that she accepted Ruby's apology and she was glad that the two of them could still be friends. The two women decided that Dot's German heritage should go no further; not that it was a secret as such, but you never knew how people might react. And then – even better – Dot had offered to come round to Ruby's house after work that evening to help her make the Christmas cake. Ruby had accepted with alacrity and then, before she knew it, Leah and Elspeth had somehow been roped in too. Then, one of them suggested that they make it a full-on Christmas preparation evening – complete with a production line making cotton-wool snowflakes.

Ruby decided that it all sounded rather fun. Maybe she might even be able to persuade Ma to join in. She debated lying in wait for Jack outside the main detonation shed and apologising to him – maybe even inviting him along – but decided against it. He had already pointed out that making cakes was not his forte and, anyway, she would see him the next day at the clinic.

That was soon enough.

Ruby dashed home straight after her shift finished, wondering if Ma would mind three friends descending on the house later in the evening.

Ma barely reacted.

She had, she said, left work early that day and had picked up some chops and vegetables on the way home; if Ruby didn't mind giving her a hand getting tea on the table and washing up afterwards, Ma would make herself scarce and Ruby could have the kitchen to herself.

'And the cake, Ma?' clarified Ruby. 'We don't have to make the cake tonight. Only it's the first of December tomorrow and . . .'

Ma just shrugged. 'You make the cake, love, if it's so important to you,' she said. 'I'll take meself off upstairs after we've eaten.'

Ruby hesitated.

Why exactly *was* making the Christmas cake so important to her?

Would it really hurt them not to have a cake that year or even to buy one readymade from the bakery?

Ruby found that she didn't really have an answer.

Partly, of course, it was to do with symbolically carrying on in the face of adversity; their world might have been rocked, but they wouldn't let themselves go under because of it.

But there was more to it than that.

It was about remembering Harry by observing all the

little rituals and routines that had meant so much to him when he was alive. Ruby could clearly remember her brother stealing some of the steeping fruit from the pantry. She could remember Ma saying that he could have one spoonful of the raw cake mixture and Harry reappearing with a twinkle in his eye and brandishing a soup ladle. And, of course, she could remember him eating big slabs of cake on Christmas day and polishing off Ruby's unwanted marzipan to boot. Ruby didn't even like Christmas cake that much!

And, so, Ruby was determined to honour her brother by making the darned cake.

It was the very least she could do.

For once, both Aunt Maggie and Charlie were home by the time the food was ready, supper was eaten without fuss and everything had been cleared away before the first knock on the door.

Dot was first to arrive.

Ruby had wondered if there would be an element of awkwardness all round in the light of the new revelations but, to her relief, Dot didn't seem to be bearing any grudges.

'I've got something for you, Mrs A,' she said as soon as she was through the door. 'I'm not sure if Ruby's already mentioned it?'

Ruby shook her head – she hadn't wanted to get Ma's hopes up unnecessarily – so, with a little flourish, Dot produced the black-and-white school photograph.

'What's all this, then?' said Ma with a little frown on her face.

She scanned the photo and then, hand fluttering to her heart, she gave a sharp intake of breath. 'My boy,' she said simply. And then, clasping the photograph to her bosom, she kissed Dot on the cheek and disappeared upstairs without another word.

Ruby watched her mother go with a lump in the throat.

Ruby had wondered if Charlie and Aunt Maggie would also make their excuses and scarper now that tea was over, but not a bit of it. When Leah and Elspeth arrived together a couple of minutes later, both were still installed in the kitchen and looking very much like they were there for the duration.

'I've bought cotton wool and string from Woolies,' said Elspeth in a sing-song voice, gesticulating to the various bags strung about her person. I've got old wrapping paper in case we want to make paper chains and all. It won't take all of us to make the cake, so I thought I might concentrate on the decorations.'

'I'll give you a hand,' said Aunt Maggie. 'Why don't we sit on the sofa so we're out of the way of the cooks.'

And, before you could say Bob's your uncle, the two women were sitting side by side on the sofa, unpacking Elspeth's treasures, laughing together, thick as thieves. Tess was unimpressed by all the noise and activity. Getting up from her place in front of the fire, she stretched and stalked haughtily towards the kitchen door. Leah reached out a hand and stroked her flank and then turned to Ruby.

'Did you know she's got a lump on her side?' she said.

Ruby's heart leapt in her throat. 'Yes?' Maybe she shouldn't have been so quick to dismiss it.

Leah patted her arm. 'I wouldn't worry,' she said. 'I've seen dozens of lumps since I've been at the clinic and most turn out to be benign cysts; they come up quickly and then disappear a few weeks later. Has Tess been herself recently?'

Ruby cast her mind back. 'She's been a bit hangdog-y now I come to think of it,' she said, suddenly feeling guilty that she hadn't followed through on it. 'She's been off her food and she gets grumpy more easily. Like now – she wouldn't normally stalk off just because there are people here.'

'I'd just keep an eye on her,' said Leah. 'If she's not herself in a week or so, maybe get Jack or Robert to look at her.'

Ruby's heart thumped uncomfortably again – this time at the mention of Jack and, again, the word 'coward' leapt unbidden into her mind.

Goodness.

She had to stop this!

She busied herself going to and from the pantry, fetching all the ingredients that she needed and trying to banish thoughts of both Tess and Jack from her mind. No sooner had she put the various tins and packets down on the table, than Charlie's hand reached out for a piece of angelica.

'Oi,' said Ruby, reaching out to slap his hand. 'Either make yourself useful or get out of here.'

'I rather think we should make him help us with the cake,' said Leah, with a grin. 'After all, it's 1916 and if women can make munitions, then men can jolly well help with the cooking once in a while.'

'Hear, hear,' said Dot. 'I'm happy to supervise.'

'Challenge accepted, 'said Charlie, with a sideways grin at Leah. 'At least you recognise that I *am* a man now, unlike some people around here,' he added, narrowing his eyes at Ruby.

Ruby looked back at him in surprise.

Was he *flirting* with Leah?

Goodness; it seemed only yesterday that he was wearing short trousers!

Leah, for her part, was taking it in her stride and obviously enjoying it enormously.

'You're a handsome lad, Charlie Archer, and no mistaking,' she said, with the ghost of a wink. 'You're going to have all the lasses after you before you know it. But your fingers are absolutely *filthy*. You look like you've been gardening with your bare hands all afternoon. For heaven's sake, go and give them a wash before you touch the food.'

Charlie had the grace to look a little sheepish as he dutifully trotted off into the scullery.

Ruby watched him go, thoughtfully. She never had worked out what Charlie had been doing after school until after five these past few weeks, and now she remembered that Nellie had told her that he and his friend Joe had been looking after stray cats a few months ago. Maybe he still was and, if so, she could stop worrying.

'You still looking after those cats?' she asked pleasantly, as Charlie came back into the kitchen.

Charlie responded with a grunt, which sounded very much like an affirmative mixed with a 'mind-your-own-business' and Ruby knew she would have to be satisfied with that.

She busied herself getting scales, sieve, baking tin

and all the other paraphernalia out of drawers and cupboards and then watched with amusement as Charlie attempted to cream the butter and sugar together with a wooden spoon. Both his enthusiasm and energy were commendable, but his technique was somewhat lacking and Ruby smothered a smile as the ingredients stubbornly refused to combine and sugar began to splatter the table.

Then Leah offered to have a go.

To be fair, her efforts weren't much better and Ruby had to remind herself that Leah probably had a whole fleet of servants back at home in St John's Wood and that even her shared accommodation in Silvertown came fully equipped with a landlady who took care of tedious things like cooking. In the end, Dot showed them both how it was done and the mixture duly complied and turned appropriately light and fluffy. It was back to square one, however, with cracking the eggs – and Ruby wasn't sure whether it was her brother or Leah who was making more of a hash of it. Either way, there was a good deal of hilarity involved in extracting small pieces of shell from their feeble attempts before Dot pronounced them fit to add to the mixture – and then casually cracked the final egg with one hand to really put them both in their place.

Then it was all hands on deck to fold in the flour and spices, to add the soaked fruit and to dollop in a couple of spoonfuls of Ma's secret ingredient – marmalade. They poured the mixture into the cake tin – which Ruby had already greased and lined with parchment paper – and popped the whole thing in the oven.

'Hurrah,' said Leah, sitting back in her chair in satisfaction and clapping her hands together. 'What a team! Charlie, I think you and I should open a bakery together.'

'Talent like ours shouldn't really go to waste,' Charlie shot back. 'Sorry, Dot, but it looks like Fishers might have competition.'

'We're quaking in our boots,' said Dot with a good-hearted grin.

Everyone roared loudly together and, even though it was barely three weeks since Harry had died, somehow it didn't seem at all inappropriate.

In fact, Ruby felt that Harry would have approved.

'You're looking rather lovely tonight, Maggie,' said Elspeth apropos of nothing as the laughter subsided.

'She is,' agreed Dot. 'I were just thinking the same meself.'

Ruby glanced with surprise at her friends and then turned her attention to Aunt Maggie, sitting on the sofa with a pile of cotton wool on her lap. Ruby wasn't really in the habit of noticing changes in her aunt's appearance – Aunt Maggie just 'was', like the range or the kitchen table or the aspidistra in the corner of the room – but, yes, there did seem to be something different about her that evening. It wasn't just that Aunt Maggie had given herself a bit of a waist, nor that her hair was nicely set – it was the sparkle in her eye and the flush to her cheeks and the smile playing at the corner of her usually pinched mouth . . .

How hadn't Ruby noticed before?

'I reckon Aunt Maggie has got herself a gentleman admirer,' said Leah, her eyes merry behind her spectacles.

Ruby expected her aunt to immediately shut down that line of questioning with an airy wave or a 'stuff and nonsense' or even by tartly telling them all to mind their own business.

What she didn't expect was for Aunt Maggie to go bright pink and to concentrate very hard on pulling the cotton through the next cotton-wool ball on her lap.

'Oooh, she has,' said Leah, triumphantly. 'Good for you, Aunt Maggie. Do tell all.'

Aunt Maggie didn't need much encouraging.

It turned out there was a very nice widower called Ernest who had recently moved into the house next door to the one that she owned in Whitechapel. Ernest had been very amenable in helping Aunt Maggie track down glaziers, plumbers and, well, one thing had led to another. They had enjoyed the odd coffee together and that had progressed to long walks, the cinema and dinner . . . but she hadn't liked to say anything, especially after Harry had died. She had just made sure that she was out of the house so as not to intrude on the family's grief.

Ruby reached out and patted her aunt on the knee.

'You *are* family,' she said. 'We want you here and please never ever feel that you're intruding.'

Aunt Maggie gave her a warm smile and Ruby felt something in her heart stir.

Life was going on and good – if surprising – things were still happening in amongst all the misery and gloom.

Ruby thought that Harry might rather have approved of that as well.

13

Friday, 1 December 1916

Ruby made a point of talking to Jack as soon as she arrived at the hospital for their regular Friday shift the next morning.

She found him in his consultation room, in the process of taking the stethoscope from its hook on the wall and putting it around his neck. He turned and looked at her calmly – his face expressionless – as she entered, and Ruby's heart began to pound. He really did look very handsome, but also very stern, and by contrast she felt a little like a naughty schoolgirl about to be given a dressing-down.

'I'm sorry I were so grumpy yesterday,' she said. 'I really don't know what got into me.'

Jack's face relaxed an iota, but, still, he didn't smile. 'Apology accepted,' he said. 'I do understand your brother has died and it's a very difficult time for you all . . . only there seems to be something more to it than that . . .'

Elspeth popped her head round the door. 'Mrs Henderson's here,' she hissed, cutting off Jack in full flow.

'Oh, goodness.' Ruby couldn't help but be relieved that their conversation had been interrupted. She smoothed down her skirts, smiled an apology to Jack and hurried down the passage to reception.

In their exchange of letters, Ruby had asked Mrs

Henderson to report for duty at eight-thirty, fully expecting her old employer to casually swan in at closer to ten, swathed in silks and satins, wearing totally impractical shoes and with Boniface yapping at her heels. She would, Ruby had anticipated, either have got lost in the East End – her chauffeur totally unfamiliar with navigating the tangle of roads around the docks – have stopped off to see someone or do something far more important en route, or have simply assumed that the eight-thirty start was merely a suggestion, which applied to everyone else but not to someone as important as herself. However, to give Mrs Henderson her due, she had arrived at precisely three past the half hour and, as there was no sign of a motor – let alone a chauffeur – outside, it looked very much as if she had got the train.

Wonders would never cease!

Better still, from what Ruby could see, Mrs Henderson was dressed sensibly in an outfit not entirely dissimilar to the 'uniform' worn by Ruby, Leah and the others - a skirt that fell to just above the ankle and stout leather boots. There was also no sign of Boniface: Ruby would dearly have loved to see the little terrier again, but it was certainly one less thing to worry about. Now she just had to worry about someone stumbling across the letter from the RVC in the bottom drawer – maybe she should take it home – and Chien secreted in the old stable . . .

'Good morning, dear,' said Mrs Henderson, shaking out her wet brolly and showering Ruby from head to foot. 'Devil of a place to find and it's raining cats and dogs out there. But look at this dear little hospital. I'm not sure what I was expecting, but this is really most impressive.'

She slipped off her fine woollen coat and handed it peremptorily to Ruby. Startled, Ruby meekly took it from her and was just about to hang it up in the cupboard under the stairs when Leah suddenly appeared and swept it from her hands.

'I'll hang that up for you, Ruby,' she said in her most la-di-da voice and with a little sideways 'look' at Mrs Henderson. Ruby felt a rush of gratitude at the intervention.

Mrs Henderson started in surprise. 'You're Bernard and Cissy's daughter, aren't you?' she said, peering shrewdly at Leah.

'I am,' replied Leah, matter of factly.

'Your father is a client of my husband's,' Mrs Henderson continued.

'Very possibly,' said Leah, briskly – although even Ruby knew full well that he was.

'I *thought* I recognised you,' said Mrs Henderson, triumphantly. 'Why don't we have a nice cuppa and then you can tell me all about your little set-up.'

Leah shot Ruby an I-can't-believe-what-she's-saying-either look.

'I'll hang up your coat and let Miss Archer here brief you on her set-up and on what needs to be done today,' said Leah firmly.

And off she went.

Ruby smiled at Mrs Henderson, noticing that her shirt was white as opposed to the darker, more forgiving, colours preferred by the regulars. If Mrs Henderson wasn't careful, it would be stained with blood, mud and worse within a couple of minutes. Still, what was the point in saying anything?

'Let me show you around,' said Ruby politely. 'This is reception where the owners wait with their animals. If the queue isn't too long, we triage them here and make an assessment on which need to see a vet and which we can deal with ourselves. If the queue is very long, we might go outside and work down the line there instead.'

'Even on a cold, wet December day like today?' said Mrs Henderson with a little shudder.

'*Especially* on a cold, wet December day like today,' said Ruby with a smile. 'No point in folks waiting for hours in the rain if all they need is a quick pill or potion or a word of advice.'

Without waiting for a response, Ruby swept Mrs Henderson down the back passage to show her the consultation rooms. Mrs Henderson, it had to be said, appeared supremely disinterested in Jack but she perked up enormously when she saw Robert.

'How marvellous,' she said, rubbing her hands together. 'I must admit I'm very pleasantly surprised to see a *proper* vet volunteering here.'

'I'm honoured to do what I can to assist, Fanny,' replied Robert, pleasantly. 'It's a very important cause.'

'And you're a man as good as your word,' said Mrs Henderson. 'When you offered your services to Ruby at Clara Williams' concert, I thought you might just be trying to show your old man up. But here you are, rolling up your sleeves and getting stuck in.'

'It's almost time to open up,' said Ruby. 'Perhaps you would like to sit behind the desk, Mrs Henderson. We'll get you a cup of tea and you can watch what's going on.'

'Oh, no, dear. I'm here to help.'

'Of course. Well, what about hanging up some paper-chains or cotton-wool snowflakes? We had great fun making them yesterday and, despite the war, we plan to make a big splash with our decorations this year to cheer everyone up.'

'So brave after all you've been through, dear,' murmured Mrs Henderson. 'But I must insist on being hands-on with the animals.'

'Your lovely white shirt, though . . .'

'I have plenty more.'

Ruby sighed. Outgunned and outmanoeuvred, she had no choice but to back down gracefully. It didn't matter. Really, the only thing she had to make sure of was that Mrs Henderson didn't find out about Chien. They had just about reached the ten days and it was only just occurring to Ruby that there was a real danger Mrs Henderson might find out what they had done and feel it her duty to report them to the authorities. Particularly, were she also to find out about the letter . . .

Where would *that* leave them?

'Fair enough,' she said. 'How about booking people in as they arrive? Once they're settled in reception, we go around and fill in a form about them and their animal. Would that be something you'd like to do?'

Or wouldn't Mrs Henderson be satisfied until she had carried out a full-scale lobotomy single-handedly?

'That's more like it,' said Mrs Henderson with a nod. 'Although wouldn't it be easier to just circulate clipboards and pens and get them to do it themselves?'

Oh, dear.

'Many of these people can't read or write,' Ruby

reminded her gently, and Mrs Henderson had the grace to look a little shamefaced.

The shift started and reception soon filled up.

Leah and Ruby started doing the rounds, with Mrs Henderson shadowing them. After she had watched once or twice, Ruby allowed her old employer to take the lead on the next one and she had to agree that – although her demeanour ricocheted between patronising and bombastic – Mrs Henderson was competence personified. After a while, Ruby left her to it and she and Leah walked down the raggedy queue outside to see what sorts of animals and ailments they were going to have to deal with that day. It was a good ten minutes before they'd finished and Ruby's heart ratcheted up a gear as she approached the hospital and heard Mrs Henderson's strident voice booming away through the closed glass door.

In trepidation, she pushed the door open.

Yes, Mrs Henderson seemed to be admonishing an owner sitting in one of the corner seats.

'No, you cannot bring that dog in here,' she was saying, emphatically. 'Look at him, covered in all sorts! This is a hospital and hygiene is imperative, don't you know?'

Ruby rushed over and took in the little scene.

A young girl, dressed in nothing more than dirty rags, was visibly cowering under Mrs Henderson's verbal onslaught, eyes wide with mortification. Her dog, a large, smelly mongrel, was busy licking his nether regions. He was, it had to be said, absolutely filthy – covered from head to foot in the mixture of animal manure and urine that the locals politely referred to as 'mud' and which lay inches deep in some of the poorest areas of Silvertown.

The recent rain had made it all ten times as bad and the dog had obviously seen fit to lie down and have a good roll around in it.

Mrs Henderson no doubt had a point – but that wasn't how things worked at the Sanctuary Lane Animal Hospital.

'Mrs Henderson,' said Ruby, firmly. 'Everyone – and I mean *everyone* – is welcome at this hospital.'

'But look at the state of him,' countered Mrs Henderson, wrinkling her nose up in disgust. 'Covered from head to toe with goodness knows what. We can't allow him to stay in here.'

'We can,' said Ruby. 'And, in fact, I insist that he does. It's wet and muddy out there and it's no one's fault that he's dirty. What's his name?' she added kindly to the young girl.

'Beau,' said the girl, without a shred of irony.

Ruby smiled and turned back to Mrs Henderson. 'Why don't you continue doing the rounds and I'll finish off getting Beau booked in.'

Mrs Henderson gave Ruby a hard stare and, for a moment, Ruby thought her old mistress was going to refuse to comply. Oh, Lordy; what on earth would she do then? But, to Ruby's relief, Mrs Henderson made a harrumphing sound and moved away. Ruby exhaled gently and carried on taking down the details of Beau's digestive problems, all the time keeping half an eye on Mrs Henderson's progress.

And, a couple of minutes later, it was clear that Mrs Henderson had hit problems again.

Ruby subtly repositioned herself so that she could see and hear what was going on.

'Tell me again what's wrong with your dog,' Mrs Henderson was asking in a confused tone.

'Reggub's plates of meat are off,' a male voice replied solemnly.

Oh, goodness.

Mrs Henderson would have no idea what that meant.

'Yes, that's what I thought you said,' said Mrs Henderson, sounding totally perplexed. 'But I have no idea what you *mean*. I'm assuming Reggub is your dog's name? And the meat you're feeding him has gone bad, is that what you're trying to tell me? Has your dog got food-poisoning?'

Ruby smothered a giggle.

She and everyone else in the room, with the possible exception of Leah, would understand exactly what the man was saying. He was telling Mrs Henderson – in a mixture of costermonger back-talk and cockney rhyming slang – that there was a problem with his dog's paws. Reggub was simply 'bugger' backwards and 'plates of meat' was Cockney-speak for 'feet'.

Ruby debated whether to step in.

She really didn't want to intervene again so soon but then again . . .

Then she looked up and clearly saw the man give the ghost of a wink to the owners sitting around him.

'I suppose he's having no end of trouble with the apple and pears?' the man on his far side interjected affably.

'To say nothing of the frog and toad.' To Ruby's surprise, the third voice belonged to Billy – handsome Billy! – standing in the middle of reception, hands deep in his pockets. He was clearly there to pick up Chien and Ruby instinctively positioned herself between him and Mrs Henderson. It was of the utmost importance that Mrs Henderson remained in the dark about the quarantine.

Meanwhile, she realised that the original fellow had been trying to bamboozle Mrs Henderson on purpose. He had been deliberately attempting to exclude her – presumably as punishment for having insulted one of their own.

And now everyone else was joining in!

'Apples and pears' meant 'stairs' and 'frog and toad' was 'road' and it really was all very funny . . .

'Apples and pears,' echoed Mrs Henderson, in vexed tones. 'You really shouldn't be feeding fruit to a dog.'

'Indeed, you should not,' said someone else, with a guffaw. 'Frogs and toads ain't too tasty either and gives you no end of a rumble in the gut. But, don't worry, once the vet gives him a lump . . .'

Oh, goodness.

'Lump of ice' – shortened to 'lump' – meant 'advice', which made total sense if you were in the know but sounded like absolute rubbish if you weren't.

This was getting out of hand.

Ruby needed to say something.

Mrs Henderson might come across as an upper-crust, stuck-up old matron, but she was a good stick really and, of course, she had been very generous to the clinic . . .

Crash!

A loud smash of breaking glass made everyone jump. It sounded so close that Ruby was slightly surprised to see the hospital windows were still intact. Heart thumping, she ran outside with several others and . . .

Oh, goodness!

The bakery window next door had been smashed to smithereens, shards of glass scattered in a wide arc across the pavement and onto the road. On further inspection, it was obvious that this had been no accident; a large brick was lying almost obscenely across a tray of cream cakes on the front counter and a dark-clad figure, cap pulled low, was disappearing at a run around the corner and onto the High Street.

A couple of men – including handsome Billy – took off in hot pursuit and Ruby stared after them all in consternation. She had only caught a glimpse of the chap running away, but there was something horribly familiar about him and, indeed, about the whole situation.

Charlie!

She could hardly believe it.

As if they didn't all have more than enough to contend with after Harry's death and the blasted war and everything else.

And Ma worked in the bakery, for goodness' sake.

Ma.

Mrs Henderson, Aunt Maggie, Nellie and a couple of the other animal owners had come outside with her. There was no sign of Jack, she noticed – and she couldn't help rather uncharitably wondering if he had heard the crash and was cowering under his examination table. No, that was unfair – Robert hadn't come out either and there was a good chance that the two of them hadn't even heard the commotion from their examination rooms at the back of the hospital. She must stop being so uncharitable towards Jack.

With a sigh, she turned back to the matter in hand. 'You get back inside,' she said to the little group who had left the hospital with her. 'Maybe move people and animals away from the windows, although it rather looks like the danger has passed.'

Or, rather, the danger had run away.

Swallowing a sudden surge of rage, Ruby crunched over the broken glass and into the bakery, both to check on Ma and to see what she could do to help. Mrs Fisher was standing in the middle of the shop. Surveying the little scene with her hands on her hips, she looked more angry than frightened.

'All ruined,' she said to Ruby, gesticulating to the display of cakes and breads in the front window. 'Even if we remove the obvious glass, we can't risk selling any of this on. What a darned waste, especially with all the shortages and the price of flour so high. Who would do something like this? And why?'

Ruby thought she had a very good idea on both counts.

'More importantly, is everyone alright?' she asked. 'No one's been injured?'

'Fortunately, not,' said Mrs Fisher. 'Although that were more by luck than by design. Someone could easily have been hit in the eye by a piece of glass . . .' She broke off as Dot, who had been helping Jack in his consultation room, came rushing to her side. 'It's alright, darling,' she added, seeing her daughter's stricken face. 'We've come through worse.'

'Where's Ma?' asked Ruby. 'Is she alright?'

'Luckily your mother left an hour ago,' said Mrs Fisher, putting an arm around Dot's shoulder. 'She were awfully pale and said she had a terrible headache, so I sent her home. I'm glad she missed this after all she's been through.'

Ruby nodded. 'Poor Ma,' she said. 'Now what can we do to help? I could send some people around to sweep up the glass . . .'

'Nothing,' said Mrs Fisher briskly. 'You've got your own business to run. Mr Fisher has gone to fetch the glazier – although last I heard he was off to France – the girls will clear the display and some of the customers have kindly said that they will help sweep up. You get back to your animals.'

'If you're sure.' Ruby sighed. 'I've got me old employer volunteering today and she's proving a bit of a liability, so I probably should get back . . .'

Despite the circumstances, Mrs Fisher laughed and patted Ruby on the shoulder and Ruby felt immediately conflicted. 'It sounds like you've got it almost as bad as me,' she said.

Ruby and the others drifted back into the hospital. Robert and Jack had appeared but, when it was clear there was no further danger and nothing they could do to help, they headed back to their consultation rooms. Handsome Billy, who had given chase, arrived back shortly afterwards.

'Couldn't catch the fella,' he grunted. 'Reggub ran into one of the closes and disappeared. Probably lives in the tenements and knows the closes much better than me.'

Ruby wasn't sure whether to be relieved or disappointed.

'It's a pity Bruce's paws are crook or he'd have bought the reggub down,' said the man who had given Mrs Henderson a hard time. 'But why attack the bakery?'

'Makes no sense,' said Billy. 'Must admit I had some

sympathy when they used to go for this place, it being owned by Germans and all.'

'Yes. The Huns is fair game. But the Fishers is one of us.'

Ruby exhaled a ragged breath.

It really wouldn't do for it to get out that the Fishers were, in fact, German – not least because it was common knowledge that they owned the whole building. And if it came out that Ruby knew full well that the Fishers *were* German and had happily based her hospital in their premises nonetheless . . . how long before the animal hospital was next?

Ruby pushed that thought to one side and turned to Billy. 'Thank you for giving chase,' she said.

Billy grinned. 'To be honest, I'm a bit browned off I didn't catch the chap,' he said. 'I obviously ain't as fit as I thought I was.'

'You ain't gone back to the front either,' said Ruby. It was none of her business – she knew it wasn't . . .

'No.' Billy shook his head. 'Nowhere to go back to now the Somme is over, although I'll be back training soon enough.'

Ruby swallowed hard. The Battle for the Somme had finished so soon after Harry's death.

'That's marvellous news,' she said. 'Your family must be so relieved.'

'Too right,' said Billy. He paused a moment and then added, 'And me fiancé is pretty happy too.'

Ruby was surprised – and shocked – by her surge of disappointment. She was in love with Jack – she shouldn't care less whether Billy had a sweetheart or not.

But she just nodded and said, 'I'm delighted Chien is well. Mum's the word where Mrs Henderson is concerned, if you please. Let me take you out the back and show you where he is. The vet thinks he just had a nasty bug, which were making him grumpy, but you might think about a little training so he ain't a danger to other animals.'

Billy nodded. 'I think it were his illness making him so bad-tempered, but I take your point. And thank you to you and to the vet for doing this for me.' He hesitated and then added, 'If I were to know of any other dogs being smuggled back from France, might I point them in your direction?'

Ruby opened the door to the stable that Chien was being held in and unlocked his cage. It was hardly going to help their case with the RCVS if she said yes, and she should really bounce it off the others first. But then again . . .

She turned to Billy. 'Yes, I think you might,' she said, stepping back as owner and dog had a rapturous reunion. 'Goodbye Private Reid. It were very nice to meet you.'

Ruby walked back inside feeling thoughtful.

What a morning!

She wondered if it would all have proved too much for Mrs Henderson. As if being excluded and ridiculed by the animal owners wasn't enough, the shop next door had just been attacked in broad daylight. Ruby wouldn't have been at all surprised if her erstwhile employer had already departed for Hampstead in a state of high dudgeon.

But not a bit of it.

In fact, it seemed that Mrs Henderson's attitude had totally changed in the interim.

She insisted on persevering with booking in animals and owners but, instead of throwing her weight around in a highhanded manner, she was now much more measured and respectful. The woman was no fool; she understood precisely what had taken place before, she had taken measures to change her own behaviour and Ruby could only stand back in admiration. And, of course, the attitude of the owners changed towards *her*. There was still a good deal of cockney slang – of course there was – but this time it was not intended to ridicule and exclude. And, this time, Mrs Henderson simply asked the owner to explain what 'barnet' or 'hammers' or 'jam jars' meant and wrote it down without comment.

What was even more lovely – and, frankly, amazing – was the way Mrs Henderson openly deferred to Ruby on a couple of occasions. Did the little mongrel who was a bit off-colour need to be seen by Robert or Jack or could it just be sent on its way with a tonic? What was the best way to handle a dog who was being bad-tempered and aggressive?

Who would ever have believed *that* might happen back in March when Ruby had still been in service?

'It's been lovely to have you here,' said Ruby, quite sincerely, towards the middle of the afternoon. 'You'll be wanting to get off before it gets dark, I expect.'

'On the contrary,' said Mrs Henderson. 'I have kept the evening free of engagements for once and I fully intend both to stay until the end of the shift *and* to help with the clearing up if you think that I might be useful? Although I would be grateful if one of the young men would be kind enough to walk me to the railway station afterwards.'

'Of course,' said Ruby. 'I'm sure either Jack or Robert would be happy to do so. In fact, Robert's got his motor out the back so he might well be able to give you a lift in that.'

She smiled to think of the alternative – Mrs Henderson perched at the front of Mayfair's scruffy old cart next to Jack – although, given how strange the day had been, she wouldn't put anything beyond the realms of possibility.

'Ah, Jack,' said Mrs Henderson, archly. 'I gather you're stepping out with him.'

Ruby stiffened, first wondering if there was an edge to Mrs Henderson's voice and then double-guessing herself for wondering why on earth there should be.

'I am,' she said neutrally, not offering further elaboration.

Mrs Henderson smiled and clapped her hands together. 'I've been hearing all day what a wonderful young man he is,' she gushed, in apparent sincerity. 'Everyone seems to love him – the owners, the animals, the other staff. And, might I say,' she added, her hand fluttering to her pearl choker, 'he is extremely handsome, to boot. You make sure you hang onto him, *dear*. It sounds like you're onto a good thing.'

'Thank you.' Ruby smiled and returned to her duties.

Mrs Henderson was right.

Jack was wonderful.

She had to stop comparing him with Harry and Billy . . . and with every other solider.

She had behaved badly but she had apologised and, surely, they could get back onto an even keel. Maybe she would even confide in him about the letter . . .

But, at the end of the day, Jack left abruptly, even before Mrs Henderson and before the clearing up was properly finished. A family birthday celebration, he said. It really wouldn't do to be late. He smiled warmly at everyone and even kissed Ruby on the cheek, but still Ruby was left staring after him in confusion and consternation.

Why hadn't she known about the family celebration?

And, more to the point, why hadn't she been invited?

14

'I know it were you, Charlie.'

Finding her brother doing his homework in an otherwise empty kitchen early that evening, Ruby furiously flung her hat and bag onto the sofa next to Tess, who was dozing peacefully, and steeled herself to give Charlie a good piece of her mind.

Charlie looked up from his books, all brown-eyed innocence. 'What am I meant to have done this time?' he said, putting his pencil in his mouth and chewing on it insolently.

'It ain't funny, Charlie. You know exactly what you've done.'

'I have no idea what you're talking about,' Charlie mumbled around the pencil.

'Yes, you *do*,' hissed Ruby. 'Take that pencil about of your mouth and stop being so rude. You've been totally irresponsible and the worst thing is that, for all you knew, you could have hurt Ma. Shame on you, Charlie Archer. *Shame* on you.'

Charlie narrowed his eyes but at least he took the pencil out of his mouth. 'I would never, ever hurt Ma,' he said, coldly. 'Shame on *you* for even suggesting it.'

'A brick through the bakery window could have hurt *anyone*,' said Ruby. 'You can't predict where it will land or where the glass will shatter.'

'And why on earth would I put a brick through the bakery window?' asked Charlie, starting to twirl the pencil between his fingers.

Infuriated, Ruby snatched the pencil from his fingers, snapped it clean in two, and dropped the pieces back onto the table.

'Because somehow you must have overheard me telling Ma that the Fishers is German,' said Ruby. She had mulled it over at the hospital and the pieces had dropped into place whilst she was getting the registers up to date. 'You must have come in the back door without us hearing you and lollygagged in the scullery, eavesdropping on our conversation.'

'Poppycock,' said Charlie, dismissively.

Ruby ignored him. 'And here was you ribbing Dot yesterday, as friendly as can be,' she continued. 'Teasing her about opening a rival bakery whilst all the time planning to smash hers up. Look, I understand how much you hate the Hun, I really do. I hate them too. I can even understand you wanting to hurt the Fishers for what they represent. But you hadn't thought it through, had you? You never think *anything* through. Because you can't possibly have known that Ma had been sent home and that's what I can't forgive you for.'

'I wouldn't do that,' said Charlie, standing up and giving Ruby a shove.

'You *did* do that,' shouted Ruby, shoving him back even harder.

Tess jumped down from the sofa in consternation and cowered under it.

'What on earth is going on in here?'

It was Aunt Maggie coming in from the back door, laden down with plump parcels wrapped in newspaper. Ruby and Charlie sprang apart like guilty toddlers, but not before Charlie had given Ruby one last sly poke under her ribs – just as he used to do when he was a little boy.

'Ruby's accusing me of doing things I ain't done,' Charlie spat out.

'Oh, you've done them, alright,' Ruby shot back furiously.

Aunt Maggie slapped the packages down on the kitchen table. 'Hark at the pair of you,' she said. 'I don't care what either of you have or ain't done, but I do care that your mother is upstairs grieving and that you two are squabbling like a couple of jackdaws down here. Charlie, take your things to your room and Ruby, help me lay the table for supper.'

Charlie duly gathered up his books and papers and left the room, giving Ruby a little shove as he passed. Ruby stuck her tongue out at his departing back and, with a deep sigh, started laying out the plates and cutlery for supper. From the enticing smells they emitted, Ruby deduced the packages contained both fish and chips *and* pickled eggs and her stomach duly started growling. No wonder Tess was now prowling impatiently around.

'Everything alright?' Aunt Maggie asked more mildly, pouring boiling water into the teapot.

Ruby hesitated.

Despite Charlie's denials, she didn't have even a shadow of doubt that he was guilty and that there should be repercussions. But surely Aunt Maggie must realise – or at least suspect – it too and the fact that she wasn't saying anything made Ruby bite her tongue. Aunt Maggie and – especially – Ma had enough on their plates without this to deal with as well.

'Everything's fine,' she replied equally mildly. 'Just a little spat.'

Aunt Maggie nodded. 'It's hard for your brother,' she said, apropos of nothing. 'He's bound to lash out sometimes.'

Ruby didn't answer.

It's not all about Charlie.

It's hard for me as well!

'Just a lad with his only brother dead and him next in line to enlist,' Aunt Maggie continued. 'No wonder he's moody sometimes.'

Again, Ruby didn't say anything. Then she noticed there was a sheet of paper in Charlie's handwriting on the floor underneath the kitchen table. She picked it up and glanced at it disinterestedly. The same short line repeated over and over again on both sides of the paper in increasingly untidy writing . . .

I must not play truant from school.

Well, there it was in black and white.

Proof that Charlie had left the school premises to commit his dastardly deed and had, presumably, been caught on his return.

Ruby was tempted to throw the piece of paper into the fire and to make Charlie write the lines out all over again, but then she recalled that being set lines at school was often preceded by having one's hand caned to really drum the message home. Ruby had only received this punishment once – the time she had dallied on the way to school to help a cat with its back leg caught in wire – but she could still recall the vicious sting of the beating and the agony of writing shortly afterwards.

Despite everything, sympathy set in and, muttering an excuse about checking in on Ma, Ruby left the kitchen and set off upstairs to return the paper to Charlie. She knocked gently and opened the door at the grunt that followed. Her eyes went straight to his prized bricks from the Zeppelin strike on the chest of drawers.

One was missing.

Further proof of Charlie's guilt.

Ruby was a little surprised he had relinquished one of his precious souvenirs so readily.

'What do you want?' asked Charlie surlily.

'You left this downstairs,' she said, passing over the piece of paper.

Charlie grunted his thanks. His outstretched hand had livid purple weals across the palm.

There was no point in further discussion; Ruby had made her point and Charlie had denied it.

And there was no point in taking it to the police because Ruby really didn't want it getting out that the Fishers were German.

She gave Charlie the ghost of a smile and went to check in on Ma.

Ma was lying flat on her back with a flannel over her forehead and Mac was lying on the bed next to her. Mac was not officially allowed upstairs and Ma would never normally have countenanced such a thing.

Ruby sat down on the purple patterned eiderdown, took her mother's hand in one of her own and rested the other on the top of Mac's head.

'You still feeling rotten, Ma?' she asked, giving the cold clammy hand in hers a little squeeze.

A silly question.

Back in the day, it had been almost unheard of for her mother to take to her bed in the middle of the day. Ruby hadn't been living at home to know whether or not she had done the same after Pa had died, but she felt sure that Harry would have let her know had that been the case.

Ma duly nodded her head. 'It all just seems too much,' she said, her voice sounding as if it was coming from a long way away.

Ruby's heart plummeted. 'But you've still got us, Ma,' she cajoled. 'And your lovely job at the bakery. You love it there, don't you? Much nicer than working at the laundry.'

Ma sighed. 'I'm sorry, love, but I just ain't up to it at the moment,' she said. 'I'm going to tell Mrs Fisher tomorrow that I need some time off.'

'Are you sure, Ma?'

'I'm sure, sweetheart. I'm sorry . . .'

'Don't be sorry,' said Ruby. 'We all just want what's best for you. Maybe take a break from it all until the New Year and just concentrate on Christmas. You've always loved Christmas, haven't you? We'll decorate the house – I'll go up to Silvertown market this weekend and get some bits and pieces and we'll make the most of it – you'll see if we don't.'

But Ma just sighed again. She turned her head towards the window, but not before Ruby saw one fat tear roll down her cheek and soak into the pillow.

'What's the point of Christmas without me boy?' she said.

15

Saturday, 2 December 1916

The next morning, Ruby accompanied Ma to hand her notice in at the bakery.

Ruby had tried to dissuade her mother, but to no avail, and, in the event, it went surprisingly well. Mrs Fisher – to give her credit – was absolutely marvellous about it all. Of course, Ma could take some time away from the bakery. Everyone would understand. But, no, she wouldn't accept Ma's resignation; Ma was free to take off all the time she needed and her job would be waiting for her if, and when, she wanted to return.

Ruby had felt like hugging Mrs Fisher.

And then – to make things even better – Aunt Maggie had suggested she take Ma's place in the interim – except for her Fridays at the hospital. She had gone straight to the bakery to offer her services and Mrs Fisher had gladly accepted. Aunt Maggie started her first shift that very day.

Given the circumstances, it was all very satisfactory.

Less satisfactory was her afternoon date with Jack.

Not that anything went *wrong*, as such. The film was light-hearted and amusing – nothing to shout out about in *that* – and they had a good mooch around the market beforehand. Ruby duly picked up some colourful streamers to decorate the house – and they even had a perfectly pleasant meal in their favourite pie and mash shop afterwards. Jack was his usual funny, charming and kind self, the conversation didn't falter and he had explained that the family party was for his stepfather's brother and a terribly dull affair, so there was nothing at all to worry about there.

It was just . . .

It was just . . .

Oh, Ruby didn't really know *what* it was.

She just knew that on some level things didn't feel the same and that she was continually looking to find fault in Jack.

Like when they were standing in front of the toy stall at Silvertown market and Jack was wondering what to buy his stepbrother Archie for Christmas. That year, anything to do with the British Expeditionary Forces was immensely popular and so the stall was heaped high with toy soldiers, ships, tanks and guns. Jack was making a big fuss about how he didn't think they were suitable gifts for a child and that he would get Archie a toy train instead and, for some reason, that really narked Ruby. Who was he to dismiss the war and all its associated paraphernalia so casually – he might have got out but there were very many who hadn't? And then she berated herself for being so stupid; she was hardly planning to buy Charlie a toy gun – not that she was planning to buy him anything, the way things stood between them! – and Archie, for heaven's sake, was barely two.

Or when they were looking at some toiletries in the

chemist window and Ruby asked Jack what he was planning to buy his mother for Christmas. Jack had laughed and said it didn't matter what he bought – the only thing his mother wanted was his stepfather home on leave from Mesopotamia and she had just discovered that her wish was to be granted. And Ruby had had to bite her lip very hard not to cry because, of course, Harry would never be coming home on leave . . .

And then there were the soldiers marching by, or sitting in the cinema in their greatcoats, and hanging around on the street corners, all of them doing their duty for King and Country – and all Ruby could think was that Jack had had it easy.

Too easy.

She knew she was being silly and unfair and . . . wrong, but she couldn't help how she felt, could she?

And then, when Jack had come to kiss her goodnight, she had been hard-pressed not to turn her face away so that his lips landed on her cheek instead.

She *loved* him.

She knew she loved him.

So, what on earth was going on?

And then, to make matters worse, Jack pushed a note through her door on Sunday night telling her that he was poorly. It was nothing to worry about – just a bad cold that had gone to his chest – but he would keep his distance for fear of passing it on. He was unlikely to be at work for a few days and he would almost certainly miss the Tuesday evening clinic at the animal hospital.

And all that just made Ruby feel even worse.

*

Over the next day or two, Ruby made a point of going home at lunchtime to check on Ma.

Aunt Maggie tried to pop home when she could but, as lunchtime was one of the busiest times in the bakery café, it wasn't often practical.

Ruby didn't mind; it was the least she could do for Ma, even though it felt strange to be out of the factory during the working day and she constantly had to remind herself that she wasn't playing truant. Leaving the site wasn't forbidden, but very few people did so unless they happened to live very close by. By the time you had been searched on your way out and navigated security on the way back in, it was hardly worth it and the centre of town and Sanctuary Lane were both a good fifteen minutes' walk away. Still, it gave her a chance to try and get some lunch down her mother – although she couldn't really tell if Ma was actually pleased to see her – and she could also check on, and make a fuss of, the animals. Tess still looked very down in the dumps and was almost permanently camped in the basket in front of the fire and Aunt Maggie had even mentioned a spot of blood on her blanket. With Jack poorly and unable to pop over and check on her, Ruby – with a twinge of guilt – vowed to bring Tess into the surgery on Friday.

A couple of days later, however, Ruby was starting to feel miserable. Lunchtimes were really her only time to get together with Leah, Dot and Elspeth and Ruby sorely missed both their company and the chance to put the world to rights together.

She could feel herself growing gloomier by the day.

Thursday, 7 December 1916

The next day, Leah was waiting for Ruby outside the detonation shed when she emerged at lunchtime.

'Are you free for lunch today?' she asked. 'It seems like ages since we've caught up.'

Ruby hesitated.

She could think of nothing nicer than a chinwag with her friend. As time went by, she dearly wanted to confide in someone about the letter and, really, who better than Leah? On the other hand, her family responsibilities weighed heavily on her.

'I'd better not,' she said regretfully. 'Much as I'd love to, I ought to check on Ma and Tess.'

'Would you like me to come home with you?' asked Leah. 'We can chat on the way there and back and, at the very least, I can make you both a cup of tea.'

Ruby smiled at her gratefully. 'Would you?' she said. 'I'm worried about Tess and I feel so guilty that I ain't had no time to make her me priority.'

'Of course,' said Leah. 'Come on, grab your hat and coat. We haven't got long.'

The two women walked briskly through the streets of Silvertown towards Sanctuary Lane.

It was a cold winter's afternoon with a sharp wind buffeting down the streets and rain in the air.

'Hang onto your hat,' said Leah with a grin. 'It's a blustery one.'

'It is,' said Ruby, holding onto her navy boater. 'Freezing

too. I hope Ma ain't let the fires go out but she's probably still in bed.'

But Ma was standing outside the house on Sanctuary Lane, deep in conversation with Annie-Next-Door. Surely that was a good sign . . . wasn't it?

Ma turned as Ruby and Leah drew closer. 'What are you two doing here?' she said. Her face was still drawn and pinched, but it looked very much as though she had been smiling.

That was . . . unexpected.

'We've come to check on you, of course, Mrs A,' said Leah cheerfully. A discarded piece of newspaper, dancing in the wind, wrapped itself around her legs and she disentangled herself without fuss. 'How are you today?'

'There's absolutely no need to come back every day,' said Ma, firmly. 'I'm right enough and you've both got enough on your plate at the moment.'

Ruby started in surprise.

This was a very different Ma speaking and a welcome development, indeed.

'I'm always here to keep an eye on your ma,' added Annie-Next-Door. 'She'd do the same for me – you know she would.'

Ruby shot her a grateful glance; Annie-Next-Door might be a busybody but she was a kind one. 'I'm glad you're feeling a bit better,' she said. 'And how's Tess? Aunt Maggie had mentioned a spot of blood and I wanted to check . . .'

Ma's face clouded over. 'You'd better go and check for yourself,' she said. 'It's clear enough what the diagnosis is now.'

'Yes, it don't take a vet to work out what's wrong with her, poor mite,' added Annie-Next-Door, solemnly. 'Someone's got a lot of clearing up to do.'

'Oh, no,' said Ruby. 'Has she eaten something she shouldn't and sicked it up? Or has it come out . . . the other end?'

'Ruby! For shame,' said Annie-Next-Door. 'In front of Miss Richardson, to boot.'

'Oh, I don't mind at all,' said Leah, cheerfully. 'You should see what we have to put up with at the hospital. So, what *is* wrong with Tess?'

'We know,' said Annie-Next-Door, in a sing-song voice. 'Tess might have been able to flummox you, but there's no pulling the wool over *our* eyes.'

'Maybe we should start volunteering at your hospital instead of you,' added Ma, with a definite glint in her eye.

And she and Ma started cackling like a pair of old witches.

'Oh, for goodness' sake,' said Ruby. 'You're both talking in riddles. Where is she?'

'In Maggie's room,' said Ma.

Ruby marched to the open front door and headed inside, throwing her hat to one side. It was dark in Aunt Maggie's room and it took a while for her eyes to adjust to the gloom, but what were all those little squeaks?

They sounded almost like mice.

Ruby looked a little closer and . . . yes!

There was Tess, lying full-square on Aunt Maggie's bed surrounded by one, two, three . . . no, *four* squirming little bodies – one black, two tabby and one ginger – nuzzling up to their mother.

Ruby turned to Leah, started to say something . . . and then just burst out laughing.

'Kittens!' she spluttered.

'So, I see.'

'Tess was in the family way.'

'Most evidently.'

'We had no idea!'

'It's a good thing we haven't tried to set up an animal hospital or anything!'

The two women dissolved into laughter, which soon degenerated into the sort of hysteria that involved clutching their sides and then clutching each other for support. Tess regarded them both with dignified consternation – and then carried on licking her kittens clean.

And here was Ma, bustling into the room and – praise be! – joining in with the merriment. Mac followed her in and just stood there looking totally flummoxed by the kittens.

'Oh, Ma,' said Ruby, giving her a hug. 'Why didn't I know?'

'Why didn't *any* of us put two and two together?' said Ma. 'The blessed cat were growing larger by the day!'

'You don't mind, do you?' persisted Ruby. She sat on the bed and, to her delight, one of the kittens immediately nuzzled against her. 'I mean, she's made a bit of a mess of Aunt Maggie's counterpane but . . .'

'Counterpanes can be washed,' said Ma, laughing at the kitten. 'In fact, I shall set to and do just that this very afternoon. After all, I ain't got nothing else to do. And, of course, I don't mind. New and unexpected lives just beginning – it's just what the doctor ordered. I'm sure we can find lovely homes for them all.'

Ma bustled off but Ruby and Leah stayed sprawled on the bed, trying to check the gender of each kitten, and bandying around possible names for them all. They had rather randomly settled on Midnight, Daisy, Millie and Winston just by their faces – without having any real clue as to their sex – when Leah suddenly sat bolt upright.

'Goodness me,' she said. 'I've just seen the time! We've only got a couple of minutes before we need to get back.'

Ruby scrambled to her feet and caught sight of herself in the mirror over the mantelpiece. 'Oh, Lordy, I look a right mess.'

Leah came and stood up beside Ruby and made a face at her reflection. 'Look at my *hair*,' she wailed. 'I look a complete *sketch*.'

Ruby grinned. 'Ain't no one going to take you seriously as a manager looking like that,' she said. 'I suppose we should tidy ourselves up before we head off. Not that there's really much point whilst it's blowing a gale out there.'

Leah nodded and there was silence as the two women busied themselves with combs and hairpins. Then, with a final stroke for Tess, a last cluck over the kittens and a wave goodbye to Ma, they were off. That had been one of the strangest lunchbreaks ever, but how lovely that they now had a litter of kittens to distract them all – and how wonderful to see a glimmer of the old Ma again.

'Thanks ever so much for coming with me,' said Ruby

as they waited for their passes to re-enter the factory site. 'You're a real pal.'

'I wouldn't have missed it for the world,' said Leah, with a grin. 'Wonderful to see you're on top of your game where animals are concerned.'

'You too.' Ruby gave Leah a friendly shove. 'I'm surprised the Royal Veterinary College ain't already given you some fancy initials to recognise your unrivalled expertise.'

She felt a sudden pang of anxiety.

That letter was still being studiously ignored in the bottom drawer of the reception desk. She really should do something about it. She really should tell Leah . . .

Leah was laughing. 'This stays between us, by the way,' she said. 'No telling Jack and Robert.'

'Absolutely not!' said Ruby. She would tell Leah about the letter later. 'Can you just imagine their ribbing? It would be never-ending and merciless.'

Another wave of worry and concern washed over Ruby at the mention of Jack's name. She still felt conflicted about him and she didn't even know if he was back at work yet. Hopefully he would recover soon and she would see him at the animal hospital the next day . . .

'We haven't got long,' said Leah, grabbing her pass and cutting across Ruby's thoughts. 'But we've probably got time for a quick bite and it wouldn't do to start the afternoon shift on an empty stomach. Why don't we dump our stuff in reception and then go to my canteen. We'll probably be served more quickly in there?'

'Right you are,' said Ruby. 'I'll just take me hat back to the shifting shed.'

'Leave it in reception, if you like,' said Leah. 'That's what I'm going to do.'

The two women surrendered their newly issued passes to the bored-looking policewoman waiting at the second barrier and walked briskly over to the reception building where Leah was based. Inside, a middle-aged woman in a broadbrimmed hat was standing by the reception desk, waving a telegram, and sobbing incoherently. Mrs Clark, Leah's colleague, was trying her best to calm her down.

Ruby's stomach constricted in sympathy for the poor woman.

Just another distraught wife or mother who had received the most unfathomable of news and who had come to fetch a hitherto unsuspecting family member home.

It was just dreadful, especially as the Battle of the Somme was over and one might have dared to hope for some reprieve.

How many more senseless deaths would they all have to endure before this terrible war of attrition was finally over?

The sobbing woman partially turned towards them and – with a start of shock – Ruby suddenly realised she knew the redhead with the waspish waist.

It was Elspeth's mother, Mrs Carson.

Ruby had only met her a couple of times . . . but there was no doubt it was her.

Ruby stepped forward.

'Mrs Carson?' she said tentatively, touching the older woman on the shoulder. 'Not bad news, I hope?'

What a stupid, stupid question.

It would hardly be good news that was making the poor lady shake with sobs.

Mrs Carson turned around, her face red and distorted and her weeping intensifying in volume.

'It's Mr Carson,' she said, her words thick and almost incomprehensible. 'I'm afraid he's been killed. My poor, poor Elspeth, her daddy gone.'

Ruby put her arm around Mrs Carson's shoulder. 'I'm so sorry . . .' she muttered hopelessly, trailing off as the right words eluded her.

What on earth could she *say*?

'Would you like me to go and get Elspeth straightaway, Mrs Carson?' interrupted Leah, calmly. 'Or would you rather have a cup of tea first . . .'

Leah didn't finish her sentence but her inference was clear. Would Mrs Carson appreciate a moment to calm down before her daughter was summoned or did she want to be reunited with Elspeth as soon as possible?

'Please get her for me now,' said Mrs Carson, wiping her eyes.

'Of course,' said Leah, soothingly. 'And should I just say, "Your mother is here and I'm afraid she has some bad news," or would you prefer I told her something else?'

'Just say there's bad news, please,' hiccupped Mrs Carson. 'I should be the one to tell her what's happened. Although, I really don't know how I can . . .'

'You will find the words,' said Leah, gently. 'I'll go and fetch Elspeth now. Ruby, perhaps you could stay here and make Mrs Carson a cup of tea.'

'Of course,' said Ruby, looking at Leah with newfound respect.

Her friend had been sitting cross-legged on Aunt Maggie's bed cooing over kittens and snuffling with giggles not fifteen minutes earlier – and now here she was dealing with the most stressful and distressing of situations with calm professionalism. Just one lone curl tumbling over her ear as she removed her hat gave away the fact that she had not spent her lunch hour demurely reading a book . . .

And then she was gone.

In the event, one of the staff bustled off to make tea, so Ruby picked up Leah's hat and coat and shepherded Mrs Carson into the back office.

What was she going to say to her?

'Elspeth loves her father,' said Mrs Carson, making a visible effort to pull herself together. 'A right little daddy's girl, she is. Or was, I should say.'

'I'm so sorry,' said Ruby. 'It'll be right hard on her – on you all. But at least you know he died doing his duty and that you can be as proud of him as I know he will have been of all of you.'

Hark at her!

Where were these words coming from?

'That's very kind of you to say,' said Mrs Carson. Her bottom lip was trembling but she was much more composed. 'Is your pa still around?'

'He died a few years ago,' said Ruby. 'An accident at the docks. But me brother Harry died six weeks ago at the Somme, so I understand something of what you're going through.'

'The club that no one wants to be part of,' said Mrs Carson sadly.

And here was Elspeth in her tan trousers and tunic, her

hair still swept up into its drawstring cap. She rushed into the room, looked questioningly at her mother and, at the answering nod, flung herself into her mother's arms without a word.

The two women clung together, rocking silently. Then Elspeth, still locked in her mother's embrace, pulled off her cap and flung it onto the table.

Ruby started in surprise.

Gone were Elspeth's long, abundant blonde curls – the source of much envy around the factory. In their place, one of those sleek, modern bobs – jaw length and all sharp lines and angles.

Ruby stifled a squawk of shock.

It just looked so different.

Modern and audacious and . . . fabulous.

Mother and daughter both swung to look at Ruby. Clearly her squawk hadn't been as stifled as she had intended.

Mrs Carson gave Ruby a wry smile. 'I suppose the only good thing is that her father ain't here to see it,' she said, her laughter quickly turning back to tears.

Ruby gave them both a smile. 'It looks marvellous,' she said. 'But now ain't the time or place. I'll give you some time alone, but I'll be right outside if you need anything.'

She was about to creep out when Elspeth suddenly reached out and tapped her on the shoulder.

'Something was happening to Leah in there,' she said almost absentmindedly. 'You might want to go and check.'

Ruby blinked at Elspeth, confused.

What on earth could she mean?

Had Leah fallen?

Had some sort of accident?

Oh, goodness.

'What sort of something?' she asked. 'And in where? On the factory floor?'

'Yes,' said Elspeth. 'She came in and told me that Ma were here and that there were bad news and suddenly everyone were crowding around and then there were a big commotion.'

'What kind of commotion?' persisted Ruby, by now thoroughly confused.

'I think she dropped a hatpin,' said Elspeth.

'Oh, goodness.' Ruby was thoroughly shocked. 'Are you sure?'

Anything metal – no matter how small – was strictly prohibited on the main factory floor because of the risk of sparks and explosions. It had been drummed into them all time and time again that any transgressions – even accidental ones – would result in the harshest repercussions.

Elspeth nodded and her new hairdo fairly shimmered and bobbed. 'Pretty sure,' she said. 'But, then, I were so shocked by what she were telling me that I couldn't really make sense of it all.'

Ruby exhaled loudly. Then she consoled herself with the fact that Dot had been caught red-handed in similar circumstances a few months ago and – despite all the fearmongering – had escaped with a slap on the wrist. Hopefully, there was nothing unduly to worry about.

Even so . . .

'That's so unlike Leah,' said Ruby, looking at Leah's cloche hat sitting innocently on the desk. Sure enough, there was no corresponding hatpin to be seen. 'She'll be *furious* with herself for doing that. But we'd just got back from lunch and she ripped off her hat in her rush to get to you, so I suppose it must have still been in her hand. Still, no harm done.'

'No, you don't understand,' said Elspeth, urgently. 'This is serious. I think she's being arrested.'

Ruby didn't stop to wait for details.

Repeating her condolences to Mrs Carson and Elspeth, she fled the little room and the reception building. Then she dashed across the compound to the main factory building – the one that she had started work in all those months before and where Elspeth and Jack worked now.

Ruby stopped by the main factory doors. As usual, they were shut and there was a policewoman standing guard on either side. There was no sign of any disturbance. In fact, it all looked as it always did. Maybe Elspeth had got it wrong.

Yes, that was bound to be it.

Any moment now, Leah would come out, a little pale and shaken by having had to break the bad news to Elspeth. She and Ruby would grab a bite to eat and talk about poor Mr Carson and then both of them would start their afternoon shift as usual.

But there was no sign of Leah.

Maybe she had already come out and gone straight to the canteen without Ruby. No, she wouldn't have done that; she would have planned to return with Elspeth.

Ruby approached the factory door, unsure of what else to do. One of the policewomen immediately sprang to attention.

'Do you have business in here?' she asked.

Ruby hesitated. It was obvious that she didn't – she wasn't dressed in the tunic and trousers combination of all the main factory-floor workers and she certainly wasn't wearing clogs in order to minimise the risk of sparks. Besides, she had three or four hairpins pinning back her thick, wavy hair *and* possibly a coin in her pocket – and she really didn't want to end up in the same predicament as Leah.

'Is Miss Richardson in here?' she asked instead.

The policewoman stared back impassively.

'Miss Richardson?' Ruby persisted. 'The lady from personnel? Wears spectacles?'

The policewoman gave a terse nod of her head.

Suddenly the doors were flung open and . . .

Oh, goodness!

Leah was being led out of the factory floor in handcuffs.

And the person leading her was none other than Cook.

16

For a moment, Ruby could only stand in shock.

It was all too much.

One minute, Leah had simply been going to fetch Elspeth and the next . . . this!

It couldn't be happening.

She stepped forward, right in front of Cook and Leah, forcing them both to stop walking. Leah, she noticed, looked pale and worried, but she seemed calm enough.

'Stop!' said Ruby. And then, 'What on earth are you doing?'

'Step aside, Miss Archer,' said Cook sternly.

'But you *can't* arrest her,' said Ruby. 'She were just fetching Elspeth and when Dot accidentally did the same thing, she were just transferred to my department.'

'I am not discussing this with you,' said Cook, more firmly. 'Move out of the way, or I will have no choice but to arrest you too for obstruction and wasting police time.'

'No . . .' started Ruby.

'Don't, Ruby,' interrupted Leah, 'There's no point in you getting in trouble as well.'

Reluctantly, Ruby took a step back and the two continued on their way, Cook fairly pulling Leah along. The next shift had started so luckily the compound was reasonably empty, but those who were around had stopped what they were doing and were craning in Leah's direction.

Ruby's cheeks burned with second-hand embarrassment and shame. Her friend was a manager, for goodness' sake, and this was all so heavy-handed and unnecessary.

Ruby knew that she should really start her afternoon shift but, against her better judgement, she followed Cook and Leah at a discreet distance to the perimeter of the site and arrived just in time to see Leah being put into the back of a police motor and driven away.

To Ruby's disgust, Cook was smiling as she turned away and re-entered the site.

Ruby marched up to her.

'It's you again,' said Cook. 'Always turning up like a bad penny, you are.'

'Where is Leah being taken to?' asked Ruby, desperately.

Cook pursed her lips. 'I'm not at liberty to say,' she said and Ruby's fingers itched to slap away her self-satisfied smirk.

'Come on, Cook,' she said, trying to keep the frustration from her voice.

'It ain't "Cook" here,' said Cook, tetchily. 'I'll thank you to remember I ain't no one's servant no more. It's WPC Fletcher, now, if you please.'

Ruby took a deep breath. 'Alright, WPC Fletcher,' she said. 'I'm proud of you for the position of authority you find yourself in – or, should I say, that you've *earned* – and I know that you're fulfilling your duties with exemplary care and attention.'

'Too right, I am,' said Cook, fairly puffing out her chest.

'And I'm sure it's within your powers – should you so choose – to tell me where Miss Richardson is being taken. In similar situations, I've heard tell that the police have been kind enough to share the location so that relatives can arrange to bring in clothes and suchlike. I'm sure her parents would be ever so grateful.'

Ruby crossed her fingers behind her back. She had no idea whatsoever if any of this made sense or was a load of old baloney, but it was worth a try.

Cook hesitated, then lent down to Ruby.

'Miss Richardson will be detained at Bow Police Station,' she said with evident relish. 'There she will be interrogated and, given she were caught red-handed, charged under the Defence of the Realm Act. Given the nature of the offence, I would imagine your friend is looking at a hefty stretch in prison. That will rub the edges off her, let me tell you.'

There was no time to lose.

Without replying to Cook, Ruby turned on her heel and hurried away back to the reception building. All was quiet. There was no sign of either Elspeth or her mother and Mrs Clark was back behind her desk.

She stood up as soon as Ruby walked in, wringing her hands together in distress.

'What's happening?' she asked. 'Where's Leah? There's been ever such a lot of kerfuffle – top management coming in and out – but nobody tells me anything.'

Ruby and Mrs Clark were hardly best friends, but, for the moment, it seemed that they were brothers in arms.

Leah's been arrested,' said Ruby, simply. 'In all the shock about Elspeth's father, she apparently went onto the factory floor with a hatpin.'

Mrs Clark recoiled and her hand flew to her turkey neck. For a moment, Ruby wondered if smelling salts would be required, but then the older woman rallied.

'I can hardly believe it!' she said, taking a deep breath and fanning herself with her other hand. 'Such a sensible and responsible girl. Now, some of the others I could mention . . .'

'She's on her way to Bow Police Station,' interrupted Ruby, briskly. 'I don't suppose I could use the telephone?'

Mrs Clark pursed her lips and Ruby steeled herself for the inevitable refusal.

'Strictly speaking . . .' But then, Mrs Clark stopped herself. 'Who do you want to call?'

'Robert Smith,' said Ruby. 'He's . . .'

'The veterinary practitioner from Hackney,' finished Mrs Clark, briskly. 'Yes, I've heard rather a lot about *him*. I gather Leah's rather smitten.'

'I'd go to the police station myself,' said Ruby, anxious to get the conversation back on track. 'Only I'd have to walk to the bus stop and then change buses and it would take all afternoon. Robert Smith has a motorcar and could be there in a jiffy. He might not be in his surgery, of course, but his secretary might be able to get him a message if he's out on call, and it's surely worth a try. It would take her parents hours to get here . . .'

'Of course,' said Mrs Clark. 'He's a gentleman and, like it or not, these things matter, even in this day and age.'

That wasn't exactly what Ruby had meant – in fact, she hadn't meant that at all – but Mrs Clark was already leading her into the little office and barking down the phone to the operator. Seconds later, they had been connected to Robert's number and Mrs Clark was handing the receiver to Ruby. Against all the odds, Robert *was* there, taking a late lunch. And then Ruby was explaining the whole situation, hearing his sharp intake of breath, and trying her best to answer his barrage of questions.

It all still felt entirely unbelievable – almost as if her voice and her words belonged to someone else.

And then Robert was telling her he would drive round to the police station and that he would get word of what was happening to Ruby as soon as he could.

Ruby started to answer him . . . but he had hung up.

Ruby handed the receiver back to Mrs Clark, and wandered out, feeling totally discombobulated.

What on earth was going to happen now?

As it turned out, Ruby didn't have too long to wait.

Ruby had, naturally, found it hard to concentrate on her work that afternoon. How much had happened since she and Leah had been laughing over the unexpected kittens at lunchtime. To be honest, she wasn't even sure that she had done the right thing by coming back on duty, but she wasn't sure what else she could have done. She did hang around the main factory floor at breaktime, hoping to find Jack, but, to her disappointment, one of his colleagues told her that he was still off work with his chest infection. That was a little worrying. Luckily, her team were ahead of their quota for that week and she could screw on detonation caps without thinking too much about it, which left her mind free to ruminate on all that had happened and to wonder how Robert was getting on. Fingers crossed that Leah had already been released – a horrible misunderstanding – and they could put the whole ridiculous, frightening, bizarre episode behind them. Ruby didn't have any firsthand knowledge of prisons, but she had read the newspaper reports about the poor imprisoned Suffragettes before the war and their experiences had sounded both utterly grim and completely petrifying. Leah was generally a resilient sort of person but, given her upper-crust background, Ruby imagined that she would be finding the whole thing far from easy.

As Ruby's shift was drawing to a close, a message arrived for her. Robert was wating in reception for her and she was granted permission to finish work a little early for the day.

Ruby didn't need telling twice.

She fairly ran through the drizzling rain to the shifting shed and stripped off her overalls in double-quick time. Flinging on her coat and cramming her hat on her head, she presented herself at reception less than five minutes after she had been summoned.

Please let it be good news.

Robert stood up in one fluid movement as Ruby hurried over to him, his narrow, intense face pinched with worry.

'Come and talk to her for me,' he said, without preamble.

Ruby blinked at him in confusion. 'Pardon me?' she said.

'I'm meant to be visiting her again in a minute, but I think you might get more sense out of her.'

'So, she ain't been released?' I'd hoped . . .'

'She's still detained at Bow Police Station,' interrupted Robert, sounding simultaneously panicked and exasperated. 'And, for reasons best known to herself, she's hellbent on pleading guilty to all charges.'

'Oh, Lordy,' breathed Ruby. 'Why on earth would she do that?'

'My sentiments exactly,' said Robert. 'It's all a goddamn mess, pardon my French. She won't listen to me, but I wonder if *you* might be able to talk her around.'

'*Me*?' Ruby puffed out her cheeks. 'What about her parents? Or someone from here, for that matter.'

'Her parents don't know,' said Robert. 'Not yet at least – and she's determined it stays that way. She says she doesn't want them getting involved and pulling strings. She's forbidden me from contacting my father for the same reason. And as for this place? Once the munitions factory police have arrested her, there doesn't seem to be much they can do.'

'It were Cook,' said Ruby, miserably. 'She's always hated Leah, for some reason. But what can I do? I ain't got influence over no one.'

'You're Leah's closest friend,' said Robert. 'You might at least be able to get her to consider her options. Remind her that if she does plead guilty, there's every chance she'll end up in Holloway. My colleague told me the authorities are granted significant powers to deal with suspected threats nowadays and often without the same level of judicial oversight.'

Ruby swallowed hard. 'It were a *mistake*,' she said. 'Leah's hardly a criminal. Look, if you think it's got a chance of helping, of course I'll go.'

'Thank you,' said Robert. 'My motor's outside. I'm booked in for a visit in about half an hour.'

Ruby nodded. 'Then there ain't no time to lose,' she said.

*

Ruby had only been in Robert's smart green-and-gold motor once a few months previously, when they had been ferrying goods for the animal hospital. It had been a sunny day, the roof had been down, and, feeling like the queen of the world, she had revelled in the attention and in every exciting second.

Today couldn't have been more different.

Inching through the busy streets – it was nearly five o'clock and the roads were clogged with all kinds of both motorised and four-legged traffic – and with the roof up against the rain, Ruby was aware only of gnawing anxiety in the pit of her stomach. Robert, beside her, was quiet too; staring ahead at the greasy road, leather-clad fingers drumming on the steering wheel every time they got stuck behind a horse and cart or a platoon of soldiers marching down the middle of the street.

Leah couldn't go to prison.

It was *unthinkable*.

It seemed both an age and no time at all that the car slowed down outside the police station on the Bow Road. A handsome, three-storey redbrick building with fancy bay windows and tall brick chimneys, it looked more like somewhere that Mr Darcy and Elizabeth Bennet would have danced the night away than a place of detention. Only the lintel inscribed with the word POLICE gave the game away and Ruby's nervousness ratcheted up a gear.

'I'll drive round the back,' said Robert. 'I left the motor out here earlier on and was given no end of an earbashing by the duty sergeant.'

He duly parked in a side street, bounded out of the car, and opened the passenger door for Ruby. Her eyes went straight to what was obviously the cell block out the back; a series of small windows set high in the wall, most with cast-iron bars but three replaced with glass blocks. Ruby hoped fervently that Leah was housed in a cell with the latter; a room open to the elements would be particularly grim.

There was no time to dwell on that because Robert was already tucking her hand in his arm and walking her around to the front of the building. Seconds later, he was announcing their arrival to the supremely bored-looking duty sergeant behind the front desk and explaining that Ruby would like to visit Leah in his place.

'I'll wait for you here,' said Robert as Ruby signed in and was waved through a panelled door. A young female police officer accompanied her down a flight of stairs, Ruby's hand shaking slightly on the cold iron handrail. This certainly wasn't how she had thought her day would pan out. She had planned to go round to Jack's house to see how he was feeling and to tell him all about the kittens. It seemed like ages since she had seen him . . .

The police officer paused outside another wooden panelled door.

'I'll need to pat you down,' she said, matter-of-factly.

Ruby shrugged. 'I'm patted down several times a day at the munitions factory, so it don't bother me a bit,' she replied.

'Pity your mistress weren't patted down more often,' said the police officer, with a sympathetic smile.

Ruby made a rueful face and let the mistress comment slide. And then she was being ushered into an almost empty, windowless room lit by a single swinging light-bulb. Leah was sitting at a small table all by herself and looking very small. She started with surprise at seeing Ruby but didn't look unduly disappointed that Robert wasn't there.

Ruby rushed across the room, sat down in the chair opposite Leah, and grabbed her hands. Leah's hair was untidily pinned and she was even paler than usual – the dark smudges under her eyes magnified several times over by her spectacles.

'No touching,' said the policewoman mildly, staring impassively into the middle-distance.

Ruby let go of Leah's hands. 'We're going to get you out of here,' she hissed.

Leah gave her a small smile. 'I don't think you are,' she said, as though comforting a small child.

'Leah, you've got to fight,' whispered Ruby urgently. 'What's all this nonsense I hear about pleading guilty to the charges?'

'Because I *am* guilty,' said Leah, simply, making no effort to lower her voice. 'I went onto the factory floor with a metal pin in my hair. There are no two ways about it.'

'But surely it ain't as clear-cut as that?' said Ruby. 'You went onto the factory floor in a hurry to fetch Elspeth because you'd just heard her father had died. You was doing her and her mother a *favour*, for goodness' sake. No one would find you guilty for that.'

'I think if the building had gone sky high, *everyone* would find me guilty,' said Leah with a hollow laugh.

'Yes, but it didn't,' said Ruby, beginning to feel thoroughly frustrated. 'And you know as well as me that Dot did exactly the same thing a few months ago and *she* got away with a slap on the wrist.'

Leah smiled sadly. 'Yes, but your Cook has clearly decided to make an example of me,' she said.

'She ain't "my" Cook!'

'I know,' said Leah. 'Sorry. None of this is your fault. It's just the luck of the draw.'

'But it's so unfair,' said Ruby. 'Come *on*, Leah. Stop being so defeatist.'

Leah sighed. She took off her specs, wiped them on her skirt and then put them on again. 'Look,' she said. 'I'm going to plead guilty and that's that. There are plenty of people who *have* been jailed for the same offence and, as I've loudly argued for equal rights for everyone, why should I be treated more leniently than working-class women who commit the same offence?'

'But you'll go to *prison*.'

Leah nodded. 'From what I gather, I'll probably get three to six months. But if I can help in some small way to break down the antiquated class system, then maybe it will be worth it.'

Ruby hesitated. It didn't appear that way to her. It was a noble proposition, but it seemed both a little simplistic and farfetched.

'Can you do a couple of things for me?' said Leah, before Ruby had had a chance to respond.

'Of course,' said Ruby. 'Anything.'

'Can you go to my lodgings and pack me up some clothes and toiletries and maybe my sketching things. I would have asked Robert, but I don't particularly want him rifling through my smalls!'

‘Of course,’ said Ruby. ‘I’ll do it on me way home, although it rather feels like accepting defeat. And what was the other thing?’

‘Just tell Elspeth that I don’t blame her in the slightest,’ said Leah. ‘None of this – absolutely none of it – is her fault.’

Ruby blinked in surprise.

She hadn’t even considered that this might be an issue.

True, Leah had gone onto the factory floor in search of her . . . but that was hardly Elspeth’s fault. And it certainly wasn’t Elspeth’s fault that Leah had had a metallic object on her person.

‘Alright,’ she said, somewhat dubiously. ‘I’ll let Elspeth know when I next see her.’

‘Please make a point of it,’ insisted Leah. ‘Promise me that you’ll do that for me.’

There was something in Leah’s expression that Ruby didn’t understand. But she just gave a little sigh and said, ‘I promise. I very much doubt she’ll be at the clinic tomorrow, but I’ll seek her out at the factory on Monday if she’s back by then. Otherwise, I’ll go around to her house.’

Leah gave a little nod of satisfaction. ‘Thank you,’ she said, simply.

Not caring what the hovering policewoman might do, Ruby reached out and squeezed Leah’s hand. ‘You’ll miss Christmas,’ she said. ‘And the bazaar.’

It was a last stab . . . and they both knew it.

Leah just made a little face. ‘Not a word to my parents,’ she said, avoiding the issue.

Ruby nodded and stood up, preparing to leave. She

didn't turn around until she reached the door of the visiting room, when she allowed herself one last glance.

Leah was silently crying.

If Robert was disappointed that Ruby hadn't manage to persuade Leah not to plead guilty, he didn't let it show.

The two drove straight to Leah's lodgings near the factory in Silvertown, consoling themselves on the way that they would, no doubt, have days in which to try and persuade Leah to change her mind before her case came before a judge. With a bit of luck, she would be released on bail before that and they could attempt to talk her round. In the meantime, Leah's landlady swallowed their story about Leah needing to go home in a hurry and together they packed a small bag of everything they thought she might need in custody. Then Robert dropped Ruby back at Sanctuary Lane on his way back to the police station to drop it off.

Ruby went back inside to tell her family the news as if in a dream.

What a day.

17

Friday, 8 December 1916

Ruby thought long and hard about whether or not there should be a clinic at the animal hospital that day.

They would be very down on numbers – there would be no Leah and no Elspeth, of course – and Robert would, more than likely, be visiting Leah at the police station. And, as for Jack, well, she really had no idea. It was getting on for a week since she had heard from him – by far the longest they had been apart since they'd started stepping out – and with all that had been going on, she had no idea if he would be well enough to volunteer . . .

Really, the only people she could be sure of were herself, Dot, Aunt Maggie and Nellie – and, to be honest, Ruby could do with a day of rest herself after the past few tumultuous weeks. She just wanted to stay at home and watch the kittens whilst also making an extra fuss of Mac, whose nose had been put very out of joint . . .

In the event, Ruby decided to go ahead with the clinic. Regardless of how she felt, there were animals who needed to be treated. At the end of the day, the animal hospital was bigger than any of them – and she had no right to cancel. She would put a notice on the door warning owners that they would be operating with a skeleton staff but, apart from that, they would put their best feet forward and just get on with it.

Onwards and upwards.

When Ruby arrived at the hospital bright and early that morning, she was surprised – and somewhat concerned – to find Robert leaning over the front desk with a furrowed brow.

'I didn't expect to see you here,' said Ruby. 'Is everything alright? Leah . . . ?'

Robert straightened up. 'Good morning,' he replied. 'I managed to see her last night when I dropped her bag off and she seems to be holding up well. But they told me I can't visit again until this afternoon, so I thought I ought to show my face here in the meantime.'

'That's very good of you when you have so much on your mind,' said Ruby. 'Even a morning will make ever such a lot of difference.'

Robert made a little face. 'I'm hoping that it might take my mind off things, to be honest,' he admitted. 'By the way, I know it's not my remit, but I picked up the post a moment ago and this one caught my eye.'

He held out a thick, creamy white envelope and, without even looking at it, Ruby knew – with a sinking heart – exactly what it would be.

Almost reluctantly, she glanced at the letter. Sure enough, RCVS was printed in bold capitals on the front.

Oh, gracious.

Ruby hadn't exactly forgotten about the letter she had received several weeks before – of course she hadn't. On occasion, she had woken in a cold sweat thinking about it – and every time Leah had rummaged in the bottom drawer of the reception desk, it had been on the tip of Ruby's tongue to say something. But she hadn't. She had just hoped that the problem would 'go away', or – at the very least – she had told herself that she would deal with it when she was a little less busy and fraught.

That day had never come.

'What could the RCVS possibly be wanting with *us*?' Robert was saying, turning the letter over and over in his hands.

Ruby couldn't meet his eye. 'I'm not sure,' she said disingenuously, busying herself with hanging up her coat and hat. 'I'll take a look later; I've got a hundred and one things to do before we open up today . . .'

'Don't you think we should take a look now?' interrupted Robert. 'Whatever it is, I'm afraid it's unlikely to be good news. I very much doubt the RCVS are writing to congratulate us on this little venture.'

'I'm not ignoring it,' said Ruby. 'I'll make it me top priority later.'

'Ruby. Please . . .'

Robert held the letter out to her and there was something in his expression that suggested he knew there was more to Ruby's response than met the eye. Feeling like a guilty schoolgirl, Ruby almost snatched the letter from him and ripped it open.

What choice did she have?

Maybe she could brazen it out and suggest that it was a reply to a question about some veterinary matter that she had written to them about. No, that wouldn't work; she had already claimed that she had no idea what the letter was about and, anyway, she would hardly have written to them in the first place without first running it by Robert . . .

Maybe she would be lucky and the letter would make no reference to the previous one and she could feign surprise and dismay . . .

No such luck.

A quick scan of the contents and Ruby knew she didn't have a leg to stand on. This letter was short, more strident and to the point. It expressed regret that Ruby had not acknowledged their previous correspondence and demanded immediate closure of the clinic. If this was not undertaken voluntarily, there would be a legal deputation two weeks from today, which would forcibly foreclose the operation.

Oh, Lordy.

Icy water ran down Ruby's spine as she handed Robert the letter and shut her eyes.

What terrible, terrible timing.

Beside her, Robert was entirely still as he – presumably – read the letter.

Ruby waited for his outburst or for his cold fury and tried to work out which would be worse.

She had rarely felt so out of depth in her life.

Why, oh, why had she ever thought she was up to opening and running an animal hospital?

She was just a girl from Sanctuary Lane . . .

'I presume you did receive the previous letter?' Robert was asking.

'Yes,' said Ruby, in a small voice, hanging her head in shame.

Whatever would he think of her?

'Well, I'd say you did the right thing in ignoring it,' said Robert briskly. 'Always a chance they were calling our bluff.'

Ruby opened her eyes and looked at Robert in surprise. That really wasn't what she had been expecting him to say.

'To be honest, that ain't really why I ignored it,' she admitted. 'The truth is that I just stuffed it away in panic and tried to forget about it.'

'That's another approach,' said Robert, with a laugh in his voice. 'You didn't burn it then?'

'No. It's right here in the bottom drawer.'

She opened the drawer, rummaged around, and pulled out the offending letter, spreading it on the table next to the new one.

The front door opened with a jangle, making her jump.

It was Jack, bag over his shoulder, sauntering in without an apparent care in the world. It was a week since they had last been together – a very long seven days – and her heart constricted with excitement at seeing him again. The height and breadth of him, his handsome face with its lopsided grin. It had been far too long and Ruby wanted nothing more than to run towards him and to fling herself into his arms . . .

Except, something was stopping her.

Decorum was part of it, of course – it would hardly be seemly to start kissing and cuddling in front of Robert – but there was more to it than that. It was partly because Jack was whistling something that sounded suspiciously like 'Roses of Picardy' and Ruby would hate that song for evermore. And, despite her never wanting there to be any lies between them, it was partly because she really, really didn't want him to see the letters and to think that he – as an unqualified veterinary practitioner – was a big part of the problem. Plus, there was still that 'something' niggling at her and the word 'coward', which somehow hadn't gone away.

She settled for a smile and a little wave as she positioned herself carefully in front of the table.

'Anything wrong?' asked Jack, swinging his bag off his shoulder, and coming over to join them.

'Nothing,' said Ruby, cheerfully, moving slightly so that she was blocking his view of the letters. 'At least,' she added, because it was abundantly clear that she wasn't behaving naturally, 'It's nothing which need concern you. More importantly, how are you? I've been worried about you.'

'Have you?' Jack gave her a long, level look, his jaw set firm. Ruby tried to meet it, to hold it – even to outstare him – but found that she couldn't.

Flushing slightly, she dropped her gaze.

'Very well then,' said Jack, stiffly. 'I'll go and get set up then, shall I?'

'If you please,' said Ruby. 'Are you quite recovered from your illness?'

'Almost completely, thank you.'

Without waiting for an answer, Jack swept passed her and Robert and headed off to his consultation room.

It was as though they were strangers.

A short silence persisted in his wake.

'You don't want to involve him?' asked Robert mildly. 'After all, this affects Jack as much as the rest of us.'

'No.' Ruby exhaled softly. 'I don't think so.' She took a deep breath. What, exactly, *did* she want? 'Maybe it's better to keep it between the two of us until we know where we stand. It might not be necessary to worry everyone at this stage.'

'Jack isn't "everyone" though, is he?' persisted Robert.

'He ain't,' conceded Ruby.

'Does he know about Leah?'

'Oh, Lordy; he doesn't,' said Ruby, clamping her hand to her mouth. 'At least not from me.'

'Well, we definitely need to tell him about *that*,' said Robert.

'Of course,' said Ruby. 'I just don't want to tell him about the letters because he will see himself as part of the problem.'

'We're *all* part of the problem,' said Robert. 'You, he and the others because you're not qualified, and me because I *am* qualified but am knowingly working alongside people I know not to be. Still, if you don't want Jack to know yet – for whatever reason – I won't tell him. Let's work out what we're going to do about these threats and then we'll focus on telling him about Leah.'

'Thank you,' said Ruby.

She had always appreciated the way Robert had never tried to take over at the hospital. He had never pulled rank or tried to lord it over her. Now, looking at his narrow, intense face as he read the first letter, Ruby realised that he possibly had more to lose than any of them. She didn't really understand how these things worked, but might he lose his position as a veterinary surgeon – and therefore his livelihood – for choosing to work alongside them?

The thought sobered her.

'I don't suppose we can ignore this letter too?' she said, half-jokingly.

Robert gave her a rueful smile. 'I'm afraid I think they mean business this time,' he said. 'I wonder who told them?'

Ruby paused. She had a pretty good idea who it might have been, but far better for Robert to work it out for himself.'

The silence persisted until Robert gave a little groan and ran his hand over his face. 'Dash it all,' he said. 'You think my father's behind it, don't you?'

Ruby gave an almost infinitesimal shrug. 'It's possible, ain't it?' she said. 'He's always hated the hospital and he certainly resents you giving up your services for free. Maybe he's back for round two?'

It was fair to say that Ruby and Sir Emrys had a long and chequered history. Sir Emrys been a regular visitor to the Henderson's home in Hampstead back when Ruby had been in service – and one who had been known for his repulsively wandering hands until Ruby had taken matters into her own hands and poured scalding coffee into his lap. He had, of course, also taken exception to Ruby setting up an animal hospital without the relevant training, fearing it would put qualified veterinary practitioners, like his son, out of business. Indeed, he had done everything in his power to scupper Ruby's plans – pulling the plug on her first intended premises and publicly branding her a charlatan.

'Oh, Lord; that's more than possible,' said Robert grimly. 'The rum cove! And the problem is that no matter how much I remonstrate with him, once the RCVS have got the bit between their teeth, they sure as hell aren't going to back down. I'll collar my father about this, don't you worry, but it seems we've already got a battle on our hands. The RCVS clearly don't want to set a precedent of unqualified people setting up a clinic behind their backs.'

'But that's so unfair,' said Ruby, close to tears of frustration. 'It wasn't behind their backs. I actually *visited* them and asked for their help.'

'Did you?' said Robert, perking up.

'Yes! And a beastly man called Mr Cotter thought I were applying to be his secretary and when I told him me plans, he laughed in me face and practically threw me out. But he never said I were breaking the law or the regulations or whatever we're supposed to have done. He never told me I weren't allowed to go ahead. He just told me it were a daft idea.'

'Hmmm. Cotter,' said Robert, thoughtfully. 'Short, rotund, ridiculous moustache . . . ?'

'That's the one. Do you know him?'

'I think so,' said Robert. 'And, just to be sure, this was in Camden Town?'

'Yes. The Royal Veterinary College.'

'And what made you think to write there?'

Ruby thought back to the chain of events that had led to that ill-fated meeting. 'It were the lady in the library. I said I wanted to write to a veterinary organisation and she gave me their name and address.'

'Ah. I think that's where she – and therefore you – went wrong,' said Robert. 'The Royal Veterinary College – where the odious Mr Cotter is employed – is a teaching institution. It's where all veterinary surgeons are trained.

These letters,' he tapped the papers in front of them, 'are from the Royal College of Veterinary Surgeons.'

'They sound ever so similar,' said Ruby, wrinkling up her nose.

'They *do* sound much the same but they are, in fact, different institutions with completely different functions,' said Robert. 'The Royal College of Veterinary Surgeons is the one that is responsible for licensing vets and giving them authority to practise.'

'Well, Mr Cotter might have said,' said Ruby crossly.

'He probably just wanted to get you out of his hair,' said Robert. 'But technically, you *did* try to tell the authorities of your plans – even if they turned out to be the wrong authorities – and that might work in our favour.'

Hope flared in Ruby's chest. 'You think we should try and fight them?' she said.

'Hell, yes,' said Robert with a laugh.' Don't you?'

'*Yes!* But you've got so much to lose and with Leah in custody and . . .'

'On the other hand, can you imagine Leah's face if she finds we've allowed the animal hospital to close down in her absence?'

Ruby gave a snort of laughter. 'Our lives wouldn't be worth living.'

'Indeed, they would not.'

Robert's dark eyes were dancing with merriment and Ruby suddenly wondered how she could ever have found him unattractive. There was something about his calm, capable manner that was just very appealing.

To Ruby's guilt – her s*hame* – she felt the first vague stirrings of attraction.

'So, what do you think we should do?' she said, carefully keeping her voice brisk and business-like. 'Write back and say that I *did* approach them?'

'Absolutely that,' said Robert. 'Claim that you haven't replied yet because you're planning to seek legal advice. That will rattle them and it's not an outright lie – we may well end up getting advice. Then make it clear that you did your best to get permission from the relevant authorities before you opened the clinic. and that, as you weren't specifically told to cease and desist, you took it as tacit permission to proceed. It will buy us a little time and, at the moment, it's the only thing we've got to go on.'

The doorbell jangled as Nellie entered and Ruby put the letters back in the bottom drawer. Then it rang again and James Coleman – the student vet who sometimes helped out at the hospital – walked in, summoned because Ruby had assumed they would be very low on numbers.

'I'll draft something at lunchtime,' she said to Robert, straightening up and smiling at the new arrivals. 'But I'll need your help with all them fancy phrases. And we'll tell Jack about Leah at tea break; I expect he'll already be wondering why she's not here. Oh, Lordy: I can hardly believe this is all happening. There certainly ain't no rest for the wicked.'

From the moment the morning shift started, there was barely a moment to think. The queues seemed even longer than normal, there were many serious injuries and illnesses, and Ruby missed Leah's calm, steady presence by her side. There was nothing for it but to plod on methodically through her list of duties.

At eleven o'clock, Mrs Fisher came through with her usual tray of tea and cakes. Ruby poured a cup for herself and for Jack and picked him out the biggest, stickiest Chelsea bun. As soon as his latest patient – a ginger moggie with a thorn in its paw – was carried through reception by its relieved-looking owner, Ruby took her haul round the back to his consultation room. With both hands occupied, she kicked gently on the door with her foot and it immediately swung open.

'I thought you might like some refreshments,' she said cheerfully. 'I've got you your favourite bun.'

Jack looked at her with a face like thunder and made no attempt to relieve her of her wares. Ruby put them down carefully on the table and turned to face him.

'I've got something to tell you,' she said. 'And I'm afraid it's rather serious.'

Jack pursed his lips. 'If it's about Leah being detained under the Defence of the Realm Act for bringing a metal object onto the munitions factory floor, *I'm* afraid you're rather too late,' he said coldly.

'Oh!' The wind was quite taken out of Ruby's sails. 'How . . . ?'

'How?' repeated Jack, incredulously. 'Well, Dot mentioned it just now, for starters. A fellow I work with at the factory told me as I was walking here this morning, for another. Me own mother had heard about it from someone who lives three doors down *last night* – do you want me to go on. A manager at the factory being arrested is quite a big deal, Ruby – in fact, there were no way I *weren't* going to hear about it, even though I weren't at work yesterday. What I don't understand is why you and Robert went out of your way to conceal it from me this morning. "*It's nothing that need concern you*,"' he ended up by mimicking her sarcastically.

Oh, goodness!

'It weren't like that,' said Ruby.

'Well, it looked very much like that to me.'

Ruby hesitated.

She still didn't want there to be any lies between herself and Jack.

Not now.

Not *ever*.

But neither did she want to burden him with the letters from the RCVS and have him believe that he was the source of all their problems. On balance – and despite it completely going against her principles – she reluctantly decided that it would be best to keep him in the dark.

But, in the meantime, what to say?

'None of this is Robert's fault,' she said eventually.

That, at least, was true.

Jack looked at her sadly. 'I dare say not,' he said.

Ruby cast her mind about for how to continue and was almost relieved when Nellie knocked on the door with a poorly pug and Jack gestured for Ruby to leave.

Almost.

Ruby threw herself back into her work, booking animals in and treating those that she felt able to. Several animals needed urgent treatment and lunchtime came and went without either Robert or Jack reappearing. When Robert *did* finally re-emerge, he was flushed and distracted.

'That's it for me for now,' he said, cramming his hat on

his head. 'I really don't want to miss seeing Leah. I'll be back in a couple of hours,' he added, 'and we can finish off that letter when the clinic closes.'

'Right you are,' said Ruby. 'I ain't even had a chance to start writing it, to be honest. Give me love to Leah, won't you, and do try to talk her round.'

'Will do,' said Robert, with a distracted smile.

He touched Ruby lightly on the shoulder, and was gone.

And then, not an hour later, a tall, middle-aged gentleman wearing a formal charcoal suit and a bowler hat marched through the front door. Someone, in other words, very unlike the usual clientele of the Sanctuary Lane Animal Hospital.

Ruby's first – panicked – thought was that the RCVS were making good on their promise and were coming to shut them down two weeks early. Suddenly, she felt physically sick. Then she took a second look at the gentleman – thin face, florid complexion, haughty expression – and realised that she recognised him.

It was Sir Emrys Smith, Robert's father.

Ruby blinked at him in surprise.

Coming so soon after her conversation that morning, she wondered if Robert had already managed to have a conversation with his father. Maybe he was there to confront his son, to confirm that he had, indeed, reported the hospital to the RCVS. Maybe – and this was, admittedly, far less likely – he was there to apologise for how matters had escalated.

Ruby plastered a smile on her face and went over to him. She had nothing to feel defensive about and every reason to feel proud. Despite Sir Emry's best efforts, the hospital was busy and thriving – every inch a success.

'Good afternoon, Sir Emrys,' she said, as politely as she could. 'What . . .'

'Is my son here?' interrupted Sir Emrys, rudely.

Ruby sighed. It seemed her old adversary had lost none of his charm.

'He's not,' said Ruby, in the same calm, measured tone.

'I thought he volunteered here on a Friday.'

'He does, ordinarily,' said Ruby. 'But I'm afraid he has an urgent appointment this afternoon.'

It sounded like Robert *hadn't* spoken to his father.

What on earth could Sir Emrys *want*?

Sir Emrys lent towards her. 'I need to see him *right now*,' he hissed. 'Is he nearby? At his clinic in Hackney?'

Ruby crossed her fingers behind her back. 'I have no idea,' she said smoothly. 'He's not at his clinic and he said he'd be back here in a couple of hours. There's a teahouse next door, if you'd care to wait there?'

Sir Emrys' face dropped and he suddenly looked ten years older. 'Robert's my last hope,' he said, in a hoarse voice that had lost much of its certainty. 'Please help me.'

Ruby blinked at the change in tone and demeanour. 'With what?' she asked.

'With my dog, Queenie,' said Sir Emrys, a note of desperation in his voice. 'She's in the most appalling pain. I've telephoned our usual vet but he's been posted to France and I've tried the numbers I was given instead, but they're either not answering or not available. The one person I did manage to get hold of said it sounds like appendicitis – rare in dogs – and would need operating on immediately.

I didn't know where to turn and then I remembered Robert works here on a Friday. Believe me, I wouldn't have come unless it was an emergency.'

Ruby ignored the insinuation that the Sanctuary Lane Animal Hospital was the last resort and also pushed away the question of whether the hospital should be treating – let alone prioritising – the animals of the upper classes.

After all, an animal in agony was an animal in agony and simply couldn't be ignored.

'Please wait here,' she said to Sir Emrys.

She dashed down the little passageway that led to the examination rooms. Jack and Nellie were just emerging with a smiling middle-aged woman who was holding a rabbit.

'Would you be able to operate on a suspected emergency appendicitis?' she asked without preamble.

Jack pursed his lips. 'Tricky operation,' he said, doubtfully. 'I did a couple at the front under the supervision of me officer so, in theory, I should know what to do. If James next door is free to jog me memory and help with the chloroform, I'm happy to give it a go. Between the three of us, we should be able to work it out.'

For a moment, Ruby thought that Jack was including her as the third and her heart leapt with a mixture of terror and excitement. Then she realised – half disappointed, half relieved – that he meant Nellie, already cracking her knuckles in anticipation.

'That's marvellous,' she said, neutrally. 'I'll go and fetch Queenie now.'

She rushed down the passage to reception, deep in

thought. Although she had heard Robert say that he would trust Jack with his life – let along a dog's – Ruby had a feeling that Sir Emrys wouldn't share the same sentiments – especially if he knew that Jack didn't have a single qualification to his name. James Coleman might fare a little better – at least he was a student at the RVC even if he hadn't yet graduated – but, as for Nellie . . .

All in all, it would be far better simply not to tell him.

Equally, she wouldn't tell Jack and the others who owned Queenie. No one needed that sort of pressure on top of everything else and, anyway, it really shouldn't matter whether Queenie belonged to the King or one of the disabled soldiers begging on the street corner.

There was no sign of Sir Emrys in reception, so Ruby hurried through the front door. There was a very grand navy-blue motor parked on the kerb and Sir Emrys was sitting on the back seat tenderly cradling a yellow Labrador groaning loudly in pain.

'I didn't want to bring the old girl inside if there was no chance of anyone treating her,' he said when Ruby opened the door.

Ruby nodded. 'There's a couple of experienced practitioners who's free to operate on Queenie,' she said, hoping that Sir Emrys wouldn't ask any awkward questions. 'I'm happy to bring her through, if you like.'

Sir Emrys nodded. 'Thank you,' he said. 'We don't want the good folks inside getting upset that I've pulled rank,' he added, with unexpected perceptiveness.

'You're not pulling rank,' she said firmly. 'We treat everybody the same and there ain't no other emergencies at the moment.'

Sir Emrys nodded and planted a kiss on Queenie's head. 'Good luck, old girl,' he said.

When he looked up again, Ruby saw that his eyes were shiny with tears.

Ruby was hovering – she couldn't help it! – when Jack, James and Nellie emerged from the operating room half an hour later.

To her relief, despite looking exhausted, they were all wreathed in smiles.

'Nasty case,' said Jack. 'It were touch and go, to be honest. We got in just before it burst; an hour or so later and the old lady would have been a goner.'

'Thank goodness for that,' said Ruby, with feeling.

'Well done, Jack,' said James. 'I learned a lot from you just then.'

'Couldn't have done it without you,' said Jack, clapping him on the back. 'You helped me fill the blanks in very nicely.'

James smiled. 'Hope it comes up in the exams!' he said. 'Right, I'd better get back on duty.'

And he headed back to the second examination room.

'Where does Queenie have to get home to?' asked Jack. 'If they ain't got no transport, I'll put her in Chien's old cage for now and take her home after me shift. I've got Mayfair and the cart round the back.'

'That won't be necessary,' said Ruby. 'There's a motor waiting for her out the front.'

'A *motor*?' said Nellie with a grin. 'You don't often hear that around here.'

'That's because it ain't your usual type of owner,' said

Ruby. 'Queenie is owned by none other than Sir Emrys Smith.'

'Who's he?' Jack looked totally blank.

'My father,' said Robert, choosing that moment to saunter in from the courtyard out the back.

'Your *father*?' echoed Jack. 'What the devil?'

'I'm as surprised as you are, old chap,' said Robert. 'I've just arrived back and I saw the old man in his motor out the front so I thought I'd nip in through the back entrance and find out what he wanted. So, you've operated on Queenie, have you? Mind if I take a look?'

Jack shook his head and they all crowded into the little operating room. Robert bent low over the table, taking his time to examine a very groggy Queenie, and then straightened up to inspect something – presumably the offending appendix – in a white bowl on the side. Finally, he offered his hand to Jack.

'Well done, old chap,' he said. 'You too, Nellie. Nice neat job from what I can see, and not a moment too soon from the look of things.'

'Thank you,' said Jack. 'James lent a hand too and luckily it all came back to me as I operated. Just a pity you couldn't have done it.'

'Not at all,' said Robert. 'I'd probably have asked you to do it anyway; conflict of interests and all that. Sounds like you didn't have a clue who she was, though?'

'I thought it best you didn't know beforehand,' Ruby admitted.

Ruby held her breath. Hopefully, she had done the right thing.

But the look Jack gave her made her insides shrivel.

'There seem to be an awful lot of things you've decided it's best I shouldn't know about nowadays,' he said coldly.

Ruby couldn't meet his eye. There was an awkward silence, broken only by Sir Emrys hurrying down the passageway towards them, Dot in tow.

'I'm so sorry,' said Dot. 'I did tell the gentleman that this part of the hospital is out of bounds.'

Sir Emrys ignored her. 'I couldn't wait any longer,' he said. 'Ah, Robert, you're back. 'How is she? Did she pull through?'

'She did, Pa,' said Robert. 'A classic case of appendicitis from what I've been told and caught just in the nick of time. Jack here has done a sterling job.'

Sir Emrys face sagged in relief. 'I'm forever indebted to you, old chap,' he said, reaching out to pump Jack's hand. 'Did you train alongside Robert?'

Jack laughed. 'Did I heck!' he said, and Ruby could have sworn he was deliberately making his East End accent even stronger. 'I learnt me trade out at the front, working alongside a vet. And, of course, I were ably assisted by Nellie here, who's something of an expert on dogs.'

'And I learned what *I* know through dogfighting,' added Nellie, with a wheezing laugh.

Sir Emrys face was a picture and, for once, he was speechless. He went over to Queenie, lying quietly on the table. The Labrador gave a little thump of her tail and started licking her master's face and Sir Emrys patted her tenderly in reply.

'Good girl,' he murmured. 'So, we live to fight another day.'

Ruby went over to him. 'Yes,' she said bitterly. 'If only the same could be guaranteed for this hospital.'

It was out before she could stop it, heart bypassing brain. Luckily, Robert, Jack and Nellie were busy tidying up and hadn't heard, but Sir Emrys straightened up and gave her a piercing look, his cheeks flushing even redder. Ruby walked away before he had a chance to reply, but his expression had already told her all she needed to know.

As she had suspected, Sir Emrys *was* the snake in the grass.

'Can I have a word?' said Jack, as Robert helped his father move Queenie to the motor.

Ruby smiled at him. 'Of course,' she said. 'And I'm ever so sorry I didn't tell you about Sir Emrys. I really thought I were doing the right thing . . .'

'Not now,' interrupted Jack. 'After we finish here. I think we need to have a proper conversation.'

Ruby puffed out her cheeks. Of course, they needed to talk. For many, many reasons.

'I really want to talk to you, Jack. But I can't after the shift. Robert and I . . .'

She trailed off.

She had to write that letter.

But how to tell Jack . . . ?

'Oh, of course,' said Jack, grimly. 'I expect Robert and you have things to talk about that don't need to concern me.'

'Yes. No. It's not like that . . .'

'Just leave me alone for a few days, will you?' said Jack.

'Jack! No!'

But Jack had already walked away.

'How was Leah?' asked Ruby, as soon as Robert returned.

Please let it be good news.

After all the day had thrown at her, she really didn't think she could cope with anything else.

To her surprise, Robert slumped into a chair with a groan. His face was tight and pinched and he suddenly looked ten years older.

'What?' asked Ruby, in alarm.

'I have bad news, I'm afraid,' said Robert, rubbing the bridge of his nose. 'I didn't like to mention it in front of Pa but, unbeknownst to us all, Leah was taken in front of a judge this morning. She pleaded guilty to taking a metal object into a munitions factory and later this afternoon, she is being transferred to serve three months in Holloway Prison.'

18

Ruby was left reeling by it all.

She could hardly believe that Leah had been *imprisoned.*

Even when she read about it in the hastily purchased *Sketch* and *Mirror* the next day: '*Gilded Cage: Debutante Manager Detained After Security Breach at Munitions Factory*', '*Luxury to Lockup: Socialite Jailed Following Munitions Security Incident*' – it didn't really sink in. Ruby read the articles – '*has Miss Richardson been unlucky to have an example made of her as an upper-class woman or has she been wantonly negligent and lucky to get away with only three months?*' – as though they were referring to a perfect stranger.

It had all just happened so *quickly*.

And why hadn't Leah at least *tried* to fight her corner? No one at home could understand it. Even if she was guilty, there was a chance that she might have been let off – as many others *had* been before her. As it was, by the time her frantic parents found out from Robert that Leah had been arrested, it was too late for them to do anything. Robert had popped round to Sanctuary Lane on the Saturday evening and told Ruby and her family that they were exploring all avenues – including pleading temporary insanity – but that did seem to be a longshot.

And, meanwhile, Leah was incarcerated in Holloway Prison, notorious for its draconian conditions and infamous for the recent force-feeding of hunger-striking Suffragettes, several of whom had died as a result. Bow Police Station would, no doubt, seem positively genteel by comparison.

It was all just heartbreaking and Ruby found it hard to concentrate on anything that weekend. It was all made worse by the fact that Jack seemed to be keeping her at arm's length. But she diligently made holes in the Christmas cake with a skewer and 'fed' it with more rum. She rushed around the market to start her Christmas shopping. (She had hoped to make this a more leisurely and considered affair this year – perhaps involving a trip to Selfridges to really push the boat out – but needs must.)

But all the time she worried.

Worried about Leah.

Worried about the future of the animal hospital, which all hinged on the letter she and Robert had sent and were waiting to hear back on. Unless things started going their way, the whole thing could be nothing but a memory by Christmas . . .

Worried about Charlie, who was still not speaking to her although, at least, he was around all Sunday, sitting with the kittens and taking Mac for a long walk.

And, of course, Ruby worried about Jack. She had respected his wish for the two not to see each other over the weekend – and, in some ways, it made things easier because she *still* didn't want to tell him about the letter. But, by Sunday evening, she was beginning to miss him terribly.

She would make a point of talking to him at work the following day.

They loved each other – that was the most important thing. Everything else was just incidental.

Surely, they could patch things up?

Monday, 11 December 1916

But the first thing that Ruby did when she got into work on Monday morning was to check if Elspeth had reported for duty. As well as wanting to comfort her friend on her very recent bereavement, Ruby hadn't forgotten she'd promised Leah she would make a point of having a word.

Elspeth – looking drawn and tired – *was* at work and gratefully accepted Ruby's suggestion of a cup of cocoa at breaktime.

'I didn't see any point in staying at home,' said Elspeth, as they sat down in a relatively quiet corner of Elspeth's canteen together. 'It won't bring Pa back and, surely, it's better to stay busy? But I know now what you meant by "that look" after your brother died. I feel like everyone's staring at me wherever I go.'

Ruby screwed up her face in sympathy. Once upon a time, Elspeth would have revelled in being the centre of *any* attention, good or bad, but these days she tended to go about her business without fuss or drama.

'The hair probably don't help either,' said Ruby, smiling at Elspeth's short, swinging bob.

Elspeth grinned. 'At least it stops the men making passes,' she said. 'Last week, one lad actually told me I'd die an old maid now me hair's short.' She stopped smiling and took a swig of cocoa. 'People are also probably staring because if Pa hadn't died, Leah wouldn't be in prison and I do feel bad about that.'

Ruby reached out and touched her hand. 'Don't,' she said. 'Leah specifically asked me to tell you that none of this is your fault.'

Elspeth wrinkled her nose. 'I know it ain't my *fault*, as such,' she said. 'But the fact remains that if Leah hadn't come onto the factory floor to find me, none of this would have happened. It's just terrible. I've got a card here for her and a book on sketching. Are you going to see her soon, or should I post them?'

'Give them to me,' said Ruby. 'Robert's got me booked in for visiting hours after work today. Now, about the Christmas bazaar. I quite understand if . . .'

Elspeth held up a hand. 'It's going ahead, so don't say another word,' she said. 'It'll give me something to focus on and, anyway, I've farmed most of it out to volunteers. Everyone in Silvertown seems to know someone who's had an animal treated at the hospital and everyone seems to want to do their bit to help. I don't think I could stop it, even if I tried.'

Ruby resisted the temptation to tell Elspeth that pretty soon there might not *be* an animal hospital to raise money for and that she was getting more and more anxious that she hadn't heard back from her letter. Instead, she reached forward and gave her friend a hug.

'Thank you,' she said, simply. 'You're a pal.'

Ruby found Jack at lunchtime, as her break was finishing and his was just starting.

She watched from a distance as he emerged blinking

and stretching from the huge hanger housing the main factory and then started to head towards the canteen with a couple of chaps Ruby barely recognised.

No attempt to look for *her*, she noticed.

Huh!

She hurried to intercept him and caught up with him just as he reached the canteen doors.

'Jack?'

If his face didn't split into a huge grin upon seeing her, at least he didn't look positively unfriendly. 'Ruby. Hello.'

'I thought we might have a chat . . .'

'I've got to grab a quick lunch. I'm training with these guys in the second team today . . .'

'And *I* were due back on duty two minutes ago. But I thought we could make a time to meet up . . . What about a walk tomorrow morning? I know Mac would love to see you.'

Jack pursed his lips and gestured for his pals to go into the canteen without him. 'Getting a bit dark in the morning nowadays,' he said, shortly. 'And, of course, it's dark when we get out of work . . .'

Ruby's stomach lurched.

Was Jack fobbing her off?

'Come on, Jack,' she said. 'It sounds like you don't want to spend no time with me?'

Jack's face softened. 'That ain't true,' he said. 'But I'll admit I've been a bit peeved by the way you've treated me and I do think we need a proper chat to clear the air. We won't have no time at the clinic, so what about Saturday. We can have a long walk, a bite to eat and then take it from there . . .'

Ruby paused. Saturday was a long way off. She had a ridiculously busy week before that, starting with her first visit to Leah in Holloway Prison that evening. Maybe it would be good to have a bit of a break. It would also give her a chance to try to tame her unruly thoughts.

'It's a date,' she said.

Before Ruby left the factory that afternoon, she popped into reception to see if anyone had left anything for Leah that she could bring along when she visited her in prison. She had already been warned that everything would need to be checked and double-checked – and was, anyway, likely to be censored or confiscated – but she judged that it was worth it because the prison mail was apparently notoriously slow and unreliable.

Mrs Clark was waiting for her behind the desk. 'Dreadful business,' she said, with an exaggerated shudder. 'Now, there are a few cards here for you to take in for her – and I just wondered if you wanted to take her hat in with you as well? It's still in the back office and we can't have the poor girl leaving prison bareheaded when the time comes, now can we?'

'The very thought,' said Ruby, with a grin. 'I'm sure Leah is thinking of nothing else.'

'You're teasing me,' said Mrs Clark good-naturedly. 'But, given the spate of recent thefts around the site, I'd be happier if it was somewhere else. It's a little modern for my tastes, but very expensively made and it might prove too big a temptation to someone of loose morals.'

'Thefts?' echoed Ruby.

This was news to her, although she suddenly remembered

the distraught girl and the missing ring in the shifting shed all those weeks ago. 'Oh, as if we all didn't have enough on our plates at the moment.'

'I'm afraid so,' said Mrs Clark. 'So, you'll take it?'

'Yes, of course. I'm not sure I'll be allowed to take it into Holloway Prison, but I'll try. It might do Leah good to have pretty things around her and to remind her of the outside world.'

Mrs Clark disappeared and came back a moment later with both Leah's blue cloche hat and one of her ornate silver hatpins. 'I found this on the floor later that day,' she said. 'I doubt you'll be able to take it into the prison, but I'd feel more comfortable if you've taken it away from here.'

Ruby nodded absentmindedly as she signed the form Mrs Clark had pushed in front of her. 'I hadn't realised Leah had been wearing two,' she remarked idly. 'I suppose the other one is still with the police.'

'Pardon me, dearie?' said Mrs Clark, looking confused.

'The second hatpin,' said Ruby. 'The one that Leah mistakenly took onto the factory floor.'

Mrs Clark's brow furrowed. 'There *was* no second hatpin,' she said. 'It was her *hair*pin falling out which caused all this trouble.'

Really?

'Are you sure?' said Ruby. 'For some reason, I thought she'd blundered onto the factory floor with her hatpin still in her hand. She'd just taken her hat off . . .'

'Oh, no, dear,' said Mrs Clark. 'It was a silver *hair*pin. It said so in the papers. Not that it matters, of course. They're both banned, so the end result would have been the same.'

'True.'

Ruby was silent, mulling it all over. Every woman knew the difference between a hatpin and a hairpin. Hatpins were long, sturdy, often showy pieces designed to pierce fabric and hold headwear in place. Hairpins were smaller and finer and a U or a V shape – used for securing hairstyles, pinning up curls and preventing loose strands from falling. At the end of the day, as Mrs Clark had said, it didn't really matter which Leah had taken onto the factory floor, but Ruby had always assumed it was her hatpin. She was pretty sure Elspeth had said as much and then Ruby had glanced at Leah's recently discarded hat and seen that her hatpin was missing and . . .

'Are you alright, dear?'

Mrs Clark's voice seemed to be coming from a long way away as Ruby wrestled with her thoughts.

Hatpin . . .

Hairpin . . .

Ruby couldn't for the life of her think exactly *why* it mattered . . . but it did.

And then she remembered.

It was that lunchtime on Sanctuary Lane, the day they discovered that Tess had given birth. They had spent time with the kittens and then Leah had stood in front of Aunt Maggie's mirror with her hair awry. Bewailing the fact she looked a sketch, she had brushed her hair and resecured her curls with her fancy tortoiseshell hairpins.

Not metal.

Tortoiseshell.

The fact was that it wouldn't have mattered that Leah had gone to fetch Elspeth with a dozen such pins in her hair. They weren't metal, they weren't a risk to anyone and, most importantly, taking them onto the factory floor wasn't against the law.

Leah was *innocent*.

Ruby should have remembered. Possibly she *would* have remembered, but then, of course, Leah had pleaded guilty and that had been that.

A surge of exaltation rippled through Ruby and she was hard-pressed not to shout out loud and to share her eureka moment with Mrs Clark.

But she held back.

There were so many unanswered questions and she needed to talk to Leah.

Although nearly ten miles away, the journey to Holloway Prison was gratifyingly straightforward.

As luck would have it, Silvertown Station was on the North London Line, which skirted the city centre and went directly to Caledonian Road & Barnsbury Station – a mere fifteen minutes' walk away from the jail. Ruby left the station and strode briskly down the Caledonian Road, the cold air nipping her cheeks and each exhaled breath a visible mist, which lingered for a moment before fading away. The street – although a busy thoroughfare – was dark and gloomy. Usually, at this time of year, all the shopfronts would be illuminated and beautifully decorated for Christmas. Nowadays, of course, they were as dark as the grave. There were still signs that it was mid-December of course – a snatch of singing from carol-singers in one of the doorways, the pungent smell of roasting chestnuts nearby. Cotton-wool snowflakes and other decorations hung defiantly in the front windows of some of the houses – reminding Ruby that it was nigh time that they decorated Sanctuary Lane – but it was as plain as day that they were sadly still at war for a third Christmas . . .

Ruby's pace slowed as Holloway Prison loomed out of the darkness. It was an imposing castellated building – six wings radiating from a central tower and the entrance flanked by huge mythical creatures clutching keys in their claws. Ruby swallowed hard, feeling very small. She must have been only a couple of miles from the Royal Veterinary College in Camden Town but this oppressive, bleak monstrosity felt half a world away.

Poor Leah.

Ruby followed a couple of other women in through the visitors' entrance and jumped as the heavy, metal doors clanged behind her. Then, chiding herself, she threw her shoulders back and raised her chin. This was about Leah – it didn't matter how she felt about it all – and she must be calm and supportive. She resigned herself to the interminable search of her person and the items she was bringing in, and then – with the other visitors – followed a warden through several more clanging doors and into a large room filled with little groups of people clustered around wooden tables.

Leah was sitting by herself at a table in the middle of the room. She smiled and gave a little wave when she saw Ruby but, even though the dimples duly started dancing in her cheeks, there were heavy grey bags beneath both eyes and her skin had a horrible ghostly pallor.

Ruby sat down and grabbed both of Leah's icy cold hands before anyone could tell her not to.

'Oh, sweetheart, how are you?' she said.

Leah gave a little shrug and made no attempt to remove her hands. 'Not too bad,' she said, stoically. 'It's grim here, of course, but it's bearable. I have my own cell, at least – I swear conditions are better for the upper classes although that is, of course, very, *very* wrong – and I've been put to work sewing officers' uniforms with some of the other girls who are, for the most part, lovely, so at least that helps to pass the time. The food is vile of course – I crave a proper pie with parsley liquor like that time we went to the cinema – but I can put up with that.'

Ruby opened her mouth to reply, but Leah hadn't finished. 'I just feel so terrible and so embarrassed that I've let everyone down,' she continued. 'I worry that Robert won't wait for me and I worry that I won't be around to help with the Christmas bazaar but, with regards to that, I have, at least, been drawing animals . . .'

'*Animals?*' interjected Ruby, desperate to interrupt with something. Anything!

'Yes,' said Leah. 'If you think they're good enough, I thought we might use them to make Christmas cards to sell at the bazaar. At least then I'd be doing my bit – however small. What do you think?'

At last Leah stopped talking and Ruby gave her friend a long, level look.

'I think it's a lovely idea but – much more importantly – I know that it weren't your hairpin.'

Leah's mouth hung open.

'What?' she stammered. 'Of course, it was . . .'

'It weren't,' said Ruby. 'I distinctly remember us fixing our hair in Sanctuary Lane that lunchtime and your hairpins was tortoiseshell. Very stylish, very simple and – most importantly – not a speck of metal on them.'

Ruby wasn't sure what reaction she was expecting.

Confusion?

Excitement?

Elation?

But Leah just dropped her gaze. 'It was definitely mine,' she said. 'I've already admitted to it.'

'But it *weren't*,' persisted Ruby. 'If I hadn't thought it had been a *hat*pin, I could have sorted it all out . . .'

'Please don't come in here and make trouble, Ruby,' interrupted Leah.

That stung.

'I ain't making trouble,' said Ruby stiffly. 'But I know you're innocent. What's going on here? If you're worried about Robert – although I know he will stand by you – and if you're worried about the bazaar, then for heaven's sake speak up. Or do you actually *want* to stay in here to prove some stupid point?'

'Don't be ridiculous,' snapped Leah. 'I'm just trying to take my punishment and get through it one day at a time. And it doesn't help when you start coming in here spouting rubbish like this.'

'It's not rubbish,' said Ruby. 'Look, why don't you take me through exactly what happened on that day so I can get it clear in me mind.'

'Because there's nothing to tell,' said Leah. 'And because, with the greatest respect, you getting it clear in your mind really has nothing to do with anything. I've already told the judge everything that matters.'

'Please, Leah.'

'*No*,' said Leah. 'I've pleaded guilty, I'm doing my time and there's really nothing more to say. I'd like you to go now and not to come back until you can promise not to mention any of this again.'

And, before Ruby could react, Leah was standing up and gesturing to the prison warden standing in the corner of the room.

Seconds later, Leah had been escorted away and Ruby was left staring into empty space.

Ruby's heart didn't return to its normal rate until she was halfway home on the train.

None of this made any sense.

And now Ruby came to really think about it, Leah *must* have known she'd been wearing tortoiseshell hairpins herself. There would be others still in her hair, for goodness, sake.

So, why on earth hadn't she said anything and thus exonerated herself?

There were, of course, other possibilities. Maybe she had left home wearing hairpins that didn't match. Or she could have accidentally picked up one of Aunt Maggie's hairpins as they stood at her mirror. There were, no doubt, many such scenarios that fitted the facts.

What didn't make sense, however, was Leah's reaction. The fact that she had so adamantly refused to even talk about her arrest and the events leading up to it was the most suspicious thing of all.

What was she hiding?

Maybe she was she being blackmailed?

Or perhaps was she protecting someone?

Surely there was a logical answer.

Halfway through her bus journey home, Ruby suddenly had a pretty good idea exactly what that might be.

19

Wednesday, 13 December 1916

In the event, it was a couple of days before Ruby had a chance to go back and visit Leah.

She had wanted to go back immediately – indeed, she had wanted to turn around the moment she'd had her eureka moment on the train – but, alas, it wasn't that simple. Visits to the prison were strictly limited – and tended to be monopolised by Robert and Leah's understandably frantic family – and Ruby had to wait her turn. And, as it was, she managed to go back two days later because she'd persuaded Robert to let her take his turn, promising him that it was important and crossing her fingers that he wouldn't press her for details. How she wished she could talk to Jack about all this but, having agreed not to meet until the following Saturday, she felt she couldn't really lumber him with her problems.

It had, of course, occurred to Ruby that she might tell someone what she'd discovered in the meantime. Robert was the obvious candidate, as were Leah's parents – or even the police. After all, it was surely worthy of mention that Ruby distinctly remembered Leah had been wearing tortoiseshell hairpins on that fateful day. But, on balance, Ruby decided to keep it to herself. Leah had already pleaded guilty and, if she was still hellbent on denying it all, then Ruby's recollections would be dismissed out of hand.

Ruby would just have to find some other way of getting Leah to listen to her.

'It's *you* again,' said Leah, unsmiling, as soon as Ruby walked into the visitors' room. 'I was expecting Robert. And, more to the point, I thought I'd said I didn't want to see you again.'

She put both hands down onto the table in front of her and glanced over at the duty prison warden.

Ruby knew that she didn't have long to persuade Leah and she held up both hands.

'I know, I know,' she said, sliding into the chair in front of her friend. 'But I feel bad about what happened and I promise you I'm just here to talk froth and fancies this time.'

Leah looked sceptical, but at least she didn't stand up or call the prison warden over. 'Really?' she said. 'When have *you* ever been interested in froth and fancies? When have *I*, for that matter?'

She had a point. Both girls were far happier getting down and dirty with a lame dog scavenging by the kerb or an injured cat hiding in the bushes than dressing to the nines.

Ruby grinned. 'It's Christmas,' she said. ''Tis the season of froth and fancies and all things frivolous and we both need to cheer ourselves up.'

'Do we?' said Leah. 'I mean, things are pretty desperate in here' – she gesticulated around the dismal room, totally devoid of anything Christmassy – 'but I'd assumed everything was tickety-boo on the outside.' Then her face coloured. 'I mean, apart from your brother, that is. Forgive me.'

Ruby hesitated.

For a moment, she badly wanted to tell Leah that the animal hospital was in real danger of being shut down and that she and Jack were having problems. But, somehow, she couldn't. Besides, it really wouldn't be fair to burden Leah with her troubles when her friend had enough of her own to worry about.

'Nothing to forgive,' she said firmly. 'But, as I said, we both need cheering up. So why don't we start off by talking about hairdos?'

'Hairdos?' echoed Leah, a quizzical smile on her face. 'Are you feeling quite well?'

'Perfectly, thank you,' said Ruby. 'But I do have an urge to cut off me plait and to replace it with one of them newfangled bobs. All the rage, nowadays, those are.'

Despite everything, Leah was laughing. 'That's something I thought I would never hear you say, Ruby Archer,' she said, 'I do think they're perfectly marvellous, but you'd have to be pretty brave to go down that route. They've been causing all sorts of issues at the factory – women who have taken the plunge have been called bluestockings and lesbians and everything else under the sun.'

Ruby pursed her lips and nodded her head. 'Poor Elspeth, then,' she said casually.

'*Elspeth?*' spluttered Leah, sitting bolt upright and then starting to laugh even harder. 'Goodness me – has *she* had her hair cut off?'

'She has,' said Ruby.

Leah's eyebrows disappeared into her hair. 'The little devil,' she said. 'I bet it really suits her too.'

'*Everything* really suits Elspeth,' said Ruby, without rancour. 'I believe she could put Mayfair's nosebag over her head and that she would still look lovely.'

Leah laughed. 'That's true,' she said. 'We should all hate her, but she's so lovely that it's impossible to do so. On a serious note, I wonder if she got her hair cut so that she gets less male attention. Maybe that's been hard to deal with since her father died.'

Ruby paused to make what she was about to say land more strongly.

'Oh, no,' she said, lightly. 'Elspeth got her bob before she heard that her pa had passed away.' She paused again and then added casually. 'She says it's saving her a fortune on hairpins – she finds she don't need a single one anymore.'

Ruby let both comments lie and avoided Leah's eye. Instead, she busied herself with her bag, extracting the letters and cards she had brought along from the factory. When she finally looked up, Leah had gone as white as a sheet and her hands were curled into tight fists on the table in front of her.

Wordlessly, the two women locked eyes. Leah's were wide and unblinking.

'You thought it were Elspeth's hairpin,' said Ruby in a voice that was barely above a whisper.

It was a statement, not a question, and Leah gave an almost imperceptible nod of her head.

'You thought it were her hairpin and you wanted to protect her,' Ruby persisted.

Another tiny nod and Ruby shook her head. 'It weren't,' she said, sadly.

Leah dropped her gaze and buried her head into her hands.

'Oh God,' she groaned.

When she looked up again, Ruby couldn't tell if she was laughing or crying.

'I knew it,' cried Ruby. 'I knew you thought you was taking the blame for Elspeth. But why, Leah? *Why?*'

Leah sighed and shrugged her shoulders, all attempts at pretence gone.

'Mainly because Elspeth had just found out her father had died,' she said. 'Her ma and brother both *need* her and she had enough to deal with without getting into trouble at the factory. Of course, I never thought that *this*' – she gestured around the room – 'would happen. Dot got away with a slap on the wrist for bringing a pin onto the factory floor and I assumed the same would happen to me. I thought I was doing a *good* turn. I was just worried that *you* would see through it all straight away and give the game away.'

'Except *I* had got muddled between hatpins and hairpins,' said Ruby. 'I should have known that you, of all people, wouldn't have been careless enough to bring either into the factory. And now it turns out that the hairpin weren't Elspeth's anyway.'

'Evidentially not,' said Leah, with another half-laugh and half-groan. 'I've lost my reputation and my freedom and probably my job to boot and it looks like it's all been for nothing.'

'I know,' said Ruby. 'So, who the Dickens *did* that hairpin belong to?'

'I don't know,' moaned Leah. 'There were a lot of people there, crowding around. I'd asked the supervisor where Elspeth was and she sent a junior off to get her but stayed with me. And then Elspeth came back with the junior and a couple of other people for good measure and I was talking to Elspeth – comforting her – when your Cook materialised and said there was a hairpin on the ground. And I just assumed it was Elspeth's and for the reasons I told you before, I said that it was mine.'

'Even though Elspeth were wearing a cap?'

'It was askew. And I obviously wasn't thinking straight. Oh, Lordy, what a mess.'

'What a mess, indeed,' said Ruby. 'But you're innocent, so we have to get you out of here.'

'How are we going to do that, then?' said Leah. 'I can't exactly just say I've changed my mind and that I didn't do it, can I?'

'Well, that would be a start,' said Ruby. 'I'm not sure what the law is around these things and whether or not anyone would believe you, but that would be the obvious place to start.'

'After sentencing, I think the case is considered closed unless there are specific legal grounds for an appeal or a review.' said Leah. 'The defendant and their legal representation would have to present new evidence or argue that there were errors in the legal process that warrant a re-examination of the case. At least, I think that's what they said.'

'Well, we can work on that,' said Ruby. 'And does it need to be done within a particular timeframe?'

Leah wrinkled her nose. 'I don't think so. But now I

know I'm not protecting Elspeth, I'd like to get out of here as soon as possible. And certainly by Christmas.'

'Then we've got less than two weeks,' said Ruby. 'Now, first things first; what exactly did this hairpin look like?'

Ridiculous though it seemed, Ruby had no idea.

She hadn't been on the factory floor when the 'incident' occurred, and she hadn't been in court when Leah was sentenced. And, of course, because Leah had pleaded guilty, she had had no curiosity about the hairpin. She, like everyone else, had just accepted at face value that the pin was Leah's and that was that.

Leah shrugged. 'I hardly saw it myself,' she said. 'It was silver with tiny pearls arranged in a semicircle, I think. Quite fancy, vulgar even, and not at all the sort of thing that I would wear – let alone to work.'

'And, by the sound of it, far too grand and expensive to be the sort of thing that Elspeth would bring to work either,' suggested Ruby gently. 'Or even to own, for that matter.'

'Ah, but it's the sort of thing that she would *love* to own, isn't it?' said Leah. The two women's eyes met in a smile. It was true that Elspeth certainly had a love for anything fine and fancy. 'To be honest, I thought it might be fake. Or perhaps a special coming-of-age present.'

'Time's up,' said the warden, coming over to them. 'Sorry, Miss, but you're going to have to leave now.'

Ruby looked at Leah, her mind going nineteen to the dozen. 'I'll be back as soon as I can,' she said.

'What should I do in the meantime?'

'There's someone I need to talk to at the animal hospital tomorrow,' said Ruby. 'And someone else at the factory on Monday. But I suggest you set the ball rolling in the meantime by telling them you'd like to change your plea to innocent and that there were any number of people who could have committed the crime. And, fingers crossed, I should be able to get you more help by the beginning of next week.'

20

Friday, 15 December 1916

Ruby was not feeling her best as she walked up Sanctuary Lane to the animal hospital the next day.

She was bone-tired and she had a rotten headache; her head had been thumping since the evening before as she wrestled with how best to help Leah. Worse still, she had woken with a blocked nose and a sore throat – no doubt the harbingers of a very unwelcome winter cold. Given that it was the fifteenth of December, she couldn't have felt any more un-Christmassy if she had tried. Even Aunt Maggie's snowflake decorations in the Sanctuary Lane Animal Hospital window twirling away in anticipation of next week's Christmas bazaar didn't make her feel in the slightest bit festive. They just reminded her that they were still a household deep in mourning and that she was nowhere near finishing her Christmas shopping.

Gah!

Unexpectedly, Jack was waiting for her inside the hospital despite it being well over an hour until they opened for business and, despite not having had a proper conversation for days on end, Ruby's heart gave a little swoop of excitement and pleasure. She couldn't wait to spend the next day with him . . .

'Fancy a cuppa?' said Jack, with a smile.

'Yes, please,' said Ruby, her eyes falling on a cream-coloured envelope lying on the reception desk and emblazoned with the initials RCVS.

Oh, Lordy.

'That's not an answer,' said Jack.

'Yes, it is.'

'It's not. I said "would you like a cuppa or hot chocolate?" and you said "yes!" Could I please, just for once, have your undivided attention. I'm fed up with your mind constantly being elsewhere.'

'I'm sorry,' said Ruby. Maybe the letter was good news. 'It's just that there's ever such a lot going on at the moment and . . .'

'And maybe you'd like to open that letter you can't keep your eyes off,' interrupted Jack. 'I can tell I ain't going to get no sense out of you until you've read it.'

'What?' Ruby's eyes snapped to Jack's face. 'No, it's alright.'

'I insist,' said Jack, picking up the envelope. 'Or would you rather I read it to you?'

Ruby's shoulders slumped in defeat. She could tell that Jack meant business and, anyway, she did really, really want and need to know what was in the letter. She fairly snatched the envelope from Jack's outstretched hand, ripped it open and hastily scanned the contents.

Her letter to the RCVS attempting to head them off at the pass hadn't worked.

Of course, it hadn't.

The short missive thanked Ruby for her reply and acknowledged that she had approached the RVC with regards to her animal hospital idea. However, she was still running an unregulated animal hospital without appropriately qualified trained veterinary staff and, as such, the aforementioned legal deputation would be arriving next Tuesday with instructions to forcibly foreclose the operation.

Ruby put the letter on the desk with a deep sigh. That gave them – gulp! – a mere four days to think of something – *anything* – to save the hospital. The trouble was that Ruby couldn't for the life of her think what that something might be.

She had tried and she had failed.

Her lovely hospital was going to be closed and it looked like there was nothing she could do about it. Sadness and anger jostled with embarrassment and shame.

Maybe she had been a fool to try.

'Damnation!' she said with feeling, tears pricking at the eyelids.

It was over.

'Bad news?' asked Jack.

Ruby nodded mutely.

'May I?'

Ruby passed him the letter. What else could she do? Rightly, or wrongly, she had tried to shield Jack from what had been going on, but she couldn't any longer.

He would find out soon enough, anyway.

There was a charged silence whilst Jack read the letter.

Then he looked up at Ruby, his face shocked.

'Bloody hell,' he said, 'I can't believe the bastards are going to shut us down.'

'Neither can I,' said Ruby. 'I feel like I'm letting everyone down.'

Suddenly, she wanted nothing more than to put her arms around Jack and to hug him tight. She took a step towards him – but Jack backed away, one palm raised.

'Sounds like it wasn't the first time they've written to you,' he said, levelly.

'It ain't,' admitted Ruby. 'They wrote once just after Harry died and again a few days ago.'

'And yet you never thought to mention it to me?'

'I didn't want to worry you, Jack!'

'And so you replied off your own back without consulting any of us,' persisted Jack in the same dangerously, level voice.

'I told Robert,' conceded Ruby. 'He helped me draft the reply.'

'Did he now?' said Jack, equally softly.

'Come on, you would have done the same. Robert always knows the right thing to say.'

'Well, clearly he don't,' said Jack. 'Otherwise, you wouldn't have received *this*, would you?' He waved the letter at Ruby, angrily. 'Still, it's good to know you think more of him than you do of your own sweetheart.'

'Oh, Jack, it weren't like that,' said Ruby wearily. 'Robert were just there when the letter arrived.'

'It weren't just that, though, were it? I remember the day now. You was both sat there thick as thieves and when I asked what were going on, you said there were nothing to worry about. So, you could have involved me – you had every opportunity – but, for reasons best known to yourself, you chose not to. I thought it were about Leah and I were cross enough about that but . . . *this*.'

He trailed off and ran a hand through his hair. Ruby stared back at him in frustration.

'You're making this out to be much bigger than it is,' she said. 'You're making it sound like we ganged up on you, and we really didn't.'

'I know exactly why you did it,' said Jack.

'What are you talking about. *Why?*'

'It's because I'm the problem, ain't it?' said Jack bitterly. 'I'm the one treating the animals who ain't a qualified veterinary practitioner. If I weren't here, the problem would go away.'

'No, it wouldn't,' said Ruby. 'I ain't a veterinary practitioner, neither, in case you ain't noticed. Neither are Nellie, Aunt Maggie, Dot, Elspeth, or Leah, for that matter.'

'Yes, but you're all just . . .' Jack trailed off.

'We're all just what?' retorted Ruby, hands on her hips.

'Nothing,' said Jack.

'Come on,' persisted Ruby. 'We're all what? *Women?*'

'No. Of course not. Women have proved that they can do just about anything nowadays.'

'What then?' demanded Ruby.

'Well, you're support staff,' said Jack. 'You keep everything ticking over. I don't think the powers that be would have any trouble with you not being qualified.'

'Support staff?' interrupted Ruby. She could hardly believe her ears. '*Support* staff! Is that how you see me? I set this whole place up, I'll have you know. It were my bleeding idea. I fought tooth and nail for it . . .'

'I'm not saying you ain't important,' said Jack. 'But . . .'

'Oh, don't try to justify yourself,' snapped Ruby.

'And don't *you* start twisting things around,' said Jack.

'You're the one in the wrong by not including me in this whole sorry mess . . .'

A blaze of rage shot through Ruby.

'Yes. Well, maybe the *support* staff chose to talk to the *qualified* vet,' she burst out.

It was a low blow – she knew it was – but she couldn't help herself.

Support staff indeed!

Jack didn't say anything for a long moment. Then he took a deep breath. 'I can't do this no more,' he said, quietly.

'What can't you do?' said Ruby, crossly.

'Any of it,' said Jack. 'I can't put this place at risk by not being qualified, I can't carry on seeing you when you clearly don't think enough of me to confide in me and I certainly can't sit around here watching you make cow eyes at Robert no more.'

Ruby's answering splutter turned into something approaching a laugh. 'Oh, now you're just being absolutely ridiculous,' she said.

'Am I? Am I really?'

'Yes. You are. Robert is me friend's sweetheart . . .'

'And that's the only reason you'd hold off?' said Jack. 'Nothing to do with the fact that you were my sweetheart? Nothing to do with not finding him attractive?'

'Well, at least he don't go around feeling sorry for himself all the time,' Ruby shot back.

She'd gone too far.

She knew she had . . . but in the heat of the moment, she just didn't know how to pull it back.

'And what's that supposed to mean?' said Jack.

Oh goodness.

Think, Ruby.

Harry wouldn't have shouted and screamed.

'Just that millions of men are dying bravely out there, Jack. Including me own brother. And you're back here – you've been given a second chance – and . . .'

Ruby wasn't sure quite how she was planning to finish that sentence, but it didn't much matter.

Jack grabbed his cap from the stand by the door.

"I'm sorry, Ruby, but it's over,' he said, coldly.

And he stormed out without a backwards glance.

Ruby was still standing there, rooted to the ground in shock, when Robert arrived. If her life depended on it, she would have been hard-pressed to determine whether twenty seconds or five minutes had gone by.

'What the Dickens is going on?' asked Robert, by way of greeting. 'I've just passed Jack marching down Sanctuary Lane with a face like thunder and he said to ask you what's just happened.'

Ruby shook her head to bring herself back into the here and now.

What *had* just happened?

'We rowed,' she said, vaguely.

She didn't want to say anything else. She couldn't believe that Jack had just ended their courtship and saying it out loud would somehow make it true.

'Yes, I guessed *that*,' Robert was saying. 'Anything I can help with?'

'I don't know,' said Ruby. 'I think he might be gone for good.' She paused, registering the fact that Jack was possibly gone from both her life *and* from the clinic. She couldn't focus on that now. She needed to concentrate on the matter at hand. 'We got another letter from the RCVS and they're still planning to shut us down,' she said. 'Jack's furious that I didn't keep him in the loop and he also thinks he's the main problem for treating animals when he don't have the necessary qualifications.'

Robert picked up the letter with a sigh and scanned it quickly.

'I guess that was inevitable,' he said with a sigh, slapping the letter back down onto the table. 'We'll talk about Jack later, but what now? As things stand, the RCVS are arriving with the cavalry on Tuesday morning and I'm all out of ideas as to what to do next.'

'Me too,' said Ruby. 'But I ain't giving up without a fight. What about if we just ignore them and carry on regardless? We won't be here on Tuesday morning anyway.'

Robert shook his head. 'They've got the law on their side and everything could get very ugly, very quickly,' he said.

Ruby sighed in frustration. 'I suppose if Jack ain't around for now, we could truthfully say that you're the only one operating on animals,' she said. She felt terribly disloyal voicing that out loud, but maybe it really was the only way. 'We get their stamp of approval and then we get Jack back in and carry on as we were.'

Robert pursed his lips and sat on the edge of the table. 'I like the way you're thinking, but I foresee two problems. Firstly, we'll always be looking over our shoulder for another visit and if we're caught again – especially having lied to them – that really would be it. And secondly, I really don't think it's just Jack and the operations. I think they're taking exception to the rest of you diagnosing and treating animals without the necessary qualifications as well.'

Ruby huffed and sat down beside him. 'So, they want the whole bleeding lot of us to have studied at the RVC?' she said gloomily. 'Well, that just about rules out anyone from the East End, doesn't it?'

'Not necessarily,' said Robert. 'East Enders can be vets too, you know.'

Ruby gave a hollow chortle. 'In case you ain't noticed,' she said, 'Money don't grow on trees around here.'

'A conversation for another time, perhaps,' said Robert. 'Meanwhile, we have to do *something* and we have to be pretty damn quick about it.'

Ruby put her chin in her hands. 'So, what exactly is the rules about who can do what?' she said. 'It sounds like you're telling me I can't even go down the queue outside the hospital and give out tonics to poorly dogs.'

'I just know it's against the law to impersonate a veterinary practitioner,' said Robert. 'Beyond that, I'm a bit sketchy on the details, I'm afraid.'

Ruby nodded. 'Is there a library at the RCVS?' she asked. 'It might be worth popping down there to find out exactly what the rules are to see if there's something we ain't yet thought about.'

'That might be worth a try,' said Robert, thoughtfully. 'It will be shut this evening and over the weekend though, so we'd have to go now.'

Ruby made a face. 'We can't really do that,' she said.

'There ain't many of us here as it is and there's a queue of animals and their owners stretching all the way down the street already. We can't let them down – especially as it might very well be our last clinic.'

'True,' said Robert. 'So, how do you fancy another trip back to the RVC in Camden Town? There's a very good library there as well and one that *will* be open later this evening.'

'I'm not sure Mr Cotter will ever be ready for me to pay another visit,' said Ruby, with a little laugh.

'We'll give him a wide berth,' said Robert. 'But the librarian always had a soft spot for me and will hopefully lend us a hand. Somewhere in the deep, dark depths may be something that can help our cause.'

'Fingers crossed,' said Ruby, as Nellie, Maggie and a beaming Mrs Henderson arrived, ready to start their shift. 'Until tonight, then.'

The shift started and Ruby was rushed off her feet for the whole morning acutely – and miserably – aware that, with Jack missing, they were a man down. She was also acutely – and just as miserably – aware this might be the very *last* day the animal hospital was operating.

At lunchtime, however, she made a point of taking Mrs Henderson to one side.

'I wonder if I might ask you something?' she said.

'Of course, dear,' said Mrs Henderson. 'Although I'm not really in a position to make another donation at the moment. Mr Henderson insists . . .'

'No, no. It's nothing like that,' said Ruby, hastily. 'Perhaps I might buy you a cuppa next door? What I want to ask you is a little . . . unusual, and I would hate for someone to overhear.'

'How very mysterious,' said Mrs Henderson, as the two women headed next door to the Fishers. 'No more bricks?' she added, looking at the newly glazed bakery window.

'No, thank goodness,' said Ruby, crossing her fingers behind her back, as they sat down and placed their order. 'It's about Cook.'

Mrs Henderson visibly started. '*Cook?*' she echoed. 'As in Lillie Fletcher?'

'Yes.'

'Well, of all the things I thought you might want to talk to me about, Cook was not one of them,' said Mrs Henderson with a laugh.

'She works at the munitions factory now. She's one of the policewomen there.'

'Yes, I heard she'd joined the police,' said Mrs Henderson, 'But how funny you two have ended up together again. Just like old times, eh?'

'Not at all like old times,' said Ruby with a grimace. 'Mrs Henderson, I don't know if you remember that when I were leaving service, you made some comment about Cook having stolen some items? I didn't give it much thought at the time – I thought you was just angry she'd left you high and dry – but just recently . . .'

'Up to her old tricks again, is she?' interrupted Mrs Henderson dryly.

Ruby paused. She needed to be very careful. 'Well, I ain't certain . . .'

'That's the problem,' said Mrs Henderson vehemently. 'None of us ever are. When she moved to us, Isabel

Drage – her previous employer from St John's Wood – warned us to be on our guard. She said she suspected some light fingers but that it was difficult to prove anything. And it was the same with us. Little bits and bobs going missing, Cook occasionally found wandering where she shouldn't . . . but impossible to conclusively put two and two together. Oh, she's a slippery one, alright. What's she been up to at your place?'

'It's just a rumour,' said Ruby. 'And, again, it's impossible to say for sure. But that's very useful to know. Thank you. Just one more thing,' she added. 'If things was going missing, how did you know that it weren't me? After all, I had far more call to be wandering than Cook.'

Mrs Henderson gave a tinkling laugh. 'You? You haven't got a dishonest bone in your body, Ruby, my love,' she said. 'You're one of life's good people.'

Ruby was quiet.

Thinking of how she had treated Jack recently, she really couldn't be sure of that at all.

Ruby started work that afternoon feeling thoughtful but was soon swept up into the organised chaos. Then a man with bushy whiskers sitting in the corner next to old Mr Atkins touched Ruby's arm as she passed. 'You the Archer girl?' he asked.

Ruby smiled. 'I suppose I am,' she said. 'Although I don't very often get called that.'

'I'm Walter Reid,' the man said. And, when Ruby looked blank, he added, 'Billy Reid's pa.'

Ruby hesitated, trying to work it out.

Yes, the handsome soldier.

And Chien.

'How's he doing?' asked Ruby, crossing her fingers that there was no bad news.

'He's well,' replied Mr Reid. 'Back to training for the time being. He'll be home for Christmas.'

That *was* good news.

'And Chien?' asked Ruby. 'Is he why you're here?'

'No, no,' said Mr Reid. 'Me granddaughter has just gone in with her pet rat. Chien is as right as rain now and keeping us all on our toes. That were a good thing you did for us all back there.'

'It's a much-needed service,' said Ruby. 'We ain't got any "guests" at the moment, but I have a feeling the demand is going to get higher and higher.'

She turned to go, but Mr Reid tapped her on the arm again.

'I knew your pa,' he said. 'Often saw him down the boozer. Top bloke he was. Funny. Generous too.'

'Yes,' said Ruby, sadly. Pa had been all of those things and much, much more.

'Still, your boy's a chip off the old block, ain't he?' Mr Reid continued.

What boy?

Mr Reid had clearly got her muddled with someone else, which was a shame because that meant that he probably hadn't known Pa after all.

'I'm afraid I don't know who you mean,' she said, politely.

'Your brother. Charlie. He's doing a decent job at my place. Excellent with the animals, he is.'

Charlie.

'Sorry,' said Ruby. 'You mean Charlie is *working* at your place?'

Mr Reid looked confused. 'Pardon me,' he said. 'I just assumed that you knew.'

'Oh, you know Charlie!' said Ruby, with what she hoped was a carefree laugh. 'He can be such a dark horse sometimes. And . . . your place? May I ask where that is?'

'Stables down by the docks,' said Mr Reid. 'Said he needed the money.'

'I'm sure he did,' said Ruby, dryly. 'Only I dread to think what for.'

'For Christmas presents, of course,' said Mr Reid, apparently without guile. 'He were very clear on that. He wants to treat you all after your recent loss. He wants to buy your ma some Worth perfume; I ain't sure he'll manage to save enough for *that* – not on what I can afford to pay him – but he'll be able to get her something nice.'

Oh!

Lovely Charlie.

How Ruby had maligned him.

No wonder his hands were filthy.

'What sort of hours does he work?' asked Ruby, her mind going nineteen to the dozen?

'Weekdays, three until five-thirty and weekends ten until three,' rattled off Mr Reid. 'Ever so reliable, he is. Hasn't missed a single shift since October . . .'

'But he has missed rather a lot of school,' said Ruby dryly.

'School!' said Mr Reid. 'How old is your brother then?'

'Fourteen.'

'Well, I'll be blowed. Little tinker said he were sixteen and had another job on the trams!'

Ruby laughed. 'Please don't sack him for it,' she said. 'And it's clearly meant to be a secret, so please don't mention that we had this conversation either. But maybe if he carries on working for you after Christmas, he could work hours that ain't actually during the school day?'

'Leave it with me.' Mr Reid patted Ruby on the shoulder and wandered off chuckling to himself. 'Little tinker . . .'

21

It felt strange going back to the Royal Veterinary College that evening.

Arriving with Robert, Ruby felt like a different woman. Robert's smart motor hadn't hurt matters, several of the louche students dropping their cynicism and making a point of coming over to check it out as Robert swept into the courtyard. Ruby even fancied that one or two of them made a point of checking *her* out as well and that made her feel rather confused and sad.

Was it really all over with Jack?

Anyway, the point was that she no longer felt an imposter at the RVC.

She was no longer an insignificant little girl from the East End who had no right to be at the college. She might not be studying to be a veterinary practitioner, but look at what she *had* achieved. In the few short months since she had last been there in the spring, she had opened up her animal hospital and now treated dozens of sick and injured animals every week. The RCVS might want her operation shut down – but some might see the fact they clearly viewed her as a threat as a measure of her success. Either way, she had every reason to be proud.

Ruby was nervous, as well, of course. Successful or not, the Sanctuary Lane Animal Hospital was a tiny operation and here they were going up against the might of a huge, official institution with a royal charter to boot. There was every chance that they would lose, but she simply could not stand by and let that happen.

The two presented themselves at reception, where Robert showed his alumnae pass and introduced Ruby as his colleague. Ruby, rolling that around her tongue, decided that she rather liked it. Of course, everyone would assume that she was his secretary – or worse – but no matter. She knew that she had founded the hospital where Robert – a bona fide veterinary surgeon – donated his time and his expertise.

And then Robert was sweeping her across neoclassical quadrangles and down dimly lit corridors, against the crowds of braying young rakes who were heading in the opposite direction towards the bright lights of London on a Friday evening in December. It was almost as if the war wasn't happening and Ruby couldn't help wondering how they had all managed to avoid enlisting.

Maybe they all had flat feet too!

Finally, they arrived at the library, deep in the bowels of the building. The librarian, Miss Jacobson, was a homely woman with dark hair and a pronounced jaw, who not only recognised Robert, but almost fell on him with delight and excitement. Robert had, she explained, been one of her star pupils; he had not only studied diligently but had been invariably polite and well-mannered in his dealings with the library staff. Given that Robert's father was Sir Emrys Smith – not always polite *nor* well-mannered – Ruby thought again that it was nothing short of a miracle Robert had ended up as charming as he was.

Ruby stood politely whilst Miss Jacobson started getting – a clearly intrigued – Robert up to date with the fortunes of his fellow students. It turned out that a dispiriting number of them *had* gone to the front and Miss Jacobson seemed hellbent on giving Robert a detailed rundown on every single one of them. After a while, she coughed discreetly and, then, a little more loudly. This fond reunion was all well and good, but it wouldn't help them save the hospital.

'Yes. Sorry.' Robert, appeared to suddenly remember that Ruby was there. 'We're here to look at the laws governing veterinary practice, Miss Jacobson. Perhaps you could point us in the right direction.'

'Of course,' said Miss Jacobson. 'After what happened to poor Albert Wheeler when he fell foul of the law, we *all* need to make sure we stay on the straight and narrow. The various Veterinary Surgeons Acts are probably your best starting points. This way.'

She led the way across the room and pointed at some slim blue publications. 'Here you are,' she said.

'Thank you,' said Robert. 'Er, what *did* happen to Albert Wheeler? What did he do and did he get struck off?'

Miss Jacobson pursed her lips and drew Robert to one side and Ruby was left on her own. Desultorily, she pulled down the first publication. She didn't hold out much hope that it would help – and she didn't really know exactly what she was looking for in the first place . . .

This first document was the Royal Charter of 1844. It recognised the veterinary 'art' as a profession, gave the College the power to administer examinations and set out details of the Council formation. There was absolutely nothing of any interest and Ruby slid the book back into place with a little sigh.

Hopeless.

Still, she had to keep going.

The Supplemental Charters of 1876 and 1879 seemed even less promising. Allowing members to vote by post and giving Council the powers to appoint a secretary were both of absolutely no relevance, nor were sections that only referred to Scotland. This was a waste of time. She should really be at home, icing the Christmas cake with Ma or trying to talk to Jack.

And where on earth was Robert?

Ruby pulled down the Veterinary Surgeons Act of 1881. If this didn't contain anything helpful, she would give it all up as a bad job and suggest that they left. As she had feared, there was more indeterminable stuff about Scotland . . . and now Ireland too . . .

But wait.

What was this?

Ruby had been about to snap the book shut when something caught her eye. The Act made it unlawful for anyone other than a member of the College to be styled a veterinary surgeon or veterinary practitioner or to charge for performing any veterinary operation.

That seemed pretty cut and dried – and largely unsurprising. It was pretty much what Robert had already told her.

And yet, might it not also be good news?

After all, if you looked at it the other way around, there was nothing to stop any individual undertaking the treatment of animals. The act might make it illegal to claim the title of 'veterinary surgeon', but it did not make it illegal to carry out animal treatment as an unqualified practitioner, especially if you were not charging to do so.

Ruby shut her eyes.

Was she missing something?

She opened it again . . . and the clause was still there in black and white.

Swallowing her excitement, Ruby turned quickly to the other books. Notwithstanding what she had just read, there might be something in one of the subsequent charters that rendered it null and void and there was no point in getting anyone's hopes up only to have them dashed again.

But there was nothing.

And, as if on cue, here was Robert striding across the library to join her. He was rubbing the bridge of his nose, his intense, clever face almost handsome in its solemnity.

'Sorry about that,' he said. 'An awful lot of news about the chaps I studied alongside to catch up on and not much of it good, I'm afraid.'

'I'm ever so sorry to hear that,' said Ruby, sincerely. 'But I think I might have something here to cheer you up a little.'

She pointed to the relevant section of the 1881 Act and stepped back to give Robert a chance to digest it.

Had she got it right – or was there some loophole she hadn't yet considered?

Please say that she had got it right!

'By Jove,' said Robert, slapping the table. 'I think you've only gone and done it!'

Ruby's face relaxed into a beam and it was only then that she realised she had been holding her breath.

'I thought so,' she said in delight. 'There ain't nothing which says we can't treat animals – particularly if we ain't charging. Only that we can't claim to be qualified veterinary practitioners or to have graduated from the RVC.'

'Exactly,' said Robert. 'And I don't think we *do* claim that. It's a little complicated because obviously I *am* qualified and am entitled to say so – but we certainly don't claim that everyone is. Nor, clearly, do we charge. Hallelujah!'

Ruby could have kissed him, but she settled for hugging herself in excitement instead.

'Oh, this is marvellous,' she said. 'I feel like we've been reprieved. But what should we do now? We've barely got time to write a letter to the RCVS before Tuesday.'

Robert tapped the table decisively. 'Let's write the letter now,' he said. 'And then we'll drive home via their offices in Red Lion Square – it's in the West End, not too far from here – and drop it off in person. That way, we'll know decisively that they've received it well before Tuesday. Oh, this is just marvellous. They don't have a leg to stand on.'

And that was what they did. Backed up by the legislature (and Robert's impressive turn of phrase), the letter took no time to draft. Ruby wrote it out carefully in her neatest writing and then Robert was bidding farewell to an almost tearful Miss Jacobson and the two of them were on their way back through the corridors and quadrangles to Robert's motor.

'Oh, I feel like celebrating,' said Ruby twenty minutes later, after they had dropped the letter off. She stretched her arms above her head as the motor nosed down the quiet December streets. 'I can hardly believe we've pulled that off.'

She and Robert were a team, working through problems logically together.

No drama.

No bickering.

Robert turned to her. 'I *would* say don't count your chickens,' he said, 'but in this case, I think things are pretty cut and dried. If the RCVS had taken legal advice, they would have known they didn't have a leg to stand on and, to be honest, I'm surprised they didn't know it in any case. In fact, the more I think about it, I suspect they *did* know it and just thought they'd blind us with fancy terms, hoping that we would back down. They clearly feel threatened by us and by the precedent we might be setting. So, in terms of celebrating, might I make a suggestion?'

'You'd like second helpings of pie, mash and liquor?' pre-empted Ruby with a giggle.

Suddenly the thought of extending the evening with Robert seemed very appealing.

Robert laughed. 'Not exactly,' he said. 'But I happen to have a booking at The Savoy this evening. With everything that's been going on, I forgot to cancel it and, as luck would have it, it's only a stone's throw away from here. I'd be delighted if you'd accompany me there if that takes your fancy.'

Ruby was taken off guard.

This was a different Robert talking and she wasn't at all sure how to respond.

One the one hand, the booking had, no doubt, been

made for him and Leah. With Leah currently languishing in Holloway Prison, would it be terribly insensitive for Ruby to take her place?

Then again, Ruby badly wanted to say yes. This was *The Savoy* and who knew when she would have the chance to dine there again. She could almost hear Leah's voice in her ear, urging her to go ahead.

'I'm not really dressed for the occasion,' she stalled, gesticulating to the perfectly serviceable but hardly fancy skirt and blouse she had been wearing all day.

Robert laughed. 'Me neither,' he said. 'But this is wartime and I daresay no one will bat an eyelid. Besides, I have it on good authority that part of The Savoy has been given over as a place for soldiers to convalesce for the duration, so I'm not sure the old rules even apply anymore. Please say yes, Ruby,' he added, in altogether more serious a tone. 'I would be honoured to spend an evening in your company.'

Ruby paused, pushing away a slight feeling of guilt and unease. She really didn't think that Leah would mind, at all, and would probably relish hearing all the details when Ruby next visited. And, as for Jack! Ruby suddenly realised that she felt angry rather than upset where he was concerned. How dare he end their courtship so abruptly and then just storm out without giving her a chance to respond? Why did he have to be so dramatic? No matter how he might have been feeling, she was worth more than that and she would show him. A handsome man wanted to take her out to dinner at The Savoy – The Savoy! – and she was jolly well going to accept.

'Yes, then,' said Ruby, clapping her hands together in glee.

How much had changed since that evening several months ago when Robert had attended a poorly Mac at her home and had dismissed her as a silly little girl with ideas above her station. Now he was treating her as a woman – and a rather attractive woman at that – and Ruby found that she didn't mind that at all.

How could she ever have thought him ugly?

The Savoy was magical.

Ruby had heard Mr and Mrs Henderson talk about the hotel from time to time, so she knew that it stood for the height of grandeur and that its pre-war parties had been legendary throughout London. In fact, Ruby distinctly remembered Mrs Henderson telling her about an American millionaire who had hosted a 'Gondola Party', which had involved the central courtyard being flooded to a depth of four feet, the guests dining in an enormous gondola and a baby elephant bringing in a five-foot birthday cake!

There was nothing quite as outlandish on display that evening but – despite whatever privations the war might have brought to the hotel – everything was still the byword in elegance and refinement. The décor was lavish and sophisticated; the sumptuous furnishings, intricate chandeliers, and exquisite floral arrangements enough to make Ruby's head spin. And as for the Christmas decorations! There were none of Aunt Maggie's cotton-wool balls *here*, thank you very much: instead, enough beautifully bedecked and illuminated Christmas trees and garlands to light up Silvertown! And, despite Robert's assurances, it seemed that a dress code was still very much in place. The gentlemen were all wearing formal attire and the ladies were dazzling in glamorous gowns, only adding to the sense of extravagance and exclusivity.

All in all, Ruby felt as if she had been transported to another universe.

Robert tucked Ruby's hand into the crook of his arm and escorted her through to the restaurant, where they were greeted by an impeccably attired maître d'hôtel. Robert smoothly attributed their own casual dress to important charity work – goodness; how grand that sounded! – and received a gracious bow in return. And then they were being ushered to their table in the centre of the restaurant, close – but not too close – to the pianist and Robert was smiling at her and holding out her chair. Ruby sat down as if in a dream, taking in all the fine china and polished silverware – and then smothered a grin because all she could think was how hard the poor saps behind the scenes must have worked to get everything so shiny and sparkling.

'Shall I order for you?' asked Robert.

Ruby knew that this was norm amongst the upper classes but . . . absolutely not! There were several dishes she had seen Cook prepare and had always longed to try and she certainly wasn't going to pass up the opportunity without a fight.

'Would it be very forward to choose for meself?' she ventured.

'Not at all,' said Robert, with a smile. 'What do you fancy?'

'Oysters Rockefeller, duck à l'orange and peach Melba,'

said Ruby immediately, hoping that she didn't sound too greedy.

'Well, what a surprising young lady you are,' said Robert with a laugh. 'Excellent choices, if I might say so myself, and I will join you in them all. And might I suggest sole meunière as the fish course?'

'Done,' said Ruby, happily.

The wine arrived. Ruby took a deep draught – rich, heady and aromatic – and tried to imprint the scene on her memory. She loved Silvertown and she loved her family and friends, but *this* was how the other half lived. She had never seen herself belonging in this world – it had always been 'us' versus 'them' – but maybe . . .

'Here's to you. *Us*,' said Robert, raising his glass to her. 'Meeting your expectations?'

Ruby grinned back at him. '*Rather*,' she breathed out. 'It's all marvellous. But I think I feel like you did in the pie and eel shop that time we all went to the cinema.'

How much had changed since then.

Harry dying, she and Jack parting ways and Leah in prison. Part of Ruby longed to tell Robert what she had discovered about Leah being innocent, but surely that was Leah's news to impart. Besides, Ruby suddenly found that she didn't very much want to talk – or think – about Leah anymore. She just wanted to lose herself in the occasion, the surroundings and Robert's rather fine chestnut-brown eyes . . .

'You put me at my ease when I thought parsley liquor was an after-dinner drink, so I'll try to do the same here,' he said. 'These ridiculous table settings for example . . .'

'Thank you,' interrupted Ruby with a grin. 'But don't

forget I used to be in service and wait at table, so I do know how it all works, ta very much.'

Robert raised his glass to her again. 'You are elegance personified,' he said and Ruby's heart, quite unexpectedly, did a little flipflop.

Oh, Lordy.

The oysters arrived in their rich herb and spinach sauce. Their waitress, a smooth-faced redhead no older than Ruby, was wearing a name badge proclaiming that her name was Ivy. Despite her impeccable appearance and obvious training, her accent was distinctly East End and Ruby felt an immediate surge of kinship and empathy. Ruby might be being waited on today, but she instinctively understood that Ivy was bone-tired, her feet were killing her and that, behind the scenes, all was not as calm and serene as on the restaurant floor.

'Do you want to talk about Jack?' asked Robert gently, when they had exhausted talking about what they had just discovered at the RVC and Ruby had scraped her plate clean to finish off every last drop of scrumptious sauce.

Ruby sighed.

She didn't.

Not at all.

She didn't want anything to cast a shadow on this enchanted evening; the marvellous surroundings, the exquisite food, the lovely company.

Ruby put her cutlery neatly together on the plate as she had seen Mr and Mrs Henderson do a hundred times. 'It's over,' she said simply.

'Oh?' Robert sat up taller in his chair and didn't take his eyes from Ruby's.

'Yes,' said Ruby. 'He ended it this morning.'

'Oh, my dear,' said Robert. 'I had no idea.'

He lent forward and put his hand over Ruby's. Then he sat back but left his hand covering hers. His hand was warm and dry and Ruby found that she rather liked it. She pushed away the thought that Leah most definitely would not.

Goodness me.

What if . . . ?

She snatched her wine glass up at exactly the same time as Ivy reappeared with her fish course. Glass and plate collided midair, the glass wobbled and a few drops of red wine sloshed onto Ruby's lap. Robert gently withdrew his hand.

Ivy was mortified. 'I'm ever so sorry, Miss,' she gabbled, her accent getting stronger by the second. She put the plates down quickly and then grabbed a napkin, dipping it into Ruby's glass of water. 'Here,' she said, bending over and preparing to dab at Ruby's skirt. 'Let me.'

'Please don't worry,' said Ruby, taking the napkin. 'Honestly, it were me fault, waving me glass around like that. And luckily me skirt's dark, so it won't even show.'

And here was the maître d', appearing unbidden at their table, full of smooth contrition whilst looking daggers at Ivy. Ruby waved him away; she really didn't want Ivy getting into trouble on her behalf.

Order restored, Ruby tucked into her sole, which was, if possible, even more delectable than the oysters, and tried very not to think 'what ifs' about Robert.

'Jack?' said Robert gently, cutting across her thoughts?

Ruby shrugged. She didn't really want to talk about Jack. She would far rather talk about . . .

Oh, stop it, Ruby!

She took a swig of wine. 'He were furious that I hadn't kept him in the loop over the RCVS and I were furious that he called me "support staff",' she admitted.

Robert gave a bark of laughter. 'Support staff?' he echoed incredulously. 'You set the darned hospital up, for goodness' sake. No wonder you were narked.'

'I *know*,' said Ruby, feeling herself getting cross all over again.

'I suppose he has a point, though,' Robert added thoughtfully.

Ruby put down her cutlery. 'What do you mean?' she asked, indignantly.

'Well, I certainly wouldn't call you support staff,' said Robert, 'but you could be actively treating the animals, if that was what you wanted to do.'

Ruby bristled. 'I run the reception,' she said stiffly. 'I book everyone in and out and I *do* diagnosis and treat where I can.'

'I know,' said Robert. 'You do a sterling job at keeping everything shipshape and running smoothly. All I'm saying is that you aren't as hands-on with the patients as perhaps you might be.'

'But I ain't trained . . .'

She hadn't really considered any of this before. Oh, of course, back when she had been working at Nellie's dog-food barrow at the market, trying to glean anything she could about caring for sick and injured animals, she probably *had* imagined herself taking more of a pivotal role in treating the patients. But she couldn't have imagined back then that both a qualified veterinary practitioner and a man who'd had heaps of hands-on experience with animals at the front would both volunteer their services for free.

So, what was she supposed to have done?

Instructed Robert to man the reception desk whilst she wrestled with broken bones?

Told Jack to make the tea whist she operated on a twisted gut?

It was ridiculous.

Before she could formulate an answer, a new waitress arrived to clear their plates. Ruby wondered where Ivy was and then silently answered her own question. Being bawled out by the maître d' in the kitchen, no doubt. Ruby had been in the same situation many a time for a real or imagined transgression . . .

The plight of the working classes.

'Jack isn't trained either,' said Robert. 'Oh, he's got a lot of hands-on experience – even at operating – and he's wonderful with the animals, but he isn't formally qualified. You could do one better than him and train to be a veterinary practitioner.'

'I've got more chance of going to the bleeding moon.'

'But what about if someone else paid for you?' said Robert.

Ruby sighed. 'Who?' she said. 'Me fairy godmother?'

'No,' said Robert. 'My father.'

Ruby paused, glass halfway to her mouth.

'Your *father*?'

'Yes,' said Robert.

'Your father wants to pay for me to become a vet?' Ruby echoed.

It was inconceivable.

Robert laughed. 'Not exactly,' he said. 'But, after what happened to Queenie, it seems he's had a change of heart about the need for animal hospitals such as ours. And he's made a really very generous donation to me to distribute on his behalf where I think it will be most useful.' He paused and sipped his wine. 'I didn't say anything at the time because, of course, the very future of the animal hospital was in jeopardy – no thanks to him! – and we all had other things on our minds. But now that things are a little clearer, I'm wondering if we might use that money to train you up at the RVC. It won't be easy, of course – you're not at all their usual type of student – but the usual entrance qualifications might be relaxed because of the war and I would vouch for you and . . .'

'Stop!' Ruby held up a hand. 'Please. I need to *think*.'

She took a deep breath and closed her eyes, trying to calm her breathing and to get her thoughts in some sort of order.

She had never ever thought that training to be a vet might even be a possibility.

It would be beyond her wildest dreams, of course, but, at the end of the day, was it a dream that she even wanted? Oh, waltzing thought the quadrangles between lectures would have a certain charm, and learning all about animals would, of course, be just heaven.

But all those rakes, all those regulations, all that *establishment* . . .

'Can I ask you something, Robert?' she asked.

'Of course.' Robert's hand reached out for hers again.

His teeth, in the candlelight, were very white and even.

Upper-class teeth.

'Why do you think it would be a good idea for me to train to be a vet?'

Robert spread his spare hand wide on the table. 'As I hope you know, I think very highly of you,' he said. 'I know you haven't had the best start in life but training to be a vet would open doors that otherwise would remain firmly shut to you. It would be an opportunity to get out of the East End, it would open out your social circle, expose you to people who otherwise – frankly – wouldn't give you the time of day . . .'

Ivy was back, carefully carrying two plates of duck. Robert ignored her, but Ruby gave her a small smile, which Ivy returned. Her eyes were red rimmed.

'I'm sorry the service is a little off tonight,' murmured Robert as Ivy left. 'It's difficult to get quality staff during the war, but at least you can't fault the food.'

He let go of her hand, speared a bean and suddenly it was as though Ruby was looking down a kaleidoscope and all the pretty, but meaningless, colour had finally formed a coherent picture.

Like Ivy, Ruby was from the East End of London.

What was more, Ruby was proud of it.

Far from not having had the best start in life, she had been truly blessed. She'd been born to parents who loved her unconditionally and who had worked hard to make the most of what they'd been given. And, of course, Ruby wished to make the most of every opportunity that came her way, but she didn't need, or want, to escape the East End in order to do that. Jack would appreciate all this in a way that Robert could never, ever do. Jack, for all his faults, had understood her and accepted her just as she was. She hadn't had to change or to prove a single thing to earn his love.

Ruby suddenly realised with every fibre of her being that Robert had just been a distraction and she wanted Jack back. She had said some things she didn't mean – some unforgivable things that she couldn't take back, but, surely, she could try to make amends.

And as for training to be a vet? At the end of the day, Ruby just wanted to help the animals. And she had just spent all evening proving that you didn't actually need to be a vet in order to be able to do just that. Robert and Jack had both had points; she *did* want to get more involved in animal treatment, but she didn't want to pay to have a string of fancy initials after her name in order to do so. She wanted to learn on the job, as Jack had done, and that would do perfectly well both for her and for the animals that she would be honoured to treat.

She smiled gently at Robert. 'I don't want to train at the RVC, thank you very much,' she said. 'It ain't for me for all sorts of reasons – but I am very grateful to you for asking.'

Robert's gaze was steady. 'I see,' he said, simply.

The understanding that passed between them went much deeper than the words alone suggested, and the fragile suggestion from earlier in the evening quietly popped under its own weight.

Ruby finished the last ambrosial mouthful of duck and put her cutlery together. 'I would, however, like you to train me up to treat the animals,' she said. 'You've quite right, I *do* want to get more involved, but on me own terms. And you might consider Jack for the RVC instead – after all, he were the one who operated on your father's dog, so Sir Emrys might like to thank him directly. He may well give you a different answer.'

'Right you are,' said Robert.

Ruby nodded. Robert was a good man, a principled man; Leah was lucky to have him. And that was that. There was nothing more; no real attraction between the two of them – or maybe it had been real in the way that the morning mist over the Thames was real before it disappeared in the bright light of day.

She loved Jack – she knew that now – and she couldn't wait to get back to the East End and to start putting things right.

The pianist finished a rousing rendition of 'The Entertainer' with a little flourish and Ruby and Robert turned away from each other to give him a polite round of applause. When they turned back to their peach Melbas, it was as if they had made a tacit and silent agreement to put the conversation on a different footing. Robert told her all about the new ragtime music sweeping across America and Ruby, in turn, told *him* all about the raucous East End music halls she had gone to as a child. And so, the evening ended on a light note with fun and laughter and merriment.

'That were absolutely magnificent,' said Ruby, rubbing her tummy with satisfaction, as the bill arrived. 'Thank you so much.'

'Tiptop food, as always,' said Robert, counting out notes.

'I'm not sure I'll add a tip this time, though,' he added. 'War or no war, the service wasn't up to scratch.'

Ruby didn't answer. But when Robert excused himself to go to the gents, she made a point of pressing a ten bob note into Ivy's hand.

Now, more than ever, East Enders had to stick together.

22

Saturday, 16 December 1916

Ruby tossed and turned that night, unable to get comfortable, let alone to sleep.

There were a thousand and one things that could have kept her up, of course, but there was really only one thing foremost in her thoughts. Jack. She would pop round the next day and apologise . . .

Meanwhile, there was something that had niggled away at the back of her mind all through her visit to the RVC and her subsequent visit to The Savoy the day before.

And that something was the new information that she had been given by Mr Reid.

Firstly, of course, Ruby knew that she owed a huge apology to the much-maligned Charlie. Mr Reid had made a point of saying that Charlie hadn't missed a shift at the stables since October, which meant her brother couldn't possibly have thrown the brick through Fisher's front window. There were no two ways about it: Charlie was innocent and Ruby felt terrible for the way she had gone on and on at him with baseless accusations. She needed to apologise – and indeed she would – but she needed to be careful about how she handled it. Charlie clearly wanted his job to be a secret so that he could spoil them all at Christmas – and the last thing Ruby wanted to do was to spoil the surprise.

The question was: who had thrown the brick through the bakery window?

It could have been a perfect stranger of course – someone else who had discovered quite independently that the Fishers were German, or who had just randomly attacked the shop without rhyme nor reason. But Ruby felt sure that she had recognised the scoundrel – something about the build or the gait or the clothing – and, all through the small hours, the thought wouldn't leave her alone.

The first thing that Ruby did the next morning was to confront her mother as the stirred the breakfast porridge on the stove.

'I know the brick were you, Ma,' she said, without preamble, leaning down to make a fuss of the kittens.

If Ruby had expected her mother to demur, she would have been very much mistaken. In fact, her Ma gave her something suspiciously close to a smirk. 'I wondered how long it would take you to work that out,' she said.

Despite everything, Ruby felt a bolt of shock at her mother's admission.

Ma!

'It took me a while to work out,' she admitted. 'I blamed Charlie at first. But then I suddenly worked out that it couldn't have been him and it was *you*. You was wearing Harry's cap and his old Hammers jacket. I'd seen they was missing from the back of his bedroom door.'

'Bull's-eye,' said Ma, with a grin, making no effort to deny it.

'But why, Ma?' said Ruby, completely nonplussed. 'I thought you liked working at the Fishers.'

'Of course, I like working there,' said Ma, taking the pan off the stove. 'What ain't to like? The Fishers have been very good to me and it certainly beats working at the laundry.'

Ruby started taking the bowls out of the cupboard. 'Then, whatever possessed you to toss a brick through their window,' she persisted. 'There are lots of other German places which ain't quite so close to home.'

Ma shrugged. 'I just felt I had to do something,' she said. 'It might not have been the right thing to do – but it were the easiest thing to do, if you know what I mean. This blasted war! There's no one to shout at, no one to take it out on . . . you're just expected to carry on as if nothing's happened.'

'I ain't taken it out on anyone,' Ruby reminded her.

After all, she had lost a much-loved brother and she had just carried on with her job and the animal hospital regardless.

Ma gave her a look. 'I think you have, poppet,' she said, softly.

'Pardon?' Ruby was totally confused. 'I don't know what you mean.'

'I rather think you might have taken it out on Jack,' said Ma in the same gentle tone.

'Jack?' Ruby screwed her face up. 'But that's entirely different.'

'Is it?' countered Ma. 'I think they might be one and the same thing. It seems to me that you've managed by throwing yourself into activities here, there and everywhere and that you might have shut out the most important people. I threw a brick and it's over and done with and, meanwhile, you and that lovely boy ain't talking no more . . .'

Ruby held up a hand. 'No,' she said. She couldn't cope with this. 'Don't change the subject, Ma. We're talking about *you*.'

Ma smiled. 'Alright,' she said. 'Look, I don't blame the Fishers personally for what happened to Harry; I'd be a fool to do so. Remember what your pa used to say about us having more in common with working Germans than with our own powers-that-be? But, for one glorious – or stupid – moment, I managed to convince myself that the Fishers represented the Hun and all they've taken from us. I went to work and then I came home, claiming a headache. I took one of the bricks that Charlie keeps in his room and I took Harry's cap and jacket from the chest in in my bedroom and I walked back and chucked the brick through the window with all me might. It felt good, let me tell you. But, ten minutes later they had just gone back to being Anna and Fred Fisher and the feeling had gone and I felt so guilty that I resigned from my job.'

'Oh, Ma.' Despite it all, Ruby found that she was laughing. 'But the men chased after you. How on earth did you get away?'

Ma smirked again. 'I dashed into the close where I'd grown up and up the staircase of one of the tenement buildings. I know those alleyways better than just about anyone. And then I whipped off Harry's clothes, stuffed them in a bag and I was back to being me again. Just a little old lady going about her business.'

'Oh, Ma,' said Ruby again. 'You're not old. But you are very, very naughty.'

'It did make me feel better,' said Ma. 'I'll never get over losing Harry, but I do feel that I started to climb out of the hole a bit after that. And I made sure that no one were near the front counter and that I didn't hurt no one; the shop were empty – Anna Fisher had nipped round the back and the girls were all serving customers in the café.'

Ruby nodded. She had vaguely noticed – though the fog of everything else that was going on – that Ma had been a bit more herself over the past few days. Proper homecooked meals were appearing with greater regularity, Ma was taking a bit more care with her appearance and Ruby had caught her on more than one occasion laughing at the kittens. Ma had even made the Christmas pudding, although the shortages were now really beginning to hit and she had had to substitute tea for the rum and apples and carrots for the dried fruit. Still, it was lovely to see her finally throwing herself into the Christmas plans as the big day approached. Ma – and all of them – still had a long way to go, but it was a start.

In the meantime, weekend or not, Ruby still had a mountain of things to do. She bolted down her porridge, then stood and kissed Ma on the top of her head.

'I'm popping out,' she said, already halfway out of the kitchen door.

'Off to see Jack?' asked Ma hopefully.

'Perhaps.'

*

Of course, she was off to see Jack.

Ruby fairly ran down Sanctuary Lane, Mac at her heels, and only slowed down when she was standing outside Jack's house. Without giving her time to second guess herself, she knocked smartly on his door. It opened seconds later and there was Jack, leaning on the door jamb and staring down at her. Ruby looked at his dear, sweet face, the broad mouth, and the green eyes, and noticed that the mouth wasn't smiling and the eyes were as hard as steel.

'I'm ever so sorry, Jack,' she started. 'I came as soon as I could and . . .'

Jack held up a hand. 'Save your breath,' he said, coldly, bending down to pat Mac. 'I know exactly where you was last night.'

'Yes,' said Ruby. 'I went to the . . .'

'. . . Savoy. With Robert.'

'Oh! How on earth did you know?'

'Because, fool that I am, I came round to see you late last night,' said Jack. 'I thought maybe I'd been hasty, that perhaps we could talk. Charlie told me you was out, so I wandered around for a while and then I saw it all. Robert's motor, you getting out of it, kissing him and thanking him for a memorable evening . . .'

'Yes, but . . .'

'No "buts" Ruby. I really have had enough of all this. I'll going to take a break from the hospital so we don't keep running into each other and please don't come to the house again.'

One last stroke of Mac and the door shut firmly in her face.

*

Halfway up Sanctuary Lane – and almost blinded by tears – Ruby ran into Dot.

'Ooh, I'm glad I bumped into you,' said Dot. 'Hang about; are you quite alright?'

'No,' said Ruby, wiping her eyes. 'Not at all, in fact, Jack and I . . .' She broke off, not trusting herself to continue.

Dot touched her arm. 'Cuppa?' she said. 'A problem shared, and all that . . . ?'

Despite everything, Ruby swallowed a smile. She had certainly got more than she bargained for the last time Dot had offered her tea and sympathy.

'I'd better not,' she said. 'Got a lot I need to do today.'

'Right you are,' said Dot. 'I hope you patch things up and I'm always here if you need me. By the way, I forgot to mention yesterday that I won't be able to run that class on feeding your dog next Tuesday. It's a shame because people are bound to feed their dogs all sorts of unsuitable table scraps over Christmas and then wonder why Rover's being sick.'

'That's a pity,' said Ruby, with a surge of irritation.

Now that she had an inkling that the animal hospital was safe from closure, it was important to keep to their planned schedule in the run up to Christmas.

'Sorry,' said Dot, pulling a little face. 'I've been meaning to tell you; we're going away for a few days next week.'

'Right,' said Ruby. Why *hadn't* Dot mentioned it before? 'Where are you going so close to Christmas?'

'To my aunt in Gloucestershire. She ain't been well.'

'But what about the bakery?' asked Ruby. There was nothing wrong with taking a break, of course – after all, relatives got poorly, even in the middle of a war – but the timing *did* seem to be a little odd. 'Surely the run up to Christmas is one of the busiest times of the year for the bakery. And what about the factory? They letting you have time off, and all?'

Dot shrugged a little defensively. 'Aunt Louisa can't help when she's ill, can she?' she said. 'We're getting in part-time staff to do the morning bake, your Aunt Maggie is stepping up her hours, and the factory have been very understanding.'

'Fair enough,' said Ruby. That told *her*. 'Will you be back in time for the bazaar on the twenty-second?'

A wave of guilt and worry swept over her. She had barely given the bazaar a second thought and, even though she knew Elspeth had assembled a strong, committed team around herself, Ruby *had* rather neglected them all.

'Of course, I will,' said Dot. 'I wouldn't miss *that* for the world. And, I'll be back on Thursday to help set up for it. Now, shall I put a poster up saying the class next Tuesday is cancelled?'

Ruby hesitated. 'Not yet,' she said. 'I'm just thinking, *I* might run the class instead.'

'*You?*' said Dot, with unflattering surprise.

'Yes. Why not?' said Ruby.

It was her turn to be slightly defensive.

She'd never done anything like that before but, at the end of the day, why not indeed? Jack had said she was support staff and Robert had made it perfectly clear that he thought she should be getting more involved in other areas of the hospital – heck, he had even thought she should consider training to be a vet!

Surely giving a lecture would be a good place to start.

The materials were all printed out, she had time over the weekend to go through the notes . . .

She had no reason not to. And every reason to line up as many distractions as she could to stop herself thinking about Jack.

'We was pretty short-staffed anyway that evening,' she said, thinking it all through. 'Robert can't make that evening and I think Jack is . . . taking some time off . . . so maybe we'll close the hospital proper that night, just do the talk, and run the hospital clinic on the Wednesday instead. I'll ask Nellie if she can help me.'

'Just don't do me out of a job,' said Dot with a laugh. 'I enjoy running those classes.'

Next, Ruby headed to the munitions factory.

Anything to try and take her mind off Jack. Besides, there was no time to lose where Leah was concerned. Not if they wanted to get her freed by Christmas . . .

She found Cook – as usual – patrolling the perimeter fence and officiously instructing those she judged to be sitting too close to it to move along.

Ruby found herself bristling as she approached; these were hardworking women – and some men – involved in dangerous work and they were just trying to grab a bit of fresh air before they reported back on duty. The two women Cook clearly had in her sights were, to Ruby's eye, easily far enough away from the fence. Knowing Cook, she would suddenly whip out a tape measure to make absolutely sure . . .

Still, there was no point in getting worked up before she had said what she had come to say. Plastering what she hoped was a determined, yet pleasant, look on her face, Ruby strode across the grass.

Maybe Cook would make things easy for her.

'Good afternoon, WPC Fletcher,' she said cheerfully as she approached.

If her erstwhile friend and colleague waived aside the formalities and said that 'Cook' would do nicely, then surely everything would be alright?

Cook swung around. 'Good afternoon, Miss Archer,' she replied, coolly. 'You working on a Saturday now, and all? I do hope I don't have to remind you to stay well away from the perimeter of the site.'

And then again, maybe Cook was going to make things as difficult as possible.

'You do not,' said Ruby politely. 'But I *would* like to have a word with you.'

'I'm on duty,' said Cook, somewhat tartly.

'And this is concerning your duties,' replied Ruby smoothly. 'It's about Leah Richardson who, you may recall, you arrested a short while ago.'

Cook gave a sniff of satisfaction. 'And how is Madam enjoying her new surroundings?' she asked, a little smirk tugging at the corners of her mouth.

A wave of anger crashed over Ruby.

Why all this anger and bitterness towards Leah?

And what on earth had happened to the woman she had once considered a friend?

'Miss Richardson is coping very well with prison life, thank you,' said Ruby. 'But I'm here to tell you that she now intends to plead innocent.'

Cook started back as if she'd been slapped and very

quickly rallied. 'It don't work like that,' she said with a sneer. 'You can't just change your plea when you've had enough of the punishment.'

'You can when you didn't commit the crime in the first place,' countered Ruby. 'When you only admitted to it because you thought you was protecting someone else – who also turned out to be innocent.'

'No one would believe that,' scoffed Cook. 'Anyway, it ain't nothing to do with me. Now, away with you, before I report you for wasting police time. What were you thinking?'

Something snapped inside Ruby.

She had intended to go in gently but . . . to hell with that!

'I'll tell you *exactly* what I think,' said Ruby icily. 'I think that you stole that hairpin.'

Cook gasped and her hand fluttered to her neck and Ruby pressed on before she had a chance to reply.

'I think you pilfered it whilst you was patrolling the shifting sheds,' Ruby continued. 'That and half a dozen other things that have since gone missing in there. I ain't sure whether you decided to deliberately plant it on Leah or whether it accidentally fell to the floor, but, either way, I expect you couldn't believe your luck when she pleaded guilty to having brought it in.'

'Stuff and nonsense,' blustered Cook. 'I ain't ever heard such rubbish.'

She did, however, steer Ruby towards the perimeter fence and away from several pairs of curious eyes, which were beginning to turn in their direction.

'I believe it to be true,' stated Ruby calmly. 'And, if

necessary, I want you to testify in court to help prove Leah's innocence and to secure her release in time for Christmas.'

'Ridiculous,' said Cook, hands on hips. 'I can't believe you want me to go to court and tell the judge I'm guilty of a crime I ain't committed just to let that lily-livered Miss La-Di-Da off the hook.'

'I ain't asking you to do that, even though I *do* believe that you are guilty,' said Ruby. 'I'm asking you to be prepared to say in court that any number of people could have dropped that hairpin but that, because Leah immediately owned up to it, you had no reason to think it were anyone else's. And after that, I want you to resign both from the munitions factory and from the police force and to go far, far away where I never have to see you again.'

'Enough of your impertinence!' said Cook. 'I ain't going to listen to another word you say. Just be grateful that I ain't arresting you here and now for false accusation.'

Ruby stood her ground. 'I'm happy for you to do that although I *should* listen to me, if I were you,' she said. 'I should listen very carefully because I've been doing a little detective work of me own. I've been talking to Mrs Henderson *and* to your employer before that, Mrs Drage, and both of them is perfectly aware that you had a nasty little habit of stealing things from their homes. Little trinkets – bit of this, bit of that – things that on their own don't perhaps count for much but, over time, add up to quite a haul.'

She paused to take breath and glanced at Cook. The woman's face had gone a horrible deathly pallor. She opened and shut her mouth a couple of times but no words were forthcoming.

Ruby decided to press on. She took a couple more steps towards the fence and Cook followed her as though in a trance.

'I expect we're a little too close to the perimeter now,' she said, 'but it seems that you're keen no one hears what I've got to say.' Cook didn't answer. 'Anyway, both of your previous employers decided not to make a fuss at the time. But now, knowing that an innocent woman has been imprisoned because of something you've done, they are perfectly prepared to go to court and testify against you. It's up to you, Cook, but if I was you, I know exactly what I would do. I would do right by Miss Richardson.'

Ruby held her breath, her heart pounding almost painfully in her chest.

She had crossed a line here and all of this really was a dreadful risk because, of course, Mrs Henderson hadn't said anything about going to court and Ruby didn't even know who Mrs Drage *was*.

Still, it had to be worth a try.

There was a long, pregnant pause but finally Cook gave a terse nod. 'I ain't admitting to nothing,' she said. 'But if your friend does decide to plead her innocence, I will back up the fact that several people might have dropped that hairpin and that there's no way of knowing who was responsible.'

And Ruby had to be satisfied with that.

23

For the rest of Saturday, Ruby's feet barely touched the ground.

It was just over a week until Christmas Day – only five days until the Sanctuary Lane Animal Hospital Christmas bazaar – and suddenly it seemed that there was a never-ending list of things she simply *had* to do. Ruby had already promised Elspeth that she would spend Sunday at the hospital helping to get ready for the bazaar – and then she had a full and busy week of work. On top of that, she needed to get a message to Leah *and* prepare for her lecture on Tuesday. Which meant that she only had that afternoon to finish her Christmas shopping.

Gah!

The market was only open until five o'clock nowadays – the wartime blackout regulations had put an end to any nighttime trading for the duration. In an ideal world, of course, Ruby would nip up to Selfridges in the West End and treat herself to a hot chocolate in the café whist she was at it, but she really didn't have time. The Silvertown market and the shops around it had a reasonable choice and would have to do . . .

It was a dry afternoon but it had turned very cold – a real icy nip to the air – and Ruby pulled her shawl more tightly around her as she hurried through the busy streets, with Mac at her heels. She had decided to make up small hampers of toiletries for both Ma and Aunt Maggie, but as her haul thus far consisted only of the hampers themselves and a bottle of Yardley's Lily of the Valley dusting powder apiece, there was much work to be done.

And, as for Charlie, Ruby had planned to buy *him* a football. The two had occasionally enjoyed attending football matches together until Charlie's 'secret' job had put paid to *that* and she knew her brother still enjoyed an occasional kickaround in the street with the local lads. But, somehow, that no longer seemed enough. This was partly, of course, because Mr Reid had let slip that Charlie planned to really treat *her* and the rest of the family and so she wanted to follow suit, but it went deeper than that. Charlie was a young man now – a young man that she had maligned, to boot – and she wanted to give him something that would start to make amends *and* also acknowledge that she recognised he was growing up. The idea came out of nowhere as she passed the end of Sanctuary Lane. Why didn't she make him up a hamper of toiletries as well? It could contain his first razor – one of Gillette's brand-new safety ones – as well as shaving soap, a badger's hair shaving brush and maybe even some brilliantine for his hair.

Ma would have a fit!

Ruby and her friends had already decided not to buy each other presents as such. They had all agreed that contributions to the war effort – purchasing war bonds or supporting charities – was more appropriate during this patriotic time. But suddenly that seemed unnecessarily austere. She *would* purchase war bonds of course – as well as donating to the Soldiers' Benevolent Fund – but there no reason that she couldn't buy little trinkets for her friends as well. Leah, of course, deserved far more than trinkets, so Ruby would make her up a little hamper as well. One thing was for certain, though; it would contain absolutely no hatpins *or* hairpins.

None.

Despite the cold and her misery about Jack, Ruby spent a happy couple of hours selecting her wares.

Soon, her baskets and bags were full of everything from Pond's Vanishing cream, rosewater soap and Pear's soap (for Ma and Aunt Maggie) to moustache wax and a compact hairbrush (for Charlie) to pretty notebooks and ribbons (for her friends). She even bought a pound of bones without knobs on from Nellie's dogfood barrow, waving away Nellie's insistence that she didn't need to pay. And then, at a nearby stall, she stumbled upon a ceramic ornament of a dog that looked almost exactly like Mac – right down to the bright, animated sparkle in his eyes. On a whim, she splashed out and bought it.

Despite everything, dare she give it to Jack?

Her shopping complete, Ruby turned to go home. The crowds were denser now and progress was slow and a minute or two later, Ruby ground to a complete halt in front of a stall selling Christmas trees, the scent of pine crisp and fresh in the winter air. Most of the trees were undecorated except the one right in the middle, which was decked in everything from glass baubles to tinsel, ribbons to strings of popcorn. The overall effect was rather like standing in an enchanted forest and Ruby stood, transfixed.

'Biggest and best trees in the market?' said the market trader, looking straight at her with a friendly smile.

Ruby knew he was just going through the motions and wasn't seriously trying to make a sale. Girls like her were far from his typical customer because Christmas trees were reserved for the houses of the rich, for public buildings and for open spaces. Mrs Henderson would have an enormous one, there was one in the canteen at work and Elspeth was getting one for the Christmas bazaar, but they weren't for the likes of her. In fact, most of these trees wouldn't even fit in the kitchen.

And yet it would be magical and maybe it was just what they all needed.

The crowds had thinned, but still Ruby stood there.

She had the money . . .

'Tempted?' asked the stallholder, coming over to her.

Ruby gave herself a little shake and shook her head.

It was ridiculous.

How on earth would she carry it home, for a start? To say nothing about Ma and Aunt Maggie's predictable comments about getting ideas above her station.

But, just then, she saw Charlie coming towards her, carrying a couple of bags, and whistling quietly to himself. He started when he saw Ruby, clutching his bag to his chest to conceal the contents. And somehow, seeing her brother there, at just that instant, was so unlikely that somehow it seemed meant to be.

'What do you reckon, Charlie?' she said by way of greeting, gesturing towards the trees.

Charlie looked at the trees and then back at Ruby, unsure whether she was joking.

'It would be marvellous, wouldn't it?' said Ruby.

'Coo, yes,' said Charlie, eyes wide. 'But . . .'

'And wouldn't our presents look magnificent displayed underneath it? No more hiding them in our rooms until Christmas morning.'

Charlie's eyes widened even more. 'That would be wonderful,' he said. 'Like something from the films.'

'I'll throw in some clips to attach candles to the branches,' said the trader, sensing the possibility of a sale. 'Hell, it's Christmas; I'll even throw in some tinsel and a couple of baubles. You can't say fairer than that.'

'It's a deal,' said Ruby, decisively. She pointed to a perfectly proportioned medium-sized tree. 'If you could tie it up with string, we'll carry it home now.'

Charlie clapped his hands together in glee.

'Am I doolally?' she said to Charlie, hoisting the back of the tree onto her shoulders as they walked home.

'Perfectly,' said Charlie, with a grin. 'Ma and Aunt Maggie will have your guts for garters.'

'Oh no,' said Ruby. 'Ma and Aunt Maggie will love it. But I've spent all day worrying that I've got too much to do, and now I've gone and added to the list.'

'It's worth it, though,' said Charlie.

'It is,' said Ruby. 'By the way, I want to apologise for accusing you of throwing the brick through Fisher's window. Don't ask me how I know it weren't you, but I do.'

'It were Ma,' said Charlie. 'I knew immediately because she took one of me bricks, but I didn't want to drop her in it.'

Brother and sister looked at each other, and then both burst out laughing.

And as they carried the tree home together in the frosty air, Ruby felt closer to her brother than she had in a long, long time.

Ruby was right.

After a predictable chorus of disbelief, Ma and Aunt Maggie seemed excited and enchanted by the Christmas tree. Charlie was dispatched to borrow a bucket to stand it in from Annie-Next-Door, who duly came around to admire it together with the guests that she was hosting for the afternoon. Before long, there was a regular little party in the kitchen of Sanctuary Lane, all helping to clear the furniture and to install the tree in pride of place. And, if it meant that the sofa was now at rather a rakish angle in the middle of the room, even Aunt Maggie didn't complain. Instead, they all made a huge fuss of Tess's kittens, who were being ever so sweet and playful. Before long, they had agreed that the Archers would keep two of the fluffiest kittens and Annie-Next-Door's guests would give homes to the others.

It was all perfect.

Rather regretfully, Ruby left them to it in order to catch her bus to Holloway Prison. As she had rather anticipated, she was not allowed in to see Leah without an appointment, but the duty sergeant was prepared to pass on a letter and, after a bit of persuading, even gave her the wherewithal to write one. So, Ruby installed herself into a quiet corner of the waiting room and wrote, explaining to Leah that Cook was more than happy to testify on her behalf. She couldn't resist adding a sentence or two telling Leah all about dinner at The Savoy with Robert and how marvellous it had all been – both because it was true and because she hoped that any jealously it might instil in Leah would encourage her friend to fight even harder for her freedom.

By the time she got home, all the guests had departed, but the Christmas tree was already looking magnificent with candles clipped to the branches and the decorations the stallholder had given them artfully arranged. Aunt Maggie had even festooned some of her cotton-wool snowflakes all around, and the whole effect was very pretty. She and Ma were at the kitchen table cutting out paper angels and Charlie – *Charlie* – was covering a card-board star with silver foil to go on top of the tree. Mac was curled up asleep in front of the range, but Tess was intrigued, batting the baubles, and even attempting to climb the branches.

Ruby looked around at them all with love and affection and swallowed the lump in her throat.

How Harry would have loved it all.

24

Suddenly it really was the run up to Christmas.

Preparing for the Christmas bazaar at the animal hospital on the Sunday was hard work but, even though Ruby wasn't really in the mood, it was a lot of fun. She spent much of her time rather inexpertly helping to paint a large picture of Mayfair, which Elspeth's mother had sketched onto a board and which would be used for pin the tail on the donkey. Then she helped paint poles for the coconut shy, priced up bric-a-brac and folded up umpteen pieces of paper for the tombola. All in all, it was pleasant work – and jolly nice not to be in charge for once! She did, however, nip out to check the room in the stables where she would be holding her talk on Tuesday. To her relief, Dot had left everything shipshape and Bristol fashion with neat rows of seats, a blackboard at the front and even – bless! – a good-luck note on the desk she would be standing behind.

She could only hope that she was up to the task.

Tuesday, 19 December 1916

First thing on Tuesday morning, Ruby ran up Sanctuary Lane to the animal hospital.

Today was supposed to be the day that the RCVS turned up – with the full weight of the law behind them – to shut down the hospital. Robert was already there and, as she pushed the front door open, he started waving a piece of paper at her in obvious jubilation.

'I know I shouldn't have opened it, but they've backed down,' he said, face shining. 'They knew they didn't have a leg to stand on and they've ruddy backed down.'

Ruby snatched the paper from him – to hell with decorum! – and quickly scanned the contents.

Dear Miss Archer,

We appreciate your prompt response to our previous communication and the detailed clarification provided regarding the operations of the Sanctuary Lane Animal Hospital.

After careful consideration, the Royal College of Veterinary Surgeons acknowledges the compliance of the Sanctuary Lane Animal Hospital with the relevant regulations and the Veterinary Surgeons Act of 1881.

We trust that your institution will continue to uphold the highest standards of professionalism and animal care. However, if there are any changes in the operational structure of the Sanctuary Lane Animal Hospital in the future, or if you require further clarification on regulatory matters, please do not hesitate to contact this office.

Thank you for your cooperation,

And there it was in black and white. Not the warmest or the most conciliatory letter but that didn't matter.

It was enough.

Ruby did a little dance of delight on the spot and then went to hug Robert.

If only she could tell Jack.

'Thank you,' she said sincerely.

'You did it,' said Robert. 'I was too busy reminiscing about my old university chums whilst you quietly saved the day.'

'We both did it,' said Ruby firmly. 'We're a team, remember? Now, I know you can't make the clinic tonight, but any chance of making one tomorrow instead?'

'It would be my pleasure,' said Robert. 'I'm off to visit Leah, now. She's being very cagey at the moment; I'm not sure what she's got up her sleeve.'

It was on in the tip of Ruby's tongue to tell him, but it wasn't really her place to do so.

'Send Leah my love,' she said, instead.

Ruby raced home after work to change ready for her talk at the hospital.

She found Ma alone in the kitchen, sitting on the sofa by the Christmas tree, a letter dangling from her fingers.

'It's about Harry,' she said by way of greeting, offering the letter to Ruby.

'Oh.'

Ruby sat down beside her mother, trying to gauge Ma's expression but came up empty handed. She took the letter and started reading.

Dear Mrs Archer,

It is with profound sorrow that I extend my deepest condolences to you upon the loss of your son, Henry Archer. I wish there were words to make this news easier.

You will know by now that Harry was killed in the line of duty and I write to inform you that he very sadly lost his life in the trenches due to an incoming shell mere minutes after arriving at the front. It was quick and he didn't suffer long and I want you to know that he wasn't alone. His fellow soldiers were there with him and he was surrounded by men who respected and cared for him. War is a brutal and unforgiving place and sometimes there is simply no way to make sense of it.

I am truly sorry for your loss. I will remember Harry as a happy-go-lucky soul, always quick with a joke to lighten the mood. I am also convinced that, should he have been put to the test, he would have faced the darkest of moments with resilience and bravery.

Whilst we cannot change the course of events which led to this sorrowful outcome, please know that Harry will be remembered with honour and respect. The bonds formed in the crucible of war are strong, and the memory of your son will endure among those who served alongside him.

I extend my deepest sympathies during this awful time and, if there is anything I can do to provide support, please do not hesitate to contact me.

With heartfelt condolences.
Yours sincerely.

It finished with the name, rank and regiment of Harry's officer and was dated almost three weeks previously.

Ruby put the letter down carefully on the table in front of them without comment.

She didn't know what to think.

What to *feel.*

‘So wonderful,’ said Ma. ‘I’m so relieved it were quick. And the officer talks about his resilience and bravery – as well as his sense of humour. Your Pa would be so proud.’

Ruby took a deep breath and hugged her mother. ‘Thank the Lord he didn’t suffer,’ she said. ‘Thank goodness he didn’t lie in no-man’s-land for hours on his own, horribly injured and slowly dying of his wounds. I’ve worried about that. *Dreamed* of it.’

‘Me too,’ said Ma. ‘I couldn’t get it out of my head that he were calling for me and that I didn’t get to him in time. That I somehow let him down.’

‘You didn’t let him down, Ma. And he didn’t let us down neither. It was just one of those things; like his officer said, you can’t make sense of nothing in this awful war.’

The two women clung together for a moment longer and then Ruby gently extricated herself.

‘I’ve got to go up to the hospital to give this talk,’ she said. ‘I’ll be back in a couple of hours and we’ll have a cup of cocoa and read the letter again together and think of Harry and remember his sacrifice.’

‘No hurry, love,’ said Ma. ‘Maggie suggested the flicks this evening with her and her new gentleman friend and I’ve a mind to join them. I’ll need to leave now to get there on time, though.’

Ruby nodded. How lovely that Ma seemed to be entering the land of the living again.

She kissed her mother on the cheek, put Mac on his lead, stroked one of the kittens and was gone.

*

Dot had told Ruby to expect between twenty and thirty people to attend the lecture but, in the event, she had an audience of precisely . . . five.

There were, of course, several irritated owners who had turned up in the expectation of having their animals treated and Ruby had to repeat, over and over again, that they weren't running the clinic that evening and that there was no one available to take a look at their sick animals until the next session. Time and again, she pointed at the poster on the window that explained all this but, as one frustrated owner explained to her, he couldn't read, so the sign was about as much use to him as a one-legged man in a kicking contest.

'Look at all those empty chairs,' said Ruby, when the last such owner had been gently but firmly given his marching orders. She wasn't sure whether to be relieved or disappointed by the terribly low numbers.

'Too close to Christmas, I suppose,' said Nellie, sucking on her teeth. 'They'll turn up if they're at their wits' end about a sick animal, but it's just too cold to be lectured at. Can't blame them really.'

'It ain't a lecture,' said Ruby. 'It's to *help* them. But I take your point and maybe we should have anticipated it. Should we cancel?'

'Tempting,' said Nellie. 'It *is* a bit parky in here; that oil heater the Fishers left for us is worse than useless. But these good folk have come out and it gives *you* a chance to practise on a small audience.'

Ruby made a little face. 'We could move inside,' she suggested. 'The fires ain't lit but it's less drafty.'

Nellie shook her head. 'There's no curtains and we'd

just have people knocking at the front door and hollering at us to have a look at their animals in there,' she said. 'Let's stay put and get through it as quickly as we can before we all freeze to death.'

Ruby nodded. 'You're right,' she said. 'At least we've got some dog tonics to give away, which should keep people happy. Before we start, I think I'll just lock the doors from the courtyard to the street so we don't get more people wandering though that way in the hope of seeing a vet.'

'You mean to stop the audience from escaping?' said Nellie, with her wheezing laugh.

Ruby grinned and nipped out into the courtyard. Quickly, she took down the signs advertising the lecture, pulled the tall courtyard doors shut and slid home the bolts.

Less than an hour, and she would be home.

The five people who had given up their Tuesday evening to attend the lecture were a motley crew and, to Ruby's surprise, she didn't recognise most of them.

There was a girl of about twenty dressed in little more than rags on the back row and clutching a filthy shawl about her shoulders. There was a florid middle-aged man who looked suspiciously rotund to hail from Silvertown, sitting on the front row with his legs splayed wide and a large notebook open expectantly on his knees. Something about his posture and his gaze unnerved Ruby; she wasn't sure exactly what it was, but she knew she would have to mind her p's and q's around *him*. Between the two was a middle-aged couple with the same thinning sandy hair and sharp, pinched features. Brother and sister? Ruby couldn't be sure. The group was completed by the only person she did recognise: Mr Atkins from the house at the top of Sanctuary Lane, which backed onto the very room they were sitting in. Ruby wondered what had brought them all here on this particular evening. She knew that, as usual, Mr Atkins would only be attending in the hope of a bit of warmth – fat chance of *that*! – and company. Maybe that was true for them all. Well, they were destined to be sorely disappointed on the heat front, but at least Ruby could try to make the session rewarding for them.

'As there are so few of us, shall we gather together rather than spreading out around the room,' she said, clapping her hands together for attention.

Hark at her; just like a teacher.

'We might need to huddle together for warmth, as well,' added the rotund, red-faced man with a grin. He *sounded* jolly enough but that definitely wasn't a Silvertown accent. Not as posh as Leah or Robert's, the gentleman was clearly neither working class, nor from the East End.

'I'm sorry it's so cold,' said Ruby, conciliatorily. 'The heater don't seem to be throwing out as much heat as it should. In fact, why don't we forget these rows and pull our chairs as close to it as we can?'

'Looks like we've been beaten to the best position, though' said the sandy-haired woman with a laugh as they shuffled their chairs into a circle. Ruby followed her gaze. Mac was curled up in a little ball – chin on tail – right in front of the heater, no doubt relieved to be away from those bothersome kittens for a while. With a little snort of laughter, Ruby reached down and scratched him between his ears.

Darling boy.

'Let's make a start,' said Ruby, once everyone was in position. She glanced at Nellie for reassurance and Nellie gave her a wide gap-toothed smile in return. It was better like this, but it was almost scarier because she could see the whites of everyone's eyes and she didn't have her blackboard and easel to hide behind. 'What do you think is the most important thing to get right in feeding a dog?'

And they were off, into a lively debate about the importance of a balanced diet, portion control, consistency, and the downsides of table scraps. Ruby was just starting to relax when . . .

Boom!

The noise came from nothing . . . turning the world upside down.

A second later, the lights went out. Where once had been a little group of people chatting round a heater, there was now just inky blackness.

Ruby was hurled from her chair and started falling. There was the shattering of glass, the rumble of collapsing masonry, and something hard landed – crack! – across one of her legs. Dust and debris filled the air, coating her mouth and making her cough and splutter, but she couldn't see a thing.

What on earth was happening?

What had happened to the others?

Would she ever see Jack and her family again?

25

Ruby lay there in shock and disorientation and tried to control her raggedy breathing.

She was alive, she was sure of it, and, at that moment, the searing pain arrived in her right leg as if to underscore the fact. There had clearly been an explosion, and the floor beneath her had given way. Cautiously, Ruby felt beneath her with her hand. Yes, wooden floorboards had been replaced by stone or concrete. She must have fallen into a semi-basement beneath the old stable buildings; not that she had previously realised that one existed. She could wriggle her toes – although her right leg hurt like billyo when she did so – but she couldn't move her legs because there was something large and wooden across them, pinning them down.

She was trapped.

For a second, as the explosion died away, there had been an eerie and unnatural silence. But now, thank goodness, there were moans and groans from those around her.

'Hello?' Ruby offered up into the darkness. Her mouth was full of something – dust and grit certainly, blood probably judging by the strong metallic tang – and her words came out as little more than a mumble. She groped into her pocket for her hankie. Somewhat against the odds, it was still there and she used it to wipe out her mouth as best she could. Then she tried to speak again, her voice louder and stronger this time. '*Hello?*'

'I'm here, girl,' came a familiar voice. Ruby's ears were still ringing and the words sounded as though they were coming from far away.

'Oh, Nellie, thank goodness,' said Ruby. Nellie was such a calm and capable presence – as well, of course, a dear friend. 'Who else can hear me?' she added.

'Me. Hilda Bowles,' came a weak voice. 'Only, I can't move. I'm trapped by bricks . . .'

Her voice trailed away.

'Anyone else?' asked Ruby.

No one else answered; apart from more groans, there was just silence. Nothing from Dennis Bowles, the jolly rotund man, Mr Atkins, or the girl in the patchwork dress. All unconscious or . . . worse.

But what was this?

Movement next to her, stirring up the dust and making her cough all over again. A whine of excitement and something wet snuffling against her face . . .

Mac.

Joy surged through Ruby as she reached out for the little dog. Firstly, she just gave him a reassuring hug and then she nervously checked him all over as best she could for injuries. His fur was caked with dust and debris, but he seemed to be moving freely, he wasn't wet and sticky, neither was he whining in pain and distress.

Thank goodness for that.

'Come on, Mac,' she said. 'Time for us all to get out of here.'

She pushed herself up onto her elbows and tried to

wriggle out from under the large wooden beam, but all she got for her efforts was a surge of icy pain down her leg, making her retch in agony. She was wedged firm and couldn't move an inch.

She lay down again with a whimper and put her arm around Mac.

'Nellie?' she called out. 'Nellie, I can't move.'

Hopefully Nellie would be able to free her and they could hatch a plan for helping everyone else and getting out of there.

But there was no reply.

'Nellie?' called Ruby. 'Nellie, are you there?'

'I'm tired, girl.' Nellie's voice was so quiet Ruby had to strain to hear it. 'Just need a little sleep.'

No.

'Nellie, you listen to me,' said Ruby urgently. 'You stay awake and you stay with me and we'll all get out of here safely.'

But there was no reply.

All Ruby could hear was the sound of Hilda Bowles weeping softly and a man moaning loudly.

'Can *you* move, Mrs Bowles?' asked Ruby.

'No,' sobbed Mrs Bowles. 'I'm covered in bricks and I don't know where me husband is. Dennis? Can you hear me?'

There was no reply to her question – at least not a coherent one.

It seemed that Ruby was on her own. She could only hope that they were all rescued soon, but that would depend very much on what had caused the blast.

If there had been an explosion at the munitions

factory – an airstrike by the Germans or a hatpin on the factory floor – the damage would be catastrophic. It would lay waste to all the surrounding streets and it could be many hours before help arrived.

Then again, it could be something much closer to home. Maybe the oil heater had exploded? It hadn't been working very well and maybe it had been faulty – another casualty of the shortage of tradesmen and spare parts.

Or maybe it was something more sinister. Deliberate sabotage was certainly a possibility. Perhaps it wasn't a coincidence that the Fishers had chosen this very week to go away . . .

No.

The Fishers were her friends. She wouldn't allow herself to think like that – let alone to entertain the idea that Charlie might have had something to do with it. She would just concentrate on surviving and on getting everyone out.

Maybe friends and family – people who loved and cared about her – would already be searching for them. Ruby cast her mind around but drew a blank.

The Fishers were away for a few days and no one would come to open the bakery until the small hours. Ma and Aunt Maggie were at the flicks, Charlie would be goodness knew where, Robert was at some important function and Leah was in prison. Elspeth was off duty and minding her own business and Jack, of course, was out of her life . . .

There was no one – *no one* – who would be thinking about her or worrying that anything out of the ordinary had happened to her and that was a sobering thought indeed.

Then again, surely other people – strangers, passers-by – would have heard the explosion and would be able to see what had happened. But, here too, the odds were stacked against them. The hospital was closed and dark, the courtyard door shut and bolted from the inside and the poster advertising the lecture had been removed. If, as Ruby suspected, the stables had collapsed into their foundations, there might be no indication from the outside that anything untoward had happened . . .

Ruby swallowed a wave of panic. She must stay calm. She didn't appear to be mortally injured. She just needed to help the others and find a way to attract attention. She tried shouting a few times – her voice thin and reedy – and then lay back down in the darkness.

Now what?

Suddenly, Ruby noticed a sliver of light, directly above her.

It hadn't been there before, Ruby was sure of it; even allowing for the time it would have taken for her eyes to adjust, it had been absolutely pitch-black immediately after the explosion. For a moment, Ruby panicked that a fire was taking hold but the light was too white and too still . . .

It was the *moon* slowly beginning to slide into view!

And that meant, somewhere above her, there was a gap in the rubble.

A potential way out.

Ruby tried to wriggle free again but was rewarded only by another bolt of pain.

'Is anyone else there?' she called. Even if she couldn't get out, maybe someone else could.

Silence.

Oh, this was hopeless.

For a moment, Ruby gave into tears of fear and sadness. Mac, who was still by her side, sat up, licked her tears away and then lay back down in the crook of her arm.

Mac.

Even if none of the humans could get out, maybe there was a chance that Mac could. It was a slim hope – he would have to get out of the courtyard to begin with – but surely there was a chance he could attract attention and help for Nellie and the others who badly needed it.

With trembling fingers, Ruby located her handkerchief. She had embroidered it with her initials – in pathetic imitation of Leah's – and it was bound to be smeared with her blood, to boot. It wasn't much, but it was the best she could do. She tied the hankie to Mac's collar, knotting it as tightly as she could, and then pushed the little dog towards the light.

'Off you go, Mac,' she said, resolutely.

Mac didn't move. Then he started running around in circles. Maybe it was the smell of blood on the handkerchief . . .

'*Go*, Mac,' she said, more loudly and with a harder push. 'Fetch help.'

But Mac just stood there and, in the gathering light, Ruby could see him looking at her with his head on one side.

'*Go*,' she commanded a third time, with as much force as she could muster, even though her heart was breaking.

And, this time, the little dog was gone.

Ruby heard, rather than saw, him scramble up piles of rubble, sending a little shower of debris down onto the basement floor. She lost him for a while and then, for a brief moment, she had a clear view of his dear little silhouette against the night sky before he finally disappeared from view.

This time, Ruby really did break down in tears. Every fibre of her being had wanted Mac to stay by her side, but she had done the right thing. She knew that there was virtually no chance of him being able to fetch help, but at least she had given him every chance of surviving whatever horrors might lie ahead.

In the meantime, all she could do was wait.

Maybe she should try praying.

Instead, her thoughts went immediately to Jack.

Darling Jack, whose dear, stubborn, proud face she could see clearly in her mind's eye. She had really made a mess of things with him, hadn't she? In fact, she had made a mess of a *lot* of things over the past few months, she could see that now. She had concentrated on things rather than people, she had prioritised the animal hospital over just about everything else and she had, for the most part, kept her cards close to her chest rather than letting other people in. She had believed she was a principled person and yet look at what she had done. Rather than letting Jack close and involving him in the ups and downs of her life as she should have done, she had repeatedly pushed him away. Worse still, she had chosen to lie to him – time and time again – if only by omission.

It was funny that it took lying trapped and injured in the dark to work all that out.

But she had done more than that, hadn't she?

Branding him a coward and comparing him unfavourably to Harry had not only been ridiculous, it had also been cruel. How *could* she have been so judgemental and unfair? After all, look at her now; crying and whimpering with fear the first time *she* had been put to the test. Not so brave now, was she? She couldn't hug Harry and tell him she understood a little of what he had had to go through, but she hoped very much that she would live to apologise to Jack.

She had to get out.

When Ruby opened her eyes again, everything was a little lighter.

She wasn't actually sure if being able to see unfamiliar – almost grotesque – shadows on either side of her was better or worse than being in the dark, but she could see the tumble of bricks on her left-hand side – thank goodness they hadn't fallen on her face – and the fact that the beam trapping her legs was slightly higher up on that side too.

If she moved the pile of bricks, maybe she would be able to wriggle across to where the beam was higher and try to get out that way. She just had to hope that dismantling the bricks wouldn't somehow dislodge the beam and crush her legs even more.

Tentatively, she set to work. She picked up a brick in her left hand, transferred to her right, set it down on the ground beside her and started over. She had no idea how many bricks she would need to move – nor how much time was passing – but it felt good to be doing *something*. Eventually, she had cleared a space all the way down to the beam, which, fortunately, stayed where it was. Now that it was a little lighter, she could see that the beam was actually supported by a higher pile of rubble further to her left so – unless she was very unlucky – it shouldn't come crashing down onto her.

Slowly, Ruby propped herself on to her elbows and tried to wiggle her legs sideways. Her left leg moved but her right leg refused to play ball, merely rewarding her with another jolt of pain, which made her yelp in agony. So, biting her lip, she reached forward and physically manhandled her right leg, scooting her bottom along as she did so. She repeated the process and gradually shuffled clear of the beam. It crossed her mind that she might be doing some irreparable damage to her leg – when an animal was hurt, the hospital's first advice was to immobilise the injury – but, on balance, she decided she had no choice. The structure might collapse further at any moment, there was the new – and deeply unwelcome – smell of burning somewhere in the distance and, most importantly, there were injured and unresponsive people lying not yards away who badly needed her help.

Finally, she was free.

Ruby took a deep breath, pulled up her skirts and took a look at her right leg. It was bent at a funny angle and obviously broken, which explained the pain, but there didn't seem to be any obvious puncture wound or bleeding to stem. In an ideal world, she would apply a splint . . . but there was nothing obvious to hand.

Right.

How to get them all out?

A quick glance up towards the jagged opening and Ruby could see that it was hopeless. She might be free of the beam, but the route Mac had taken out involved both climbing and jumping. With a useless leg, Ruby just didn't stand a chance of even trying. She glanced around, hoping for an alternative, but there were no other obvious options.

'Anyone there?' Ruby called out, suddenly feeling strangely calm.

There were a couple of indistinct moans.

'Anyone?' Ruby called out again. 'Nellie.'

More grunts and groans and Ruby set off towards the nearest moan, using her arms and her good leg to propel herself along the ground. It was hard work, not least because of the piles of bricks and rubble that she had to navigate, but it was getting lighter all the time as the moon made its stately progress across the opening above her head. She only had a matter of time before it disappeared again, plunging them all into darkness.

She arrived at a huge pile of bricks – if she had her bearings right, it was what used to be the wall separating the old stable from the neighbouring house on Sanctuary Lane – and recoiled with shock when she saw a hand protruding from it.

A limp, male hand, white and terrible in the moonlight.

Tentatively, Ruby reached out and touched it. 'Are you alright?' she whispered.

A stupid question. The hand was cool to the touch and clearly not alright.

Is that what Harry had looked like?

Ruby shuffled on.

And here was Nellie, lying flat on her back mere inches away from Mrs Bowles who, as Ruby already knew, was trapped from the chest down by bricks from the same wall that had buried the dead man. Ruby assessed them quickly. They were both moaning quietly – clearly alive – but Ruby judged them both to be in a bad way. Nellie had a deep gash to her forehead and a wound just above her elbow, which was bleeding stickily onto the rubble and Mrs Bowles' face was cold and clammy, her breathing fast and erratic . . .

There was no immediate sign of the girl in the patchwork dress and the three men.

Ruby took a couple of deep breaths, trying to think clearly. What had she learned during her time at the animal hospital? All those weeks triaging the animals as they queued with their owners down Sanctuary Lane? It wasn't quite the same of course, but surely the principles still held . . .

Should she deal with Nellie or Mrs Bowles first?

She could see Nellie's injuries and she didn't know quite *what* had happened to Mrs Bowles. But, if she removed the bricks to release Mrs Bowles, Nellie might bleed to death. Then again, if the bricks were crushing Mrs Bowles and suffocating her, maybe she should be the priority . . .

Ruby's hands – and maybe her heart – set to work whilst her brain was still trying to decide. She remembered Robert using a tourniquet on a dog with a badly mangled leg and imagined that the technique would work just as well on humans. She didn't have any straps or bandages, of course, but strips of petticoat would surely do in an emergency.

She set to work pulling hers apart; it wasn't easy but eventually, using hands and teeth, she managed to rip off some passably long strips. She tied one as tightly as she could to Nellie's upper arm to try and stop any further blood loss and wrapped the other around Nellie's head, although the wound there seemed more superficial.

'You'll be alright, love,' said Ruby, bending over and planting a kiss on Nellie's grime-encrusted cheek. She had no idea if that was the truth but knew from her work at the hospital that reassuring the patient was all-important. Either way, Nellie suddenly reached out and grasped Ruby's forearm in a surprisingly strong grip.

'Thank you, girl,' she rasped.

Ruby started pulling herself across to Mrs Bowles, horribly aware that the smell of burning was getting stronger. It was beginning to burn her throat and she fancied she could hear the crackle of flames getting closer.

Ruby started pulling bricks off Mrs Bowles, as fast as she could, praying that it wasn't too late for them all.

Crash!

There was an unearthly creak and the groan of a structure under unbearable pressure. Plaster dust splattered onto Ruby's forehead and she closed her eyes.

Please don't let the building fall onto them all.

'Help,' she cried as she frantically pulled bricks off Mrs Bowles. 'Someone. *Please.*'

It was getting hotter in there, and, for the first time, Ruby was aware of smoke twisting amongst the rubble and the first flames licking around the collapsed wall of bricks. There would be oil on the ground from the broken heater . . .

Oh, God.

Swallowing hard on the sob in her throat, Ruby started pulling off the bricks more and more frantically. It was probably too little too late – for all of them – but there was nothing else she could do . . .

'Ruby?'

At first Ruby thought she was hearing voices.

It was – no doubt – just a manifestation of her wildest hopes and borne out of fear, pain and despair. It was like a parched man in a desert spotting a mirage and futilely changing course . . .

Mustn't change course.

Must free Mrs Bowles.

But then it came again, a little louder this time.

'Ruby?'

It *was* a voice – and not just any voice, either.

It was Jack.

26

Ruby craned towards the moonlight streaming in through the gap in the roof, hoping against hope that it wasn't her imagination playing tricks on her.

But, no; there was Jack, silhouetted against the night sky and peering down anxiously at her.

'Jack!' she called out, a quaver in her voice. 'We're here. *Quickly*.'

Jack started clambering down towards Ruby, carefully easing himself down the piles of rubble. 'We didn't know anyone were here!' he shouted. 'Everything were locked and shuttered.'

A moan from Mrs Bowles reminded Ruby of her task and she continued removing the bricks with renewed energy.

'An explosion,' she called back. 'Out of nowhere.'

'The stables have collapsed.' Jack's voice was coming closer. 'You can't see a darned thing from outside.'

'I sent Mac to get help.'

'He found me.'

And then Jack was by her side, his arm around her shoulders.

Ruby smiled up at him in utter, blessed relief.

' 'I love you,' she said.

'I love you too.'

'And I'm sorry about everything.'

'Me too.'

'You took your bloody time.'

After that, everything seemed to be happening at once.

Ruby – continuing to remove bricks from Mrs Bowles – quickly gave Jack a rundown of who had been at the meeting and the current position and condition of those she had thus far located. Jack quickly surveyed the scene, offering words of reassurance where he could, and then helped to remove the last of the bricks from Mrs Bowles. Her right arm was torn and mangled but there were no other visible injuries, save a large swelling bump on her head.

Then Jack turned to Ruby.

'Right, let's get you out of here,' he said, briskly. 'That fire's too darn close for my liking.'

Ruby shook her head.

She wanted nothing more than to get out of there, but something held her back.

'The others should go first,' she said. 'They're more badly injured than me.'

That was the protocol and they shouldn't deviate from it, even now.

Jack puffed out his cheeks. 'Ruby, I'm in charge of this rescue, so just do as you're told, please,' he said. 'Put your arms around me neck. We ain't got long.'

Right on cue, there was crash behind Ruby and everything turned red and golden.

Terrified, Ruby turned her head. The fire wasn't quite upon them, but Jack was right.

They had minutes at most, perhaps less.

'Take Nellie first,' she said frantically. 'I can scoot away from the fire and buy meself a little more time, but she can't move at all.'

Crash.

Another beam tumbled and burst into flame and Jack gave an almost unearthly howl of fear. He stumbled to his feet and Ruby could only watch in horror as, without a backwards glance, he scuttled up the piles of rubble towards the jagged hole in the roof.

For a moment, he was silhouetted against the sky . . . and then he was gone.

Ruby sat stock-still, numb with shock.

Jack had *left* her.

The flames and the devastation and the roaring and the cracking . . . it had all been too much for him.

He was saving himself.

Ruby's numbness melted into unutterable sadness. However logical Jack's behaviour – and maybe it *did* make sense in the cold light of day – he had betrayed them all.

Because there was absolutely no hope of rescue now.

She had done what she could, but you had to know when you were beaten. There was nothing for it but to succumb to the inevitable as bravely as she could.

Ruby pulled Nellie's head onto her lap, took Mrs Bowles's hand in her own and shut her eyes.

This was it.

Oh, please don't let it hurt too much.

Ruby's thoughts were of her family: Ma and Pa, Harry and Charlie. She was full of sadness to be leaving Ma and Charlie, but hopefully Pa and Harry were out there somewhere, waiting for her. She should have had years left – she wouldn't even be twenty-two for another month – but hundreds of thousands were dying before their time nowadays, so why should she be any different? She had tried to live a good life and to make a difference and she really didn't want to die but . . .

Oof!

Ruby's eyes snapped open.

She was soaking wet . . . and the water was *freezing.*

And here was Charlie standing on a nearby mound of rubble and spraying everyone and everything with the hose that was used to wash down the horses.

Hope – pure, exquisite hope – flared in Ruby's chest again.

Seconds later, Jack was bounding down the debris followed by at least six other men. Ruby watched joyfully as some of them came towards her, Nellie and Mrs Bowles, whilst others fanned out to inspect the tumbled wall and the furthest reaches of the basement.

Jack stayed by her side. 'I thought you'd abandoned me,' said Ruby, as Jack scooped her up into his arms.

'Never,' said Jack. He lent closer so that their faces were almost touching. 'I would never abandon you, Ruby. But I suddenly realised I didn't have time to get you all out on me Todd, so I went to fetch reinforcements. Do you understand?'

Ruby nodded, cradled in the arms that felt like home. And, even though the pain shooting through her leg was almost unbearable, she had never felt as happy.

She was getting a second chance.

Outside, all was blessed fresh air and moonlight.

Ruby, her head against Jack's shoulder, gulped in great

shuddering breaths and surveyed the scene. The courtyard was covered in roof tiles and rubble and the doors to the street were hanging at an angle. The animal hospital, the bakery and the Fisher's flat above were all pretty much intact, although the windows had been blown out and the backdoor was hanging skew-whiff on its hinges. But, turning the other way, the familiar landscape had completely changed. As Ruby had surmised, the stable block had collapsed into the basement in a pile of twisted beams and the structure had completely disappeared. Where once had been buildings, there was now just smoke and dust and a sky stained grotesquely orange by fire.

Had the whole of Sanctuary Lane gone up in smoke?

'Oh, Lordy,' said Ruby. 'Is Ma alright?'

Jack, picking his way carefully over the rubble, smiled at her reassuringly. 'She's tickety-boo,' he said. 'Charlie says she's at the flicks with your aunt.'

Ruby sagged against him with relief.

'And the house?'

'Still standing.'

'So, it's not the factory? It hasn't exploded or been hit by a Zep?'

'Not this time,' said Jack. 'It looks like it were a gas explosion in old Mr Atkins house. They're searching the rubble, but so far there's no sign of him.'

'He were at the meeting,' said Ruby. 'Just trying to keep warm, I reckon. I didn't hear hide nor hair of him after the explosion, though, so I reckon his number's up.'

'Poor old soul,' said Jack, stumbling slightly as he negotiated some slippery tiles on the cobbles. 'There will be time enough later to pay our respects but let's just concentrate on getting you to hospital.'

'Where's Charlie,' said Ruby, craning over her shoulder for her little brother. 'We can't just leave him.'

How brave her little brother had been. Rushing in with the hose without a thought as to his own safety.

'Here he comes now,' said Jack.

And, indeed, here he was, emerging from the rubble, carrying a mumbling Nellie as though she weighed nothing at all. 'You alright, Sis?' he asked, as they drew level.

'Yes,' said Ruby. 'Me leg's hurt but I think it's just broken. It's Nellie I'm worried about.'

'I'm alright, girl,' mumbled Nellie and Ruby's heart surged with joy and relief that her friend was conscious again.

'Did you apply that tourniquet?' asked Jack, glancing at Nellie's arm.

Ruby nodded absentmindedly.

'Pretty professional job,' muttered Jack in approval.

'I learned from the best.'

As they emerged out into Sanctuary Lane, a little crowd of onlookers on the opposite side of the street burst into spontaneous applause and Ruby felt a wave of gratitude and pride that both Jack and Charlie had overcome their nerves in order to rescue her.

Ear-piercing sirens shattered the calm as both ambulances and fire engines rattled around the corner and screeched to a halt outside the animal hospital. And suddenly the professionals were taking over; assembling hoses, corralling the crowd around the corner onto the high street and triaging the injured. Nellie and a couple of other people were bundled into ambulances and driven away.

'We'll be back for you as soon as we can,' a young nurse told Ruby sympathetically. 'But, as your injuries aren't life-threatening, I'm afraid it may be a while.'

'That's alright,' said Ruby. She suddenly felt desperately tired. 'Maybe I'll just go home . . .'

'Where are you taking the injured?' interrupted Jack.

'To the clinic in Limehouse in the first instance and we'll reassess from there,' said the nurse. 'It's less than a mile away but . . .'

'Then we'll make our own way there,' said Jack firmly.

'If you could,' said the nurse. 'We'd be very grateful.'

And she was gone.

'You going to carry me all the way there?' asked Ruby, with the ghost of a grin.

'I can do better than that,' said Jack, kissing her on the cheek.

He walked round the corner onto the high street – Charlie in tow – and there was Mayfair standing at the kerb and munching placidly from her nosebag. Next to her, Mac – tied to a lamppost – started wriggling and barking furiously.

'Your transport, Ma'am,' said Jack, with a laugh in his voice.

And then Jack and Charlie were helping Ruby onto Mayfair's back, her good leg finding the stirrup, her broken leg hanging free. It hurt like anything, of course, but no more – to be honest – than when she had been being carried by Jack.

'Thank you, kind sirs,' she said.

'I'll head back,' said Charlie. 'See if there's anything else I can do to help. I'm glad you're alright, Sis,' he added gruffly.

Ruby watched him lope off with a lump in her throat. A matter of months ago, he had seemed half-man and half boy, but there was no doubt he had truly come of age. Ruby couldn't have been prouder of him.

Jack untied Mac and took hold of Mayfair's halter.

'I never want to see Mac tied to a lamppost again!' said Ruby, smiling down at the little dog. 'Hoist him up here, will you? He's the hero of the day and I want to give him a hug.'

So, Jack carried Mac onto Mayfair's back and settled him in front of Ruby and Ruby, in turn, put her arms around the little dog and held him tight.

'He came to find me, you know,' said Jack. 'Ma said he came in the scullery door, barking away, very insistent. I'd already heard the explosion, of course; I were taking Mayfair back to the depot and I'd come to see what I could do to help. Ma said that when I weren't there, Mac rushed away. He found me on Sanctuary Lane and when I found your hankie covered in blood attached to his collar, I were in a right state. The rescue work had just started on the houses, but none of us had any idea that Fisher's stables had also collapsed, let alone that anyone were trapped under the rubble.'

'He saved my life,' said Ruby simply, burying her nose into his fur. 'You both did. I'll never be able to thank you enough.'

'I can't work out how Mac got himself out of the courtyard,' said Jack, beginning to lead Mayfair up the High

Street. 'The courtyard doors was locked and there were no obvious way out.'

Ruby smiled. 'Maybe we don't need to know,' she said. 'Maybe it were a Christmas miracle.'

Jack returned her smile and then lent over, kissing her gently on the forehead.

And the man, the woman, the dog, and the donkey walked slowly through the frosty streets of London as the first snowflakes of winter began to gently settle around them.

27

As she had already surmised, Ruby's right leg was shattered below the knee. It was broken in three places and needed immobilising, but she should be discharged from the Royal London Hospital in time for Christmas and the doctor was confident that she would make a full recovery.

Ma told her that Mr Atkins hadn't been so lucky – the limp hand protruding from the rubble had belonged to him – and the only good news was that he would have died instantly. The explosion had been caused by a gas leak in his house, and Ma said it was already prompting a newspaper debate about how the inability to get household appliances fixed nowadays had led directly to this tragedy. Ruby privately rather expected that Mr Atkins had just absentmindedly left the gas on before he went out, but she kept her thoughts to herself. She hadn't known him well, but he had been attracted to her animal hospital – if only for a little warmth and company – and she mourned his loss.

But, to Ruby's surprised delight, everyone else in the stable that evening had survived.

Nellie and Mrs Bowles had far more extensive injuries than she did, but both were expected to make a full recovery. The medics judged that Ruby had been directly responsible for saving Nellie's life – without the tourniquet hastily cobbled together from her petticoat, the old woman would certainly have bled to death. And Mrs Bowles, who had been slowly suffocating under the weight of the bricks on top of her, had a lot to thank Ruby for too. Everyone else had been thrown into in a far corner of the basement and had various injuries of different severity – although none of them were thought to be life threatening.

It could all have been so much worse.

Ruby was only allowed two visitors a day in the ward. Ma came in whenever she could, of course, and her other main visitor was Jack. The two talked and talked and talked and, despite their differences over the past few months, Ruby knew that she was as deeply in love with him as ever. She loved the way he made her feel – a deep golden glow that lit her up from inside. No one else had ever made her feel like that before – and she couldn't imagine that anyone would again.

'Three pieces of news . . .' said Jack, when he visited her for the second time.

'Leah?' interrupted Ruby hopefully.

Jack shook his head sadly. 'You did marvellously there,' he said. 'Leah has pleaded innocent but it seems the wheels of justice turn very, very slowly.'

'So, the poor girl is still looking at Christmas behind bars,' she said. 'That ain't right.'

Jack screwed up his face in sympathy and Ruby slumped back against the pillows. She *had* hoped that there might have been some movement on that front and she was devastated that there clearly had not. At this rate, Leah would have served her whole sentence before they released her.

'What about the Christmas bazaar?' she asked, dejectedly.

Jack was laughing. 'What is this?' he said. 'Twenty questions? But, yes, the Christmas bazaar is one of the things I wanted to talk to you about. It's had to be cancelled, of course. With the stables and the courtyard out of action, we've nowhere to hold it and, of course, a lot of the goods for it have gone up in smoke.'

Ruby nodded. She had suspected – known – as much.

'Poor Elspeth,' she sighed. 'All that work. And it was going to be something lovely and Christmassy to pull us all together.'

'There's always next year,' said Jack, gently.

Ruby nodded. 'What were your other news?' she asked. 'Something more cheerful, I hope?'

'Rather,' said Jack, brightening up. 'Wait for this: Robert has offered to pay for me to study to become a vet.'

Ruby smiled and did her very best to express surprise. 'Congratulations,' she said. 'That's marvellous news.'

'It is. Very exciting and very flattering.'

'I shall have to start minding me p's and q's around you from now on,' said Ruby with a giggle.

'Quite right too,' said Jack with a smile. 'I expect nothing less – even though I ain't accepted, of course.'

'Oh!' Ruby blinked in surprise. 'Why ever not?'

Jack gave her his lopsided grin. 'For the same reason you didn't,' he said. 'I found out later Robert had made the same offer to you and that you had said what I did. That if we don't need a qualification from the RVC to treat animals, there ain't much point in training for five years to get one.'

'Exactly,' said Ruby, leaning forward. 'I'm ever so pleased you feel the same way I do, although I do want to get more involved in treating the animals. But maybe, with neither of us training, we could use Sir Emry's money to buy the animal hospital an x-ray machine. You should see the pictures of me leg, Jack. It's like magic and it will make all the difference to the animals.'

Jack nodded. 'A splendid idea,' he said. 'There's more good news from Sir Emrys as well,' he added. 'He's offered to put up the money to repair the courtyard and the stables, as well. That way we don't have to move premises.'

'Oh, that's marvellous,' said Ruby, clapping her hands together in glee. 'I'm ever so glad that Dot and her family won't have to pay for that.'

Jack paused and ran a hand over his face. 'Robert did make me another offer, though,' he said, 'One that I *did* accept.'

'Oh? What was that?'

Jack hesitated again before he spoke. 'He told me about a new condition called shellshock,' he said, eventually. 'It's only just been given a name but apparently lots of chaps who have been at the front are like me. Lots of us have terrible feelings of panic or fear; some have lost their ability to reason and others can't sleep, walk or even talk. The good news is that Robert knows of a clinic in London that is starting to offer help and support and he's put me forward for it.' Jack stopped and took a deep breath before ploughing on. 'I know sometimes you can't help thinking I'm a bit of a coward or that I've got off lightly and I don't blame you, but . . .'

Ruby reached forward, took Jack's hand and held it tightly on the starched hospital sheet. 'I promise you I don't think either of those things now and I'm sorry I weren't always that sympathetic before,' she said earnestly. 'Besides, I can't cast stones. Every time I shut me eyes, I'm back in that basement – trapped and with the fire getting closer – and the nurse told me I cried out last night. So, I do understand what it's like for you and how you don't have a *choice* in how you react to these things. Your body just does what it damn well pleases and there's nothing you can do about it.'

Jack put his spare arm around Ruby's shoulder and kissed her cheek. 'I'm glad you understand,' he said. 'I love you. Ruby Archer.'

'And I love you too, Jack Kennedy.'

Saturday, 23 December 1916

When the time finally came to go home, Ruby was cock-a-hoop that Robert had offered to pick her up and take her back to Silvertown in his smart green-and-gold motor.

This beat taking the bus – or even dear old Mayfair's back.

'I feel marvellous,' she beamed, as he and Jack half-carried her into the front seat and placed her crutches next to her. 'Home, James!'

Her heart was soaring as the car purred along Commercial Road. She had only been in hospital for four nights, but it seemed like forever, and she couldn't wait to make herself comfortable on the sofa in the kitchen with Mac at her feet and Tess and a couple of the kittens next to her and to start wrapping up her Christmas presents.

'I'm sorry about Leah,' she said to Robert as they approached Silvertown. I had hoped . . .'

Robert reached across and patted her arm. 'Don't be sorry about anything,' he said. 'It's thanks to you that she changed her plea and has a chance to getting out early at all. She's very grateful – as are we all.'

Ruby settled back into her seat. She'd be home in a couple of minutes. But . . . wait.

Instead of turning off the High Street on to Sanctuary Lane, Robert had carried on, towards the docks.

'This ain't the right way,' said Ruby as the car nosed slowly towards North Woolwich.

'Just quickly need to do something en route,' muttered Robert.

Ruby didn't answer. It was very kind of him to give her a lift home . . . but it *was* a little strange to be running errands at a time like this. She was an invalid, for goodness' sake.

Robert pulled the car to a stop outside St Mark's Church and Ruby glanced disinterestedly at the gothic architecture and decorative brickwork. Whatever could Robert want here? He didn't even live in Silvertown, so he was unlikely to be enquiring about the Christmas services or asking after the vicar's wife. Ruby could only hope whatever it was wouldn't take long and that they would soon be on their way.

But now Robert was opening the door to the car and ushering Ruby out with an elaborate bow. And here was Jack, proffering her crutches, with a huge grin on his face.

'Perhaps Madam would like to come with us,' he said, gallantly.

Ruby glanced from one to the other in confusion. This was getting stranger and stranger. But she just shrugged and allowed Jack to help her down from the car and to set her up with her crutches and then she slowly swung herself across the forecourt towards the church hall behind the two men.

Honestly!

Robert flung open the doors to the church hall and Ruby started in shock at the sound of cheering. She went and joined Robert and Jack in the entrance and . . .

Wow!

Inside, an exuberant Christmas fair was in full swing. And not just any old Christmas bazaar. A huge sign above the stage proclaimed that this was none other than the Sanctuary Lane Christmas Bazaar.

And what a bazaar it was.

The hall was bedecked with paperchains and cotton-wool snowflakes and there was an enormous Christmas tree in one corner, fairly laden with baubles and tinsel and with a golden angel perched on the top. There were hundreds of people thronging the colourful stalls or trying their hands at the various games on offer – but, for now, they had all turned towards *her*, smiling and clapping. There was even a brass band playing a jaunty version of 'When the Boys Come Home'.

Somewhat overwhelmed, Ruby turned to Jack and Robert. 'What the . . . ? Did you . . . ?'

'We all did it,' said Jack, firmly. 'It's amazing what a group of people working together can do when they put their mind to it. Robert's father kindly found and paid for the hall and everyone else pitched in where they could. Luckily, not everything had been stored at the Animal Hospital and people have rallied around brilliantly filling in the gaps. It seems that everyone thinks rather a lot of you, Ruby Archer.'

'I can hardly believe it,' breathed Ruby.

And then she was hobbling around the bazaar on her crutches with Jack by her side, trying to take it all in and accepting everyone's well wishes and congratulations.

There was Mrs Henderson attempting to pin the tail on the donkey and attaching it on the poor creature's ear. 'Such fun,' she trilled, whipping off her blindfold and patting Ruby exuberantly on the back.

Here was Ma rushing over to envelop Ruby in a huge bearhug and – goodness me – was that really Mr Reid in tow, a twinkle in his eye and a coconut tucked under his arm?

Aunt Maggie was promenading with the most distinguished-looking gentleman with luxuriant whiskers. Charlie was manning the tombola with his friend Joe and shouting something about moving into the boxroom and giving Ruby the big bedroom, and Dot and Elspeth both rushed over to tuck their arms through Ruby's and to exclaim over her plaster cast.

Oh, it was all just wonderful.

'There's one more surprise for you,' said Jack, when they had completed a circuit of the hall and Ruby was still catching her breath. 'Someone that you really wouldn't expect to see here.'

Ruby turned to him, a huge grin on her face.

It was Mac.

It had to be!

'Oh, Jack!' she said. 'Is that really a good idea? There will be chaos and carnage! The tree will be down and the stalls in disarray before you can say Bob's Your Uncle. You know that's true!'

'Charming,' came a voice behind them. 'I might be a little clumsy, but I'm not *that* bad.'

Ruby's heart leapt with excitement and joy.

She recognised that voice. It was rather grand and la-di-da and . . .

She swung around and – yes – it was Leah, eyes shining behind her thick-rimmed specs.

'Leah!' Half-laughing and half-crying, Ruby attempted to hug her friend, almost taking someone's eye out with her crutches. 'You're here!'

'I *am*,' said Leah. 'I can hardly believe it. Your plan worked like a charm, you clever, clever girl. I told them I wanted to change my plea and then your Cook vouched for me and said the pin could have been dropped by anyone and . . . they let me go. I'd love to thank Cook in person, but no one seems to have seen hide nor hair of her since.'

Before Ruby could answer, a voice asked for everyone's attention over a loud speaker. Ruby glanced around and there were Jack and Robert up on the stage. Jack made an elegant little speech about the difference the animal hospital was making to the animals and owners of Silvertown and then voices started calling for Ruby to join them on stage. Ruby started to demur but eager hands were already taking her elbows and helping her to navigate the steps.

And then Ruby – her eyes blinded by tears – called for Dot, Elspeth, Leah and Aunt Maggie to come up as well and, just when she thought the day couldn't get any more surreal or any more wonderful, Jack actually led Mayfair and Mac out from the wings.

The resultant storm of clapping and cheering was almost deafening.

And then the cheering turned to shouts of 'speech, speech' and Ruby stepped forward, somehow finding the words. She spoke about family and community and the importance of East Enders pulling together and doing things for themselves. Because that, really, was what the animal hospital – if not life itself – was all about.

As applause rang out, a light flashed in her face and Ruby blinked in shock to see it came from a camera held by the red-faced man who had been caught in the explosion with her. He was sitting in a wheelchair; the same notepad open on his lap.

'He's apparently a reporter from the *Sketch*,' muttered Jack. 'He's very impressed by the animal hospital and he's planning to write a spread on it. You don't mind, do you?'

'Of course, I don't mind,' said Ruby. 'After all, "any publicity is good publicity".'

As everyone started streaming off the stage, she suddenly felt happier than she had ever done before. She smiled up at Jack – his dear, handsome face – and had an impulsive urge to formalise things and to show him how much she loved him.

It was too soon.

It was *much* too soon.

She had only known him for a matter of months and, for quite a lot of time, they had been at loggerheads.

But then she heard Harry's voice in her head, as clearly as if he was standing next to her. Lovely, laughing Harry, telling her that it was *never* too soon to follow her heart's desire because no one knew what was coming next and because there were too many who had forever lost the chance.

I'll take you with me, wherever I go, Harry.

'I need to sort the animals out,' Jack was saying, one hand on Mayfair's halter and the other on Mac's lead.

Ruby nodded and bending down, kissed the little dog on top of his head. 'I'm a bit worried about Mac,' she said, straightening up.

Jack's brow furrowed in confusion. 'In what way?' he said as Mac wagged his tail at the mention of his name. 'He seems happy enough to me and Charlie said he would keep an eye on him until it's time to go home.'

'Yes, but he's confused,' said Ruby. 'He used to live with you, then he came to me, back to you, back to me . . . he can't know if he's coming or going. Surely, we should make things clearer for him . . . especially after his Christmas miracle.'

'He seems to be doing alright to me,' said Jack, giving Ruby a strange look.

Oh, for goodness' sake.

'I'm asking you to *marry* me, Jack!' Ruby burst out, halfway between laughter and tears.

The words were out.

She couldn't take them back, even if she wanted to.

Jack hesitated for a horribly long time.

'You've been through a terrible time . . .' he started gently.

'That's as maybe,' interrupted Ruby. 'But I've never been thinking so clearly in me whole life. If you don't want to, that's fine; you're under absolutely no obligation to do anything but . . .'

She broke off as Jack's face relaxed into a grin

'Of course I bloody want to,' he said. 'It were on the tip of me tongue to ask *you* in the hospital, but I thought that were a bit unfair when your leg were hoisted up and you couldn't run away . . .'

Ruby started laughing. 'Jack Kennedy, will you please just shut up and kiss me?' she said, as the brass brand struck up 'Oh Come All Ye Faithful.'

And Jack leant over and kissed her gently on the mouth.

'Merry Christmas, sweetheart,' he said.

Acknowledgements

As ever, I have a host of people to thank, without whom *A Christmas Miracle on Sanctuary Lane* simply wouldn't have been written.

Thank you to my lovely agent Safae El-Ouahabi for your enthusiasm and for always having my back (to say nothing of the delicious caramel milkshakes!). Thank you to the marvellous team at Michael Joseph for your faith in me and for buying the series on a partial (although I always get confused and refer to you as Michael Douglas!). Thank you especially to my fabulous editor Madeleine Woodfield for your unfailing support and good humour and for steering the book through the editing process with ne'er a ruffled feather. Thank you also to Bea McIntyre, Hattie Evans and Kay Halsey and to the whole PMJ team.

Thank you again to Bruce Vivash Jones – an absolute font of knowledge on UK veterinary history – who has answered my many and varied questions with grace and good humour. Thank you to UP for putting us in touch. Needless to add, any mistakes are mine alone.

I've said it before, and I'll say it again – writing can be a lonely old business so thank heavens for lovely friends. Thank you, especially, to the NaNs, the Sister Scribes, the Saga Sisters and the Coppa Crew. You guys have helped me more than you can know.

A big shout out to the DB clan – Mum; Ingrid, David,

Iain, Alexander and Anna Hamilton; Tonia, Richard, Matthew and Laura Lovell and, of course, UP.

And the biggest thank you of all to my immediate family: John, Tom and Charlotte, and our fluffy moggies: Oscar and Ozzie. You all mean the world to me. Xxx

In case you missed it, turn over for an extract from the first book in the Sanctuary Lane series!

Available to buy now

NURTURING WRITERS SINCE 1935

Prologue

1905

Ruby crouched in the bushes, heart thumping.

She was well hidden here, the only way through the dense foliage a small gap on the river side. The others would take ages to find her. She settled on to the damp earth, spreading her skirts, surveying her hiding place. The leaves were still trembling from the morning's rain. There was a little spider eyeing her from the tatters of its web; she must have broken the delicate threads as she crawled in. Sorry, little spider.

Oh, no.

What was that?

Running footsteps. Closer now. Ruby held her breath. Too soon . . . far too soon.

'Found you!'

Darn. It was her older brother, Harry. How on earth had he found her so quickly? He was twelve and usually too old for hide and seek and he didn't know the park nearly as well as she did. But here he was, crawling in and settling the leaves a-rustle again. He grinned at her, merry brown eyes a-sparkle, a leaf atop his dark, curly hair.

'Careful,' whispered Ruby, shuffling up and pointing at the spider. It was dangling from the end of a new thread, its work destroyed for the second time in as many minutes.

Harry shrugged. 'It's only a spider,' he mouthed back, sitting down beside her. 'And stop talking. The others are coming.'

The two children sat silently as the footsteps outside their hiding place grew ever closer. But these footsteps were too heavy and slow to belong to any of the children they were playing with. And, heavens, what was that *noise*? High-pitched screams; plaintive, desperate . . .

A man came into view, striding towards the river. He was tall and thickset, his cap pulled down low over his face. There was a large brown sack over his shoulder, moving with a life of its own. And from its depths came the most heart-tugging cries. It sounded exactly like their younger brother Charlie as a baby . . .

'It's babies,' she hissed to Harry. 'There are *babies* in that bag.'

Harry's eyes met hers, round and wide in horror.

They watched as the man crossed the grass, vaulted the low stone wall and disappeared. Ruby was out of the bushes in a trice, blinking in the light, brushing down her dress. Harry appeared beside her.

'Found you!' shouted one of their playmates from somewhere behind them.

'Shhh!' hissed Ruby and Harry, without turning around.

As one, they ran to the wall just in time to see the man wade out over the mudflats and splash up to his knees in the gunmetal water. Then, without ceremony, he swung the bag off his shoulder and in a wide arc into the Thames. There was a loud splash before the bag billowed across the surface and slowly began to sink. The cries grew in volume but the man didn't look back. He waded back through the water and across the mud further downstream, over towards the Brunner Mond factory. If he saw the children, now crouched behind the wall, he didn't acknowledge them.

Ruby waited until the man had disappeared round the bend. Then she climbed over the wall – just as the other children skidded to halt beside her. Hitching up her skirts, she set out across the mud. It oozed over her boots, sticky and unforgiving, slowing her down.

'Ruby,' yelled one. '*Don't.*'

'You'll drown!' shouted another.

'You'll get your dress all wet and muddy,' added Harry in a quieter voice.

Ruby ignored them all. She ploughed on, keeping her eyes on the exact spot in the water where the bag was disappearing. And here was Harry, appearing without ceremony by her side. Together they splashed into the water, slipping and sliding on the stones and in the mud. The water was icy cold, tugging at Ruby's dress, weighing her down . . .

Hurry.

Must hurry.

'Here. It was here,' panted Ruby.

She reached into the water, fingers straining for the coarse material. It was much heavier than it had looked. Harry helped her lug it clear of the water and together they struggled back to the bank. Then, with shaking fingers, they untied the thick canvas knot.

The bag contained kittens – two black, one ginger, one tabby.

'It's not babies,' said Harry dismissively. 'It's just cats.'

Ruby didn't answer. The kittens were still and quiet and, for a horrible, heart-searing moment, she feared that she been too late. Then, to her exquisite relief, three of the little bodies began to wriggle and mew. Only the tabby – the smallest and presumably the runt of the litter – didn't stir.

Ruby crouched down beside them all, not sure whether to laugh or cry. Who cared if they were cats and not babies? They had feelings. They would have known what was about to happen.

And they would been terrified.

She scooped up the three living kittens, trying to dry them with her dress, whilst hastily formulating a plan. They would bury the poor runt with dignity right here on the foreshore and she would carry the rest to a stray cat who she knew had recently given birth near the Brunner Mond factory.

It was all she could do.

'Ruby. Your dress!'

Ruby glanced down at herself. Her pleated cotton Sunday-best with its pretty purple flowers was covered in thick brown river sludge.

And they all knew what that meant.

'I'm proud of you, Ruby.'

Ruby blinked. That made no sense at all. Her father was about to *beat* her. He'd just beaten Harry and now it was her turn to bend over the arm of the parlour chair.

Ruby's father followed her gaze to the strap in his hand. 'Necessary, I'm afraid, for ruining your Sunday clothes,' he said. 'But trying to rescue those kittens? That was spirited.'

Really?

Now didn't seem to be the time to ask her father how she should have attempted the very brave rescue *without* getting her clothes all wet and muddy. Should she have taken her dress and apron off? Gone into the river in her drawers? It was almost funny . . .

Except it wasn't.

Her father indicated her forwards and Ruby duly assumed the position.

She heard the strap whistle down and, a second later, a line of fire exploded across her bottom. Five more – and an extra one if she cried out. How on earth could she stand it? She bit her lip. Harry hadn't made a sound when it was his turn – and she wouldn't either.

Besides, the sting of the strap was worth it.

Worth it because she had managed to save three of the kittens who, hopefully, would live to fight another day.

And worth it because she now knew, once and for all, that even a working-class girl from the East End of London could make a difference if she followed her convictions and instincts.

That was something she would never, ever let herself forget.

1

Hampstead, London
March 1916

The back doorbell rang just as Ruby started to lay the dining room table.

More deliveries.

She smoothed down her wavy, honey hair as best she could and nipped down the stairs to the back entrance of the mansion block. Elsie from Number 8 was already there, leaning against the doorjamb, watching Mrs Henderson's flowers being unloaded in the pouring rain. Elsie *always* seemed to be there – regardless of whether she was expecting a delivery – waiting to make eyes at the delivery boys. Ruby nearly laughed out loud when she saw that this delivery 'boy' was actually a girl.

'*Another* soirée?' asked Elsie, as Ruby signed for the order.

Ruby understood the implication all too well. With the country at war, parties and soirées were unpatriotic. Extravagance was unpatriotic. Everyone knew that. There were posters all over London encouraging people to cut back and to do their bit. But regardless of what Ruby personally thought about the matter – and actually she had given it a great deal of thought – it wouldn't do to badmouth Mr and Mrs Henderson. Elsie wasn't the most discreet of people and Ruby didn't want anything getting back to them.

Not until she had decided what she was going to do.

So, she just said, 'You can't eat flowers,' smiled politely at Elsie and headed back upstairs with her armfuls of sweet peas and roses.

The preparations for that evening were in full swing.

War or no war, the Hendersons were hosting a dinner party for some of Mr Henderson's business associates. Ruby quite liked soirées – they were a welcome break from the everyday – but, goodness, they didn't half add to the workload. Unlike many households, the Hendersons still had a cook, and, even more luckily, Mrs Henderson had called Agnes in today. Agnes usually only came in on a Monday to help with the washing and to do the windows, but she was already in the scullery making a start on the spuds while Cook wrestled with the leg of lamb. But even with Cook and Agnes sorting the food, there was still a great deal to do and Mrs Henderson would make her feelings abundantly clear if Ruby fell behind on her own allotted list of tasks. There was no time to waste, so she quickly but carefully carried the Chinese vases into the kitchen to make a start on the flowers.

'I'd be quite looking forward to tonight if "he" weren't coming,' she commented to Cook as she filled each vase with water.

'He', of course, was Sir Emrys. Most of Mr Henderson's clients weren't too bad; dreadfully dreary and impossibly la-di-da, of course, but they kept their hands to themselves. Sir Emrys was different. Horribly different. Just about every time Ruby proffered him a serving platter, he would run one leisurely hand up her leg; up and up until it was almost cupping her bottom. And Ruby just had to stand there, holding the blasted dish steady and with a pleasant smile on her face. Every time it happened, she marvelled that Mr and Mrs Henderson didn't say anything. That Sir Emrys' *wife* didn't say anything. Surely, they all knew. Surely, if nothing else, Ruby's flaming cheeks always gave the game away . . .

Cook, inserting garlic and rosemary slivers into the leg of lamb, straightened up and tucked a few stray wisps of sandy hair back under her cap. 'If I had a penny for every time I've heard you say that,' she said, not unsympathetically. 'You're twenty-one years old and you've got to learn to stand up to these people. Otherwise, Sir-Bleeding-Emrys ain't got no reason to stop grabbing your arse, has he?'

'How am I supposed to do that?' wailed Ruby, as she started to snip the bottom leaves off the roses. 'Scream blue murder? Slap him? Oh, it's perfectly fine for you and Agnes to laugh – there ain't no one trying to pinch *your* bottoms in here.'

'I'd like to see them try,' muttered Cook with a grin. 'I'd have their guts for garters before you could say Jack Robinson.'

Ruby smothered a smile. She didn't doubt that Cook would be as good as her word. Cook rarely had anything nice to say about Mr or Mrs Henderson – or anyone from the upper classes, for that matter – and her manner towards them was habitually just short of surly. Ruby had a sneaking feeling that Mrs Henderson was a little bit afraid of her, as were they all; Cook was hot-headed, quick-tempered, and certainly didn't suffer fools gladly. But, despite all that – and despite the fact that the two were a generation apart – Ruby was very fond of Cook. She was certainly the closest Ruby had to a friend at the Hendersons' and their sense of loyalty and camaraderie had only grown since the war had started and thrown everything up into the air.

'At least you'll get to meet Clara Williams,' said Agnes, poking her freckled face in from the scullery. 'I reckon it'll be worth getting your arse pinched black and blue just to hear her sing.'

'Almost,' agreed Ruby, fanning the roses out prettily in their vases.

Her dread of the imminent arrival of the repulsive Sir Emrys *was* slightly offset by the evening's guest of honour. Clara Williams was not only a second cousin of Mrs Henderson but she was also a famous singer. Mrs Williams had sung for King George, and King Edward before him, and even for Queen Victoria. Ruby's mother loved Clara Williams; she had once seen her at a concert to raise money for the soldiers at the People's Palace and hadn't stopped going on about it for months. And now Ruby was going to meet her! She had already polished Mrs Henderson's cutlery until she could see her dark-blond hair under its snowy cap reflected back in each piece . . .

'A word please, Ruby,' said Cook, once Agnes had retreated and Ruby had nearly finished arranging the sweet peas in amongst the roses.

'One tick,' said Ruby, picking up a vase. Cook was bound to want to give her more advice on handling 'him', but Ruby knew she'd never have the audacity to carry any of it through. 'I'd better get these flowers in position before Mrs H gets back from her walk.'

She took the first vase, manhandled it into the lounge and carried the second one into the dining room overlooking Hampstead Heath.

'Not done in here yet, Ruby?'

It was Mrs Henderson, long, thin face radiating disapproval. She was clutching armfuls of ivy, her terrier Boniface at her heels. A trail of leaves and muddy pawprints followed in her wake.

Ruby bobbed a little curtsey. 'Just finishing the flowers, Ma'am,' she replied.

She would, she reflected, be a lot more 'nearly finished' if she now didn't have to sweep and mop the floor all over again. Why oh why hadn't Mrs Henderson taken both the ivy and Boniface straight to the kitchen? It would have been the sensible and the considerate thing to do, but Mrs Henderson had never shown herself to be overly endowed with either quality. Not that it was Boniface's fault, of course. Ruby adored the terrier and she knew the feeling was mutual. Boniface was, even now, looking at her with his head on one side and Ruby fancied that he was trying his best to apologise.

Still, with the table all laid up, the dining room really did look beautiful. Like the drawing room, it looked directly over the ponds and meadows of Hampstead Heath and it was hard to remember that they were only a few miles from the centre of London. Aside from their wonderful, open views – dull and misty as they might be on this March day – both rooms were papered in the modern ivories and creams. With electric lights throughout the house, there was no need to mask the soot stains as they had to in the East End. Everything looked fresh and clean because everything *was* fresh and clean.

Even Mrs Henderson seemed charmed by it all.

'Even if we have to cut back on food nowadays, at least Jerry can't stop us using our best china and silver,' she said, running her finger over one of the side plates.

Ruby found it hard to suppress her smile. Oyster soufflé, mutton with anchovies and several other courses might be Mrs Henderson's idea of cutting back – but most of London couldn't contemplate such a meal regardless of whether they were trying to be patriotic. She had overheard Cook saying the lamb had cost ten shillings! *Ten shillings!* Back in the day, Ma had to run her entire household – rent and all – on about a pound a week.

'I've picked some ivy from the Heath to make the flowers go further,' Mrs Henderson was saying. 'I wanted to order more but the florists were out of stock. You'll need to redo those vases. Come along. Spit spot!'

By the time the guests were gathered in the drawing room after dinner at ten o'clock that evening, Ruby was exhausted. Proper right-through-to-your-bones exhausted. Too exhausted to appreciate Clara Williams seated at the piano and singing 'It's a Long Way to Tipperary' and 'When Tommy Comes Marching Home'. Too exhausted to be concerned that the gentlemen were saying Britain had merely been marking time in the war and that efforts needed to be stepped up. Too exhausted even to be relieved that an unusually subdued Sir Emrys had kept his hands to himself all evening.

Thank goodness Agnes was doing the washing-up.

Ruby started circling the room with a pot of coffee and a jug of cream. Two of the wives were perched on the turquoise sofa together, deep in conversation. They didn't look up as Ruby approached.

'I hear Cook is off,' one was saying. 'No notice, of course. Off to join the *police*, of all things.'

Ruby concentrated very hard on not splashing the coffee.

It didn't have to mean *Cook*.

'Fanny's devastated,' the other woman replied. 'But it might be a blessing in disguise. Those oyster soufflés *were* very heavy.'

Ruby's arm shook involuntarily as she finished pouring the coffee. Mrs Henderson's first name was Fanny and the soufflés had looked uncharacteristically on the stodgy side tonight . . .

Shocked, *stunned*, Ruby hurried out of the room, not much caring much what it looked like to the guests. Cooks were leaving households all over London, of course – Ruby knew that. They were off to 'do their bit', enticed by new opportunities and larger wage packets . . .

But she simply hadn't reckoned on Cook joining their ranks that evening. Her only ally; upping and offing and leaving her in the lurch!

One thing was for certain; the police would be lucky to have Cook.

One look at Cook's face and Ruby saw that it was true.

'I tried to tell you earlier,' said Cook, filling up the coffee pot. 'To be honest, I only found out today that I'd been accepted.'

'I know you did,' said Ruby. 'And then we both got swept up in all the preparations. But – oh, Cook. I will really miss you. And who's going to do the cooking now?'

Cook gave an elaborate shrug. 'Buggered if I know,' she said. 'It's a topsy-turvy world out there nowadays and I'll not lie; they'll find it hard enough to replace me. I reckon Mrs H will have *you* knocking up a roux before the month's up.'

Ruby had an uncontrollable urge to laugh. She put her sleeve over her mouth to drown her giggles.

Her?

Cook?

Cook was taking off her apron. 'By the way, love, young Agnes has got a terrible headache and I've sent her off home. I've left the worst of the dishes soaking and I'll be in at midday tomorrow, but until then, I'm afraid it's all down to you.'

The urge to laugh disappeared and suddenly Ruby was on the verge of tears. She was tired. So very tired. And the washing-up would take *hours*.

And then the kitchen door burst open.

'There you are,' Mrs Henderson hissed at Ruby. 'I knew I'd find you malingering in here. Sir Emrys is asking for more coffee. Now!'

Ruby picked up the coffee pot. 'Yes, Ma'am,' she said.

'And when you're tidying up, don't you dare touch any of the leftover lamb,' Mrs Henderson called after her retreating back. 'That's *all* for Boniface.'

Ruby slunk back into the drawing room.

Clara was still at the piano, leading a rousing rendition

of 'Keep the Home Fires Burning'. Voices rose and fell and twisted around each other and suddenly Ruby wanted to cry for quite a different reason. She wanted to cry for the whole mad world and especially for her brother Harry who had recently been conscripted into the 47th (London) Division and who might never come home – no matter how brightly the home fires burned.

Ruby tiptoed around the room, offering coffee, topping up cups. As she bent over to fill up Sir Emrys' cup, she suddenly felt his meaty hand on her thigh. It paused and then leisurely moved higher until it was resting right on her bottom.

Impotent rage surged through Ruby. What could she do? A girl like her didn't have choices. She was a nobody, a dogsbody, unfit even to eat the leftover meat.

But then she heard Cook's voice in her ear and another thought – nothing more than an impulse, really – surged through her.

She *did* have choices.

The choices might have repercussions – but that didn't mean that she didn't have them.

Calmly, almost casually, she straightened up and looked Sir Emrys in the eye. Then, giving him a wide smile, she poured scalding coffee straight into his lap.

She would hand in her notice in the morning.